For Emily

Blessings

Bill

The Historical Jesus for Beginners

The Historical Jesus for Beginners

A Primer on Contemporary Biblical Scholarship

WILLIAM M. LINDEN

WIPF & STOCK · Eugene, Oregon

HISTORICAL JESUS FOR BEGINNERS
A Primer on Biblical Scholarship

www.wipfandstock.com

ISBN 13: 978-1-55635-338-3

Cataloging-in-Publication data

Linden, William M.
    Historical Jesus for beginners : a biblical scholarship primer / William M. Linden.

    xxiv + 144 p.; 23 cm.
    Includes bibliographical references.

    ISBN 13: 978-1-55635-338-3

    1. Jesus Christ—Historicity. 2. Bible. N.T. Gospels—Criticism, interpretation, etc.
I. Title.

BT301.2 L58 2008

Manufactured in the U.S.A.

Contents

Acknowledgments

THE AUTHOR AND PUBLISHER wish to thank the following for the material included in this edition.

Selections from eighteen pages from Chapters 2, 3, 4, and 5, as specified, from *Meeting Jesus Again for the First Time* by Marcus J. Borg. Copyright © 1994 by Marcus J. Borg. Reprinted by permission of HarperCollins Publishers.

Selections from three pages from Chapter 7, as specified, from *Jesus a New Vision,* by Marcus Borg. Copyright © 1988 by Marcus J. Borg. Reprinted by permission of HarperCollins Publishers.

Selections from seventeen pages from Chapters 1 and 5, as specified, from *The Heart of Christianity* by Marcus J. Borg. Copyright © 2003 by Marcus Borg. Reprinted by permission of HarperCollins Publishers.

Selections from twenty pages from Chapters 2, 4, 7, 12, and Epilogue, as specified, from *Why Christianity Must Change or Die* by John Spong. Copyright © 1998 by John Shelby Spong. Reprinted by permission of HarperCollins Publishers.

Selections from *The God of Jesus* by Steve Patterson. Copyright © 1989 by Steve Patterson. Reprinted by permission of Continuum International Publishing Group.

Selections from *Jesus the Man* by Marvin F. Cain. Copyright © 1999 by Marvin F. Cain. Reprinted by permission of Polebridge Press.

Preface

THIS BOOK IS ABOUT the historical Jesus. But beneath the surface, it is also about my own spiritual journey. As you will see, my journey led me into a quite remarkable church named the Episcopal Church of the Redeemer which I describe in this Preface and which I believe could be one possible model for what a church might be if it encapsulates and follows many of the teachings and the life of the historical Jesus. The quest for the historical Jesus has brought new life to my faith. It has enabled me to be a scientific person of the twenty-first century and a devout Christian all at the same time. I have written this book in the hope that the same result might be true for you.

The pursuit of God, of knowing God as one person knows another in a relationship, is a corporate journey. We worship together, we study scripture together, and we share the details of our lives together. But the pursuit of God is also an extremely individual effort. Each of us has our own spiritual journey that is unique to ourselves. No one travels the road in exactly the same way as another person.

In my own spiritual journey, I would like to say that God's hand was guiding me all along, but I'm not sure of that. Sometimes it seems to me that I move from one way to seek God to another without knowing whether it is God leading me or it is just my own personal hunger for God. But either way, I believe that God has honored my footsteps just because I have always had the desire to know God and to please God.

Perhaps some of you can resonate to what is said here and even find some commonality to your own journey. But that is for you to say. At least, your knowledge of my own spiritual journey will explain the reason I wrote this book.

Why is the quest for the historical Jesus important? There is a different answer to that question for each person. Some may find it totally unimportant. But for others, like me, it is of vast and life-giving importance for the nourishment of Christian faith.

I am not alone in this quest for the historical Jesus. Indeed, I am but one of a growing group of people who can say that nothing has more surely captured our imagination than the current scholarly quest for the historical Jesus. Who are those people? They are people within Christian churches who are only lukewarm in their attendance and participation in the Church because they cannot bring themselves to believe some of the current doctrines of the Church that are so at odds with their modern worldview. And this group of people includes those who have left the Church altogether for the same reason. One scholar has called them the "Church Alumni Association." These people often feel alienated from organized religion in general and from Christianity in particular. Then one day they pick up a copy of *Time, Newsweek,* or *U.S. News and World Report* and they see an article outlining the quest for the historical Jesus. Or they see an announcement of a college course or a television program on that topic. They find that biblical scholars are concluding that the message of the historical Jesus did not encompass the Church doctrines that are contrary to scientific knowledge. Those doctrines were not introduced by Jesus but by the Church, decades or centuries after the life of Jesus. Their eyes have been opened to new truth. They begin their own quest. The number of these people is growing. To quote one scholar, "Interest in the 'historical Jesus' has continued unabated since the Enlightenment. Each year new books and magazine articles appear, the media offer new programs, and since the 1970s, college courses on the topic have been overflowing in enrollment."[1]

For most of Christian history, the figure of Jesus was simply what could be seen on the surface of the four New Testament Gospels, all blended together. With the advent of the scholarly study of scripture that became possible with the Enlightenment, and more particularly with the studies of recent text discoveries in the past twenty years, it became possible for the first time to determine with some degree of probability what the human Jesus actually said and did. Thus, the Gospels can now be seen as a combination of history and metaphor, a combination of the actual sayings and actions of the historical Jesus and the faith-based interpretations that the writers of the Gospels added and the later Christian church also added. It is now possible to separate the historical Jesus from the Christ of faith. Both are vitally important as a foundation for the Christian religion.

1. Amy-Jill Levine, "Introduction," in *The Historical Jesus in Context*, 1.

But for purposes of study and development of Christian theology, we can and should study the historical Jesus. It is my hope that this small book will make a contribution to that worthy task.

I grew up in a family in which the Christian church was on the periphery of life. My mother and two aunts, but not my father, took me to the Methodist Church on Sundays in the small town of Denison, Texas, just north of Dallas. My memory of the Church in my early life is rather vague but I do know that the Church was not very important. What was supremely important was education, and I was encouraged from earliest days to excel in school. After a brief career as a petroleum engineer, I became a lawyer, specializing in Federal Income tax law, retiring after twenty-five years as a partner in a firm of more than nine hundred lawyers.

My wife and I were members of a conservative Episcopal church in Houston during our early years there. I was on the Vestry of the church but I had a very meager spiritual life. I read the Bible literally in much the same way as I read the Internal Revenue Code, which had to be literally true because it was all passed by Congress. I got fairly good at reconciling the differences in the Code and I was also quite good at the same reconciliation process applied to the Bible. But I no longer read the Bible in such a simplistic manner. For me now, the Bible is far more complex—in its oral and literary histories as well as the depth of its imagery. I think of the changes in my biblical interpretation as a maturing experience.

A glacial change in my spiritual life came on a Friday night during our fifth year in Houston. Martha Ann and I were invited by a friend to attend a service in an Episcopal church on the "wrong" side of town, the so-called East End of Houston. It was the Church of the Redeemer. I really didn't want to go. But the friend who had invited us was so thrilled about this church she had discovered that I did consent to go more out of curiosity than anything else. We were late for the 7:00 service. My first clue was the lines and lines of cars that crowded the streets around the church. As we approached the church, I saw a very large man, an usher, standing in the front door greeting the latecomers as they streamed into the building. He was hugging every person who passed, saying, "May the Lord bless you tonight." I thought, "Well, it's too late to back out now so maybe I just have to be hugged." I was stiff as a board. Inside, the church was packed and the service had already started. The congregation was singing what sounded like a folk song rather than a traditional hymn. Our friend pulled us toward the sanctuary and found an acquaintance on the back pew who would scoot aside enough for us to cram in.

Years later, when reminiscing with other people about our first time at Redeemer, most of my friends would say that they were impressed with the music or the teachings. But what I most remember was the congregation. As we sat there on the back pew, I saw something I had never seen before. I saw people worshiping God with a heart-felt intensity that was new to me. The service lasted about 3 hours without an intermission. It consisted of teaching, congregational singing and spontaneous testimony from various people who would come forward. And, during those three hours, people would mill around, leave briefly to go to the bathroom, and talk with each other in the isles. All that happened while the service was still going on in the front of the church. And what I saw amazed me. I saw what appeared to be people from every walk of life loving each other with deep hugs and sparkling eyes. They were the rich and the poor, the educated and the uneducated, the older and the younger, men and women. People were loving each other without regard to the barriers that usually result in human separation. Of course, at that time I had no way of knowing the details about those people except by their dress and general demeanor. But later, I found that my initial impression was correct. Their diversity was astounding and their love for each other was genuine. What I was seeing, for the first time in my life, was what St. Paul called the "Body of Christ," a living, breathing organism that was living the life of God. All I knew was that I had to be a part of that or die.

This first encounter with the Church of the Redeemer came quite soon after I was admitted into the partnership in the Law Firm of Vinson & Elkins, L.L.P. Partnership had been my focus for years, and now that the goal had been reached, I found that it was shockingly unfulfilling. I was like a greyhound running around the track chasing the little rabbit. But I caught the rabbit and it tasted awful. It was made of cotton. So inwardly I began an unconscious search for the meaning of life. In the Church of the Redeemer I found my new life.

Let me give you a thumbnail of the life and theology of Redeemer. The principal emphasis was always upon what we called "Community" by which we meant a deep sharing of life between people, a sharing of life so complete that we knew both the good and the bad of each other. We found and experienced God, which is equivalent to experiencing the Spirit of Jesus, in each other *collectively*. We often thought of it as a life of concentric circles. In the inner ring were three or four people with whom you shared all of life. The next ring had seven or eight people with whom much of life was shared. Next came ten or fifteen people who were close friends in the Lord, and after that were twenty or so who were acquaintances and outside of that was the remainder of the congregation and those outside the Church. The rings were interlocking. A person who was in my innermost ring might be in the third ring of someone else. In that way, the whole Community was held together as one Body. And the rings of relationship were always in a state of flux. People would move from my third ring to my second ring or the other way around. And that happened naturally without any external administration. Where were marriage partners? Ideally, and for most of us, they were in the inner ring. But that was not always the case with everyone in the Community. At its height, the Community at Redeemer consisted of about two hundred people who led and served in the ministries of the Church and there were about twelve hundred people in the congregation in attendance on Sundays. People moved freely in and out of the Community by their own choice, but while they were in Community they were expected to be involved in ministry and share their lives as I have described above.

My quest for the historical Jesus began long after most of my time at Redeemer. In reflection, however, many of the facets that scholars have highlighted about the historical Jesus were present in our life at Redeemer. Let me compare my experience at Redeemer with what I later learned about the historical Jesus.

The first experience was the music which at Redeemer was an integral part of our life. And the music folded me into a worship experience that connected me to the living God. The historical Jesus is sometimes viewed as a Spirit person, one of those people to whom the Spirit was an experiential reality. Thus, the music at Redeemer accomplished the same result in me in which the historical Jesus participated—a first-hand connection with God.

In addition, the music at Redeemer celebrated life—our life in God. While acknowledging the penitential seasons of Lent and Advent, the overriding theme of the music was not fear or sorrow, it was celebration. In fact, one of the Communities which spun off from the Church of the Redeemer which is now located in Aliquippa, Pennsylvania, is named the "Community of Celebration." All of that direction seems consistent with viewing the historical Jesus as one who celebrated God's life in the here and now. Thus, when my attention turned to the scholarly quest for the historical Jesus, I found the same values in Jesus character that were present in Redeemer's music.

One of the most countercultural facets of Redeemer's life was the inclusion of women in leadership of the ministries of the church. Women in leadership was not just a token, it was a reality—leadership in the pulpit, in the joint leadership of the households and house-churches, in the leading of worship and in the leadership of every other ministry. Typically, ministries were led by a *team*, which included both men and women. This was intentional. There were at least two persons in the team because it takes two or more to reflect community. And the two or more consisted of both men and women because it takes both genders to make a whole vision for the ministry. So, joint leadership was the rule. The male viewpoint is different from the female viewpoint and it takes both of them together to be complete. The teaching ministry at Redeemer, usually consisted of two leaders—a woman and a man together. Whenever I teach today, I always look for a woman partner either to teach with me, if there is a woman available with a gift in teaching, or, if not, to plan the content of the teachings with me. It's not just a luxury, it's a necessity. Redeemer showed us a way that there can be *joint* leadership with *both* men and women equally yoked in the leadership effort. At Redeemer, we thought of ministry emanating out from the community of both men and women. The teaching or other ministry proceeded from their relationship, their fellowship together. We had the idea that the closer was the relationship of the leaders, the more of God was in it and the more of God's life would proceed from their ministry.

Team leadership of two or more persons at Redeemer reflected the custom that the historical Jesus sent out his followers for ministry in pairs instead of singly. The Redeemer ministries with *joint* leadership of *both* men and women equally yoked was a reflection of the life and ministry of the historical Jesus. The portions of the Gospels which go back to the historical Jesus show us that women were deeply involved in his ministry. In fact, recent discoveries suggest that Mary Magdalene could have been on a par with Peter, James, and John as the leaders of Jesus' community. Thus, it seems that it was no accident that the historical Jesus included women in his ministry. It was his deliberate choice. Women in leadership also pervaded Paul's communities—as reflected in his authentic letters. So the earliest versions of the Jesus movement continued the practice of the historical Jesus to include both men and women in joint and equal leadership. The intentional inclusion of women in leadership at the Church of the Redeemer simply reflected the practice of the historical Jesus.

Noon Eucharist at Redeemer happened each week day. The Eucharistic prayers were offered and then the bread and wine were simply passed from one person to another in the large group collected around the alter without prior form or plan. One person, holding the basket containing the bread would pinch off a bit of bread and serve it to a person standing nearby, calling them by name and saying a few words of the element's significance. Then, the person who had received the bread would take the basket, turn and serve someone else the bread. At the same time, cups of wine were making the rounds. Each person would serve wine to another person nearby, calling them by name and saying a few significant words. Then the cup would be handed to that person to serve wine to the next person. All of this was without regard to the clergy status of any of the people. This practice symbolized the egalitarian ethos which I later found in the portraits of the historical Jesus.

We considered ourselves a family—not blood kin family, but instead a family of disciples. The teachings at Redeemer constantly emphasized the kind of family that we found in scripture, and which I later realized went back to the historical Jesus.

> And he came home, and the multitude gathered again to such an extent that they could not even eat a meal. And when his own people heard of this, they went out to take custody of him; for they were saying he has lost his senses. (Mark 3:20–21)

> And his mother and his brothers arrived, and standing outside they sent word to him, and called him. And a multitude was sitting around him, and they said to him, "Behold, your mother and your brothers are outside looking for you." And answering them, he said, "Who are my mother and my brothers?" And looking about on those who were sitting around him, he said, "Behold, my mother and my brothers. For whoever does the will of God, he is my brother and sister and mother." (Mark 3:31–35)

For Martha Ann and me, the family of disciples was (and is) a supplement and enhancement of blood-kin family. But some people in our Redeemer Community had such a negative experience of blood kin family that the disciple family became almost their sole family of choice. That seems to be the case described by Mark about the situation in the life of the historical Jesus.

Those in the Community viewed ourselves jointly as the Body of Christ. Sometimes poetry can convey the message clearer than prose. Pat Beall Gavigan composed this poem when she was a member of the Community at the Church of the Redeemer in Houston, and a student at the University of Houston:

WE TOGETHER

are Jesus:
we form his body, seen by others

We together
become one:
we are one in Christ, one by Christ

We together
offer our lives
our life
to celebrate, to proclaim, the Good News!

We together
grow in maturity:
in the expression, the revelation
of who we are
each one, together.

Not only was our love for each other paramount, we also offered love to the surrounding world outside of our community and congregation. It was our experience that we were serving them, as well as serving each other, with the hands of Jesus. This was lived out in free tutoring in an elementary school, a free medical clinic, and free legal aid, among other ministries. All of these activities at Redeemer were a reflection of the character of the historical Jesus in his advocacy of a loving life in the family of disciples and a social world of compassion.

It is also the same concept that James M. Robinson describes in his insightful book, *The Gospel of Jesus*:

> Jesus' message was simple . . . trust God to look out for you by providing people who will care for you, and listen to him when he calls on you to provide for them.[2]

He continues:

> [The] "kingdom of God" (or "kingdom of heaven") is Jesus' favorite term for talking about God acting in our own world . . . . Jesus must have realized that God is not always fully reigning now, since so much evil still prevails.[3]
> Rather, God reigning is something that actually happens from time to time as God participates in the living experience of people. . . . Jesus could call people to "seek" the kingdom. . . .[4]

Finally, Robinson restates his thesis in expanded form:

> There is explicit reciprocity in what Jesus has to say about God reigning: we receive from God through what he motivates other people to do for us, and other people receive from God through what he motivates us to do from them.[5]

One of the most outstanding characteristics of the historical Jesus was that he was a teacher about the Kingdom of God. For him, this was not a Kingdom in the hereafter, but the place where God reigns here and now in our lives. The community at the Church of the Redeemer was that kind of place where we glimpsed the Kingdom of God.

But it exists no more. People from the Redeemer Community now are scattered all across the United States and the United Kingdom. Some of them still live in Houston and some of the old relationships are still in my life. There is a tiny congregation of an Episcopal Church of the

2. Robinson, James M., *The Gospel of Jesus*, viii.

3. Ibid., 164.

4. Ibid., 169.

5. Ibid., 171.

Redeemer still present in the East End of Houston. But the community as we knew it is completely gone. I think that there might be a natural life-cycle for intense community. It is born, it grows, it matures, it grows old and it dies. The Redeemer community followed that pattern. But is lasted for more than twenty-five years and I am deeply grateful that God let me be a part of it. It has left an indelible impression on my life.

As you can see, my memory of Redeemer fits with my understanding of the historical Jesus. It has been a progression in my life. After I retired from my law practice and after the Redeemer Community vanished, I was attracted more and more to the academic study of scripture. For three summers I attended the Graduate Theological Union in Berkeley, California, and then moved to England for a year where I earned a Post Graduate Diploma in Theology from Oxford University. For three autumn terms, I have taught a course in the historical Jesus at the School of Continuing Studies of Rice University in Houston. I am an Associate member of the Westar Institute, which sponsors the Jesus Seminar, a member of the Society of Biblical Literature, and I am Chair of the Board of the Foundation for Contemporary Theology here in Houston. Martha Ann and I are members of St. Martin's Episcopal Church in Houston, and I teach in many Houston churches.

The vision of a vibrant organism of the Body of Christ has never left me. Deep in my soul I know that if we together *are* the Body of Christ, then we together are the Spirit of Jesus. It follows that we together can participate in the religion *of* the historical Jesus instead of a religion *about* him.

Perhaps the quest of the historical Jesus is a signal to the elements that must necessarily be in place before God can and will build an intense community of people. For me, and perhaps for others, understanding the historical Jesus and building upon that understanding a compatible Christ of Faith as the meaning of Jesus' life, can lead to the same kind of life among us now which Jesus lived and modeled long ago. It can lead to a re-visioned Christianity built upon a foundation that has a theology to which people can give themselves unreservedly and completely as those who live in the scientific world of the twenty-first century.

The earliest Christians were known as people of "the Way," and it seems to me that having the historical Jesus as a foundation is the Way. It can lead to the kind of intense community that we had at Redeemer. It also seems to me that God does not create anything twice in exactly the same form. So the Church of the Redeemer, as it once was, will never return. It is my hope, however, that as more and more people understand the life of the historical Jesus, a lifestyle like we had at Redeemer can emerge and flourish in a new form again.

Introduction

IN THE LAST FEW decades, there has been a resurgence of the scholarly quest for the historical Jesus. Since the term "historical Jesus" is used extensively in this book, perhaps it is best to define the term as quickly and clearly as possible. The historical Jesus is a collection of the words and deeds that probably can be attributed to the human Jesus who walked the hills of Galilee some two thousand years ago. The quest for this historical Jesus is the scholarly effort to find those words and deeds within the range of probability.

You might not be aware of the scholarly quest for the historical Jesus, and the reason is simple: scholars write and talk to other scholars for the most part, using their own technical language. That leaves 99% of the Christians unaware of their discoveries. So, even though you may have studied the Bible for years, you still may be a historical Jesus beginner. The title of this book may describe you.

After the life of Jesus, his followers began to develop their memory of his sayings and actions. Then, year after year, and century after century, the tradition grew until it became Christianity as it is known in the twenty-first century. What if we could go back in time and delve under all the layers to find what Christianity would be if it were based upon the historical Jesus and not on later Church pronouncements? That is what this book is all about. If you are a person who would like to begin to be informed, this book is for you.

This book contains a group of readings for members of the general public who are just beginning to learn about the academic analysis of the Christian Gospels. Most scholars and clergy know about the concepts described in what I call "Basic Scholarship" below, because the topics have been taught in universities and seminaries and have progressively developed over the last two hundred years. In most cases, however, this information has not been passed on to the ordinary Christians in the pew and has not been made available to the general public who might be interested in Christianity.

It is my goal to explain in ordinary English language what many of the academic scholars now are writing about the Christian Gospels. In order to accomplish that goal, this book will present to you excerpts of the writings of various scholars with a preface defining the scholarly terms and with an epilogue summarizing what has been said. In addition, the last Chapter of this book is my own creation that will describe not the historical Jesus himself but, instead, the Spirit of the historical Jesus which survived his death—a concept often called the "Christ of faith." I hope that you will learn from these readings enough to capture your interest as well as deepen your Christian faith in a manner that does not deny the advancing scientific and intellectual knowledge of the past two centuries.

It may interest you to know how the current manuscript came into being and why it approaches the subject the way it does. Several years ago someone suggested to me that Biblical scholarship needed a reading list at four different levels: the entry level for those who are totally new to what scholars call "the historical-critical" method of Bible study, the second level for those with some knowledge, the third level for those with more experience and a fourth level for serious academics. On each level the reading list would not only be the titles of books, as in a Bibliography, but also a five or six sentence summary of the content of each book. The project intrigued me and I began working on levels one and two completing most of the first drafts of the work. After further examination, I decided that people in the "entry level" might well be very intelligent people but they would have limited time and limited interest in the subject matter and they were unlikely to go out and purchase 10 or 15 books and then read them. What they might do, however, is purchase and read one book containing excerpts from those other books. Thus, the book you are reading is intended for the audience I have just described. It also is intended to preserve the integrity of each scholar and therefore contain their writing without explanation and without any attempt to draw inferences or comparisons. It is intended to be like a Public Broadcasting Station (PBS) television program, which interviews different historical Jesus scholars. I would be in the role of the "host" simply to introduce them and let the scholars speak for themselves. Then, hopefully, the readers might choose to purchase books on a similar topic or, even, books in general about early Christianity. I set to work on that manuscript.

As the manuscript developed, the excerpts seemed a bit bare and I decided to use the tried and true teaching technique of: (1) tell them what the scholar is going to tell them, (2) let the scholar tell them, and (3) tell them what the scholar has said in summary form. The introduction to the excerpt would contain an explanation of scholarly terms with which the readers might not be familiar. That is the way this book began and was formulated.

The historical Jesus readings fall into four separate categories: first, Basic Scholarship, secondly, the most recent scholarly "quest for the historical Jesus," third, the problems in the Christian church today, and fourthly, possible solutions to the problems using the scholarship of the quest for the historical Jesus. As you will learn in this book, the "historical Jesus" is a term used by scholars to distinguish between (a) the Jesus of history, the human being who walked about Galilee in the first century, and (b) the Christ of Faith which the later Church glorified in its theological reflections on the meaning of Jesus's life. Because the Christ of faith is such an important part of the Christian religion, in addition to the focus upon the historical Jesus, the last chapter of this book is my own creation instead of an excerpt to discuss briefly this important topic. There I step out of the role of PBS interviewer and into the role of scholar, giving you my understanding of the Spirit of the historical Jesus that survived his death and has continued to inspire allegiance down through the centuries.

If these readings are fruitful for you, perhaps you will want to continue your biblical literacy education by reading more of the writings of the authors presented here, and the authors of books listed in the Epilog. Thank you for your interest. Enjoy the learning experience of a lifetime.

One

The Basics of Contemporary Biblical Scholarship

IN CONNECTION WITH OUR quest for the historical Jesus, it is necessary to acquaint you with some of the foundations of Biblical scholarship. First we will look at the way scholars view the "nature of the Bible." In short, is the Bible a divine document which has words directly from God? Or is it a Human Document which tells of the valid *experiences* of God by the ancient Israelites and the ancient Christians, but which recognizes that their *explanations* of those experiences are rooted in their own time and place? Next, we will examine the Sources used by Matthew and Luke when they were composing their Gospels and we will discuss how these two Gospels, along with the Gospel of Mark, are interdependent. The Gospel of John is in an exceptional category and we will look at why this is the case. Then, we will look at the scholarly arguments whether the historical Jesus believed the world was coming to an end in his lifetime. In scholarly language, this issue is referred to as whether or not the historical Jesus was "apocalyptic." We will see how the answer to this question influences the way we interpret many of the characteristics of the historical Jesus. In the final portion of this chapter, we will examine the way some scholars view the "layering" of some of the ancient texts to be vital to the explanation of their meaning.

THE NATURE OF THE BIBLE

We begin with an issue foundationally critical for the academic study of the Christian Gospels—the nature of the Bible. In this short excerpt from a lecture and subsequent essay, Marcus J. Borg (Oregon State University) sets forth the issue clearly and convincingly from an academic standpoint. Borg's full essay is titled "Re-visioning Christianity."

1

In . . . [the last portion of] this lecture, I focus on the Bible. I do so for two reasons. It is foundational for the Christian tradition; and confusion and conflict about the Bible is the central theological issue in the church in North America today. Conflict about the Bible is the major source of division between fundamentalist and conservative churches, on the one hand, and mainline denominations, on the other hand. Moreover, the conflict exists within the mainline denominations themselves.

The re-visioning of the Bible that I suggest has five points.

1. Seeing the Bible as a human product. To make the implicit contrast explicit, we need to see the bible as a human product, not a divine product. It is easy to understand why the older conventional understanding saw the Bible as a divine product. In the Christian tradition, we have consistently spoken of it as "the Word of God" and "inspired by God," language which readily suggests that the Bible comes from God in a way that no other collection of writings does. Near the end of this lecture, I will suggest another way of understanding this language.

When I say the Bible is a human product, I mean simply that it is the product of two ancient communities. The Hebrew Bible (the Christian Old Testament) is the product of ancient Israel, and the New Testament is the product of the early Christian movement. As the product of these two communities, the Bible tells us about their life with God— about how they saw things and how they told their stories.

When we are not completely clear and candid about the Bible being a human product, we create the possibility of enormous confusion. I provide two quick illustrations of the difference it makes.

The first concerns the Genesis stories of creation. If we think of the Bible as a divine product, then these are God's stories of creation. As God's stories, they cannot be wrong. If we go very far down this road, we may find ourselves involved in scientific creationism and perhaps even in school board conflicts about whether Genesis should be taught alongside of evolution in public school biology courses. But if we think of the opening chapters of Genesis as ancient Israel's stories of creation, we realize that ancient Israel (like virtually every culture known to us) had its creation stories. And if we ask, "What are the chances that ancient Israel's stories of creation contain scientifically accurate information?" The answer would be, "About zero." And if they did, it would be sheer coincidence. Let me add that I think Israel's creation stories are profoundly true—but true as metaphorical or symbolic narratives, not as literally factual accounts.

The second illustration concerns the laws of the Bible. If we think of the Bible as a divine product, then the laws of the Bible are God's laws. To use one of the hot-button issues in the contemporary church to make the point, consider the single law in the Hebrew Bible prohibiting homosexual behavior between men. The prohibition is found in Lev 18:22, with the penalty (death) found two chapters later in Lev 20:13. If we think of the Bible as a divine product, then this is one of God's laws, and the ethical questions becomes, "How can one justify setting aside one of the laws of God?"

But if we think of the bible as a human product, the laws of the Hebrew Bible are ancient Israel's laws, and the prohibition of homosexual behavior tells us that such behavior was considered unacceptable in ancient Israel. The ethical question then becomes, "What would be the justification for continuing to see this matter as ancient Israel did?" The question becomes even more acute when we realize that this law is embedded in a collection of laws that, among other things, prohibits planting two kinds of seed in the same field and wearing garments made of two kinds of cloth. How many of you are wearing blends today? My point is that we readily recognize some of these laws as the laws of an ancient culture which we are not bound to follow. Why then single out some as "the laws of God"?

2. Seeing the Bible as a combination of historical memory and metaphorical narratives. The meaning of "historical memory" is evident: some events reported in the Bible really happened, and the community preserved the memory of

their having happened. The meaning of "metaphorical narratives" takes a bit longer to explain. They are of two kinds. Sometimes a historical event lies behind them, but the way the story is told gives it a metaphorical meaning as well. For example, ancient Israel did have her origin in the exodus from Egypt, but the way the story is told gives it metaphorical or symbolic meanings. Sometimes metaphorical narratives are purely metaphorical; that is, no particular historical event lies behind them (for example, the creation stories, the stories of Jesus walking on water and multiplying loaves).

It seems that the ancient communities which produced the Bible often metaphorized their history, and then we have often historicized their metaphors. To make the same point only slightly differently, they often mythologized their history, and then we have literalized their mythology. But when one literalizes a metaphor, the result is nonsense. On the other hand, when one recognizes a metaphorical narrative as such, the result is a powerful story. This leads directly to my next point.

3. Seeing the Bible as stories about the divine-human relationship. The Hebrew Bible is ancient Israel's story of her relationship with God. The Christian Testament is the early Christian movement's story of her relationship with God as disclosed in Jesus.

Moreover, these stories are not just about the divine-human relationship in the past, but also in the present. A particularly illuminating way of making this point is with the way the exodus story is understood in the Jewish celebration of Passover each year. A liturgy accompanies the Passover meal, and it includes the following words (slightly paraphrased):

> It was not just our fathers and our mothers who were Pharaoh's slaves in Egypt, but we, all of us gathered here tonight, were Pharaoh's slaves in Egypt. And it was not just our fathers and mothers who were led out of Egypt by the great and mighty hand of God, but we, all of us gathered here tonight, were led out of Egypt by the great and mighty hand of God.

4

What is the meaning of this language? It does not mean that we were there in the loins of our ancestors, as if it were our DNA that was there. Rather, the exodus story is understood to be true in every generation. It portrays the human condition or predicament as bondage, and it proclaims that it is God's will that we be liberated from bondage. The story of Israel's bondage in Egypt and her liberation by God is a metaphor for the divine-human relationship.

4. Seeing the Bible in a state of post-critical naïveté. Given the above, a major need in the contemporary church is helping people move from pre-critical naiveté through critical thinking to post-critical naiveté. I turn now to explaining these three phrases.

Pre-critical naiveté is an early childhood state in which we take it for granted that whatever the significant authority figures in our lives tell us to be true is indeed true. To illustrate, I recall the way I heard the Christmas stories when I was a child. I took it for granted that the birth of Jesus really happened the way Matthew and Luke and our Christmas pageants portrayed it: that there really was a special star guiding the wisemen; that angels really sang in the night sky to the shepherds; that Jesus really was born to a virgin, and so forth. It didn't occur to me to wonder, "Now, how much of this is historically factual, and how much is metaphorical narrative?" I simply heard these stories as true. Moreover, it took no effort to do so. In particular, it didn't require faith. I had no reason to think otherwise.

Critical thinking begins in late childhood and early adolescence. One doesn't have to be an intellectual or go to college for this to happen; rather, it is a natural stage of human development. In this stage, consciously or quite unconsciously, we sift through what we learned as children to see how much of it we should keep. Is there really a tooth fairy? Are babies brought by storks (are children ever told that anymore)? Were Adam and Eve real people? In modern western culture, as noted earlier, critical thinking is very much concerned with factuality, and is thus deeply corrosive of religion in general and Christianity and the Bible in particular. In this state, we no longer hear the biblical stories as true stories or, at the least, their truth has become suspect: now it takes faith to believe them. And faith becomes believing things that you would otherwise reject.

Post-critical naiveté is the ability to hear the biblical stories once again as true stories, even as you know that they may not be factually true, and that their truth does not depend upon their factuality. My favorite way of illustrating this state is with words used by a Native American story-teller. Each time he tells his tribe's story of creation, he begins, "Now I don't know if it happened this way or not, but I know this story is true." If you can get your mind around that statement, then you know what post-critical naïveté is.

Importantly, post-critical naïveté is not a return to pre-critical naïveté. It brings critical awareness with it, even as it integrates that awareness into a larger whole. It is the ability to hear the Christmas stories once again as true stories, even though you know that the story of the star and the wisemen bringing gifts is most likely Matthew's literary creation based on Isaiah 60, that Jesus was most likely born in Nazareth and not Bethlehem, that there was no massacre of the infants, and so forth. For now the truth of the stories lies in their meanings as metaphorical narratives that speak about the divine-human relationship.

Though the movement from pre-critical naïveté into critical thinking is inevitable, there is nothing inevitable about moving into the state of post-critical naïveté. One can remain in the state of critical thinking all of one's life. Though the initial movement into critical thinking can be experienced as liberating, if one remains in this state for decade after decade, it can become a very arid and barren place, like T. S. Eliot's "wasteland." We need to be led into the state of post-critical naïveté, and this is one of the major tasks in our time for Christian educators, clergy and laity alike.

5. Seeing the Bible as lens and sacrament. For my last point, I use a double metaphor: Bible as "lens" and "sacrament." I move into the point by contrasting this way of see-

ing with two other ways of seeing the Bible. The first affirms that the Bible is a divine product, and that's why it matters. The second affirms that the Bible is a human product, and draws the inference that it is therefore nothing special. This is what many of our fundamentalist and conservative Christian brothers and sisters fear—that if one lets go of the notion that the Bible is a divine product, it becomes just another ancient text of no particular importance.

The third option—the Bible as lens and sacrament—is the one with which I will conclude. I illustrate this option with a story. Each year at Oregon State I teach an introductory level course on the Bible. From teaching the course for two decades, I know that about twenty percent of the students who sign up for it will be conservative Christians. Either they grew up in a conservative Christian church and family, or they are recent converts to a conservative form of college Christianity such as Campus Crusade for Christ or Navigators or Intervarsity Fellowship.

Because I know this, I use the whole of the first class period to explain as clearly as I can the perspective or vantage point from which the course will be taught. I tell my class that the perspective is the academic discipline of biblical scholarship. I tell them about the origins of the discipline some three centuries ago, dip into its history for exciting and illuminating episodes, and emphasize that it sees the Bible as a human cultural product, not as a divine product (as I did earlier in this lecture).

Furthermore, I tell them that I am emphasizing this the first day so that, if this doesn't sound like their cup of tea, they can drop the course and sign up for another course before it's too late. I also tell them that I'm not trying to get rid of them, and that I hope they will stay. To their credit, they almost always do stay. But in spite of all this careful explanation, the first few weeks of each term typically involve a lot of squabbling between me and the more bold and articulate conservative students. I don't mind, and the conflict is most often pedagogically useful.

One year I happened to have a Muslim engineering student in the class. A Muslim from the Middle East and not from North America, he signed up for it because he needed one more humanities course in order to graduate, and this one met at the right time. About two weeks into the term, after listening to the continuing conflict between me and some of the conservative students, he came up to me after class and said, "I think I'm beginning to understand what's going on here. You're saying that the Bible is like a lens through which we see God; and they're saying that it's important to believe in the lens." I looked at him and said, "Yeah, that's what I'm saying."

The distinction between "seeing the Bible as a lens" and "believing in the lens" is crucial for the re-visioning I am suggesting. Ever since much of the Bible began to be called into question by Enlightenment modes of thought, many Christians have thought that being a Christian meant "believing in the lens" in spite of rational reasons for not doing so. Christian faith began to mean "believing in the Christian tradition." The lens became the object of belief rather than a way of seeing.

But ultimately the lens metaphor is inadequate and I need to supplement it with a second metaphor: the Bible as sacrament. Within the discipline of religious studies, a sacrament is a mediator of the sacred, a means by which God becomes present to us. The point is not to believe in the sacrament, but to let it do its work. As I see it, the Bible is not simply a lens through which we see God, but also a sacrament—a means whereby the Spirit of God continues to speak to us to this day. This is most obvious in the private contemplative and devotional use of the Bible, but it can also happen in the public use of the Bible in Christian worship and preaching.

Seeing the Bible as sacrament also enables us to understand what it means to say that the Bible is "the Word of God." The older conventional way of seeing the Bible understood

"Word of God" to mean that the Bible is a divine product. But I find it significant that the Christian tradition does not speak of the Bible as "the words of God" (lower case "w" and plural), but as "the Word of God" (capital "w" and singular). The former would suggest that the Bible is a divine product. But the latter suggests that the "Word" is being used in a special sense, indeed that it is being used metaphorically. A word is a means of communication, a means of disclosing oneself, a bridge. To speak of the Bible as "the Word of God" is thus to affirm that it is a means whereby the Spirit continues to speak to us to this day. In short, as sacrament, the Bible is "Word of God" in its function, not in its origin.[1]

Now you may understand why our journey into biblical literacy must begin with an analysis of how we view the Bible. If it is viewed as a divine document, then, as Borg has said, its creation stories are God's creation stories and they must be literally accurate. If we think of the laws of the Hebrew Scriptures (the Christian Old Testament) as God's laws then, in the simplest approach, they must all be obeyed. However, some of my conservative friends have told me that the Hebrew Scripture laws are no longer God's laws because Jesus' death freed us from obedience to them. But, it seems to me that this argument carries the fatal flaw of allowing each person a choice of *which* laws are still God's laws, and a part of a divine document, and which are not. Who is to say? And doesn't that undercut the whole idea that the Bible is a divine document?

Viewing the Christian New Testament as a divine document has a parallel dimension to the reasoning applied to the Hebrew Scriptures. If the Bible is a divine document, then all the stories about Jesus must be literally true.

But if we think about the Bible as being the product of the ancient Israelites and the early Christian movement, then we can see it as a mixture of history and metaphor. It conveys truth in those two different ways. We can apply scholarly methods to examine it. And it allows the Bible to convey God's truth to us in a manner that does not require us to park our minds at the Church door.

Borg has suggested that when we begin to analyze the Scripture, we will pass through three stages: pre-critical naiveté, critical, and post-criti-

---

1. Borg, "Re-visioning Christianity," 55–61.

cal naiveté. A student in one of my classes suggested that these stages more properly could be called, "pre-critical *acceptance*, critical, and post-critical *acceptance*. This terminology has the double advantage of avoiding the negative implications of the word "naiveté" and also it states directly that we are dealing with two different ways we can experience the acceptance of the Scriptures: accepting them without analysis, or accepting them by using critical analysis. Whatever terminology is used, the first stage is believing the Scriptures to be literally true. The second stage is an analysis of Scripture that has the hazard of disregarding the metaphorical truth of Scripture. The third stage, to which we must try to evolve, is seeing the Scripture as a combination of historical memory and of metaphor so that the Scripture is true again in a totally different way. Borg cautions that we can get "stuck" in the critical stage and it should be a major task of the church to help us move on to the third stage.

Borg then states that the Bible can be viewed as a lens through which we see God without worshiping the lens itself, and it can be viewed as a sacrament through which God comes to us by teaching us the truth by means of both history and metaphor. On this point, Bishop John Shelby Spong, retired Episcopal Bishop of New Jersey, is fond of saying that the ancient Israelites and early Christians had valid *experiences* of God, and they must be honored as true; but their *descriptions* of those experiences are rooted in their own time and culture and cannot be taken at face value. Instead we must translate their descriptions of their God-experience into our own time for it to have meaning in our lives.

If you have been convinced by Borg's arguments, and can view the Bible as the product of ancient Israelites immersed in their own culture and the product of the early Christian movement, with each of its writers imbedded in the culture of the first century, then you will be able to move on to the next set of readings and begin to understand how the Christian Gospels were formulated. The Gospels did not drop from the sky into the hands of the Gospel writers. How then, did the Gospel writers put together their books? Jesus died about the year thirty in the first century. For many years, the stories about him and his sayings were transmitted simply by speech from one person to another; this stage is called the "oral tradition." Slowly, some of these stories and sayings were put into writing and, as we will see, the Gospel authors had some literary "raw material," as well as the continuing oral tradition, before they began to write. Then they carefully crafted their Gospels as *theological* documents intended to convey the truth about God and Jesus *from the point of view of the Gospel writer*. Each of the Gospel writers had a different point of view.

Before you begin the next section of this book, it is necessary to acquaint you with a semi-technical term used by the scholars. The word "synoptic" means to "see together" and it is applied to three Gospels: Matthew, Mark, and Luke, but not to the Gospel of John. The reason will become clear to you as you read the next section. Matthew, Mark and Luke can be seen together in scholarly studies because they have some foundational similarities.

Also, in the material that follows, you will see references to the Gospel of Thomas and you may have never heard of that book. The Gospel of Thomas is a collection of some of the sayings of Jesus. Its dating is uncertain but it may have been put into writing some time in the middle of the first century. But it was lost for many centuries. Then in 1945, an ancient library was discovered near the town of Nag Hammadi in Egypt and in it was the Gospel of Thomas. Many scholars believe that the discovery of the Nag Hammadi library is just as important in the study of Christian scriptures as was the discovery of the Dead Sea Scrolls in the study of Hebrew scriptures. Thus, scholars make extensive use of the Gospel of Thomas, as you will see in the next section.

THE RELATIONSHIP OF THE NEW TESTAMENT GOSPELS

Next we turn to an analysis and evaluation of the Christian Gospels. As we shall see, scholars have analyzed the Christian Gospels first by noting that the Gospel of John is quite different from the synoptic Gospels of Matthew, Mark, and Luke. The Gospel of John could be characterized as a theological reflection on the meaning of Jesus' life, while Matthew, Mark, and Luke contain some information that can be traced back to the historical Jesus. The text I have chosen for your consideration is an excerpt from the Introduction of a book entitled *The Five Gospels*, which is a product of The Jesus Seminar. Here you will learn how scholars believe that the Gospels were constructed from earlier sources and it should help you to read these Gospels with more understanding and better interpretation. Here is the excerpt.

> The establishment of a critical Greek text of the gospels is only the beginning of the detective work. To unravel the mysteries of the nearly two centuries that separate Jesus

from the earliest surviving records, scholars have had to examine the gospels with minute care and develop theories to explain what appears to be a network of complex relationships.

The first step is to understand the diminished role the Gospel of John plays in the search for the Jesus of history. The two pictures painted by John and the synoptic gospels cannot both be historically accurate. In the synoptic gospels, Jesus speaks in brief, pithy one-liners and couplets, and in parables. His witticisms are sometimes embedded in a short dialogue with disciples or opponents. In John, by contrast, Jesus speaks in lengthy discourses or monologues, or in elaborate dialogues prompted by some deed Jesus has performed (for example, the cure of the man born blind, John 9:1–41) or by an ambiguous statement ("You must be reborn from above," John 3:3).

Such speeches as Jesus makes in Matthew, Mark, and Luke are composed of aphorisms and parables strung together like beads on a string. In John, these speeches form coherent lectures on a specific theme, such as "light," Jesus as the way, the truth, the life, and the vine and the canes. The parables, which are so characteristic of Jesus in the synoptic tradition, do not appear in John at all.

The ethical teaching of Jesus in the first three gospels is replaced in John by lengthy reflections on Jesus' self-affirmations in the form of "I AM" sayings.

In sum, there is virtually nothing of the synoptic sage in the Fourth Gospel. That sage has been displaced by Jesus the revealer who has been sent from God to reveal who the Father is. . . .

The differences between the two portraits of Jesus show up in a dramatic way in the evaluation, by the Jesus Seminar, of the words attributed to Jesus in the Gospel of John. The Fellows of the Seminar were unable to find a single saying they could with certainty trace back to the historical Jesus. They did identify one saying that might have originated with Jesus, but this saying (John 4:44) has synoptic parallels. There were no parables to consider. The words attributed to

Jesus in the Fourth Gospel are the creation of the evangelist for the most part, and reflect the developed language of John's Christian community.

[Next we will consider what scholars call] the synoptic puzzle. The primary information regarding Jesus of Nazareth is derived from the synoptic gospels, along with the Gospel of Thomas. The relationships among Matthew, Mark, and Luke constitute a basic puzzle for gospel scholars. The three are called "synoptic" gospels, in fact, because they present a "common view" of Jesus. Most scholars have concluded that Matthew and Luke utilized Mark as the basis of their gospels, to which they added other materials. There are powerful arguments to support this conclusion:

1. Agreement between Matthew and Luke [in the story line] begins where Mark begins and ends where Mark ends.

2. Matthew reproduces about 90 percent of Mark, Luke about 50 percent. They often reproduce Mark in the same order. When they disagree, either Matthew or Luke supports the sequence of Mark.

3. In segments the three have in common, verbal agreement averages about 50 percent. The extent of the agreement may be observed in the sample of the triple tradition reproduced [below], where the lines have been matched for easy comparison. (Scholars have adopted the convention of referring to segments the three synoptics have in common as "triple tradition.")

4. In the triple tradition, Matthew and Mark often agree against Luke, and Luke and Mark often agree against Matthew, but Matthew and Luke only rarely agree against Mark.

These facts and the examination of agreements and disagreements have led scholars to conclude that Mark was written first. Further, scholars generally agree that in constructing their own gospels, Matthew and Luke made use of Mark.

A gospel synopsis, in which the three synoptics are printed in parallel columns, permits scholars to observe how

Matthew and Luke edit Mark as they compose their own versions of the gospel. Matthew and Luke revise the text of Mark, but they also expand and delete and rearrange it, in accordance with their own perspectives. The basic solution to the synoptic puzzle plays a fundamental role in historical evaluations made by members of the Jesus Seminar and other scholars. Mark is now understood to be the fundamental source for narrative information about Jesus. The priority of Mark has become a cornerstone of the modern scholarship of the gospels.

Mark 2:16–17	Matt 9:11–12	Luke 5:30–31
And whenever the Pharisees' scholars saw him eating with sinners and toll collectors they would question his disciples: "What's he doing eating with toll collectors?"	And whenever the Pharisees saw this they would question his disciples: "Why does your teacher eat with toll collectors and sinners?"	And the Pharisees and their scholars would complain to his disciples: "Why do you people eat and drink with toll collectors and sinners?"
When Jesus overhears, he said to them: "Since when do the able-bodied need a doctor? It's the sick who do."	When Jesus overheard, he said, "Since when do the able-bodied need a doctor. It's the sick who do."	In response, Jesus said to them: "Since when do the healthy need a doctor? It's the sick who do."

[Next, we turn to] the mystery of the double tradition. In addition to the verbal agreements Matthew and Luke share with Mark, they also have striking verbal agreements in passages where Mark offers nothing comparable. There are about two hundred verses that fall into this category. Virtually all of the material—which may be called "double tradition" to distinguish it from the triple tradition—consists of sayings or parables. As a way of explaining the striking agreements between Matthew and Luke, a German scholar hypothesized that there once existed a source document, which he referred to as a *Quelle*, which in German means "source." The abbreviation "Q" was later adopted as its name.

The existence of Q was once challenged by some scholars on the grounds that a sayings gospel was not really a gospel. The challengers argued that there were no ancient parallels to a gospel containing only sayings and parables and lacking stories about Jesus, especially the story about his trial and death. The discovery of the Gospel of Thomas changed all that. Thomas, too, is a sayings gospel that contains no account of Jesus' exorcisms, healings, trial, or death.

Verbal agreement in the material Matthew and Luke take from the Sayings Gospel Q is sometimes high. . . . [as illustrated in the passages below which Matthew and Luke copied from Q. It is significant that Mark has no equivalent text].

Matthew 3:7–10	Luke 3:7–9
When he saw that many of the Pharisees and Sadducees were coming for baptism, (John) said to them	So (John) would say to the crowds
"You spawn of Satan!	"You spawn of Satan!
Who warned you to flee	Who warned you to flee
from the impending doom?	from the impending doom?
Well, then, start producing fruit	Well, then, start producing fruit
suitable for a change of heart	suitable for a change of heart
and don't even think of	and don't even start
saying to yourselves	saying to yourselves
'We have Abraham for our father'	'We have Abraham for our father'
Let me tell you	Let me tell you
God can raise up children for	God can raise up children for
Abraham right out of these rocks	Abraham right out of these rocks
Even now the ax is aimed	Even now the ax is aimed
at the root of the trees.	at the root of the trees.
So every tree not producing	So every tree not producing
choice fruit gets cut down	choice fruit gets cut down
and tossed into the fire."	and tossed into the fire."

At other times the agreement is so minimal it is difficult to determine whether Matthew and Luke are in fact copying from a common source. Further, the Q material Matthew and Luke incorporate into their gospels is not arranged in the same way. It appears that Matthew and Luke have inserted Q material into the outline they borrowed from Mark, but they each distributed those sayings and parables in very different ways. In general, specialists in Q studies are inclined to think that Luke best preserves the original Q order of sayings and parables.

The general acceptance of the Q hypothesis by scholars became another of the pillars of scholarly wisdom. It plays a significant role in assessing the development of the Jesus tradition in its earliest stages. It is also worth noting that, inasmuch as both Matthew and Luke revised Mark and Q in creating their own texts, they evidently did not regard either source as the final word to be said about Jesus.

The hypothesis that Matthew and Luke made use of two written sources, Mark and Q, in composing their gospels is known as the two-source theory. That theory is represented graphically [as follows:]

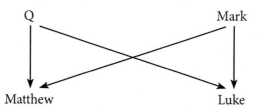

After scholars extract Q from Matthew and Luke (about two hundred verses), and after they identify the material drawn from the Gospel of Mark, there is still a significant amount of material left over that is peculiar to each evangelist. This special material does not come from Mark, or Q, or any other common source. Matthew and Luke go their separate ways when they have finished making use of Mark and Q. It is unclear whether the verses—including parables and other teachings—peculiar to Matthew and Luke reflect written sources from which the two evangelists took their material, or whether the authors were drawing on oral tradition for what might be termed "stray" fragments. "Stray" refers to stories and reports that had not yet been captured in writing. In any case, the materials peculiar to Matthew and Luke constitute two additional independent "sources."

The view that Matthew and Luke each had three independent sources to draw on in composing their gospels is known as the four-source theory. . . . Each evangelist made use of Mark and Q, and, in addition, each incorporated a third source unknown to the other evangelist. Matthew's third source is known as "M," Luke's third source is called "L."

Sources M and L contain some very important parables, such as those of the Samaritan (L), the prodigal son (L), the vineyard laborers (M), the treasure (M), and the pearl (M), which scholars think may have originated with Jesus. The parables of the treasure and the pearl have parallels in the newly discovered Gospel of Thomas.

A significant new independent source of data for the study of the historical Jesus is the Gospel of Thomas. The Coptic [i.e., the language descended from ancient Egyptian] translation of this document, found in 1945 at Nag Hammadi in Egypt, has enabled scholars to identify three Greek fragments, discovered earlier, as pieces of three different copies of the same gospel. Thomas contains one hundred and fourteen sayings and parables ascribed to Jesus; it has no narrative framework: no account of Jesus' trial, death, and resurrection; no birth or childhood stories; and no narrated account of his public ministry in Galilee and Judea.

The Gospel of Thomas has proved to be a gold mine of comparative material and new information. Thomas has forty-seven parallels to Mark, forty parallels to Q, seventeen to Matthew, four to Luke, and five to John. These numbers include sayings that have been counted twice. About sixty-five sayings or parts of sayings are unique to Thomas. (Complex sayings in Thomas, as in the other gospels, are often made up of more than one saying, so that the total number of individual items in Thomas exceeds one hundred and fourteen.) These materials, which many scholars take to represent a tradition quite independent of the other gospels, provide what scientists call a "control group" for the analysis of sayings and parables that appear in the other gospels.

In making judgments about the age and authenticity of various sayings and parables preserved by the gospels, scholars are understandably concerned to distinguish independent from derivative sources. Based on the two-source theory...combined with the four-source theory,...scholars accept four independent sources behind the three synoptic gospels. They are (1) Sayings Gospel Q, (2) Gospel of Mark, (3) Special Matthew, and (4) Special Luke. In addition, the Gospel of Thomas is now available and provides a fifth independent source for the sayings and parables of Jesus.

The present edition of the Gospel of John incorporates an earlier written source, a Gospel of Signs, in the judgment of many scholars. This brings the total number of independent sources to six. The Gospel of Signs, as a part of the Gospel of John, contains very few aphorisms and no parables of the synoptic type. As a consequence, it contributes little to the search for the authentic sayings of Jesus. . . .

The letters of Paul and other early Christian documents, such as the Teaching of the Twelve Apostles (also known as the Didache, an early instructional manual), sometimes quote Jesus and these, too, constitute independent sources.

Present knowledge of what Jesus said rests mostly on the evidence provided by the first five independent sources listed above.[2]

In summary, then, as previously noted, scholars have analyzed the Christian Gospels first by noting that the Gospel of John is quite different from the synoptic Gospels of Matthew, Mark and Luke. The Gospel of John could be characterized as a theological reflection on the meaning of Jesus' life, while Matthew, Mark and Luke contain some information that can be traced back to the historical Jesus.

2. *The Five Gospels*, 9–16.

Next, most scholars agree that the Gospel of Mark was written first and that the authors of Matthew and Luke copied Mark, adding to it their own refinements.

But the similarity between Matthew and Luke does not end there. Where Mark is silent, Matthew and Luke have substantial agreements, often word-for-word, principally in the sayings of Jesus—his parables and short pithy statements called aphorisms. When similarity is so precise, the conclusion is that somebody was copying. Of course, Matthew could have copied Luke or Luke could have copied Matthew. But there is strong evidence that neither of these events occurred because there are important parts of Matthew which are not in Luke and, similarly, there are important parts of Luke that do not appear in Matthew. Most scholars conclude, therefore, that Matthew never saw Luke's gospel and Luke never saw Matthew's gospel. There is in general a scholarly consensus that there once existed a document which is called "Q" containing many sayings of Jesus. Q has been lost in antiquity but both Matthew and Luke (but not Mark) had it available as they wrote and copied from it. In addition, both Matthew and Luke had their own sources, either written or oral, which was not available to any other gospel writer.

The Gospel of Thomas is another collection of the sayings of Jesus. Because there is no word-for-word agreement with the synoptic gospels, even when the substance of the saying is the same, Thomas is regarded as another independent source and has been of enormous help in tracing sayings back through the oral tradition and to the historical Jesus.

Knowledge of the sources behind the Christian Gospels is a foundational part of biblical literacy. Next we will consider another vital part—the issue of whether the historical Jesus did or did not think that the world was coming to an end in his lifetime. It is a hotly debated issue at the present time and it is to that topic that we now turn.

THE NON-APOCALYPTIC JESUS

One foundational issue in the interpretation of the Gospels is whether or not Jesus, in his earthly life, was "apocalyptic." This is a technical term that refers to the end of history coming soon by overpowering divine intervention. Apocalypticism is one form of eschatology—another technical term meaning a set of beliefs about the end of the world. The question is whether Jesus thought that the end of the world, by God's intervention, was going to occur during his own lifetime. Scholars are divided on this issue. Albert Schweitzer, the physician humanitarian in Africa, was a theologian during his early life and set the tone for some seventy-five years. He believed that Jesus was apocalyptic, as he argues in his famous book, *The Quest for the Historical Jesus.* Almost all scholars of his day followed his lead. In the last quarter of the twentieth century, however, there has been a decided shift of opinion and now perhaps a slight majority of scholars believe Jesus was non-apocalyptic, that he did not believe the world was coming to an end in his lifetime. The issue in Biblical scholarship is vital because, as you will see later in this book, many other issues rise or fall upon the determination of apocalypticism. For your consideration of this vital issue we will present excerpts from a recent book which contained a written debate on the issue: *The Apocalyptic Jesus: A Debate.* Please consider the following excerpt from the introduction in that book. It contains a full explanation of the terms eschatology and apocalypticism, something you need to know in order to understand the scholars in their debate.

> At this point, we need to clarify our terminology by defining two key terms: *eschatology* and *apocalypticism.* These words can cause confusion because different writers use them in different ways, sometimes without defining them. Since this book is an exchange among scholars with different positions, it is crucial to make sure everyone agrees on the meanings of key terms lest disagreements about the historical Jesus result from misunderstanding one another's terminology.
>
> The term *eschatology* comes from the Greek word *eschaton*, which means "end." In a general sense eschatology is a set of beliefs about the end of the world. In biblical studies it refers to a way of thinking that is centered on the end of history. For Jews and Christians this end is understood to be a culmination, not a cessation: the end of history is the fulfillment of God's plan for humanity. Both Judaism and Christianity exhibit a variety of eschatologies. Some of them envision the literal end of the world, in the sense of the destruction of the material universe. Some of them envision not the end of the physical earth, but rather the end of the world as we know it, that is, the end of all the established orders that create injustice and misery. Some eschatolo-

gies envision God transforming the natural world so that it becomes miraculously abundant and free of disease and natural disasters. Some eschatologies are more specifically focused on the social, political, and religious transformations that will ensure that people live according to God's will. Despite these variations in Jewish and Christian eschatological hopes, all biblical eschatologies are united by the fundamental conviction that God will prevail in the end. In terms of the specific concern of this book, to say that the message and mission of the historical Jesus was eschatological, is to say that it was focused on the culmination of history and the fulfillment of God's plan for humanity.

Apocalypticism is one kind of eschatology. Thus, all apocalypticism is eschatological, but not every eschatology is apocalyptic. Apocalypticism is a complex phenomenon that appears in a variety of expressions. In this book apocalypticism is understood as a kind of eschatology that envisions the end of history coming soon and brought about by an overpowering divine intervention. This occurrence will be evident to all people and will be preceded by cataclysmic events. Thus to describe Jesus as an apocalyptic prophet is to claim that he taught that in the very near future, within the lifetime of his contemporaries, God was going to intervene directly and decisively to bring history to its divinely planned fulfillment.[3]

While several arguments are presented on each side, one vital argument in favor of seeing Jesus as apocalyptic is what I call the "sandwich theory." Jesus' immediate forerunner and mentor, John the Baptist, certainly was apocalyptic. Jesus' early followers including Paul and the writer of the Gospel of Mark were quite apocalyptic. Thus, the argument goes, if all of those people were apocalyptic on both sides of the chronology of the historical Jesus, it stands to reason that Jesus also was apocalyptic. Here is Dale C. Allison's argument from the book:

> ... the conventional paradigm of Jesus [is] as an apocalyptic prophet. Here are the reasons for thinking this:

3. Miller, ed., *The Apocalyptic Jesus: A Debate*, 5–6.

Passages from a wide variety of sources show us that many early followers of Jesus thought the eschatological climax to be near. Consider the following, from six different first-century Christian writers:

Acts 3:19–21: "Repent, therefore, and turn to God so that times of refreshing may come from the presence of the Lord, and that he may send the Messiah appointed for you, that is, Jesus, who must remain in heaven until the time of universal restoration that God announced long ago through his holy prophets."

Rom 13:11: "Besides this, you know what time it is, how it is now the moment for you to wake from sleep. For salvation is nearer to us now than when we became believers."

1 Cor. 16:22: "Our Lord, come!" (a traditional formulation; see Rev 22:20)

Heb 10:37: "In a very little while, the one who is coming will come and will not delay."

James 5:8: "You must also be patient. Strengthen your hearts, for the coming of the Lord is near."

1 Pet 4:17: "For the time has come for judgment to begin with the household of God."

Rev 22:20: "The one who testifies to these things says, 'Surely I am coming soon.'"

We also know that, in the pre-Easter period, Jesus himself was closely associated with John the Baptist, whose public speech, if the synoptics are any guide at all, featured frequent allusion to the eschatological judgment, conceived as imminent (see Luke 3:7–17, which preserves material from the Q source). Jesus indeed was baptized by John. Obviously then, there must have been significant ideological continuity between the two men. So, as many have observed again and again, to reconstruct a Jesus who did not have a strong eschatological or apocalyptic orientation entails discontinuity not only between him and people who took themselves to be furthering his cause, but also between him and the Baptist—that is, discontinuity with the movement out of which he came as well as with the movement that came out of him. Isn't presumption against this?[4]

The argument on the other side is that the historical Jesus was primarily a sage of wisdom about how to live in the here and now and was a social prophet proclaiming God's justice in the here and now. These teachings simply do not fit with apocalypticism because if the world is coming to an end day after tomorrow, why bother with knowing a wise way to live and why bother with social justice? Therefore, the argument goes, Jesus was non-apocalyptic. Here is Marcus J. Borg's argument from the book:

> So I do not think Jesus had an apocalyptic eschatology. Or if he did, it was secondary, and not primary. I don't think it was the animating vision generating his mission. My own hunch is that his animating vision flowed out of his experience of the sacred, his familiarity with the traditions of Israel (whether only in oral or also in written form, I do not know), and his observation of the conditions of peasant life.
>
> As a wisdom teacher, I think he taught a way or a path that provided immediacy of access to God, one that was open to marginalized peasants and outcasts. As a social prophet proclaiming the kingdom of God, I think he was a radical critic of the domination system of his day, and that he threatened it with destruction in the name of God. There is urgency and crisis in his words and deeds. But I think it is the urgency of a social prophet, not the urgency of apocalyptic eschatology. The movement which he initiated, whose meal practice emphasized both sharing food and breaking social boundaries, embodied his social vision of what Israel was to be. But I don't think his passion was about preparing people for the last judgment.

4. Ibid., 20–21.

And so the questions remain. Which of these paradigms—the paradigm of primary apocalyptic, or a non-apocalyptic paradigm—better accommodates the data that we find in the synoptic gospels? And beyond that, which paradigm better enables us to see "the whole" in a way that accounts for the persuasive and compelling power that these traditions have had through the centuries?[5]

For purposes of analysis, it would be too lengthy to present the paths that can be taken on both "branches" of the apocalyptic debate. Therefore, in this book, I will take the position which I believe has the better reasoning and I will assume that Jesus was non-apocalyptic. However, the issue is not yet closed. We will find additional evidence and additional arguments later in this book about whether or not the historical Jesus was or was not apocalyptic.

THE LAYERING OF Q AND THOMAS

Now that you know something about the Sayings Gospel Q and the Sayings Gospel of Thomas, and you know something of the debate about whether the historical Jesus was apocalyptic, you may be interested to peer deeper into Q and Thomas to find how some scholars believe both of these gospels have multiple additions or "layers" which were added over a period of time. Stephen J. Patterson (Eden Theological Seminary) has written an essay with exactly that description and then has compared Q and Thomas with some surprising results. Patterson's essay is titled, "Wisdom in Q and Thomas," and his theory will help you read Matthew, Luke, and Thomas with new eyes. It will also explain why you find in Matthew's Gospel and Luke's Gospel certain words which are attributed to Jesus predicting the immanent, apocalyptic end of the world.

Patterson's essay has to do with the "wisdom" sayings and to understand it you should know that there was a long tradition of wisdom sayings in the Hebrew Scriptures. They can be found in several books of your Bible, including Job, Psalms, Proverbs and Ecclesiastes. Wisdom has to do with how to live wisely in this life. But are there wisdom sayings in the Christian Scriptures? In his essay, it is Patterson's contention that both Q and Thomas contain some of the wisdom sayings of Jesus.

5. Ibid., 48.

There is a technical term in the first sentence of the excerpt below with which you should become familiar. The term "genres" means particular categories of literature. In our own day, the short story and the novel would be examples of two different genre. In his essay, Patterson contends that the sayings collection as found in Q and Thomas are one of wisdom literature's favorite genres.

Also included in Patterson's essay is the term "CE." This is an abbreviation of the term "Common Era" which scholars use to designate the year numerology used by all cultures and religions. Scholars use it instead of the term "AD" which stands for Anno Domini, the "year of our Lord," a specifically Christian expression.

Here is the first excerpt from Patterson's essay:

> Two of the oldest Christian documents that survived antiquity (directly or indirectly) are cast in the form of one of wisdom's favored genres, the sayings collection. They are the sayings gospel known as Q and the Gospel of Thomas. Their presence at the very beginning of early Christian literary activity raises acutely the question of the role played by wisdom in Christian origins. This essay addresses this question through a tradition-historical study of these two documents.[6]

Then, Patterson gives us a brief introduction to both Q and Thomas, most of which you already know, but which is important to set the stage for his essay.

> Q is an early Christian document widely held to have been used by Matthew and Luke in the composition of their respective Gospels. The Q hypothesis is one-half of the most commonly held explanation for the extensive parallels between the first three canonical Gospels: Matthew, Mark, and Luke. This hypothesis—commonly referred to as the two-source hypothesis—was made popular by Heinrich Julius Holtzmann in the late nineteenth century. It holds that Matthew and Luke made independent use of two sources: the Gospel of Mark and a second source, Q. (The siglum Q derives from *Quelle*, the word for "source" in German, the

6. Patterson, "Wisdom in Q and Thomas," 187.

language in which the hypothesis was first proposed and discussed.) This second source was composed mostly of sayings attributed to Jesus. Unfortunately it did not survive antiquity and must therefore be reconstructed on the basis of Matthew's and Luke's use of it. However, that it was indeed a written document and not simply a commonly shared body of oral tradition is suggested by the extensive verbal correspondence found in parallel texts ascribed to Q. Further evidence for its existence as a written source can be adduced from the fact that while Matthew and Luke tend to insert sayings from Q into different contexts in the Markan narrative, they nonetheless frequently make use of Q sayings in the same relative order. Though the actual document used by Matthew and Luke has been lost, scholarly convention assigns all of the parallel texts shared by Matthew and Luke, but not found in Mark, to this sayings source. That Matthew and Luke made use of it necessitates a date for Q sometime before the mid-80s CE (the date normally assigned to Matthew), but Mark's probable knowledge of some Q texts makes a date of around 60 CE more likely, though an earlier date is not ruled out.

The *Gospel of Thomas*, like Q, is a collection of sayings attributed to Jesus. And like Q, the *Gospel of Thomas* disappeared sometime after the close of the early Christian period. In fact, it was lost to the modern world until 1945, when a chance discovery in the sands of Egypt brought it once again into the light of day. The fact that this noncanonical text shares so much in common with Matthew, Mark, and Luke (about half of *Thomas*'s sayings are found also in the Synoptic Gospels) at once made it both the object of much attention and the center of much controversy. At issue were its relationship to the canonical tradition and its date. While a full-scale discussion of these important issues is not possible here, my own position may be summarized as follows: the *Gospel of Thomas* derives for the most part from oral and written traditions that are parallel to, but not derived from the canonical Gospels and their sources. . . . The primitive nature of its sayings, its independence from the canonical tradition, and its genre all suggest a date in the first century. Without a compelling reason to date it later, one should probably regard it as roughly contemporaneous with Q.

As a pair, then, Q and *Thomas* make up one of the earliest strata of Christian literary activity. Both documents are sayings collections. This fact has not gone unnoticed in the study of early Christianity, and its significance may be considerable.[7]

First, Patterson sets forth some of the scholarly analysis of Q and Thomas, and then he summarizes their findings. To understand his perspective, however, there are two technical terms of which you should be aware. The first term, you have already encountered in this book. The term "apocalyptic" means the overpowering intervention of God to bring about the end of the world. The second term may be new to you. It is "Gnosticism" which is a Greek word that means "knowing." One branch of Gnosticism is a Christian spirituality that focused upon persons "knowing" themselves and thereby "knowing" God. This kind of Gnosticism is similar to the spirituality of Christian mystics, which has been present throughout Christian history. In another branch of Gnosticism, however, and in its extreme form, Gnosticism rejected the material world as evil. For this reason and perhaps for reasons of "Church politics," it was branded a heresy by the early Christian orthodox church. It is this latter meaning which Patterson focuses upon in his work.

Patterson follows the lead of many other scholars in concluding that the early forms of both Q and Thomas were purely wisdom documents, but that later additions to those documents altered their character. These later "layers" of writing moved Thomas in the direction of Gnosticism while Q moved toward apocalypticism. Patterson quotes two other scholars to make his point, Helmut Koester (Harvard University) and John Kloppenborg (University of Toronto).

> Koester points out that when one compares the content of Q and Thomas, one finds that conspicuously absent from Thomas is any of the apocalyptic expectation so typical of Q.[8]

7. Ibid., 188–91.
8. Ibid., 192.

Here is a summary by Patterson of Kloppenborg's work.

> Kloppenborg discovered that the compositional structure that underlies the Q document as a whole is a series of wisdom speeches. . . . To this foundational layer in Q . . . are affixed, at irregular intervals, a number of sayings whose character may generally be described as "the announcement of judgment. . . ."[9]

Patterson continues by saying:

> It is Kloppenborg's hypothesis that this second . . . layer of Q . . . was added as the Q community came ever more to the realization that their initial preaching was not being received with enthusiasm. Their frustration with this course of events inspired the strains of judgment spoken against "this generation. . . ."[10]

Patterson continues his summary of Kloppenborg's research:

> . . . while Q in the form used by Matthew and Luke was an apocalyptic document, the Q tradition nonetheless had its origins in an early Christian sapiential [i.e., wisdom] tradition that focused not on judgment and in imminent, cataclysmic end to history, but on Jesus' words.[11]

After finding that Thomas contains Gnostic sayings and Q contains apocalyptic sayings, Patterson concludes:

> It seems clear from this work that in Q and *Thomas* we have the remnants of an early Christian tradition in which emphasis was placed on Jesus' words;....In its later manifestations...this early . . . orientation gave way to . . . Gnosticism and apocalypticism. . . ."[12]

How could Thomas and Q have a common wisdom tradition and yet be independent of each other to the extent that their later trajectories took

9. Ibid., 193.
10. Ibid.
11. Ibid., 194.
12. Ibid.

them in different directions (Gnosticism and apocalypticism)? Patterson offers his opinion.

> It seems probable that those who proffered the oral tradi-
> tions that eventually found codification in Q and *Thomas*,
> respectively, simply knew one another and consequently
> shared traditions.[13]

Over the course of a few years in the early Jesus movement, the optimistic, but counter-cultural messages of the Q community and the Thomas
community both were rejected by the culture around them, driving the
Q community into apocalyptic thought and the Thomas community into
Gnosticism.

Patterson, summarizes his own conclusions of what drew them away
from their original optimistic wisdom tradition of finding meaning in the
world of human existence and into only a hope for personal salvation.

> Wisdom is about the quest for insight into the nature of
> the world and human existence in it. If one experiences the
> world as a benevolent place, or if one at least sees this possi-
> bility, wisdom can be a theological exercise in optimism and
> confidence. But what if one's experience indicates that the
> best one can say about the world is that it is evil? Then there
> are other traditions close at hand that can be drawn upon to
> give this experience its own proper expression. When early
> Christians experienced the world in this way they turned
> to apocalypticism and Gnosticism. Apocalypticism and
> Gnosticism lie close to wisdom when the sage experiences
> the world as evil, and the quest for meaning in social struc-
> tures, perceived as unalterable, collapses in despair. This is
> what happened ultimately to the early Christian wisdom
> movement that produced Q and *Thomas*.[14]

As you may have surmised, the theories presented by Patterson necessarily assume that Jesus was non-apocalyptic and that these portions of
Q (in Matthew and Luke) were added as a later layer during the Christian
traditions after the death of Jesus. And it is in the comparison of Q and

13. Ibid., 196–97.
14. Ibid., 221.

Thomas which makes these layers most apparent. If Patterson and the other scholars he cites in his essay are correct, it explains why you will find Jesus seem to be saying things in your Bible about the imminent end of the world. It is most likely that the historical Jesus never said those things or believed them. The apocalyptic sayings were added by later traditions decades after the death of Jesus and simply attributed to him by the writers of the Gospels.

In summary, then, the comparison of Q and Thomas permits us to view separately each of the earliest layers of both Gospels, both of which contain the wisdom sayings of Jesus. Although many of these wisdom sayings are similar in content, their dissimilarity in wording indicate that they came from two different and independent strains of the oral tradition. This analysis sheds light on who the historical Jesus was and sheds additional light on who these early Christians were. This implication is possible because the *earliest* independent layers of both Q and Thomas are the first written records of the Jesus Movement coming out of the oral tradition (probably 60 CE or earlier) and therefore the most likely to reflect accurately the life of the historical Jesus and the faith of those in the Q community and the Thomas community who followed Jesus.

The historical Jesus was a wisdom sage teaching people how to live in this world. The early Christians who recorded these sayings were interested only in Jesus' teachings and how to follow them. That is where they found the meaning of Jesus' life. These early Christians were not at all interested in Jesus' birth or his passion, death, and resurrection to find the meaning of Jesus' life. It was only a separate theological reflection that must have produced the thoughts that Jesus was a victim of the Roman Empire's domination system and also that Jesus was a martyr in the Israelite tradition. Then Jesus' death took on new meaning and his resurrection became a divine affirmation of his life. But all these concepts must have developed from traditions that were generated separately from Q and Thomas.

The letters of Paul were written during the same time interval as the early layers of Q and Thomas but they contain almost nothing of the life of the historical Jesus, and very little of his teachings. For Paul, Jesus death and resurrection were paramount. Therefore, perhaps Paul was reflecting the separate traditions described above in focusing upon Jesus' death and resurrection in thinking about the meaning of Jesus' life.

A later layer of Q contains apocalyptic material, but Thomas has no apocalyptic sayings. A later layer of Thomas contains Gnostic material, but Q has no Gnostic sayings of the branch of Gnosticism viewing the material world as evil. Thus, while the early layers of both Q and Thomas contain only Jesus' wisdom teachings, the later layers of Q and Thomas reveal trajectories into apocalyptic thinking for the Q community and into material-evil Gnosticism for the Thomas community. Both of these later layers reflect a pessimistic view of life in this world.

Patterson believes that it is possible that during the time of the early layers, the Q and Thomas communities experienced the world as a benevolent place and their wisdom was a theological exercise in optimism and confidence. But later, when their teachings and way of life were rejected by the surrounding culture, both communities experienced the world as evil. The Q community turned to apocalypticism and the Thomas community turned to material-evil Gnosticism, both of which lie close to the wisdom tradition and explain the reaction the Q community and the Thomas community to their rejection by the surrounding culture.

Two

The Renewed Quest for the Historical Jesus

SINCE THE "ENLIGHTENMENT" IN Western culture beginning about two hundred years ago, biblical scholars have been interested in deploying the skills used in the examination of any ancient document and applying those skills to the Gospels of the New Testament. The first step must be to determine, as the best scholarship will allow, which are most probably the words of the historical Jesus. We will examine that scholarship below. Using that raw data, various scholars have drawn the first level of inference, the first level of conclusions based upon that raw data, in developing "portraits" of what the historical Jesus might have been like. What was his purpose, what did he hope to accomplish and how did he go about that endeavor? We will examine the portraits of the historical Jesus by four noted scholars.

We begin with our effort to isolate which words attributed to Jesus in the Gospels probably can be traced to the historical Jesus.

THE WORDS OF THE HISTORICAL JESUS

The Gospels contain two voices, that of the historical Jesus, the man who lived in the first third of the first century, and the voice of the later Christian tradition, principally the voice of the communities within which the Gospels were written. It is the task of the historian to separate these two voices. It must be emphasized that just because certain words are deemed to have originated from the Christian communities rather than from the historical Jesus, does not mean they are wrong. Conversely, they may be very, very right because they represent the experience of the Christian community. For example, the words of Matt 18:20, "... wherever two or three are gathered together in my name, I will be there among them," are believed by many scholars to have originated in Matthew's community rather than the words which were spoken by the historical Jesus. But that doesn't diminish their truth. It simply means that it was the *experience* of Matthew's community. When two or three of them were gathered together in the name of Jesus, they found that in some way Jesus was in their midst. They found it to be true. When you think about it, that may be an even more powerful statement than a mere promise of the historical Jesus to be with his people.

How then, do scholars go about separating the two voices? How do they determine which words probably go back to the historical Jesus? In a recent book titled *Jesus the Man*, author and scholar Marvin F. Cain gives us an explanation of his method:

> Before we begin our look at the historical Jesus, a word about axioms is in order. After all, scholars who have written books on the historical Jesus have employed a wide variety of assumptions and methods; thus it is that they often work with the same materials but view them differently. So let me state what are the foundation stones of my attempt to get back to the historical Jesus. The first is that Jesus, in his earthly ministry, was a real person of history. He was a Jew who was born and lived in the real world of first-century Palestine. Jesus said and did real things, and he was crucified. The details and circumstances of his life are the legitimate subject of historical study.
>
> Second, as to the sources of our information, I rely most heavily on the synoptic gospels of Matthew, Mark and Luke. Like most scholars, I also regard Mark as the earliest of these and hold that Mark provided the basic outline and much of the material for the writers of Matthew and Luke. I also share the widely held view that before the gospels were written, collections of Jesus' words and deeds were made and circulated among his followers. One of these we have in the newly discovered Gospel of Thomas (Thom) and another, the so-called "Q" document, can be reconstructed from the sayings material common to Matthew and Luke. Very likely, Mark and John drew on similar collections of Jesus' deeds. In addition, all the gospel writers undoubtedly relied on oral

traditions, though by the time the gospels were written the original followers of Jesus had died. There may also have been available to them a passion account of Jesus' last days on earth.

Because the Gospel of John differs so markedly from the synoptic gospels, and because virtually all scholars see John as later and much more theologically developed than the other gospels, its value as a source for data on the historical Jesus is considerably less than that of Mark, Matthew or Luke. Apart from isolated bits of data and sayings, the Gospel of John will be used very sparingly in fleshing out the historical Jesus.

Third, for determining the historical plausibility of a given saying or deed of Jesus, I mainly utilize five criteria which are commonly used by all historians today. The first is *multiple attestation*. That is, if a saying or deed of Jesus is found in several early, independent sources, it has a higher degree of historical plausibility than a saying or deed that occurs only in a single later source. For example, the Parable of the Mustard Seed occurs in Mark (4:30–32), Q (Luke 13:18–19 = Matt 13:31–32) and Thomas (Thom 20:2–4); thus it is multiply attested. By contrast, nearly all the sayings of Jesus in the Gospel of John are found only in that gospel, written a decade or more after the other gospels. Consequently, many of the sayings of Jesus in the Gospel of John are considered as likely unhistorical, even though for many Christians they are the most beloved sayings of Jesus.

The second criterion is *embarrassment*. This holds that if a saying or deed of Jesus was such an embarrassment to the later church, that they felt obliged to explain it, it probably is historical. The church would hardly create problems for itself to solve. Two examples of this are the crucifixion of Jesus and the baptism of Jesus by John the Baptist. As problems that the church struggled to explain, both are certainly historical.

The third criterion is *coherence*. That is, if something is stated in only a single source, but agrees in substance with what has multiple attestation elsewhere, it has a high degree of historical plausibility. An example of this is the Parable of the Good Samaritan (Luke 10:30–35). While it occurs only in Luke, it is so like other better attested parables of Jesus that it, too, is highly likely to be authentic.

The fourth criterion is *dissimilarity*. This means that if Jesus is reported to have said or done something that is unlike what either contemporary Judaism or the later Christian church said or did, the report has a high degree of historical plausibility. An example of this is Jesus' use of the intimate Aramaic term *Abba* (literally: "Daddy") to address God. That was something neither contemporary Judaism, nor the early Church normally did, so it too probably goes back to Jesus.

The fifth Criterion is *historic continuity*. This means that a word or deed must be in accord with later history. Whether we like it or not, the outcome of Jesus' ministry was crucifixion. Whatever we deem historical about Jesus must agree with that central fact. A Jesus, who offended no one by what he said or did, is fictitious. And a Jesus whose crucifixion is incomprehensible is a non-historical Jesus.[1]

To summarize Cain's criteria for determining the words of the historical Jesus from Matthew, Mark, and Luke:

1. Multiple attestation: finding the saying in more than one independent source.

2. Embarrassment to the early Christian Church: such as Jesus crucifixion and Jesus' baptism by John the Baptist.

3. Coherence: agreement with a text which has multiple attestation elsewhere.

4. Dissimilarity: something unlike what contemporary Judaism or the later Christian Church said. Great care must be taken with the first part of this criteria because, if carried too far, it will rule out the things which make Jesus totally Jewish—something that he undoubtedly was.

---

1. *Jesus the Man*, 6–8.

5.   Historic continuity: in accord with later history, such as Jesus' crucifixion.

Now that you know something of the criteria which scholars use to determine which words probably go back to the historical Jesus, we can use these tools and combine them with our examination of the "layering of Q and Thomas" to re-examine an issue considered previously: whether the historical Jesus was non-apocalyptic.

1.   We found that a comparison of the earlier and later layers of Q and Thomas produced the conclusion that the earlier layers of both Gospels were similar in content, even though their words were not identical. Thus, they are two independent sources, both of which attest to the same ideas of Jesus the wisdom sage.

2.   We found that the later layer of Q contains apocalyptic sayings which are not found at all in Thomas. Also, the later layer of Thomas contains Gnostic sayings which are not found at all in Q.

3.   Thus, the wisdom sayings of both Q and Thomas (the earlier layers) have the attribute of "double attestation" and according to the rules set out above, this means they are from a much earlier part of the oral tradition which may indeed go back to the historical Jesus.

4.   On the other hand, the apocalyptic sayings of Q have only single attestation since they are not found in Thomas.

5.   Similarly, the Gnostic sayings of Thomas have only single attestation since they are not found in Q.

6.   We can then draw the conclusion that the apocalyptic sayings of Q and the Gnostic sayings of Thomas do not go back to the historical Jesus but instead originated in the Q community and the Thomas community, respectively.

7.   The ultimate conclusion, then, is that the historical Jesus was a sage, but that he was not Gnostic and he was not apocalyptic.

8.   In an earlier section of this book, we found several arguments that the historical Jesus was not apocalyptic. The layering of Q and Thomas produces an additional argument which seems very strong. The evidence is mounting that the historical Jesus, indeed, was non-apocalyptic.

We now turn to the groundbreaking work of a group of scholars called the Jesus Seminar who have been the pioneers in the current quest for the historical Jesus. The Jesus Seminar is a group of some two hundred scholars who have worked together in various size groups and with various scholarly continuities. Since 1985 they have collaborated in an effort to identify which words attributed to Jesus in the Gospels actually can be traced to the historical Jesus. Using criteria similar to those articulated by Cain, as well as several others, the Jesus Seminar Fellows (i.e., the scholars) debated with each other in open forum. Their first agreement was that they would attempt to arrive at consensus by voting on each saying attributed to Jesus. Then, to quote from the Introduction to the Jesus Seminar's book *The Five Gospels*,

> The ... agreement reached by the Seminar at the beginning of its work—again, only after agonizing review—was to create a critical red letter edition of the gospels as the vehicle of its public report. We could not readily report the exchange that regularly followed the presentation of technical papers. We required some shorthand and graphic model—one that could be understood at a glance by the casual reader.
>
> The model of the red letter edition suggested that the Seminar should adopt one of two options in its votes: either Jesus said it or he did not say it. A vote recognizing the words as authentic would entail printing the items in red; a vote recognizing the words as inauthentic meant that they would be left in regular black print.
>
> Academics do not like simple choices. The Seminar adopted four categories as a compromise with those who wanted more. In addition to red, we permitted a pink vote for those who wanted to hedge: a pink vote represented reservations either about the degree of certainty or about modifications the saying or parable had suffered in the course of its transmission and recording. And for those who wanted to avoid a flat negative note, we allowed a gray vote (gray being a weak form of black). The Seminar employed colored beads dropped into voting boxes in order to permit all members to vote in secret. Beads and boxes turned out

to be a fortunate choice for both Fellows and an interested public.

Fellows were permitted to cast ballots under two different options for understanding the four colors.

Option 1

red: I would include this item unequivocally in the database for determining who Jesus was.

pink: I would include this item with reservations (or modifications) in the database.

gray: I would not include this item in the database, but I might make use of some of the content in determining who Jesus was.

black: I would not include this item in the primary database.

Option 2

red: Jesus undoubtedly said this or something very like it.

pink: Jesus probably said something like this.

gray: Jesus did not say this, but the ideas contained in it are close to his own

black: Jesus did not say this; it represents the perspective or content of a later or different tradition.

One member suggested this unofficial but helpful interpretation of the colors:

red: That's Jesus!

pink: Sure sounds like Jesus.

gray: Well, maybe.

black: There's been some mistake.

The Seminar did not insist on uniform standards for balloting. The ranking of items was determined by weighted vote. Since most Fellows of the Seminar are professors, they are accustomed to grade points and grade-point averages. So they decided on the following scheme:

red   = 3

pink   = 2

gray   = 1

black = 0

The points on each ballot were added up and divided by the number of votes in order to determine the weighted average. We then converted the scale to percentages—to yield a scale of 1.00 rather than a scale of 3.00. The result was a scale divided into four quadrants:

red: .7501 and up

pink: .5001 to .7500

gray: .2501 to .5000

black: .0000 to .2500

This system seemed superior to a system that relied on majorities or pluralities of one type or another. In a system that made the dividing line between pink and gray a simple majority, nearly half of the Fellows would lose their vote. There would only be winners and losers. Under weighted averages, all votes would count in the averages. Black votes in particular could readily pull an average down, as students know who have one "F" along with several "A"s. Yet this shortcoming seemed consonant with the methodological skepticism that was a working principle of the Seminar: when in sufficient doubt, leave it out.[2]

The results of the deliberations of the Seminar are presented in [a] red letter edition of the five gospels.[3]

The Five Gospels was published in 1993.

2. The Jesus Seminar, *The Five Gospels*, 36–37.
3. Ibid., 38.

The Jesus Seminar is not without its critics. Some of that criticism, and answers to it, can be found in *The Jesus Seminar and Its Critics* by Robert J. Miller. In a chapter titled "History is Not Optional," Miller sets the scene.

The most significant development in biblical scholarship over the past two decades has been the resurgence of interest in the historical Jesus. It has generated a vigorous debate that has spilled out of the usual academic venues, where it would otherwise still be proceeding in obscurity, and into the public arena. The national print media, sensing its potential for controversy, have paid close attention to it. For example, the 1996 Easter week issues of *Time, Newsweek, and U.S. News & World Report* all featured cover stories on the scholarly debate about the resurrection. Until recently the media took virtually no notice of the Bible (apart from bogus tabloid reports on such things as the alleged discovery of Noah's ark) and even less of serious biblical scholarship.

Journalism about the new Jesus scholarship consistently spotlights the disagreements among scholars and can foster the impression that the experts cancel each other out. . . . Those who follow the historical Jesus debate from the sidelines may find it fascinating but also a bit bewildering. . . . Christian observers of the debate may well be scandalized by what they hear or read. Many Christians are disconcerted, to say the least, when some of their cherished beliefs about Jesus, long considered non-negotiable in orthodox Christianity, are publicly called into question by credentialed biblical scholars, many of them on the faculties of Christian colleges and seminaries. Several theologically conservative scholars have weighed in with books that criticize the work of more liberal scholars and present portraits of the historical Jesus that leave orthodox beliefs unchallenged. Prominent among these apologetic studies is Luke Timothy Johnson's *The Real Jesus* (San Francisco: HarperSanFrancisco, 1996). Vigorously attacking scholars who (in the jargon of the Catholic magisterium) "scandalize the faithful" and taking an unqualified stand on the canon and creed, Johnson's book has been hailed as a powerful response to the troubling claims emerging from the historical Jesus debate.

Johnson does not present himself as a participant in this debate, but rather as its adjudicator. So although the book deals with the discussion about the historical Jesus, it is not really intended to contribute to it. Johnson's goal for this book is much more ambitious. He hopes his book will put an end to the debate once and for all.

The book's subtitle is *The Misguided Quest for the Historical Jesus and the Truth of the Traditional Gospels*, the first half of which sums up one of its theses: that all attempts at historical reconstruction of the life and teachings of Jesus are doomed to failure. Johnson makes his case by criticizing recent Jesus books and by arguing that the New Testament writings cannot yield reliable historical information about Jesus beyond a few biographical facts.[4]

... Johnson criticizes books by a broad spectrum of authors: Thiering, Spong, Mitchell, Wilson, Borg, Crossan, Mack, and the Jesus Seminar. In a concluding summary he lists six of their "constant traits," all of which are obviously meant as criticisms.

1. These authors "reject canonical gospels as reliable sources for our knowledge of Jesus."

2. They reconstruct the historical Jesus "without reference to other canonical sources." (Johnson refers to Acts, the letters of Paul, Hebrews, 1 Peter, and James.)

3. They portray the mission of Jesus and his movement "in terms of a social or cultural critique rather than in terms of religious or spiritual realities."

4. They all have a theological agenda, inasmuch as they "want their understanding of Jesus and Christian origins to have an impact on Christians."

---

4. Miller, *The Jesus Seminar and Its Critics*, 79–80.

5. They assume that "historical knowledge is normative for faith, and therefore for theology" and that the "origins (of Christianity) define (its) essence."

6. Although the authors (except Mitchell) "have some form of identification with Christianity," their real allegiance is to academia.[5]

Miller then analyses each of these criticisms in detail and concludes:

> Johnson's criticisms of his opponents have little substance and less merit. Criticism 1 is either an error or a stone thrown from a glass house. Criticism 2 is true but unimportant. Criticism 3 sets up a false dichotomy. Criticisms 4 and 5 fault others for doing what Johnson himself does. Criticism 6 is unverifiable and downright peculiar. While the rhetoric of these criticisms is forceful, the argument is weak. The rhetoric seems to appeal, at least in part, to readers' emotions: to their affection for a venerated tradition and to resentment toward those who question it.
>
> It is difficult to imagine how readers who have studied the authors in question could give much credence to Johnson's critique. Instead of encouraging honest critical inquiry without prior conditions, Johnson assures his audience that they need not bother to read the authors he attacks. "Poisoning the well" is an old debating trick which, like all tricks, aims to fool rather than to persuade.[6]

Later in this book, you will have the opportunity to read excerpts from some of the authors who are criticized by Johnson. Then, you can judge for yourself.

PORTRAITS OF THE HISTORICAL JESUS

The Jesus Seminar originally did not carry their work into the realm of *interpreting* the results of their historical work. They were content to uncover the bare facts of the authentic words and deeds of the historical Jesus.

5. Ibid., 82–83.
6. Ibid., 87.

Lately, however, the Seminar seems to be involved with inferences—the conclusions based upon the facts of the authentic words and actions of the historical Jesus. But this is a new development. Originally, inferences were left to each individual scholar if he or she chose to do so. In other words, each scholar of the Jesus Seminar (or any other scholar or person, for that matter) was free to take the words attributed to the historical Jesus and determine a portrait of what that man might have been like, what his values might have been and what his vision of the Kingdom of God meant. Many books have been published on that topic since 1993 and space here does not permit even a summary of all of them. For our purposes, inferences by the Jesus Seminar itself will not be presented. Instead, we will consider the work of individual scholars. Only four Portraits will be discussed. First we will look at the Portrait by Robert W. Funk, the former chair of the Graduate Department of Religion at Vanderbilt University and founder and co-chair of the Jesus Seminar. Then there is the portrait by Marcus J. Borg, the Hundere Distinguished Professor of Religion and Culture at Oregon State University. Next is the portrait by the late Marvin F. Cain, previously Executive Director of Mid-Columbia Center for Theological Studies in Pasco, Washington. Both Borg and Cain have been long time members of the Jesus Seminar. Finally there is a portrait by John Dominic Crossan, co-chair of the Jesus Seminar and Professor Emeritus of Religious Studies at DePaul University in Chicago.

The Portrait by Robert W. Funk

We start the portraits of the historical Jesus by reading several excerpts from Robert W. Funk's comprehensive book, *Honest to Jesus*. First, Funk observes the side of Jesus's personality that focused on his humor.

> Jesus was a comic savant. He mixed humor with subversive and troubling knowledge born of direct insight. That was also the technique of Mark Twain and Will Rogers, who might also be described as comic savants. A comic savant is an intellectual—better, a poet—who is redefining what it means to be wise. That is the real role of the court jester: tell the king the truth but tell it as a joke. Jesters consequently

enjoyed a limited immunity for their jokes. New truth is easier to embrace if it comes wrapped in humor.[7]

What was the social status of the historical Jesus? Funk explains:

> Economically and socially Jesus was a peasant. He was also probably technically illiterate—he may not have been able to read and write. Yet by virtue of his linguistic skills he belonged to the wisdom aristocracy. He could therefore be compared to David and Solomon in the popular culture: he is referred to as a son of David, and there is a Q saying to the effect that Jesus is wiser than Solomon. Attributions of this type eased the way for the transition from Jesus the sage to Jesus the messiah. His rhetorical skills bordered on the magical—he was a word wizard. The combination of his style with the content of his discourse marked him as a social deviant. That may be the reason he was both feared and adored.[8]

Next, our focus is drawn to the side of Jesus that called for a celebration of life. Here is what Funk has to say.

> Jesus' discourse and deeds are filled with celebration. A woman celebrates the recovery of a lost coin; a shepherd ritualizes the finding of a lost sheep, a father solemnizes the return of a prodigal son. A royal dinner party is given for the homeless and destitute. Jesus himself reclines at public table with toll collectors and prostitutes in defiance of the social code. His initial public meal took place at a wedding, according to the Gospel of John; his final meal with a celebration with his intimate followers. Jesus acts in accordance with the contours of his own vision.[9]

> Jesus initially followed his mentor, John the Baptist, into the wilderness to escape the evils of urban life and to repent, fast, and pray. As a follower of John, Jesus would have become an ascetic. John neither ate nor drank, and folks used to say he

---

7. Funk, *Honest to Jesus*, 158.
8. Ibid.
9. Ibid., 161.

was demented. Jesus soon rejected the options offered by the Baptist. He returned to hellenized Galilee and feasted rather than fasted. His rule was not merely to simplify, simplify, simplify, like Henry David Thoreau, but to celebrate, celebrate, celebrate.

Because Jesus is confident God will provide and because he is willing to trust human generosity, he strongly recommends celebration. He congratulates the hungry and promises them a feast. Jesus shows up both eating and drinking, and so people call him a glutton and a drunk, a crony of toll collectors and sinners. He advises his critics that the groom's friends can't fast as long as the groom is around. His parables are filled with parties—over the recovery of a lost coin, a lost sheep, a lost son—and Jesus pictures the arrival of God's rule as a dinner party. He is the proverbial party animal, as one of our colleagues in the Jesus Seminar has put it.[10]

If such generalizations do in fact represent Jesus' views, he can hardly have shared the apocalyptic outlook of John the Baptist, Paul, and other members of the early Christian community. The apocalypticism of the book of Revelation is entirely foreign to Jesus' convictions about God's rule. We can understand the intrusion of the standard apocalyptic hope back into his gospel at the hands of his disciples, some of whom had formerly been followers of the Baptist: they had not understood the subtleties of Jesus' position, they had not captured the intensity of his vision, and so reverted to the standard, orthodox scenario once Jesus had departed from the scene.[11]

We now turn to an aspect of Jesus's teaching and life that caused a shock wave in first-century Galilee and can be equally shocking today in our own lives. Jesus devalued the natural family and elevated, in its place, the family of God. It is the group of disciples who follow God who are drawn together into bonds of kinship that are so strong that they become family for each other. Those who experience this kind of family some-

10. Ibid., 208.
11. Ibid., 168.

times call it the "family of choice." How often have you heard a sermon on this theme? Never? It is hard to get our minds around it and the concept is still so very, very counter-cultural. But this is a foundational part of what Jesus called the Kingdom of God. Funk puts the spotlight on this controversial subject.

> Two of the most powerful social forces, the family and kin-ship, were immediately drawn into the vortex of the kingdom as Jesus understood it. Kinship extended, of course, beyond the immediate family formed by marriage and procreation; it embraced those who considered themselves descended from the same ancestor or who belonged to the same clan. Contrast Jesus' vision of the family in God's domain with what went before. Here is the fifth commandment in the Mosaic code:

>> Honor your father and mother that your days may be long in the land the Lord your God is giving you.

> This is what Jesus has to say:

>> If any of you comes to me and does not hate your own father and mother and wife and children and brothers and sisters— yes, even your own life—you're no disciple of mine.

> How are we to account for this harsh new directive? Jesus knew of the extended family running to three or four gen-erations living in the same house, dominated by an aging patriarch with absolute authority over the family, especially over women and children. Respect for and obedience to the family head was at the top of the traditional-values list. Yet, in these words, Jesus insists that in God's kingdom the old family ties are to be broken in favor of new liaisons and loyalties.

> We should remember that many things Jesus said can-not be taken entirely literally. Yet a strong saying like this certainly cuts across the commandment to honor one's fa-ther and mother. And the attitude toward filial responsibili-ties to parents is underscored by another saying:

>> Another potential follower made this request, "First, let me go and bury my father." Jesus said to him, "Leave it to the dead

to bury their own dead; but you, go out and announce God's imperial rule.

And when Jesus' mother and siblings come to get him for fear he has gone mad, he tells the circle around him that his true relatives are those who do his Father's will. In the context of traditional family ties, it is no wonder his mother thought him demented.

The scene from the Gospel of Mark in which his family comes to take him home is abbreviated in Thomas 99:

> The disciples said to him, "Your brothers and your mother are standing outside." He said to them, "Those here who do what my Father wants are my brothers and my mother."

Does this saying, attested by both Mark and Thomas, reflect some conflict between Jesus and his family? We know there was conflict later between Jesus' brother James, a leader of the Judean wing of the budding Christian movement, and other leaders, especially Paul of Tarsus. This happened after Jesus' death, of course. The tension may have triggered some claims and counterclaims about the rights and privileges of blood relatives of Jesus. But it is also entirely conceivable that the tension goes back to Jesus himself, since he seems to have crossed frontiers in over-riding biological barriers along with religious and social lines of demarcation as a matter of principle.

In his admonitions to Judeans coming out to the Jordan valley to repent and be baptized, John the Baptist says:

> Well then, start producing fruit suitable for a change of heart, and don't even think of saying to yourselves, "We have Abraham as our father." Let me tell you, God can raise up children for Abraham right out of these rocks.

This saying suggests that John, too, made light of genealogies and perhaps passed that assessment on to Jesus.[12]

We turn now to the last facet of the personality of the historical Jesus discussed by Funk the fact that the historical Jesus challenged the valid-

---

12. Ibid., 197–98.

ity of sacred spaces (such as the temple in Jerusalem and, by implication our Church sanctuaries today). As a corollary, the historical Jesus taught and lived that to have access to God there was no need to go through a "broker" such as a temple priest or, in our day, the pastor or rector of a church. Instead, anyone could have direct access to God. Perhaps the term "broker" needs a bit of explaining because you may never have seen it used in a context of the church. A "broker" is simply a middle person. For example, a real estate broker stands between the buyer and the seller of the real estate. Instead of the buyer and seller dealing directly with each other, the buyer relates to the seller *through* the broker and the seller relates to the buyer *through* the broker. In a similar way, the priest in the temple (or the pastor or rector in today's Churches) can be a broker, and, if so, each person must relate to God through the broker instead of having direct access to God. That is the pattern that the historical Jesus subverted and declared null and void.

As another application of this principle, the historical Jesus taught that forgiveness was simply to be reciprocal. "Forgive and you will be forgiven" is the rule, instead of seeking God's forgiveness by what a priest in the temple in Jerusalem or, by implication, what a pastor or rector in our own day, might do or say. According to the historical Jesus, forgiveness is in the hands of each human being. One can be the recipient of forgiveness if, and only if, one is an agent of forgiveness. Here again are excerpts from Funk's book:

> The wall around temples in the ancient Near East—called a *temenos*—defined sacred space and set it off from profane space. The *temenos* represented the boundary between the pure and the polluted or defiled.[13]

> In the vision of Jesus, the temple seemingly lacked a *temenos* and, had he been able to foresee the future, the church would have lacked a chancel. In his view, every person had immediate, unbrokered access to God's presence, God's love, God's forgiveness. There appeared to be no sacred places in Jesus' world: all space had become sacred. The bush burned for Jesus not just on the sacred mountain in Sinai but in the marketplace, at the public well, in every poor hovel, in the

13. Ibid., 202.

interstices of the everyday. While the story is almost certainly a fiction, Jesus advises the Samaritan woman at the well that true worshipers will worship the Father without regard to place. Neither Jerusalem nor Gerizim, neither Constantinople nor Rome, defines sacred space. That advice seems to comport with what we know of the historical Jesus.[14]

Reciprocity is his fundamental principle. The standard I apply to you, he suggests, is the standard that will be applied to me. As a consequence, he makes forgiveness reciprocal: "Forgive and you'll be forgiven." One of the petitions he may have taught his disciples asks God to forgive only to the extent that the petitioner has forgiven others. One cannot be a recipient of forgiveness unless or until one is an agent of forgiveness. It's as simple as that and as difficult as that.[15]

In his book, Funk then elaborates upon what he believes the historical Jesus thought about sacred foods, sacred names, sacred seasons, anxieties, success, riches and God's Domain, rewards and punishments, death, and entering the Kingdom. For purposes of brevity in this book, we must be content only to name these characteristics by title without excerpts from Funk's book.

To summarize Funk's portrait of the historical Jesus:

1. Jesus was a comic savant (in the order of Mark Twain and Will Rogers) who mixed humor with subversive wisdom.

2. Jesus was a peasant who may or may not have been able to read and write, but his rhetorical skills bordered on the magical. He was a word wizard.

3. Jesus life and stories were filled with celebration. His rule was to celebrate, celebrate, celebrate. He was the proverbial party animal.

4. Jesus devalued blood-kin relationships. His real family was the family of God.

---

14. Ibid., 203.
15. Ibid., 213.

5. Jesus lived and taught that every person had immediate and un-
    brokered access to God. People need not go through a priest or a
    Temple (or a Church) to commune with God. There were no sacred
    places because they all can be holy.

6. Reciprocity is Jesus' fundamental principle. The standard one ap-
    plies to another is the standard that person will apply in return.
    Forgiveness is reciprocal. If one is the agent of forgiveness of oth-
    ers, then God's forgiveness is received. It is unnecessary to go to
    God for forgiveness through a religious broker (in the Jerusalem
    Temple or, by implication, in today's Christian churches).

This completes our visit with Robert W. Funk. Next we turn to another portrait of the historical Jesus, this time from Marcus J. Borg, a
sought-after lecturer and the author of many best-selling books.

The Portrait by Marcus J. Borg

We continue with the historical Jesus's characteristics described by Marcus
J. Borg in his best selling book, *Meeting Jesus Again, For the First Time.* As
you will see, Borg uses the terms "pre-Easter Jesus" and "historical Jesus"
as being equivalent. A term used by Borg in describing his sketch of the
historical Jesus is drawn from the language of psychology but which may
not be familiar to ordinary readers. It is the term "gestalt" which means
phenomena so integrated as to constitute a functional unit with proper-
ties not derivable by summation of its parts. Here is Borg's analysis.

> So what was the adult Jesus like? What did this person, born
> to Mary and Joseph, socialized in Nazareth, and discipled to
> John the Baptizer, become?
>
> Answering this question involves us in the task of his-
> torical reconstruction, which may be understood as gener-
> ating an image or gestalt that draws together into a cohesive
> whole the various elements of the tradition judged to be
> historical. The process is very much like a particular stage of
> detective work: after the evidence has been gathered, ana-
> lyzed, and weighed, it has to be integrated into an overall
> hypothesis.
>
> Doing this with the traditions about Jesus produces a
> sketch, or construal or gestalt or image, of Jesus. I prefer

these terms to *picture* or *portrait*, both of which suggest too much fullness of detail. A *sketch*, on the other hand, suggests broad strokes—a clear outline without much precision of detail.[16]

Before I turn to my sketch, it is important that I make two negative statements. The first, which counters a central element in the popular image of Jesus, is that the self-understanding and message of the pre-Easter Jesus were in all likelihood *nonmessianic*. By this I mean simply that we have no way of knowing whether Jesus thought of himself as the Messiah or as the Son of God in some special sense. According to the earliest layers of the developing gospel tradition, he said nothing about having such thoughts. They were not part of his own teaching. His message was not about believing in him. Rather, the pre-Easter Jesus consistently pointed away from himself to God. His message was *theocentric*, not christocentric—centered in God, not centered in a messianic proclamation about himself.

The second negative statement, which counters a widespread scholarly image of Jesus, is that in all likelihood the pre-Easter Jesus was *noneschatological*. That statement needs precise formulation in order not to be misunderstood: what is being denied is the notion that Jesus expected the supernatural coming of the Kingdom of God as a world-ending event in his own generation. This growing scholarly consensus is a recent development. Over the last ten years, the image of Jesus as an eschatological prophet, which dominated scholarship through the middle third of this century, has become very much a minority position.

My own sketch of the pre-Easter Jesus consists of four broad strokes. It is based upon a typology of religious figures. My research and evaluation of the best Jesus scholarship convince me that Jesus had characteristics of several different types of religious personalities, and each stroke in my sketch identifies him with one of these types. Because I

16. Borg, *Meeting Jesus Again, For the First Time*, 28.

have developed this idea in considerable detail elsewhere, I will present it here very compactly.

1. The historical Jesus was a *spirit person,* one of those figures in human history with an experiential awareness of the reality of God. . . .

2. Jesus was a *teacher of wisdom* who regularly used the classic forms of wisdom speech (parables, and memorable short sayings known as aphorisms) to teach a subversive and alternative wisdom. . . .

3. Jesus was a *social prophet*, similar to the classical prophets of ancient Israel. As such, he criticized the elites (economic, political, and religious) of his time, was an advocate of an alternative social vision, and was often in conflict with authorities. . . .

4. Jesus was a *movement founder* who brought into being a Jewish renewal or revitalization movement that challenged and shattered the social boundaries of his day, a movement that eventually became the early Christian church. . . .

These four strokes, taken in combination with the two negative statements made earlier, provide a sketch or profile of what the pre-Easter Jesus was like. Together, they enable us to constellate the traditions about him into a coherent whole.[17]

Next, Borg amplifies on each of his four strokes in his sketch of the Pre-Easter Jesus. For our purposes in this book, we will offer excerpts from Borg's book on only three of those strokes: Jesus was a Spirit Person; Jesus was a Teacher of Alternative Wisdom; and Jesus was a Teacher of Compassion, social world and politics. Then, we will take a brief look at an additional characteristic of the historical Jesus which Borg discusses in one his earlier books: the way Jesus accepted women as radically equal with men.

17. Ibid., 29–30.

JESUS AS SPIRIT PERSON AND MEDIATOR
OF THE SACRED

The first stroke in my four-stroke sketch is foundational to everything else Jesus was. The most crucial fact about Jesus was that he was a "spirit person," a "mediator of the sacred," one of those persons in human history to whom the Spirit was an experiential reality.

It took me a long time to see this. The process began with the realization that there really are such phenomena as experiences of Spirit and spirit persons. The realization came to me initially not from the study of the Bible or the Christian tradition, but from the study of non-Western religions and cultural anthropology. This illuminating category helps us see much about Jesus that we otherwise might miss.

We begin with what a spirit person is. The older, semitechnical term is *holy man*, but *spirit person* seems better. The change to *person* reflects the fact that such figures come in both genders, which makes a gender-inclusive term desirable. The change to *spirit* (*spirit* person rather than *holy* person) seeks to avoid the connotations of *holy*, which there is a natural tendency to understand as an adjective denoting a moral quality, such as *righteous* or *pious* or *revered* or *saintly* or even *sanctimonious*. Such a reading would profoundly obscure what the phrase is meant to convey: a person to whom the sacred is an experiential reality.

Spirit persons are known cross-culturally. They are people who have vivid and frequent subjective experiences of another level or dimension of reality. These experiences involve momentary entry into nonordinary states of consciousness and take a number of different forms. Sometimes there is a vivid sense of momentarily seeing into another layer of reality; these are visionary experiences. Sometimes there is the experience of journeying into that other dimension of reality; this is the classic experience of the shaman. Sometimes there is a strong sense of another reality coming upon one, as in the ancient expression "The Spirit fell upon me."

Sometimes the experience is of nature or an object within nature momentarily transfigured by "the sacred" shining through it. Bushes burn without being consumed; the whole earth is seen as filled with the glory of God (where *glory* means "radiant presence"). The world is perceived in such a way that previous perceptions seem nothing more than blindness.

[1] What all persons who have these experiences share is a strong sense of there being more to reality than the tangible world of our ordinary experience. They share a compelling sense of having experienced something "real." They feel strongly that they know something they didn't know before. Their experiences are noetic, involving not simply a *feeling* of ecstasy, but a *knowing*. What such persons know is *the sacred*. Spirit persons are people who experience the sacred frequently and vividly.

It is experiences such as these that have led the religious traditions of the world to speak of "the sacred." *The sacred* (or *the numinous*) refers to the other reality encountered in these experiences. Most often, of course, the religious traditions do not speak of the sacred abstractly; rather, they *name* it—as Yahweh, Brahman, Atman, Allah, the Tao, Great Spirit, God. This is not to suppose that all these names (and the concepts associated with them) mean the same thing. But it is to suppose that the impulse to name something as sacred flows out of the experience of the sacred. Because the most common name for the sacred in the Jewish-Christian tradition is *God*, I shall from now on most often use *God* or *(the) Spirit* when referring to the sacred.

[2] Spirit persons share a second feature as well: they become mediators of the sacred. They mediate the Spirit in various ways. Sometimes they speak the word or will of God. Sometimes they mediate the power of God in the form of healings and/or exorcisms. Sometimes they function as game finders or rainmakers in hunting-and-gathering and early agricultural societies. Sometimes they become charismatic warriors or military leaders. What they all have in common

is that they become funnels or conduits for the power or wisdom of God to enter into this world. Anthropologically speaking, they are delegates of the tribe to another layer of reality, mediators who connect their communities to the Spirit.

It is important to note that the experience of spirit persons presupposes an understanding of reality very different from the dominant image of reality in the modern Western world. The modern worldview, derived from the Enlightenment, sees reality in material terms, as constituted by the world of matter and energy within the space-time continuum. The experience of spirit persons suggests that there is more to reality than this—that there is, in addition to the tangible world of our ordinary experience, a nonmaterial level of reality, actual even though nonmaterial, and charged with energy and power. The modern worldview is one-dimensional; the worldview of spirit persons is multidimensional.

Moreover, this other reality, it is important to emphasize, is not "somewhere else." Rather, it is all around us, and we are in it. In William James's words, we are separated from it only by filmy screens of consciousness. When those screens of consciousness momentarily drop away, the experience of Spirit occurs. A spirit person is one in whom those screens of consciousness are unusually permeable—compared with most of us, who seem to have hardened rinds of consciousness instead.[18]

TEACHER OF ALTERNATIVE WISDOM

Wisdom is one of the most important concepts for an understanding of what the New Testament says about Jesus. It is central for two reasons. On the one hand, Jesus was a teacher of wisdom. This is the strongest consensus among today's Jesus scholars. Whatever else can be said about the pre-Easter Jesus, he was a teacher of wisdom—a *sage*, as teachers of wisdom are called. On the other hand, the New

18. Ibid., 31–34.

Testament also presents Jesus as the embodiment or incarnation of divine wisdom. . . .

The subject matter of wisdom is broad. Basically, wisdom concerns how to live. It speaks of the nature of reality and how to live one's life in accord with reality. Central to it is the notion of a way or a path, indeed of two ways or paths: the wise way and the foolish way. Teachers of wisdom speak of these two ways, commending the one and warning of the consequences of following the other.

There are two types of wisdom and two types of sages. The most common type of wisdom is conventional wisdom; its teachers are conventional sages. This is the mainstream wisdom of a culture, "what everybody knows," a culture's understandings about what is real and how to live. . . .

The second type is a subversive and alternative wisdom. This wisdom questions and undermines conventional wisdom and speaks of another way, another path. Its teachers are subversive sages, and they include some of the most famous figures of religious history. Within Eastern religions, the two best-known teachers of a world-subverting wisdom are Lao-tzu and the Buddha. Lao-tzu spoke of following a "way" that led away from conventional perceptions and values and toward living in accord with "the Tao" itself. At the center of the Buddha's teaching is the image of a way, "the eightfold path," leading from the world of convention and its "grasping" to enlightenment and compassion. At the fountainhead of the Western philosophical tradition, Socrates taught a subversive wisdom that involved the citizens of Athens in a critical examination of the conventions that shaped their lives. For his efforts, he was executed.

The wisdom of subversive sages is the wisdom of "the road less traveled." And so it was with Jesus: his wisdom spoke of "the narrow way," which led to life, and subverted the "broad way" followed by the many, which led to destruction.[19]

19. Ibid., 69–70.

Next in our analysis of Borg's insights, we will present his thoughts on a foundational element of Jesus's character—that Jesus's dominant social vision was centered in compassion.

COMPASSION, SOCIAL WORLD AND POLITICS

Though compassion as the content of Jesus' *imitatio dei* [i.e., the imitation of God] was rooted in the Jewish tradition, it was not the dominant *imitatio dei* of the first-century Jewish social world. Instead, a different *imitatio dei*, also grounded in the Hebrew Bible, had become the primary paradigm shaping the Jewish social world: "Be holy as God is holy."

It is in the conflict between these two *imitatio deis*—between holiness and compassion as qualities of God to be embodied in community—that we see the central conflict in the ministry of Jesus: between two different social visions. The dominant social vision was centered in holiness; the alternative social vision of Jesus was centered in compassion.

Indeed, it is only when we appreciate this dimension of Jesus' emphasis upon compassion that we realize how radical his message and vision were. For Jesus, compassion was more than a quality of God and an individual virtue: it was a social paradigm, the core value for life in community. To put it boldly: compassion for Jesus was political. He directly and repeatedly challenged the dominant sociopolitical paradigm of his social world and advocated instead what might be called a *politics of compassion*. This conflict and this social vision continue to have striking implications for the life of the church today.[20]

There is another aspect of the character of the historical Jesus which fits into the sketch of Jesus but which Borg did not discuss in *Meeting Jesus Again, For the First Time*. He did, however, outline it in another of his books, *Jesus, a New Vision*. There, Borg describes Jesus's association with women and how that contrasted with the culture of his day. The culture of Galilee and Judea in the first century, it seems, was shot through and through with patriarchy, the social organization of society marked by the

20. Ibid., 49.

supremacy of men. The historical Jesus, on the other hand, treated men and women with radical equality. Here is an excerpt from *Jesus, a New Vision*.

> One of the most remarkable features of Jesus' ministry was his relationship to women. Challenging the conventional wisdom of his time, it continues to challenge the conventional wisdom of much of the church.
>
> Rigid boundaries between men and women marked the world in which he lived. Although perhaps intensified by the politics of holiness, these boundaries were not its direct result but a perennial characteristic of conventional wisdom in most cultures: patriarchy. Conventional wisdom is typically male-dominated. Produced and written by men, it is taught by men to men and reflects a male point of view. So it was in the cultures surrounding the Jewish social world and within Judaism itself.
>
> Though there are positive statements about women in both the Old Testament and postbiblical Judaism, the dominant attitude reflected in the teaching of the sages was negative. A good wife was much appreciated, but women as a group were not thought well of. The synagogue prayer recited at each service included the words, "Blessed art thou, O lord, who hast not made me a woman". In synagogues women typically were required to sit in a separate section and were not counted in the quorum of ten people needed to hold a prayer meeting. They did not teach the Torah, and as a general rule were not even to be taught the Torah.
>
> Their religious disenfranchisement extended into the social sphere. Except among the poorer classes, men and women were rigidly separated in public life. Young women of the wealthier families were completely secluded until marriage; after marriage, they could go out in public only if veiled. They were not to talk to men outside of their families. Similarly, a respectable Jewish man (and especially a religious teacher) was not to talk much with women, apparently for two reasons. There was no benefit to be gained, for they were viewed as not very bright and as preoccupied

with trivia. Moreover women were considered to be seductive and sexually rapacious temptresses. Their voices, hair, and legs were felt to be especially enticing. Thus, in part because they were regarded as inferior and in part because of male perceptions (and fears) of their sexuality, women were systematically excluded from both the religious and public life of the social world.

Against this background, Jesus' own behavior was extraordinary. The itinerant group of immediate followers included women, some of whom—Joanna and Susanna—supported the movement financially. The sight of a sexually mixed group traveling with a Jewish holy man must have been provocative. Similarly, the occasion on which a woman who was a "sinner" washed Jesus' feet with her tears and dried them with her hair as he reclined at a banquet given by a Pharisee was shocking.

Jesus was a guest in the home of two sisters named Mary and Martha. Martha played the traditional woman's role of preparing a meal, while Mary related to him as disciple to teacher. When Martha complained that she was doing all the work, Jesus endorsed Mary's behavior. In a first-century Jewish social context, it was a radical point. Jesus treated women and men as equally capable (and worthy) of dealing with sacred matters. In a time when a respectable sage was not even to converse with a woman outside of his family, and when women were viewed as both dangerous and inferior, the practice of Jesus was startling.

The radically transformed attitude toward women continued in the early church for the first several decades, according to both Acts and the letters of Paul, where women in many of his churches were prominent enough to be greeted by name. Paul's own position was consistent with the radicalism of the Jesus movement: "There is neither Jew nor Gentile, there is neither slave nor free, *there is neither male nor female,* for you are all one in Christ Jesus."

As already noted, patriarchy is not peculiar to ancient Judaism, but characterizes most cultures, Christian ones included. Indeed, the radical attitude of the Jesus movement toward women was already modified within the church before the New Testament was even completed. One of the later New Testament documents repeats the patriarchal view of the dominant culture: women are to be submissive and modest, and *not* to be teachers of men, and are even held responsible for bringing sin into the world [1 Tim 2: 8–15]. While attributed to Paul, most scholars believe this letter was written near the end of the first century by a second-generation follower of Paul.] Cultural attitudes from the Jewish and broader Mediterranean world had begun to cloud the vision generated by the Spirit.

Such attitudes have been part of the church and Western culture ever since. Yet when one sees the rejection of patriarchy by Jesus and his earliest followers and the clear historical evidence that patriarchy reentered the tradition at a later date, representing a "fall" from the radicalism of the early movement, it is almost incomprehensible that many within the church continue to teach the subordination of women. The Jesus movement as a counter-culture stands in contrast to later Christian tradition even as it stood out in its own social world.[21]

This concludes our visit with Marcus Borg and his portrait of the historical Jesus, a person immersed in the Sacred Spirit, who taught alternative wisdom, whose core value was compassion, and who treated women and men with radical equality. We now turn to a portrait of Jesus by Marvin Cain.

The Portrait by Marvin F. Cain

Marvin Cain presents to us his portrait of the historical Jesus from his book, *Jesus the Man.* Cain's first "stroke" in the portrait is that of Jesus as a teacher.

One thing about Jesus on which nearly everyone seems to agree is that Jesus was a teacher. In fact, Christians and non-Christians alike, generally regard him as one of the greatest teachers in the world. So, what did Jesus teach? How did he

21. Borg, *Jesus, A New Vision*, 133–35.

teach? How did people respond to his teaching? These questions have been around for centuries, yet there are no simple answers. Was Jesus a great moral teacher who propounded the fatherhood of God and the brotherhood of man, as many today claim? Did Jesus lay out a plan whereby people who followed it could be assured of going to heaven when they died? Did Jesus teach about himself? As a child, I learned that Jesus taught the "Golden Rule," that we should love one another, and that if we believed in him, heaven awaited us after death. But did Jesus actually teach those things?

During the last century, the extraordinary amount of study, which has been devoted to Jesus' teachings led to the rediscovery of a key element. First noted by European scholars, but now recognized by everyone, that discovery was the recognition that whatever else Jesus may have said, his fundamental message was about "the kingdom of God." One reason that discovery was so long in coming is that for the first nineteen centuries of Christianity, the Gospel of Matthew was the gospel most widely read, and regarded as the most accurate of the four. And Matthew's gospel does not have Jesus speak of the kingdom of God. Instead Matthew generally used the term "kingdom of Heaven" which many took to mean a kingdom beyond this world. That fact caused many to think Jesus' main concern was to teach about life in the next world, or in heaven, and how to get there. Apparently, however, Matthew was trying only to avoid the use of the word "God", something many pious people do even today, and simply substituted the word "heaven" for it. The consequence of that for me, and I suspect for many others, was that though I had been brought up in the church, and attended countless Sunday School and Vacation Bible School classes, I had never been told about the centrality of the kingdom of God in the teaching of Jesus. I first learned of its vital importance in seminary. I was puzzled that such an important concept could be so long and so totally ignored in the schools of Christianity.

In addition to the importance of the term "kingdom of God" for Jesus, scholars also discovered that by "the kingdom of God", Jesus was not referring to Heaven or some state of life after death, but rather the reign or rule of God in the real world. It differed from earthly kingdoms ruled by kings, priests or the rich and powerful. And it certainly was not the kingdom ruled by Caesar! It was the kingdom where God is the sovereign, where compassion and acceptance are the norm rather than ruthless enforcement of imperial regulations. Next scholars noted that most of Jesus' parables focused on defining or explaining that sovereign rule, or kingdom, of God. A giant step forward was made when scholars noted that Jesus' parables were not simply stories to be allegorized or moralized, as is often done in sermons; rather, they challenged the listener (or reader) to be confronted by what life is like when God is truly in control. Often the stories had surprising conclusions, such as a Samaritan, an outcast in the eyes of most Jews, coming to the aid of an injured Jew. The parables were, in reality, invitations to the hearer to ponder Jesus' vision of life in God's kingdom, under the beneficent rule of a loving, caring creator.

The third contribution those earlier twentieth-century scholars made to Jesus studies was in recognizing that in his sayings, one can come closer to the historical Jesus than anywhere else. It is in Jesus' teachings that his real uniqueness comes out. For that reason, when the Jesus Seminar set out to separate the historical Jesus from the Jesus of later dogma, they started with his sayings, especially his parables. These are as close as we can get to the heart and mind of Jesus. And let us note in passing that the word "parable" is a translation of the Hebrew *mashal*, which can mean not just story, but metaphor, riddle, sharp saying, and the like. Later in this chapter, we will look at a few of the parables of Jesus in some depth.

Along with the parables, a second form of Jesus' teaching relating to the kingdom of God was soon recognized: the one-line pithy sayings called "aphorisms" which occur throughout the gospels. While the parables are essentially stories comparing the kingdom of God to a commonplace experience, the aphorisms are "one-liners" that are sharp and unforgettable. Often they express ideas that are paradoxical or contrary to common experience. Two examples of such aphoristic sayings are:

> So the last will be first, and the first will be last. (Matt 20:16)

and

> It is easier for a camel to go through the eye of a needle than for someone who is rich to enter the kingdom of God. (Mark 10:25)

These short sayings are not facts set forth to be learned by rote. Instead, they are invitations to think, to ponder about what is involved. In the everyday world, the first are first and the last are last and it is much better to be first than last. But in God's realm it is not that way. Even wealth counts for nothing in God's kingdom. The reference to the camel going through the eye of a needle is as absurd as the man with a log in his eye seeing the speck in his neighbor's eye (Q, Matt 7:3–5 = Luke 6:41–42). Yet both are unforgettable images that present the hearers with an invitation to view life from a perspective other than the worldly.

Putting all this together, we come to see Jesus not as an inspiring teller of uplifting stories, but as a teacher whose abrasive images and appeal to common experience set him apart from other teachers of the ancient world. Jesus was a revolutionary teacher, who turned the conventional wisdom of his day on its ear. Instead of putting people to sleep, as most sermons on Jesus' teachings do today, his words prompted his hearers to think, and in some cases even provoked anger and rage. Jesus' teaching involved frontal attacks on the political, religious, social, and economic kingdoms of his day.

John Dominic Crossan, probably the foremost Jesus historian today, tells this story. Three people once heard Jesus speak. One went away saying, "I don't get it. I'm out of here." A second said, "I got his message and he is threatening my way of life. He must be destroyed!" The third person, having heard the very same words as the other two, declared, "This man speaks the word of God. I will follow him." I suspect

this was typical of the reactions to Jesus' parables and aphorisms. Some liked what Jesus said and followed him, some
became angry even to the point of wanting him done away
with, and some, perhaps most, simply ignored him.[22]

Cain concludes with more comments near the end of his book:

Having looked at the Jesus of history, what can we now make
of it all? Is there anything of practical value to glean from
all the scholarly work on Jesus during the past few decades?
I believe there is. What has become clear to me is a pressing
need to get back to the historical Jesus, to discover anew his
message of God's kingdom and to share in his vision of God
and the world. But to do that means to liberate Jesus from
the various prisons in which he has been confined since
the early centuries, when the church became organized and
Jesus became the God of both the Christian Church and the
Roman Empire. I see this need for liberation in [several]
areas [including] popular piety [i.e., conventional belief or
devoutness], the ancient worldview, [and] apocalyptic eschatology. . . .

The first need is to liberate Jesus from the image of
popular Christian piety. The traditional understanding of
Jesus—the sweet, sentimental, miracle-working moralist,
who walked on water, taught the Golden Rule, and came
down from heaven to die for the sins of the world. That notion must give way to a Jesus who was much more than that.
Jesus was a real person, a first century Palestinian Jew, a man
of strength, a man of courage, who dared to challenge the
power systems of his day. He placed allegiance to God above
that owed to political, religious, economic, or social rulers.
He challenged the elite with the message that God cares for
the lowest elements of society, especially those marginalized
by rigid standards of purity that defined who was, who was
not, worthy of God's love and care.

Jesus' words were not sweet stories but sharp exhortations to view the world from God's perspective. God's high

22. Cain, *Jesus the Man*, 47–49.

standards of mercy and compassion stand in sharp contrast to those of many people today including Christians, for whom wealth, power, elitism and piety are life's highest priorities. Because of what he said and did, Jesus did not find many approving listeners, and his words angered many who heard him. In the end, the cry to crucify came not from a small group of especially evil people but from those who make up the respectable elements of every society.

Secondly, Jesus needs to be freed from the ancient worldview and the language of neo-Platonism and Augustinian metaphysics. For people to continue to speak of Jesus in terms developed at the councils of Nicea (325 CE) and Chalcedon (451 CE) is to make Jesus unintelligible to modern people. We no longer speak of things in terms of "accidents" and "substance" as did the neo-Platonists. For us to declare Jesus as being "of one substance with the Father" is to speak gobbledegook.

As for the ancient world view, it was based on a three-tiered universe: heaven, the abode of God and other spirits was above the earth; the nether world below was the domain of evil spirits and the resting place of the dead; and the earth between was a battle ground between good and evil, with evil forces largely in control. That view is no longer intelligible to people who know astronomy and physics. And the idea of God "up there" or "out there" in either time or space is an equally radical contradiction to the teaching of Jesus, who saw God in the world and in the lives of people here on earth.

Along with that, we need to liberate God from the Gnostic and medieval notions that have permeated Christian theology for nearly two millennia. Traditional Christian theology holds to a God who demands perfection; but since no human being can be perfect, all are consigned to damnation unless they are rescued by someone who comes from God. That notion of God, which arose in Gnosticism, is unacceptable for people today who see in the world, and in their lives, a God of love and compassion for all creation. That God of love and compassion is also the God of Jesus, who knew and spoke about a God as a loving father who cares for even the worst of people and who enjoins all creation to live by that same law of love.

In the first Christian centuries, Jesus, as a Jewish teacher/exorcist, was intelligible to Jews, but made little sense to sophisticated Greeks and Romans. So, early Christians sought to make Jesus meaningful to the gentile world by describing him in terms and concepts more appropriate to Greco-Roman heroes and gods. But for many people today things have come full circle and the Jewish prophet/healer makes much more sense than the Greco-Roman Jesus of the church's creeds and dogmas.

Acts 2 contains the story of Pentecost. It describes an event in which Palestinian Jews, who spoke Aramaic, were suddenly able to proclaim the gospel to people who spoke a myriad of languages. Regardless of how one might interpret the story (was it a matter of instant Berlitz or of speaking in the universal language of love and acceptance?), the point is that the gospel must be in a comprehensible language if it is to be understood and followed. What we need today is a second Pentecost, in which the gospel is made intelligible to modern people, who have been trained in the sciences and hold a scientific view of history and of the world.

The third prison from which we must free Jesus is the prison of eschatology, especially apocalyptic eschatology. For Luke to describe Jesus as ascending into heaven (remember, Luke is the only Evangelist to do so) made sense when God was "up there". We no longer view the world in terms of a three-tiered universe. The abode of God is not some place out beyond the sun, moon and stars, a place that one can reach by traveling through space. Modern cosmology not only demands a different way of viewing the heavenly bodies, but it also demands a different way of viewing the abode of God and Jesus.

And just as God's abode is not a matter of space, so it is not a matter of time either. The notion that God and Jesus are sitting "up there" waiting to return at some future day, bringing judgment and destruction of all his enemies, has done considerable mischief in the church. First, it has created an idea of God and Jesus as absentee landlords far removed from the world we inhabit. As a result, it is Satan, not God, who often seems to be most at work in the world—or even in control of it. Second, it has often created an atmosphere of resignation, as though Christians should not get involved in confronting society's ills, but quietly wait for God to act in the end time (Greek: *eschaton*). Third, it has focused attention on the individual getting ready for something to happen in the future, rather than living actively, as Jesus did, in the present world. Fourth, it portrays God as one who can accomplish his will only by destruction. According to the apocalypticists, millions of Jews, Arabs and others will have to be destroyed for God to win in the end. Such notions of God are bizarre when compared to the compassionate and loving God of Jesus and his message.

We need to rediscover Jesus' message that the kingdom of God has arrived. It is here, not up there in space, or out there in time.[23]

Thus, Marvin Cain sees the historical Jesus in the following manner:

1. Jesus was a revolutionary teacher in parables and aphorisms who focused upon what he called the Kingdom of God, and by that he meant the reign of God in this real world.

2. Jesus was not a sweet sentimental moralist, but was a man of strength and courage who challenged the power systems of his day. His sharp exhortations called people to view the world from God's perspective of mercy and compassion.

3. The real historical Jesus can be seen only if we speak of him in terms of our own scientific worldview, not the three tiered universe of the first century: heaven above where God dwells, the nether world below which is the domain of evil spirits, and the flat earth in between where there is a battle between good and evil.

4. Jesus did not believe or teach in apocalyptic eschatology – that is, he did not believe in a God who will accomplish his will only by the

---

23. Ibid., 135–37.

destruction of all his enemies. Instead, Jesus believed and taught of compassion and love.

This completes our visit with Marvin Cain and his portrait of the historical Jesus. We now turn to the final portrait in the series in this book: that of John Dominic Crossan.

The Portrait by John Dominic Crossan

Our final look at the Portraits of the historical Jesus is provided by a person who is undoubtedly one of the most outstanding Jesus scholars in the world today: John Dominic Crossan. Crossan is professor emeritus of religious studies at DePaul University in Chicago. He is the former chair of the Historical Jesus Section of the Society of Biblical Literature. We will look at excerpts from his article "Jesus as a Mediterranean Jewish Peasant," in a book that contains a collection of fourteen Portraits of the historical Jesus. The book is *Profiles of Jesus*.[24] Crossan begins his article by announcing his conclusion.

> The heart of the original Jesus movement was a shared egalitarianism [i.e., human equality] of spiritual and material resources.[25]

Then, he develops his theme by analyzing several parables as they appear in the sources of Q, the Gospel of Thomas, and the Gospel of Mark. Crossan believes that Jesus's ecstatic vision centered on eating with people from all classes, sexes, ranks and grades, all mixed up together.

> The social challenge of an egalitarian table is the radical threat posed by [a] parable and is the content of Jesus' ecstatic vision. [A] parable is only a story, of course, but it is a story that focuses its challenge on the heart of society, the table, the place where persons meet to eat, the place where they establish and confirm the social order.[26]

In Crossan's view, the historical Jesus's vision was closely linked with his social program.

24. Hooever, ed., *Profiles of Jesus*.
25. Crossan, "Jesus as a Mediterranean Peasant," 161.
26. Ibid., 164.

Yet, in all these texts, the same basic point appears: things are shared in common. There healers are not to receive alms or handouts, let alone payments of wages. They bring with them a free, open, and shared healing. In return they are to receive a free, open, and shared eating. And that explains, of course, the two items of dress code on which Q and Mark agree: Jesus' followers are not to carry either money-purse or bag. They do not need a money-purse because they are not to receive alms in the form of money. And they do not require a bag because they are not to receive alms in the form of food. For Jesus, in other words, sharing was not just a strategy for supporting the mission. That could have been achieved by the use of alms, or wages, or charges, or fees of some sort. It could have been done, for instance, by begging in the fashion of Cynic philosophers who wandered around the Greco-Roman cities. Sharing was rather a strategy for building or rebuilding the peasant community on radically different principles from those under girding an honor/shame society, a society based on patronage and clientage. Jesus' strategy was based on an egalitarian sharing of spiritual and material power at the most grassroots level. For that reason, dress and equipment were just as important as house and table.

To sum up, Jesus had both a vision and a program, which were designed originally to move from peasant to peasant among the houses and small villages of lower Galilee. And what is still visible, even in sources written down years later for circumstances quite different from those under which Jesus labored and for circumstances that differed from Christian community to Christian community, is the clear evidence that we are not dealing originally with mere begging and almsgiving, but with a common table and open sharing. The disciples do not carry a bag because they do not beg for alms or food or clothing or anything else. They share a miracle and a kingdom and in return they receive a table and a house. Here, I think is the heart of the original Jesus movement, a shared egalitarianism of spiritual and material resources. I emphasize this as strongly as possible and I insist that its material aspects and its spiritual aspects, the fact of it and its symbolic representation cannot be separated. The mission we are talking about is not, like Paul's, a dramatic thrust along major trade routes to urban centers hundreds of miles apart. Yet it concerns the longest journey in the Greco-Roman world, maybe in any world, the step across the threshold of a peasant stranger's home.[27]

This completes our surveys of scholarly portraits of the historical Jesus. Although the four portraits we have examined are not identical, they certainly do have much in common. It brings richness to our vision to see the historical Jesus from these four points of view.

We now turn from the examination of the quest for the historical Jesus to a realistic look at the Christian church of our own day.

27. Ibid., 167–68.

Three

The Problems in Today's Church

WHAT IS TO BE the result of all this theological research on the historical Jesus? Can it change the Christian church? Before we consider that question in detail, we must start with an analysis of the problem. In what way, if any, is the Christian church in need of change? Some say the church is in desperate need of a new Reformation even deeper and broader than the Reformation of the sixteenth century led by Martin Luther.

Bishop John Shelby Spong, retired Episcopal Bishop of New Jersey, has been a vocal and articulate spokesperson for the need to change the church. Although he does not say so, the views of Bishop Spong seem to apply to the Christian church of North America and Europe, and they may or may not be pertinent to the Christian churches of Africa, South America and, perhaps, China and Russia. These latter churches have their own culture and problems that may be on a different level than the church in the United States and Europe. Nevertheless, the views of Bishop Spong seem valid for our own church and culture and should carry particular weight because he is someone who is an insider, someone who has been an integral part of the American Christian church all his life, and who criticizes the church from that vantage point. Surely, that is more valuable than an outsider attacking the church.

Bishop Spong says that for the first sixteen hundred years or so of Christian history, the church envisioned God as a being in the sky, a God who intervenes in human affairs from time to time. But then, as Bishop Spong states in his book, *Why Christianity Must Change or Die,*

> ... when the modern age began to dawn, a new understand-
> ing of the shape of the universe began to grow and God's

71

place as the heavenly director of human affairs began to totter.

This revolution in Western thought began first, perhaps, with the work of Nicolaus Copernicus (1473–1573), who with relatively primitive astronomical tools began to study the sun, the moon, the stars, and the heavens in a new way. He came to some startling conclusions, which changed forever the way we would think about the skies and the God who presumably inhabited them. In this time before mass communications, the insights of Copernicus went almost unnoticed, however, until a disciple named Galileo Galilei (1564–1642), building on those Copernican insights, began to revise in a public way the perception of the universe and the place of the planet Earth within that universe. Galileo concluded that the sun did not rotate around the earth but rather that the earth rotated around the sun. It was a revolutionary idea and represented a major shift in human consciousness. This meant that the Earth could no longer be envisioned as the center of the universe and thus that God might not be quite so involved in the day-to-day affairs of human beings. This idea sent shivers down the spines of the ecclesiastical power brokers of the day, whose understanding of God depended on these heretofore unquestioned assumptions. Galileo was condemned to death as a heretic. In order to save his life, he was given the opportunity to recant, which he, not very courageously, decided to accept. His recantation, however, changed nothing. The ancient worldview against which the Christian story had been framed had been dealt a mighty blow. In time it would even be seen by some as a fatal blow. At that moment, however, it was only the first step toward our exile.

The process of adjusting to this new understanding of the world produced a long-term but inevitable trauma. The biblical view of the universe was slowly and quietly discarded. Perhaps the full acceptance of this idea was not complete until December 28, 1991, when the Vatican finally admitted officially that Galileo had been right and that the Church, as well as the Bible, had been wrong about the shape of the universe and the place of human beings and this world within that universe.

That Vatican admission came far too late. The world had for some centuries already assumed that truth. Air travel, satellite communications, and space exploration were all built on the insights of Copernicus and Galileo. When those insights became the working assumptions of human beings, the power of the Church to control life, or even to interpret it, began to fade perceptibly. That lost ecclesiastical power would never be recovered.

People began to grasp the fact that God did not sit on a throne beyond the sky looking down. Divine intervention became a problematic concept. As the knowledge of the universe grew, the religious community tried to adjust. Christianity began to shift the location of God from "up there" to "out there," as if somehow that new spatial image made God more believable. Finally, however, distances overwhelmed even this concept of God's dwelling place. The nearest star to our sun, Alpha Centauri, is about 4.3 light-years away. The large Magellanic cloud, the nearest galaxy to our galaxy, is about 150,000 light-years away. Andromeda, the nearest clearly defined galaxy, is 2,000,000 light-years away. What is a light-year? The distance light will journey in a year traveling at the approximate rate of 186,000 miles per second. One light-year equals almost six trillion miles. Our embrace of the vastness of space had the effect, finally, of removing God from the sky and then increasingly even from our human consciousness.

God was no longer either up there or out there. The heavens began to seem empty of that protecting, judging, and even caring divine presence. Yet the ancient world could envision God in no other way; neither can most of the religious systems of our contemporary world. So when believers faced the shock of an empty sky, the content that once filled the word God began a slow but certain retreat into oblivion. The modern consciousness was on the way to becoming godless, at least by traditional religious definitions. The Church began to wonder how it could continue to talk about a God beyond the sky who, according to the biblical story, had once sent fire from those same heavens to burn up the sacrifices offered by Elijah on Mount Carmel and thus to defeat the priests of an alien deity known as Baal (1 Kings 18:20–46). How could the story of Jesus ascending into the sky to return to God after his death (Acts 2) still be proclaimed with intellectual integrity? The stories of Jesus appearing out of the sky to his disciples on a mountaintop in Galilee (Matt. 28:16–20) or of Paul seeing a heavenly Jesus in that same sky on the road to Damascus (Acts 9) became increasingly problematic. Those biblical accounts were so obviously shaped by the ancient three-tiered worldview that no longer existed. People living in the new world, whose shape Copernicus and Galileo and countless others had delineated, began to awaken to the fact that they could no longer use any of the traditional language about God and a heaven "out there" that so deeply filled our ancient faith system. That language had lost its meaning.

Beyond the time of Galileo, but still within the same century, an English physicist named Isaac Newton (1643–1727) applied his brilliant mathematical mind to this growing body of scientific data first suggested by the insights of Copernicus and Galileo. Newton was determined to demonstrate in intimate detail just how the world worked and, not coincidentally, how God worked within this world. So he began to assert that there were natural explanations for many of the things that in generations past had been considered mysteries attributed solely to the power of God. At that moment the need for God as the explanation for things that previously had been inexplicable began to fade, and with it also faded the previously powerful religious categories of miracle and magic.[1]

A century or so after Newton, an English biologist named Charles R. Darwin (1809–1882) added enormously to the body of breathtaking modern knowledge and to the development of what today is called the secular spirit. The same

1. Spong, *Why Christianity Must Change or Die*, 31–34.

frightened human beings who once thought that the earth was the center of the universe, and who once believed that they basked continuously in the center of God's heavenly gaze, had consoled themselves after Galileo and Newton with the comforting thought that at least human beings were the crown of God's creation and the purpose for which God had made the world. They even bore within themselves, it was said, the divine image. People living in the pre-Darwinian world simply could not imagine a time before human life, and in their worldview all of nature was believed to exist only for human benefit. They also made the assumption that a great gap separated the human from the subhuman forms of life and that an even greater gap separated the animate world from the inanimate world. The myth of creation with which the Bible opened had long been treated as if it were literally true both geologically and biologically. That myth suggested that the man and the woman were made on the final day of God's busy first week. God finished the perfect creation with this majestic act and proceeded to take the divine rest on the seventh day, thus creating the Sabbath. In the common mind so obviously true were these tales that few people in that believing age conceived of any other possibility—few people, that is, until the writings of Charles Darwin appeared.

In 1859 Darwin's masterpiece, entitled *The Origin of Species*, was published. That book caused most of the remaining principles by which human life was understood in religious terms to go up in smoke. Darwin suggested, for example, that the world of God's creation was not yet finished, directly contradicting the literal biblical text. The world, he said, was still evolving, still being created. Even Darwin had not yet embraced the true age of this planet, but his work opened the door to vastly expanding the timeline. Darwin's insights also caused the distance between human and subhuman life to shrink perceptibly. In the book of Psalms (Ps. 8), it had been suggested that human beings were just a little lower than the angels. But now we began to recognize that we were just a little higher than the animals. Apes and monkeys came to be viewed as our cousins, and defining the moment when human beings first appeared on this earth became problematic. Guesses still range from fifty thousand to two million years ago, depending on which definition of human life one is using. There was much talk in that era about something called "the missing link," as if the various species of life were separated by a single link rather than by centuries of tiny adaptations. Pinpointing mutations in the eons of evolutionary time was difficult. Slowly but surely it dawned upon people that human beings are, in fact, highly evolved animals with superior brains. But since no ultimate worth or eternal destiny had yet been attributed to any animal, questions and doubts about the status that had been claimed previously for Homo sapiens began to be raised. Darwin's insights posed those questions and doubts in an unavoidable way so they began to rattle around in our psyches, to echo in our inner chambers, and to challenge our inflated self-perceptions. Increasingly, human beings felt themselves bound to this earth. "Dust thou art and to dust thou shalt return" became not just a Lenten note of penitence, but a statement of this newly understood reality of human life.

The Christian Church resisted Darwin with vigor, but the ecclesiastical power of antiquity had already been broken, and the Church's ability to threaten Darwin with execution as a heretic no longer existed. Besides, truth can never be deterred just because it is inconvenient. Today, whether his critics like it or not, Charles Darwin's thought organizes the biological sciences of the Western world. His work has made possible such once-unimaginable things as organ transplants using organs derived from subhuman species. They work because Darwin was right. That strange thing called "creation science" [i.e., a so-called "science" which follows the Hebrew myth of creation in Genesis and which is sometimes taught alongside the Darwin theories in American schools] is nothing more than ignorant rantings reflecting a frightened and dying religious mentality.[2]

How, then, can Christianity be changed to comport with modern scientific knowledge? How can we fashion a belief system which does not require us to park our minds at the door of the church and which is consistent with the true findings of Galileo and Darwin? Bishop Spong believes that we must change the way we think about God and about Jesus. He believes that our current condition is similar to that of the ancient Judeans when they were carried off into exile in Babylon, away from their home in Israel. They were in a strange land and had to completely revise their image of God. No longer could God be the protector of their own tribe. The image of God had to change. In a similar way, our own image of God can no longer be that of the Christian church before Galileo and Darwin. We are in exile and our image of God must change. As Bishop Spong puts it:

> The God worshiped by the Jews before their Babylonian exile was not the same God who emerged from the exile. Much later a longer-range view of Jewish history reconnected the two, but that was not the sense of the people who lived at the time of the exile. Similarly, the God worshiped in the Christian West will not survive the thought revolution that has produced our exile, though we, too, might hope for some future reconnection. The Jews came out of Babylon as a people of faith with a God who had been transformed from the tribal deity of Israel's past.[3]

> One ancient Hebrew word for God, for example, was *ruach*. Literally, that word meant "wind," a natural and even an impersonal concept. The wind or *ruach* was observed not as a being, but as a vitalizing force. It had no boundaries and no recognizable destination. Among the Hebrews the *ruach* or wind of God was said to have brooded over the chaos in the story of creation in order to bring forth life. Slowly

2. Ibid., 35–37.
3. Ibid., 59.

this *ruach* then evolved and became personalized and was called Spirit. But it is important to note that at its origin *ruach* was an impersonal life force, an experienced "what," not a "who." The *ruach* or wind of God was not external. It rather emerged from within the world and was understood as its very ground, its life-giving reality. This *ruach* was also thought to be connected in some way to human *nephesh* or breath. That also was and is an impersonal concept. Breath was a force that wells up from within each of us and was thought in some sense to be identical with our life.[4]

Turning from thinking about the concept of God to thinking about Jesus, Bishop Spong writes,

. . . the earliest Christians first referred to Jesus as a "spirit person." So to probe the Jesus experience, we need to focus on why the word spirit was the first word applied to him by his original followers.[5]

To see Jesus clearly as a spirit person, Bishop Spong returns to the concept of "wind."

So once again I pick up the Jewish word for wind, *ruach*, and the Jewish word for breath, *nephesh*, and seek to explore their Jewish meaning. The *ruach* or wind was first of all impersonal. It was conceived of by Jews to be mysterious in both its origin and in its destination. It "blows where it wills and you hear the sound of it, but you do not know whence it comes or whither it goes," said the Johannine Gospel (3:8) written near the end of the first century of the common era. That writer went on to say, "So is everyone who is born of the spirit." The wind is an analogy for the spiritual life. Wind also had an animating power. It vitalized the world, which shook and waved as a sign of the wind's power. To try to capture the wind, or to strive after the wind, or even to define the wind was vanity, said the book of Ecclesiastes (2:17, 26, 4:4). The wind was also assumed by the Jewish mind

4. Ibid., 60–61.
5. Ibid., 101.

to have come from God. "Thou didst blow with thy wind," said the book of Exodus (15:10), and "There went forth a wind from the Lord," said the book of Numbers (11:31). God might have been defined by these ancient people as a distant, theistic, personal power who lived beyond the sky, but in the very mysterious wind, which the Jews felt on their own faces, they believed they found themselves touched by God here and now.... The wind was a symbol of God's vitality, God's incorporeal status, and God's intimacy, and even though the divine one dwelled beyond this world, a God presence in this world forced God's reality upon them. So the Hebrew word for wind, *ruach*, became a synonym for spirit.

The second Jewish word for spirit was *nephesh*, breath. In the ancient Jewish story of creation, God created life in the man, Adam, when God "breathed into Adam's nostrils the breath of life and this creature became a living being" (Gen. 2:7). So the mighty wind, the *ruach*, we discover, was also sometimes understood to be the very breath of God. Hence, God's breath, or the divine *nephesh*, came to be thought of as the very source of all life, and *nephesh* or breath was identified with the vitality and animation found in every living being. Therefore, in Jewish thinking, spirit was conceived of externally as the wind, the ruach, and internally as the breath of life itself, the *nephesh*. When *nephesh* was removed from a being, that being became inert and dead. That is how *nephesh*, the breath of God within us, came to be identified with that nonmaterial part of our reality. Thus *nephesh* would later be translated as "soul" or "spirit." But at its inception and at its heart, it referred to the breath of God dwelling within us, calling us to life itself.

Once we have clarified these words and scraped them clean of later doctrinal connotations, we can begin to see the interconnections among wind, breath, and spirit all over the Jewish and Christian story. The task of spirit was always to give life. In this ancient understanding, the spiritual person was not the pious person or the religious person, but the vital, alive, whole, and real person. So the Jewish scriptures tell us that in Ezekiel's vision, when the wind or breath of God blew over the mountain and touched the dead dry bones in the valley, those bones came alive (Ezek. 37:1–10). That is the result of ruach spirit. Later in the Christian scriptures, when the Holy Spirit descended upon the gathered Christian community at Pentecost (Acts 2), we note that it came as a mighty rushing wind, a *ruach*, and it resulted in barriers being broken and community being restored. When the Christian Church formulated its creeds in the fourth and fifth centuries of this common era, it had its adherents say, "I believe in the Holy Spirit, the Lord, the giver of life." Spirit as *ruach* and *nephesh* always meant life-giver.[6]

Certainly this understanding of Spirit gives us a fuller view of Jesus as a spirit person, and leads to seeing ourselves as spirit persons filled with the breath of life. And this leads directly to the way worship in the Christian Church should now be focused. Bishop Spong continues:

> . . . worship may well have to be defined anew in every age, but worship must always be an aspect of our humanity. Since worship must be located somewhere, then something like a church as a center or place of worship must always be a part of our future. Both the activity of worship and the structure of the church may be very different, but my conviction is that we cannot be fully human without them. The question for our time is, can worship and the Church escape its theistic understandings, which will guarantee the deaths of both as we know them? Can both move from where they are today to where they must be tomorrow without a complete break with yesterday? Must a death to the past be a prerequisite to life in the future for these aspects of our humanity?
>
> We have looked at the signs of change already apparent in the activity called worship. Now let me try to sketch the future, first in broad brush strokes and later in more specific details.

6. Ibid., 104–6.

Worship beyond the exile will not be marked with chanted words to an external deity. Liturgical activity will not be a repetitious living out of a remembered tradition that celebrated the perceived activity of the theistic God. Worship in the future will be marked, rather, by the self-conscious awareness that all of us are or can be God bearers and life givers and that our deepest religious task is to give ourselves away. It will involve a call to that state of being where giving one's life away is both natural and desirable. Worship beyond the exile will not be oriented toward an external God but toward the world of our human community. That, however, will not result in a shallow humanism but in a recognition that the place where God is ultimately found is in the depths of our own humanity. So there will be no attempt in our future worship to escape life, but every attempt to expand life.

Since God will be seen as a presence at the heart of life, available to everyone and not as the special possession of the religious institution, then surely worship in the future will be less and less hierarchical and more and more circular. It will inevitably shed its denominational agenda and its territorial wars. It will lay down its royal images and its pretensions. It will cease to pretend that it speaks for God or that it is the sole channel of divine grace. It will dedicate itself to the search for truth, universal truth, rather than expending its energies in seeking to defend its narrow version of truth. It will treasure its sacred scriptures as the record of its ancestors in faith as they sought to worship God. But it will not be bound by either the cultural or the cultic limitations of those scriptures. It will recognize that the revelations of the Holy One did not cease when the canon of scripture was closed. It will call people into the fullness of life. It will not exist to support that specialized activity called religion. Those few whose being has been affirmed by the theistic patterns of the past will find themselves stripped bare. But those who hunger for God, who thirst for righteousness, and who believe that worship issues in an enhanced being for all will rejoice.[7]

Religion is . . . a human attempt to process the God experience, which breaks forth from our own depths and wells up constantly within us. We must lay down, therefore, the primitive claims we have made for our religious traditions. None of them is drawn from otherworldly revelations. None of them is inerrant or infallible. None of them represents the only way to God. None of them can be used legitimately to coerce or compel another to belief. All evangelical and missionary activities designed to convert the heathen are base born. They are the expressions of our sense of superiority and our hostility toward those who are different. The only divine mission in life that the Church of the future could possibly have is to open people to a recognition that the ground of their very being is holy and that when they are in touch with that . . . they can share in God's creation by giving life, love, and being to others. That is the task of those who claim to be God bearers. The Christians of the world are not here to build institutions, to convert other people, or even to claim that we can speak for God. Those aspects of our religions heritage must be sacrificed as the premodern misunderstandings of our primitive history.[8]

Bishop Spong ends with a personal note:

I am first, last, and always a believer. I define myself theologically as a believer who lives in exile. I have lived and worshiped as a believer. I shall continue to do so and to be so until the day I die. When that moment comes, I expect to enter even more deeply into the reality of the God in whom I have lived and moved and had my being.

I am therefore at peace.

Shalom.[9]

7. Ibid., 186–88.
8. Ibid., 225–26.
9. Ibid., 228.

Now that we have defined the problems in the North American and European Christian churches, at least as it is seen through the eyes of Bishop John Shelby Spong, we turn to what other authors believe can be the solutions of that problem.

Four

Re-visioning the Church with the Historical Jesus

MANY SCHOLARS BELIEVE THAT the changes in Christianity called for by Bishop Spong must include what scholarship has revealed about the historical Jesus. A Christian religion based upon Jesus of Nazareth might be very different from a religion based upon the traditions which developed after Jesus's death culminating in the creeds of the fourth century. Indeed, it would be a re-visioning of the Christian Church, a new vision of the Church based upon what we know of the historical Jesus. Let us look at six scholarly visions of this new Christianity. We begin with the scholarly work of Robert W. Funk, in which he places the spotlight upon certain doctrines of the Christian church that have been outmoded by the new knowledge of the historical Jesus. Next, we will look at two insights of Roy W. Hoover. First, Hoover draws a parallel between the situation of our own time and the time of the historical Jesus. Hoover then sets forth his views on how the re-visioned Christian church should conduct its adult education and its form of worship in its use of Scripture, its hymns, and its public prayers. Next, Charles Hedrick invites the Christian church to take the raw data of what we have learned about the historical Jesus and use it to develop our own inferences that are compatible with our own century of time. Stephen J. Patterson then points out that both the historical and confessional aspects of Scripture are necessary, but he implores us to confess a faith that is focused upon the historical Jesus. Finally, in the work of Marcus Borg, we are given the opportunity to view Christianity based on the historical Jesus as an Emerging Paradigm, which can change the basic groundwork of our faith. Does each aspect of this re-visioning of Christianity really amount to a new Reformation? Perhaps that is the root question.

84

OUTMODED CHURCH DOCTRINES: ROBERT W. FUNK

We begin with Robert W. Funk, who gives us his analysis in his book *Honest to Jesus*. He asks the question, "What real knowledge—knowledge of consequence for us and our time—has this thirst to know the flesh-and-blood Jesus produced?" His answer to that question can be glimpsed by the following excerpts from his book.

> What would happen if "the dangerous and subversive memories" of that solitary figure were really stripped of their interpretive overlay? Were that to happen, the gospel of Jesus would be liberated from the Jesus of the gospels and allowed to speak for itself. The creedal formulations of the second, third, and fourth centuries would be de-dogmatized and Jesus would be permitted to emerge as a robust, real, larger-than-life figure in his own right. Moreover, current images of Jesus would be torn up by their long affective roots and their attachment to pet causes severed. The pale, anemic, iconic Jesus would suffer by comparison with the stark realism of the genuine article.[1]

> This agenda takes us back to the beginnings of Christianity, to a time well before it assumed its classical form at Nicea. Just as the first believers did, we will have to start all over again with a clean theological slate, with only the parables, aphorisms, parabolic acts, and deeds of Jesus as the basis on which to formulate a new version of the faith. That is a breathtaking agenda, to say the very least.[2]

> The initial observation to be made is this: the popular forms of Christianity we now have do not require—indeed, do not even permit—Jesus to endorse them. Creedalism is a religion that supersedes Jesus, replaces him, or perhaps displaces him, with a mythology that depends on nothing Jesus said, or did, with the possible exception of his death.
>
> I am a spiritual descendant of Rudolf Bultmann and Karl Barth, Reinhold Niebuhr and Paul Tillich, and the

---

1. Funk, *Honest to Jesus*, 300.
2. Ibid., 301.

neo-orthodox movement they sponsored. I am deeply in-
debted to my mentors, and I have nothing but respect for
that legacy. Nevertheless, I now believe that neo-orthodoxy (and its Catholic counterparts) was the dying gasp of
creedal Christianity—a last effort to salvage it for the modern world. In the half century that follows the end of the
Second World War, it has become clear that neo-orthodoxy
has failed, that we have moved beyond the reach of that
noble effort. In plain language, neo-orthodoxy is dead. As
that fact dawned on me, slowly and painfully, I found myself forced to re-evaluate all those doctrines that constitute
the orthodox creed. I have done so at the behest of Jesus as
the subverter of theological litmus tests. I began to wonder
what, if anything, Jesus had contributed to the religion that
regards him as its founder. Here are the preliminary results
of my reflections, formulated as additional theses. . . . We
can no longer rest our faith on the faith of Peter or the faith
of Paul. I do not want my faith to be a secondhand faith. I
am therefore fundamentally dissatisfied with versions of the
faith that trace their origins only so far as the first believers;
true faith, fundamental faith, must be related in some way
directly to Jesus of Nazareth.[3]

Jesus made forgiveness reciprocal. Jesus tells the paralytic,
the blind man, the adulteress that they are forgiven, without
exacting penalties or promises from them. Jesus forgives
because his Father forgives and on the same terms: without
penalty or promise. The only requirement is reciprocity: one
is forgiven to the extent that one forgives. Thus, one can become the recipient of forgiveness only if one first becomes
the agent of forgiveness. By acknowledging that forgiveness
is in the hands of the human agents, Jesus precludes the
possibility of vesting that matter in the hands of priests or
clerics or even God. The power to forgive has already been
conferred upon those who themselves need and want for-

3. Ibid., 304.

giveness. Human beings can have only what they freely give away.[4]

Jesus advocated an unbrokered relationship to God. Jesus insisted that everyone has immediate and particular access to God. It is therefore not plausible that he would have commissioned certain disciples to broker that relationship in his vision of God's domain. The inauguration of a priesthood and clergy therefore appears to be inimical to Jesus' wishes.

The Jesus Seminar concluded, on the basis of the evidence, that, while Jesus enjoyed good companionship, he did not deliberately collect disciples, and he did not select "twelve" special followers or appoint leaders among them. Furthermore, he did not commission his followers to establish a church or inaugurate a world mission. The words and acts to this effect are found only in the framework stories of the narrative gospels, not in the authentic parables and aphorisms. (Awarding the keys to the kingdom to Peter in Matthew 16:16–19 and the great commission in Matthew 28:16–20 are stories without historical foundation, according to the Seminar.)

To put the matter candidly, the canonical gospels endeavor to authenticate the leadership of the church then in power. The authentic words of Jesus reject the notion of privileged position among his followers: the first will be last and the last first; those who aspire to be leaders should become slaves of all.[5]

We will have to abandon the doctrine of the blood atonement. The atonement in popular piety is based on a mythology that is no longer credible—that God is appeased by blood sacrifices. Jesus never expressed the view that God was holding humanity hostage until someone paid the bill. Nor did Amos, Hosea, or other prophets of Israel. In addition, it is the linchpin that holds the divinity of Jesus, his virgin birth, the bodily resurrection, and a sinless life together in a

4. Ibid., 310–11.
5. Ibid., 311.

unified but naive package: God required a perfect sacrifice, so only a divine victim would do.[6]

Redeem sex and Mary, Jesus' mother, by restoring to Jesus a biological if not actual father. Virginity is not necessarily godly, except in an ascetic, pleasure-denying, dualistic world. And Jesus is not necessarily a more effective savior for having been born without a father. Celebrate all aspects of life by giving Mary her rights as a woman, even if it means acknowledging that Jesus may have been a bastard. A bastard messiah is a more evocative redeemer figure than an unblemished lamb of God.

The virgin birth, in the light of other miraculous birth stories in the ancient world, is a mythical way to account for an unusual life. The gods frequently consorted with human beings in Greek and Roman mythology and gave birth to heroes and heroines. Within the limits of romantic folklore, the virgin birth of Jesus is an intriguing tale—not particularly well suited to adolescent Mary and baby Jesus, perhaps, but delightful; as a piece of literalized theology, it is contemptible. In any case, the virgin birth becomes an extraneous doctrine once the need for an unblemished sacrifice, for a blood atonement, is abandoned.

Augustine's notion that the consequences of Adam's sin is transmitted through male sperm is one of the great tragedies of theological history. He should be labeled as misguided and Manichean for his views. Furthermore, we should blow the whistle on the Roman curia for its ascetic proclivities—the self-justifying inclination to condemn sex for all purposes other than conception. Mary's plight is thereby linked to a celibate priesthood on the grounds that abstinence is godly and that sex is dirty, aside from necessary multiplication of the race, especially in Catholic countries. In Genesis the Lord did not order human beings to multiply and *destroy* the earth.

The anti-abortion movement, sponsored by both Catholics and Protestants, pretends that it is solely con-

6. Ibid., 312.

cerned with the sacredness of life, a concern contradicted by its parallel endorsement of capital punishment. In fact, the so-called prolife people are driven by a fundamental disdain for the sex act if its intent is not to produce children. In the absence of such intent, sinners who indulge and conceive accidentally should be forced to pay the price of parenting unwanted progeny. Criminalizing abortion is a way of enforcing Puritanical sexual codes.[7]

Funk's vision of the new Christian church, without the outmoded doctrines, is vastly different from any denomination we have today. No doubt that will be good news to those who find the present Christian church irrelevant to their lives or who have been injured by the Christian religion. For them, as well as for millions of others, Funk's dream of a new Christian religion can be authentic and welcoming.

Next we turn to the thoughts of Roy W. Hoover about what can be done to solve the current problems in the Christian church.

A PARALLEL OF OUR TIME AND THAT OF THE HISTORICAL JESUS: ROY W. HOOVER

Funk is not the only one who is openly speculating on what a new Christian church would be. We turn now to an essay by Roy W. Hoover titled, "Incredible Creed, Credible Faith," which was published in a collection of essays entitled *The Once and Future Faith*. Hoover is Weyerhaeuser Professor of Biblical Literature and Professor of Religion Emeritus, Whitman College. Hoover calls on us to look at the historical Jesus as a man dealing with problems in society that are similar to our own and then to compare what Jesus did with what we should do in the here and now.

> [We should] embrace the idea of thinking and speaking about Jesus as a figure of history rather than as the second person of the Trinity, as the creeds crafted at Nicea in 325 CE and at Chalcedon in 451 CE do. If Jesus of Nazareth is going to be regarded as a figure who may have religious significance for moderns, rather than only as the principal icon of the Christian tradition (and as such a figure of the religious

7. Ibid., 313–14.

past, but not of the religious present and future), then he will have to be seen in terms of his historicity rather than in terms of his scriptural and creedal authority. The Jesus who might matter to moderns is the Jesus who was involved in the same basic conditions of human life that we are and had to deal with them. . . . [The Jesus of the creeds] can only be the fictional Jesus of ancient mythical imagination, not the flesh and blood young man who grew up in northern Israel. Jesus of Nazareth met the conditions of life in his place and time not as one who was resigned to the way things were, but as one who was moved and enlightened by a vision of the way things ought to be. That made him a threat to the privileged, the established, the powerful and those who benefited from being in their employ, but a liberator to many who were bound by those in power and their servants, and by their own weak and dull resignations. He was no doubt a threat to traditionalists down as well as up the social scale too. The challenge this Jesus may pose for us is not so much to follow in his footsteps as to catch a glimpse, even a critical glimpse, of his vision of "the good life" = life ruled by God's generosity and goodness as light for paths he never walked, but we do: the pathways of the modern world.

Will people in and out of the church today be interested in such a Jesus? "I saw Jesus tonight as a three-dimensional person for the first time in my life," I heard a middle-aged woman say in a Seattle church one evening near the close of an adult education session. "I've waited forty years for this class," is what on another occasion a man in a Bellevue, Washington church said. The day after a Jesus Seminar on the Road in Rock Hill, South Carolina last November a man who had driven there from Atlanta e-mailed Westar Institute to say, "It was the first time [in my experience] people associated with Christianity had spoken my language!" I take these sample bites of anecdotal evidence as a sign of the times. They speak for others "out there" who are waiting to hear a believable word.

In the introduction to this paper I made reference to Edward Farley's apt characterization of our religious situation as one in which we are confronted with the collapse of the house of authority. I suggest that the house of authority had collapsed for the Jesus of history also, and that in this respect there is something particularly analogous between our historical moment and his that would not resonate in the same way for those who lived in an era in which the house of authority stood intact. What prompts this suggestion is the activity of John the Baptist and the fact that Jesus was initially drawn to it. John summoned people to baptism in the Jordan River. Why the Jordan? There was plenty of water available closer to population centers elsewhere in the land that would have made John's baptism more accessible to people. The most likely explanation, I think, is that John was playing on the appeal of the wilderness and the Jordan as symbols of Israel's origins when from the banks of the Jordan they first took possession of the Promised Land, according to the biblical story. That he offered baptism as a cleansing from sin in that location implies that in his view the house of authority, the Temple establishment in Jerusalem, had collapsed. It had become religiously bankrupt, incapable of mediating the spiritual cleansing and moral renewal the nation needed. To gain access to that cleansing and new beginning, Israel would have to return to the ideals of its origins, if it wanted to regain the genuineness it had lost, and to escape the fire of coming judgment. John not only was preaching this, he was also dramatizing his message by staging a bit of religious and political theatre in a location that symbolized the genuineness and purity of Israel's religious ideals. Very probably, John thought that the political house of authority had no genuine authority either. Herod Antipas certainly heard him that way. Jesus accepted the baptism John offered, but did not repeat his fiery message of judgment to come nor did he continue his baptizing practice. Jesus and John agreed about the collapse of the house of religious authority, it seems, but disagreed about what to say and do about it. What the idea of the reign of God meant to Jesus was not impending judgment, but a vision of the way things ought to be, life as ruled by God's generosity and goodness. Jesus did not follow John's script; he called it as he saw it.[8]

Jesus was not what we would call a biblical preacher: it was not his habit to appeal to the authority of scripture as the basis of his teaching. Rather, his habit was to make frequent use of parables and aphorisms, forms of rhetoric that expect their hearers to think for themselves and that seek to persuade them to accept his teaching because they recognize its truth, not because it is based on the authority of scripture. In short, Jesus offered his contemporaries what might be called "a religion of insight" as an alternative to the religion of authority represented in his day by a priestly hierarchy, Temple ritual, and sacred texts.

(This reference to Jesus' rhetorical preferences is intended only to call attention to the fact that the preaching of the gospel originated outside the then house of authority and in forms other than the dominant teaching paradigm of the scribes— commentary on scripture—not to propose that Jesus furnishes us with the only legitimate model of Christian rhetoric. Parable and aphorism no doubt can still proclaim the gospel; but they need not be regarded as the only language of the gospel.)

What would preaching be if it were not expected to conform to the dominant paradigm? If preaching were not supposed to find truth in a [biblical] text and connect it to the present, what should it be supposed to do? . . . Taking one cue from Jesus, one might say that to preach the gospel is to cultivate the imagination and wisdom to see our lives as under the rule of God's unfailing generosity and enduring goodness.[9]

8. Hoover, "Incredible Creed, Credible Faith," 92–94.
9. Ibid., 97–98.

In his recently published book, *Eyewitness to Power*, presidential advisor and journalist David Gergen refers to G. K. Chesteron's observation that America is the only nation in the world that is founded on what it believes, especially as classically expressed in the preamble to the Declaration of Independence. "It was not intended to be a statement of who we are," Gergen says, "but of what we dream of becoming, realizing that the journey never ends. It is our communal vision. That's why a president . . . need not reinvent the national vision upon taking office. He should instead give fresh life to the one we have, applying it to the context of the times, leading the nation forward to its greater fulfillment." In a similar vein one can refer to the gospel [i.e., the "good news" not a particular book of the Bible] as the founding and communal vision of Christian faith. The preacher who seeks to relate it to the context of the times and to summon his or her hearers to a new measure of its fulfillment will find it to be an infinitely renewable resource for discovering the wisdom, grace, and courage we need "for the living of these days."[10]

Hoover has drawn a startling parallel between the time and place of the historical Jesus and our own time and place. He encourages us to embrace the vision of the historical Jesus, how he dealt with issues in his own time, and to put that vision into effect in our own culture and lives.

Next we look at another insight of Roy Hoover concerning how a re-visioned Christian Church might alter its Adult Education, and change its worship in three vital areas: its use of Scripture, its hymns and its public prayers.

ADULT EDUCATION AND WORSHIP IN A CHURCH THAT IS INVOLVED IN RE-VISIONING ITS CHRISTIANITY: ROY W. HOOVER

In a different book from the one excerpted above, Roy Hoover sets forth his thoughts about the renewed adult education and public worship that Christian churches should employ. He makes a powerful and cogent argu-

10. Ibid., 99–100.

ment that Adult Education should be focused upon theological scholarship. In addition, Hoover strongly believes that the public worship in the Church should present Scripture in the context of the time and place it was composed, that hymns should reflect the new contemporary theology and that public prayers should reflect the people's life in which they feel gratitude and responsibility. Hoover's insights in these issues are vital if Christianity is to be re-visioned in the Church in a way that it will take root and become permanent. The following excerpts are from Hoover's essay entitled "The Art of Gaining and Losing Everything" in a collection of essays called, *The Historical Jesus Goes to Church.*

First, Hoover examines the education of the adult members of the local Church.

> [One] principal task confronting the churches . . . [is] in a word [the] challenge [of] *education.*
>
> We can no more expect people to embrace a new understanding of the Christian faith in the absence of information that shows why it is necessary and what its contours are than we could expect people to give up their visually reinforced notion that the sun arcs around the earth in the absence of convincing information about the solar system. Only a few need to become astronomers, but everyone needs a readable map of our corner of the universe. A viable faith also requires a readable map. An adequate faith is not possible in the absence of the requisite knowledge.[11]
>
> How can the education of the people of the church that our religious situation calls for be accomplished? An important part of an answer to that question is already under way in some churches: adult education series and programs, special classes, and small groups in which recently published biblical and theological scholarship that is addressed to a general audience is read and discussed. . . . All of these means can continue to be utilized to advantage.[12]

While the education of adults in the new theology is imperative, it is only half the battle. If the re-visioned Christianity is to become per-

11. Hoover, "The Art of Gaining and Losing Everything," 22.
12. Ibid., 24.

manent, the worship of the Church must be aligned with that theology. Hoover makes a strong and convincing argument.

> ... there is another avenue that is at least as important as any of these and in some respects is even more important: the form and content of public worship. Too often the kinds of educational programs just mentioned go on with no visible effect upon the conduct of public worship. They remain marginal activities, more often tolerated than utilized. This pattern continues the virtual divorce between biblical scholarship and the church's worship that has prevailed, for the most part, throughout the modern era. What if scholarship and worship remarried?[13]

How might one set out to design such a form of worship? ... a pertinent place to begin would be with the way in which scripture is presented. Common liturgical formulas bracket scripture readings by references to them as "the Word of God," thus affirming their authority as in some way divine in origin. Usually such reading of scripture is offered with little or no comment about its time and place of origin or the connection of the passage selected to the writing as a whole of which it is a part. In a new form of worship as I am envisioning it here, scripture would be presented as our primary source of information about the origins and early history of the faith of the church. In other words, the biblical writings should be presented as the church's earliest classical literature. As such these scriptures are the word of humans about God and about human life viewed as under God's sovereignty, not the word of God. That is, God (and God's alleged rule) is the *subject* of these scriptures, not their *author*. The biblical authors were concerned with throwing light upon human history and experience in the hope of leading it to a good end. As the word of our religious progenitors about God, the biblical scriptures are an irreplaceable source of information about the origins of a characteristic way of viewing the human situation and a pri-

13. Ibid.

mary resource for the theological reflection. Such a view of scripture is consistent with the way critical biblical scholars look at the Bible and with the methods they use to recover historical information embedded in these writings as well as the faith or religious meaning their authors affirm. To make effective use of this scholarship for the purposes of worship, I suggest, every passage of scripture read in public worship should be accompanied by information about its author, the time and place of its composition, the situation the author addressed, and the point the author wanted to make. It is the view of human life expressed in the text that needs to be made evident, or the issue raised by the text for our consideration, criticism, reflection, and on occasion for updating and correction. This way of using scripture in worship is to treat it as a valuable resource for our reflection and enlightenment, but not as an anthology of divine pronouncements nor as a compendium of eternal truths that must not be questioned.

The necessary information about the scripture read in worship can be variously conveyed: by a well-prepared introduction to the reading delivered orally, or printed as an insert in the church bulletin or order of worship, or incorporated into the sermon. But without this information scripture reading will be left either to the vagaries of free-association by the hearer, to the superstitious notion that biblical words are endowed with supernatural power and inexhaustible meanings, or to dismissal as incomprehensible or irredeemably antiquated and irrelevant. The reading of scripture in public worship is a prime teachable moment in which the marriage of faith and scholarship would be visibly and audibly celebrated. Such a practice would do much to provide worshipers with some of the most important information they need to move toward a form of Christian faith that is both modern in its literacy and credible in its claims. *Information is the source of inspiration about the contemporary meaning of Christian faith.*

This proposal does not assume that the sanctuary is to be regarded simply as a classroom, but it does assume that

it is *essential* for worshipers to know what they are reading or hearing when scripture is included as an element of
worship. Remember, we are admonished by "the great commandment" to love God with all our mind, as well as with
our heart, soul, and strength. The commandment assumes
that these four are and ought to be inseparable. May it be
so!

If the Jesus of history and his vision of the Kingdom of
God as the symbol of the union of power and goodness that
ought to rule in human life constitutes the central paradigm
for a new form of Christian worship, and if a new way of
presenting and understanding the value and importance of
scripture became a regular part of that worship, other appropriate changes would follow, some of which I can mention here, but only briefly.[14]

Thus, education in the new theology and the modification of the
presentation of scripture to reflect that theology are vital first steps to
bring about the re-visioning of Christianity, but there is more. The hymns
of the church and the public prayers of the church must also be revised.
How should the hymns be changed to anchor the new form of worship?
Hoover gives us his thoughts.

The hymnody of the church presents a major challenge to
anyone who would like to modernize public worship. Some
of the great traditional hymns may still be able to give
expression to the meaning of Christian faith in a modern
form of worship, but the lyrics of many hymns voice forms
of Christian faith that reflect [the earlier paradigm of the-
ology]. Some of these hymns may survive by giving them
substantially new lyrics. Others will no doubt have to be
abandoned as relics of an earlier age.... In any case, dealing
with the heritage of Christian hymnody is a large project
and will be accomplished only through the creativity and
the religiously literate imagination of many gifted people.[15]

14. Ibid., 25–26.
15. Ibid., 27.

The revision of public prayer in the Church is Hoover's next topic.

> One other change that a new form of worship calls for that can be mentioned briefly here is the form and content of public prayer. As has often been noted, the style of much traditional prayer is that of a lowly subject in the presence of royalty. The prayer assumes the role of a supplicant who with great deference requests the favor of the divine majesty. That posture presumably seemed fitting in the culture of the ancient and medieval worlds, but seems remote from the world of the modern West. Furthermore, the weekly use of the prayer of confession and assurance of forgiveness that is still a part of traditional worship in many Protestant churches owes more to ancient orthodoxy's theological paradigm of sin and forgiveness and to liturgical habits corresponding to it than to the actual lives of the people who assemble for worship. The weekly ritual of confession of sin by a Christian congregation appears to assume that the people of the church are capable of nothing in the future other than repeating the same pathetic failures every week their whole lives long. The real life experience of most worshipers, I submit, is quite different. They are most often people who recognize that they are part of a larger order of life for which they feel gratitude and have a measure of responsibility. They are more likely to be looking for encouragement and wisdom than they are for forgiveness. We should reserve the matters of confession and forgiveness for occasions when something really important has gone wrong that calls for a change of mind and behavior, and abandon the weekly routine of asking forgiveness for doing what we ought not to have done and for leaving undone what we ought to have done. Most of the people for whom such a traditional prayer is relevant are candidates for an appearance in criminal court or are in prison, not in church.[16]

16. Ibid., 27–28.

Hoover concludes with a quote from theologian Gordon Kaufman.

> The proper question to put . . . is not Will (or should) change
> occur . . . ? But rather, Are the churches willing and able to
> support the kind of moves that will enable [the churches] to
> continue their life-giving function? . . . This can happen only,
> I think, if there is fairly wide recognition that this is really a
> life-or-death matter for the churches; . . .[17]

Thus, Hoover ends his essay with the same warning we saw from Bishop John Shelby Spong in his book *Why Christianity Must Change or Die*, which was excerpted in chapter 3 of this book. It is a startling challenge, and no task could require more of our attention and energy.[18]

This concludes our visit with Roy W. Hoover. We turn now to the thoughts of Charles W. Hedrick.

USING THE BASIC DATA TO DRAW NEW INFERENCES: CHARLES W. HEDRICK

Charles W. Hedrick is Distinguished Professor of Religious Studies at Southwest Missouri State University. He wrote an essay titled "The 'Good News' about the Historical Jesus" in a collection of essays in a book called, *The Historical Jesus Goes to Church*. In his essay, Hedrick begins by sounding the alarm which many Church leaders feel when confronted with contemporary scholarship about the historical Jesus.

> I know of no one who has argued that the "historical Jesus"
> is "good news" for the Church, though I know many who
> think that recovering the historical Jesus is a good thing.
> On the other hand, I also know many who think that the
> work of scholars . . . has been a disservice to the church by
> undermining "faith," causing doubt. If true, that would not
> seem to be good news for the church, and I suppose that

---

17. Ibid., 29.

18. As an aside, it should be noted that many of the mega-churches seem to have found the change from traditional values in the form of entertainment. In other words, the congregation is first and foremost entertained all the time of the church service and that entertainment is looked upon as the way to satisfy the members.

makes the [work of these scholars] "the Grinch who stole Christmas."[19]

[However] the recovery of the historical Jesus, in spite of the discomfort it now causes the church and professional scholars . . . is good news. The historical Jesus contributes to the church's future by helping the church to understand its origins, and thus helping it to shape its future in the light of its origins.[20]

Hedrick then proceeds to the heart of his essay: how he thinks the data on the historical Jesus should be used by the church. He distinguishes sharply between the historical Jesus *data* and the *inferences* which might be drawn from that data. Bear in mind that "inferences" are conclusions drawn from the facts of raw data.

Properly speaking, the "historical Jesus" is not a construct, but a disassociated collection of raw data, brought together in no particular order on the basis of the most rigorous historical criteria—a hodgepodge of information and not Jesus as he actually was. . . . Thus, the criteria exclude, or should exclude, all early Christian inferences about Jesus drawn from the data.[21]

Modern historians have developed rigorous criteria for sorting through the multilayered traditions reflected in the gospels; the criteria exclude *possible* historical information in favor of what *most probably* originates with the historical man. The most probable information is the raw data recovered by the Jesus Seminar.[22]

The canonical evangelists drew different inferences from the traditions they had available to them. There is no reason in principle why other inferences may not be drawn from the historical data—even in the twenty-first century.[23]

19. Hedrick, "The 'Good News' about the Historical Jesus," 91.
20. Ibid., 92.
21. Ibid., 96.
22. Ibid., 97.
23. Ibid., 96.

There are, at least, two reasons why the "historical Jesus" is good news for the church . . .

1. The "historical Jesus" (the raw historical data) offers the church an opportunity—not available since the first century—to recreate itself and its gospel for the twenty-first century. For nearly 2000 years Jesus of Nazareth has been represented to the world in terms of later inferences drawn from his sayings and deeds rather than in terms of what he himself did and said. This second-century orthodox construct completely obscures the tunic of Jesus' own "homespun" personal history, by shrouding it in the heavy brocaded robe of myth. The peasant has become so exalted that the human is all but swallowed up in divinity. The question is: Does the church follow Jesus, or Jesus as kerygma [i.e., the proclamation about Jesus] and creed construe him?

2. The "historical Jesus" offers the church in the twenty-first century an opportunity to draw its own inferences about Jesus. The only other time in history that this was possible was in the first century.[24]

Faced with the historical Jesus, a modern seeker begins largely on the same footing as Jesus' earliest followers. Faced with the historical Jesus, the church has the option of holding to kerygma and creed, or reevaluating the data, drawing what inferences seem appropriate for a different culture and time. Reevaluation of the data is the church's first step to developing a new idiom and rhetoric for the twenty-first century.

Reevaluating Jesus is not a novel idea. The first-century church did it to develop its kerygma, and the later church did it to develop the creeds. There is precedent.[25]

Hedrick summarizes his thesis:

The way forward is by going backward to the residue of the personal history of Jesus, reassessing it, re-envisioning it,

---

24. Ibid., 98–99.
25. Ibid., 101.

drawing new inferences from the data—in short, developing a gospel for the twenty-first century.[26]

Hedrick has laid down a startling challenge for the church. He urges
nothing less than that the church use the raw data of facts about the historical Jesus to develop a new gospel which will be compatible with the
culture of the twenty-first century. Can the church meet this challenge?

The next scholar who we should examine on our topic of a re-visioning for the Christian church is Stephen J. Patterson. It is his work to which
we now turn.

THE FOCUS OF CONFESSION MUST BE THE HISTORICAL JESUS: STEPHEN J. PATTERSON

Stephen J. Patterson is Professor of New Testament at Eden Theological
Seminary in St. Louis. In his book *The God of Jesus,* Patterson reflects
upon how the quest for the historical Jesus actually enriches the Christian
faith. Patterson believes that both the historical Jesus and the "Christ of
faith" are important. Here is an excerpt from his book:

> . . . most gospels scholarship today presumes that even
> though the gospels are not historical, they do indeed contain
> historical elements. This mixture of history and confession
> in the gospels is also *theologically* important. That which is
> historical gives us a glimpse of what the earliest Christians
> experienced in the presence of Jesus that so transformed
> their lives. The non-historical elements—the confessional
> elements—proclaim that what they experienced was not just
> the effective ministry of a fine teacher, but the very love and
> acceptance of God. This confessional material is just as im-
> portant as the historical. In it, the "what" of history is trans-
> formed into a confession of who God is. However, so often,
> Christians have focused on the confessional elements of the
> gospels, such as the virgin birth or the resurrection, but ig-
> nored that which is being confessed. The earliest Christians
> did not simply proclaim that *someone* was raised from the
> dead, but that God had raised *Jesus* from the dead—Jesus,
> who pronounced blessings on beggars, who ate with prosti-

26. Ibid., 103.

tutes and sinners, who parabled his listeners into a new way of thinking. These things are not incidental. They are among the fundamentals of Christian faith, for they define for us who God is.

The search for the historical Jesus should not be about replacing the biblical stories with history, throwing out the "confessionally biased gospels" in favor of the "indisputable facts of history." If this were the case, the quest would be a false one, a futile search for certainty in the realm of faith, a realm that does not allow the comfort of certainty. Rather, the search for historical materials embedded in the gospels can be helpful, even crucial for the understanding of Christian faith, when in the end we can see the interplay between history and its interpretation in scripture. History and interpretation—they work together in these sacred texts, the gospels. The interpretive element tells us that the gospel writers saw in the events surrounding Jesus' life a significance deep enough to be called "Immanuel . . . God with us." The historical element tells us what it was about Jesus that moved them so deeply that they could only name it as "God with us."[27]

According to Patterson, the results of historical Jesus research can help us discern what Jesus thought about God, about human community, and about life. In his view, these historical facts are the very focal points for the confessional elements of Scripture. It is by understanding these historical facts about Jesus that the confessional elements come alive. This is what is being confessed. In an excerpt from Patterson's book, he explains these three topics of historical fact.

> As Jesus thought about life's ultimate questions, what did he come to believe about God, about human community, about the things that give life real meaning?
>
> First, what did Jesus think about God?
>
> Jesus believed in a God who is present in human life, not a distant reality. This is what it means to speak of the Empire of God as already present, "within you." God is as close as

27. Patterson, *The God of Jesus*, 8–9.

the human heart. And yet, this kind of closeness suggests limits to the concept of God's involvement in human life. Jesus did not experience God as a power operating in the world apart from human agency. God did not throw up a pillar of fire for Jesus to follow into the wilderness. God did not stop the world for Jesus. And though Jesus may well have been a healer, a holy person who could do for people what a shaman can do, there were many things that Jesus could not do, pray to God as he might. There were people he could not heal. There was pain that he could not stop. And there were powers in the world that would eventually overwhelm him. God could not save him from his fate. To know God as part of human life is not to know a disembodied power intervening willy-nilly at the convenience of those who call out for help, however just, however pained or pathetic their cries might be. Too many innocents have suffered and died, like Jesus himself, to think that God's presence in human life takes the form of a power that can save us from the evils that one human being can inflict upon another. To know God's power in the way Jesus knew it, as an Empire "within you," is to know God as a reality running through all of life, a basic, fundamental reality. When one responds to this reality and makes it part of one's whole life, everything changes. Sometimes even the world changes. Human life works better. It means more. It becomes richer and rises above the pettiness of our contrived realities because it becomes part of something more basic, more real, more true.

This basic reality that Jesus experienced as God had the character of love. This word has become so washed out and sentimentalized in our time that it seems hopelessly naive and corny even to say this. But our cynicism about this old liberal notion only underscores how difficult it really is to believe. Did Jesus believe it? I think he really did. He boiled his own faith down to just two propositions: to love God and to love one's neighbor (Mark 12:29–31). The writer of Matthew would later add: the second is like unto the first (Matt 22:39). This is true. To love one's neighbor is to love God. For to love God is to love love itself. That is why Jesus embodied love in his own life in a more radical way than the simple love of neighbor might suggest. He loved prostitutes. He loved sinners, traitors, tax collectors. He treated the shamed with honor and declared the unclean clean. He loved the unlovable. He loved his enemies. To love God is to be devoted to a basic and fundamental reality that runs through all of life and creation. The character of that reality is love. This is the reality that can give life its richness and ultimate meaning. This is the reality that beckons us to live better than we live. This is the reality that exists as already present, an Empire "within you," that can be as powerful in the shaping of human life and relationships as we want it to be.

But to know God in this way is to admit of divine limitation. Love does have limits. It cannot force its own way. Love cannot be coerced. It can invite, croon, cajole, mourn, weep, and summon all the persuasive powers love can afford. But it cannot force. This lies beyond the character of love. If one risks the belief that God's nature is love, then one must be willing to accept the limitations that come with this faith.

Jesus lived with limitations. Perhaps his whole life was a struggle with limitation. He was not a person of means. His place in his world was marginal. He lacked the one thing that could guarantee him a place in the ancient agrarian culture of imperial Rome: land. Whatever place his family may have had, now it had little, and Jesus had none. He was a wanderer, homeless, without family in a culture where power and possibility came from family. Yet, in spite of these limitations, Jesus still found within himself the power to love. He experienced that power as an ultimate power, one that came not from himself, but from God. And so he embraced that power, lived it, spoke of it, storied it into existence, and surrendered to it, finally accepting its limitations and succumbing to the powers of fear and hatred that crucified him. This is how, even in death, Jesus could become an experience of God to others.

Secondly, what did Jesus think about human community?

Jesus believed that the experience of God he had could be translated into human relationships and forms of community. That is why he began to speak about a new Empire of God. To speak about a new Empire, a reign, is to speak about life in its greatest corporate aspect, life *together*. How did he imagine this?

Picture a table. It is large and lavished with foods of every sort and drink. Around it are gathered the children of God. They are not your peers. They are brought here by another invitation. Each has been drawn to the table by the inviting power of God's love. They have come as they are, some in rags, some in rich finery, some washed, some not, some are alone, some sit as families, some speak your language, most do not. There is a man you know, who has so utterly destroyed his life and that of those around him that he seems beyond redemption. He waits. There is a woman whose shoulders curl in the permanent shape of shame. Her back is bowed, but her head is held high. She sits at the head of the table. There is a young child, thin and drawn, with hollow cheeks but eager eyes. She has already begun to eat. A beggar slips into a chair, unsure of his place but willing to risk it. He tries to blend in. And so it goes around this infinite expanse of table, containing practical things: food, company, belonging, care, honor—the necessities of life. Here they are offered to each; all have access to what is needed. This is the communal form of love.

Jesus' vision for what human community might be like came from his experience of God. If God is that fundamental reality running through all of life and existence, and if the character of that fundamental reality is love, then the finest, most authentic form of human community must in some way embody love. Jesus told many stories, parables offering glimpses of what authentic human community might be: the Great Feast, the story of a table that is opened to all; the Workers in the Vineyard, a parable of worth and work, in which all receive at the end of the day enough pay to meet their need, no more, no less; the Samaritan, where one's enemy becomes salvation and unexpected care renders the old maps of who belongs where utterly ridiculous; the Prodigal, a tale of lost and found, in which a brother must choose love over honor or risk losing everything. How can we imagine human life and relationships lived out of the fundamental reality of love? Jesus tried out scenarios in his parables. As stories, they are experiences of love manifest in relationships, not templates for community formation. They are not a blueprint, but invite further imaginative work: how might love be embodied in all our relationships?

This imaginative challenge is with us now more than ever. How might we imagine life together in such a way that the poor are blessed, the hungry fed, the depressed filled with laughter, and the abused made safe? How might we imagine a world in which the anxieties of those who live teetering on the margins of life, never knowing whether food will come tomorrow, or clothing and shelter might disappear in a sea of enough? Does this seem too hopelessly naive? Perhaps it is. But anyone who risks the claim that in Jesus we have come to know who God is ought at least to remember that Jesus did dream such utopian dreams. He did not spell out a complete social and political program. Perhaps his peasant imagination was not quite up to that; or perhaps he simply did not live long enough to think through all the implications of what he was doing. But he did envision human life together in terms that are vastly different from those which Christian culture has agreed to settle for. Hard work, thrift, a day's pay for a day's work, competition in the marketplace—these modern values, as admirable as they may be, were not the building blocks Jesus imagined as the foundation for human life together. Love, care, mutual nurture of one another, mercy, redemption of the lost—these were the values Jesus claimed as ultimate values. Human relationships, if they are to be fully authentic, fully grounded in what is real and true, must be grounded in these values.

Finally, what did Jesus think about life?

These are the values that Jesus believed gave meaning to individual lives as well. Human relationships that are grounded in love do not just happen. Communities of care do not simply appear with the wave of a hand or the desire of a well-wisher. People must decide to act out of love as though it were the ultimate reality running through and beyond all things. To believe in God is to believe in such a reality. It is to believe that what one can feel and taste and count and measure, what one can possess and hold and manipulate, what one can see and hear, these things are not all there is to life and existence. To believe in God is to believe in a transcendent reality, something that lies in and yet beyond all things. It is in giving oneself over to this transcendent reality that life finds its ultimate meaning. This is what Jesus meant in counseling others to give up their lives in order to find real life. To see the transcendent in life means seeing through the concrete realities that suggest themselves as so utterly important and determinative for one's daily plan. What is most urgent is not always what is most important.

Jesus' life was a failure, at least when measured against any common standard of success. He had no home. He had no family, and few friends. He died a criminal, his body hung out in shame for all to see, and to think, "Thank God I did not turn out like that." How is it that so many have come to worship a person whose life we would still most surely despise if it were not the life of our "savior"? Perhaps it is that we have imbued Jesus with such mythic power and cultic strength that his life can sink quietly into the background, a mere comma in the Apostles' Creed that jumps quickly from "born of the Virgin Mary" to "suffered under Pontius Pilate" without so much as a glance back at Jesus' sorry life. That this is at least part of the truth about us is indicated by the great shock and offense that historical Jesus research always produces among folk not used to thinking about Jesus as a real person. The historian's Jesus is an offense because Jesus was an offense. Part of the reason we can worship Jesus today as "Christ," "Savior," "Son of God" is that we have run from the historical Jesus and his challenge to see through the shallowness with which we normally conduct our lives.

But this is only part of the truth. For when we bother to read the gospels, that offensive life and challenging voice are still there, clearly audible among the enthusiastic confessional claims of his followers who had been moved by his life and his voice. And through history there have been remarkable souls who have heard this voice and experienced this life in such a way that moved them to their own radical demonstrations of what life might be like if it were lived in response to a God whose nature is love—St. Benedict, Francis of Assisi, Catherine of Siena, Menno Simons, Sojourner Truth, Dorothy Day, Martin Luther King, Jr. We are moved by such lives and drawn to them because in them there is hope. The hope they offer is that this is not as good as it gets. Life can be richer. Human existence can become more meaningful. There is a transcendent reality that can transform us if we will but let it. Jesus' life is one that draws to it a worshiping community because, even in its failure, it allows us to see through the pretense of meaning we erect around the great trophies to be won in a successful life. Jesus experienced intimately a transcendent quality to existence that was more real, more satisfying, more hopeful than what life—even a successful life—can offer. It is this transcendent quality that we call God. Its nature is love. This is what Jesus knew.[28]

Thus, in summary, Patterson begins his exposition of the way he sees a re-visioning of the Christian Church by recalling that both the historical facts of the Gospels and the confessional aspects are vital. They interplay with one another. In much of Christian history, the church has focused on the confessional aspects while ignoring *that which was being confessed, the historical Jesus*. Patterson sees the necessity of bringing the historical Jesus into the mix, not to replace, but to interact with the confessional parts of the Gospels.

In the second, and rather lengthy excerpt, Patterson focuses upon the human life that the study of the historical Jesus has revealed. When these historical facts become the focus of the confessional elements of Scripture, a re-visioning of Christianity can begin. Patterson calls our attention to three facets of the character of the historical Jesus: his thoughts about God, his thoughts about human community, and his thoughts

28. Ibid., 244–49.

about life—the things that give life real meaning. It is in understanding Patterson's explanation of these three issues that we can find his vision for the re-visioning of the Christian church. These are the characteristics of the life of the historical Jesus which must interplay with the confessional elements to bring about the re-visioning.

This concludes our visit with Stephen Patterson. We now turn to our final insight on a possible solution to the problem in the Christian church and what path the church might take for re-visioning. Here we will visit with Marcus Borg.

THE EMERGING PARADIGM: MARCUS J. BORG

We have encountered Marcus Borg previously in this book. It has been said of him that he has "Faith, Hope, and *Clarity*."

As we shall see, Borg sees that the re-visioning in the Christian church is already underway. He calls it the "Emerging Paradigm" and he will define those terms in the excerpt to follow. There is a significantly different flavor in Borg's vision: Borg sees the Emerging Paradigm (i.e., the new re-visioning) as co-existing, at least for the time being, with the earlier ways of seeing Christianity. While there is a sharp demarcation between the earlier ways of seeing Christianity and the emerging ways, Borg refuses to cast aside the earlier way but instead affirms it for those people who still find within it the nourishment of their lives. Since the Emerging Paradigm exists alongside the Earlier Paradigm, Borg characterizes the new re-visioning as a grassroots movement that *gradually* is making itself felt and visible. Here are excerpts from Borg's book, *The Heart of Christianity*.

> We live in a time of major conflict in the church. Millions of Christians are embracing an emerging way of seeing Christianity's heart. Millions of other Christians continue to embrace an earlier vision of Christianity, often ... defending it as ... the only legitimate way of being Christian.
>
> I have struggled with what to call these two ways of being Christian and have settled on the "earlier" and "emerging" ways of being Christian.[29]

---

29. Borg, *The Heart of Christianity*, 2.

So significant is this time of change and conflict in North American Christianity that some observers speak of a "new reformation" in our time comparable in importance to the Protestant Reformation of the sixteenth century. Though it is an overstatement, even overstatements can contain truth: we are living in a time of major change.

The name of this kind of change is *paradigm* change, to introduce a term central to understanding what is happening in the church today. A paradigm is a *comprehensive way of seeing*, a way of seeing a "whole."

Sometimes called a *gestalt*, a paradigm is a large interpretive framework that shapes how everything is seen, a way of constellating particulars into a whole. Our time of conflict is about more than specifics, for it concerns a change in how the Christian tradition and the Christian life are viewed as a *whole*.

The history of astronomy provides an illuminating illustration of what is involved in a paradigm change. The sixteenth and seventeenth centuries saw a change from a Ptolemaic paradigm to a Copernican paradigm, each a way of picturing the solar system as a whole and the earth's place in it. The Ptolemaic paradigm (named after Ptolemy, an ancient Greek astronomer) was dominant in Western science for about fifteen hundred years. A geocentric, or earth-centered, paradigm, it sought to understand the motion of the planets and stars in relationship to a stationary earth at the center. The Copernican paradigm is named after Nicholas Copernicus, a Polish monk and mathematician. In a book published in 1543, Copernicus argued for a heliocentric view of the solar system: the sun, not the earth, is at the center. It transformed the way the movement of the planets was seen, even as it also transformed our sense of our "place" in the universe.

Significantly, the change from a Ptolemaic to Copernican paradigm was not about a detail or two; it affected how the "whole" was seen. Both paradigms are ways of looking at the same phenomena (in this case, the solar system), *but the phenomena are seen differently.* The shift in how the "whole" was seen affected how all the details were seen.

So also in contemporary Christianity. The paradigm change is about how the "whole" of Christianity is viewed. The same "phenomena" are in view (God, the Bible, Jesus, the creeds, faith, and so forth), but *they are seen differently.* The analogy to what is happening in Christianity is not perfect, of course. Science proceeds by different rules than religion, and one may speak of the Copernican paradigm as "verified" and the Ptolemaic paradigm as "wrong." Such verification and falsification are not so readily possible in religion.

But the analogy does work in this way. Christians in North America are living in a time of paradigm change and conflict. The conflict is not about a few items of Christian theology or behavior, but between two comprehensive ways of seeing Christianity as a whole.[30]

The earlier paradigm's view of Christianity is very familiar. Most of us over age forty (and many younger) grew up with it. It has been the most common form of Christianity for the past few hundred years. Today, it is affirmed by fundamentalist, most conservative-evangelical, and many Pentecostal Christians. And because it dominates Christian television and radio, it is the most publicly visible vision of Christianity and the Christian life.

The emerging paradigm has been visible for well over a hundred years. In the last twenty to thirty years, it has become a major grass-roots movement among both laity and clergy in "mainline" or "old mainline" Protestant denominations. These include the United Church of Christ, the Episcopal Church, the United Methodist Church, the Christian Church (Disciples of Christ), the Presbyterian Church USA, the American Baptist Convention and the Evangelical Lutheran Church in America. The emerging paradigm is also present in the Catholic church.

30. Ibid., 4–5.

Yet earlier-paradigm Christians are also found within mainline denominations. Some are insistent advocates of the earlier vision of Christianity and protest the movement of their denominations away from it. Others are not as insistent, but affirm the earlier paradigm because they grew up with it and it still makes sense to them, so they see no good reason to change. Still others remain within the earlier way of being Christian because they aren't aware of an alternative.[31]

The earlier paradigm sees the Bible as a divine product. For this paradigm, the bible comes from God as no other book does. It is the unique revelation of God.[32]

The earlier paradigm interprets the Bible literally.[33]

[The earlier paradigm has its own vision of the Christian life.]

Faith as believing is central.... The afterlife is central.... The Christian life is about requirements and rewards.[34]

[The Emerging Paradigm, too, has its own vision of the Christian life.]

The emerging paradigm has been visible for well over a century. Like the earlier paradigm, its central features are a response to the Enlightenment. Though the description is mine, the vision is not. This way of seeing Christianity is widely shared among theological and biblical scholars and increasingly among laity and clergy within mainline denominations. I seek to describe something that already exists, a development well under way.

... I here provide ... [the Emerging Paradigm's] vision of the Bible and the Christian life, using five adjectives put into two phrases. The first three adjectives describe *a way*

31. Ibid., 6.
32. Ibid., 7.
33. Ibid., 8.
34. Ibid., 10.

of seeing the Bible (and the Christian tradition as a whole): historical, metaphorical, and sacramental. The last two adjectives describe *a way of seeing the Christian life*: relational and transformational.[35]

Borg then amplifies on all of these views. For his full explanation, please refer to *The Heart of Christianity*. We now turn to how Jesus is seen in the Earlier Paradigm and in the Emerging Paradigm.

> ... an earlier image of Jesus and the image of the Christian life that goes with it have become unpersuasive to millions of people in the last century. The earlier image is quite familiar. Within the earlier paradigm of hard or soft literalism, the gospels are read literally or semi literally as if they were straightforward historical documents.
>
> When that is done, the following image of Jesus results. It emphasizes his identity: that he was the Son of God, the "light of the world," the "bread of life," the promised messiah who will come again, and so forth, and that he knew and taught this about himself. It emphasizes the saving significance of his death and sees it as the purpose of his life: he died for our sins. It emphasizes the miraculous, especially the virgin birth and physical bodily resurrection. It also emphasizes that Jesus is the only way of salvation, and that Christianity is therefore the only true religion.
>
> The image of the Christian life that goes with this image of Jesus emphasizes believing all of this to be true: that Jesus is the only Son of God, born of a virgin; that he died for our sins; that he rose physically from the dead; that he will come again; and so forth. This image of Jesus no longer works for millions of people, both within and outside the church. For these millions, its literalism and exclusivity are not only unpersuasive, but a barrier to being a Christian.[36]

If Borg is correct that the Earlier Paradigm no longer works for millions of people, both within and outside of the church, and is actually a

35. Ibid., 13.
36. Ibid., 81–82.

barrier for some people to be Christian at all, how, then, does it maintain its power? Borg has a response to this question:

> Though the earlier paradigm emphasizes believing. . . . it seems clear that what energizes and nourishes [the lives of Christians who continue to subscribe to the Earlier Paradigm] is the relationship with God mediated by the beliefs. The earlier paradigm "works" because of the relationship to which it leads.
>
> The earlier paradigm has nourished and continues to nourish lives of deep devotion, faith, and love. The Spirit of God can and does work through it. It has for centuries and still does.[37]

But for those millions for whom the Earlier Paradigm no longer works, that paradigm cannot nourish their lives and these people find that they must either walk away from Christianity or find another path. The "other path" suggested by Borg, as we shall see, is the Emerging Paradigm.

We now turn to a central aspect of the Emerging Paradigm: the way Jesus is seen and experienced in this new way of being Christian. Recall that Borg has previously told us that the way of seeing the Bible in the Emerging Paradigm is historical, metaphorical and sacramental. When discussing Jesus in the Emerging Paradigm, Borg introduces two new terms. The "Pre-Easter Jesus," is his term for the historical Jesus, and the "Post-Easter Jesus," is what some scholars call the "Christ of faith," the image of what Jesus became in the experience of his followers after his death. Borg asserts that the historical-metaphorical approach matters in the Emerging Paradigm's vision of Jesus because:

> . . . the gospels contain two voices: the voice of Jesus and the voice of the community. Both . . . voices are important. The former tell[s] us about the Pre-Easter Jesus; the latter [is] the witness and testimony of the community to what Jesus had become in their experience in the decades after Easter.
>
> . . . [the gospels] combine memory and metaphor. Like the Bible in general, they are a mixture of historical memory and metaphorical narrative. Metaphor and metaphorical

37. Ibid., 17–18.

narratives . . . can be profoundly true even through not literally factual.

In our time, many need to hear about the distinction
between history and metaphor because there are many
parts of the gospels that they can't take literally. When literalized, the story of Jesus becomes literally incredible. But
it's not meant to be incredible; as good news, it is meant to
be compelling.[38]

Borg illustrates the importance of recognizing metaphor in the
Gospels with an example from the Gospel of John: the story of Jesus turning water into wine.

> . . . recognizing metaphor in the gospels matters because it
> helps us to see rich meanings in the texts that we would oth-
> erwise miss. A literal reading can flatten the text. The story
> of Jesus changing water into wine at the wedding in Cana
> in the second chapter of John's gospel illustrates the point.
> A literal reading emphasizes the spectacular deed: if Jesus
> could change 120 to 150 gallons of water into wine, he must
> really have been somebody—he must have had the power of
> God. The story becomes "evidence" of Jesus' identity, "proof"
> that he was who he said he was.
>
> A historical-metaphorical reading of this story yields a
> very different meaning. It notes its literary context: in John's
> gospel, the wedding at Cana is the opening scene of the pub-
> lic activity of Jesus. As such, it is John's way of saying, "This is
> what the story of Jesus is about" (just as the inaugural scene
> of the public activity in other gospels is an epiphany of what
> their stories of Jesus are about). The story begins in a highly
> evocative way: "On the third day, there was a wedding. . . ."
> The story of Jesus is about a wedding, and the phrase "on the
> third day" evokes the Easter story at the very beginning of
> Jesus' story.
>
> Wedding and marriage have rich metaphorical associa-
> tions in the biblical and Christian traditions. There is the
> mystical imagery of the marriage of heaven and earth, of

38. Ibid., 84–85.

God as lover and us as the beloved of God. The story of Jesus is about this. It is also earthy: a wedding banquet was the most festive occasion in Jewish peasant life. A celebration lasting seven days, it involved dancing and copious amounts of food and wine, in sharp contrast to the basic peasant diet of grains, vegetables, fruit and an occasional fish.

So what is the story of Jesus about? According to John's inaugural story of Jesus' public activity, it is about a wedding. More: it is about a wedding banquet. More: it is about a wedding banquet at which the wine never runs out. More: it is about a wedding banquet at which the wine never runs out, and the best is saved for last. The story of the wedding at Cana invites us to see that the story of Jesus is about *this*.

A literal reading can miss all of that. Instead, it generates a factual question that is a distraction and can be a stumbling block: Do you believe this really happened? By not focusing on this question, a metaphorical reading enables us to see the rich meanings of the text. Rather than being inferior to a literal reading, a metaphorical reading is richer.[39]

Borg continues in discussing the meaning of the exalted titles given to Jesus in the Gospels.

. . . a historical-metaphorical approach matters because it helps us to see the meaning of our Christological language, by which I mean the exalted "titles" used to refer to Jesus' identity and significance in the New Testament. These include Son of God, Lord, Messiah, Word of God, Wisdom of God, Great High Priest and Sacrifice, Lamb of God, Light of the World, Bread of Life, True Vine, and so forth.

. . . Within the emerging paradigm, this language . . . is post Easter. A strong majority of scholars think it unlikely that Jesus said these things about himself; he probably did not speak of himself as the Messiah, the Son of God, the Light of the World and so forth. Rather, this is the voice of the community in the years and decades after Easter. It is

---

39. Ibid., 85–86.

not the language of self-proclamation, but the community's testimony to Jesus' significance in their lives.

As such, it is very powerful. The community affirms: we have found in this person the light in our darkness, the way that has led us from death to life, the bread of life that nourishes us even now; we have found in this person the word and wisdom of God; we have found in this person the son of God, the promised messiah; he is one with God, and we address him as "My Lord and my God." Indeed, for me this language is more powerful as the testimony of a community than if I try to imagine it as language a man used about himself.

... all of this language is metaphorical.

... Metaphor means "to see as." To say, "Jesus is the light of the world," is to say, "I see Jesus as the light of the world"; to say, "Jesus is the Messiah and Lord," is to say, "I see Jesus as the Messiah and Lord." Thus, it is the language of confession ... it is also the language of commitment. It would make no sense to say, "[I see Jesus as] the light of the world," and then be indifferent to him. To use this language about Jesus is to commit oneself to him. On the other hand, simply to believe that he used this language about himself does not involve commitment. One might believe that he said all of these things about himself and yet think that he was mistaken.

... Jesus is, for us as Christians, the decisive revelation of what a life full of God looks like. Radically centered in God and filled with the Spirit, he is the decisive disclosure and epiphany of what can be seen of God embodied in a human life. As the Word and Wisdom and Spirit of God become flesh, his life incarnates the character of God, indeed the passion of God. In him we see God's passion.[40]

In many ways, Borg's *The Heart of Christianity* is a broad explanation of the Emerging Paradigm.

Now we will look at how "Sophia Theology" affects the Emerging Paradigm. In an earlier chapter of this book, Marcus Borg presented a profile of the historical Jesus. It was drawn from his book, *Meeting Jesus*

40. Ibid., 86–88.

Again for the First Time. In a manner consistent with that Profile, I included another characteristic of the historical Jesus which Borg explained in one of his earlier books: *Jesus, A New Vision.* The additional facet was how the historical Jesus related to women. In direct contradiction to the patriarchal culture of his day, the historical Jesus treated women as radically equal with men.

Recall that in Marcus Borg's Profile, the historical Jesus was a teacher of alternative wisdom. However, in the Jewish tradition and in early Christianity, wisdom was much more than an alternative way of seeing the right way to live. Wisdom was, in addition, the feminine form of God. This could be called "Sophia theology" for reasons you will soon learn. It is to that issue we now turn. We shall see how Jesus's equal treatment of women is intertwined and interdependent with Sophia theology. Here are some excerpts from *Meeting Jesus Again, for the First Time.*

> In Jewish wisdom literature, wisdom is often personified in female form as "the Wisdom Woman." Consistent with this personification, *wisdom* is a feminine noun in both Hebrew (*hokmah*) and Greek (*Sophia*). Among scholars, it has become common to name this personification Sophia, even when the reference is to a Hebrew text. The obvious reason for doing so (besides the fact that Greek texts use *Sophia*) is that *Sophia* is a woman's name in English, thereby reminding us of the female personification in a way that the neuter-sounding word *wisdom* does not.[41]

> This personification is first developed in the opening chapters of Proverbs. The Wisdom Woman, Sophia, appears in chapter 1, speaking in a public place like one of the prophets of ancient Israel:

>> Sophia cries out in the street; in the squares she raises her voice. At the busiest corner she cries out; at the entrance of the city gates she speaks:

>>> "How long, O simple ones, will you love being simple? How long will scoffers delight in their scoffing and fools hate knowledge?"

>> "Give heed to my reproof," she continues. And then she says:

41. Borg, *Meeting Jesus Again for the First Time*, 98.

> I will pour out my thoughts on you, I will make my words
> known to you.

The first half of this verse—"I will pour out my thoughts to
you"—can also be translated, "I will pour out my Spirit upon
you," a function attributed to Yahweh in prophetic texts.
This is the first hint of a possibility that will soon become
explicit: that Sophia is a personification of God.[42]

[In Proverbs 8], she speaks of her role in creation. She was in
the beginning with God before the world was created:

> Yahweh created me [Sophia] at the beginning of God's work,
> the first of God's acts of long ago. Ages ago I was set up, at the
> first, before the beginning of the earth.

Not only was Sophia with God from before the beginning,
but she participated in God's creative work:

> When god established the heavens, I was there .... When God
> marked out the foundations of the earth, I was beside God as
> a master worker.

Here is the suggestion that it was through Sophia that God
created the world. Sophia was the chief artisan who executed
the divine plan....

The Jewish personification of wisdom as Sophia, and
the attribution to her of divine qualities, becomes even
more developed in the two intertestamental books—Sirach,
and the Wisdom of Solomon....[43]

[I]t is she who was active in the history of Israel from the
very beginning of the Old Testament story. We are accustomed to hearing God spoken of as the one who led Israel
out of Egypt. But in Wisdom of Solomon, it is Sophia who
does this.

> A holy people and blameless race Sophia delivered from a na-
> tion of oppressors ... She brought them over the Red Sea, and
> led them through deep waters; she drowned their enemies,
> and cast them up from the depth of the sea.

42. Ibid., 98–99.
43. Ibid., 99–100.

Thus in the book as a whole, she has qualities and functions normally attributed to God. . . . Sophia is not simply personification of wisdom in female form, but personification of *God* in female form. Sophia is a female image for God, a lens through which divine reality is imaged as a woman.[44]

[T]here are a number of passages in the synoptic gospels that associate Jesus with the figure of Sophia. On one occasion, Jesus is reported to have said:

> Therefore also the Sophia of God said, "I will send them prophets and emissaries, some of whom they will kill and persecute, " so that this generation may be charged with the blood of all the prophets shed since the foundation of the world. [Luke: 11:49–50]

Of utmost importance for our purposes is the introductory phrase, in which Jesus speaks for divine Sophia. Speaking her words, he is the envoy or emissary of Sophia.

In another verse, Jesus speaks of himself as a child of Sophia. At the end of a passage that reports criticisms directed against Jesus and John the Baptizer, Jesus says:

> John the Baptizer has come eating no bread and drinking no wine; and you say, "He has a demon." The Son of man [a reference to Jesus himself] has come eating and drinking; and you say, "Behold, a glutton and a wino, a friend of tax collectors and sinners [outcasts]! *Yet Sophia is vindicated by her children.* [Luke 7:33–35]

Here Jesus speaks of himself (and implicitly, of the Baptizer as well) as a child of Sophia. . . . [T]hese . . . passages imply that the early Christian movement saw Jesus as both the spokesperson and the child of Sophia, and that Jesus himself may have spoken of himself in these terms.[45]

[It] is important to understand [the language of Sophia] in a tradition whose Christological and devotional language has been dominated by patriarchal imagery. Trinitarian language and liturgical formulae that speak of "Father and

44. Ibid., 101–2.
45. Ibid., 102–3.

Son" easily create the impression that this is the definitive Christian way of speaking about God and Jesus. But is it useful to realize that the dominance of father/son imagery reflects the fact that Trinitarian thinking took shape in a patriarchal and androcentric culture.

Thus it is not the case that Jesus is *literally* "the Son of God" though he can also be spoken of metaphorically in other ways, such as the Sophia of God. Rather, both are metaphors. What they have in common is that they point to Jesus as one whose relationship to God was so intimate and deep that he could be spoken of as the son of *Abba* and the child of Sophia. We do not (and probably cannot) know whether this way of speaking began while Jesus was still alive, or whether these images were present in his own consciousness. True, it is plausible to see a connection between this language and what we can surmise about his experience. The intimacy of the metaphors is consistent with seeing the pre-Easter Jesus as a spirit person. As one who knew the Spirit, Jesus *may* have imaged and /or experienced the Spirit as *Abba* and as Sophia.[46]

It is interesting to speculate about the intersection of (a) Jesus's treatment of women as radically equal with men (which I have included in Marcus Borg's portrait of the historical Jesus) and (b) the possibility that one of the historical Jesus's images of God was that of the feminine Sophia. Of course God has no gender, but our humanity often assigns God a gender unconsciously. It is without doubt that Jesus held a male image of God as evidenced by his term for God, *Abba*, and his addressing God as "Father" in what we call "The Lord's Prayer." But the Scriptures quoted above, are from a very early Christian tradition and may, indeed, go back to the historical Jesus. If so, they indicate that Jesus worshiped the feminine form of God as well as the male form. Would it not follow that if he worshiped the feminine God as well as the masculine God, he also respected and honored women as radically equal with men? Actually, those two concepts intertwine with each other. Recognizing the feminine side of God engenders respect and honor of women. The converse also is true. Respect

46. Ibid., 109–10.

and honor of women as equal with men can encourage the acknowledgement and worship of the feminine form of God.

In our own day, male pronouns for God predominate in the liturgies of our churches. It has been that way for centuries. I wonder how much of our patriarchy and the patriarchy of past centuries can be traced to this male language for God. What would happen if Sophia Theology were taught in our Churches? Would the feminine side of God emerge? Would women begin to receive the equal recognition they deserve?

Marcus Borg did not include Sophia Theology in his description of the Emerging Paradigm in his book, *The Heart of Christianity.* However, as we have seen, Borg did explain and endorse it in his book, *Meeting Jesus Again for the First Time.* I think it is not a stretch to include Sophia Theology as an integral part of the Emerging Paradigm for the purposes of this book. It should be the way we now see Christianity as a whole.

To summarize all of the excerpts quoted above, Borg first states that in our time there are two distinctly different ways of being Christian. He introduces the term "paradigm," a term with which you might not be familiar. A paradigm, he says, is a way of seeing the whole and he provides an example from the history of astronomy. For about fifteen hundred years, the solar system was viewed under the "Ptolemaic Paradigm" which had the earth as the center and all the planets and stars revolving around the earth. But in the sixteenth century, new scientific knowledge led to the abandonment of the earlier paradigm and eventually led to its replacement by a new paradigm, the Copernican Paradigm in which the sun was deemed the center of the universe and all the planets, including the earth, were seen to circle the sun. The change in paradigm was not about a detail or two. It changed the way all the data was interpreted. In a similar way, says Borg, the Emerging Paradigm in Christian theology is different from the Earlier Paradigm. Everything changes.

Borg then offers a short description of the Earlier Paradigm, which he says is unpersuasive to millions of people in our time. The Bible is seen as a divine product which came from God, faith is defined as believing a certain set of propositions, the afterlife is central and there are doctrines of requirements and rewards. The Emerging Paradigm, on the other hand, sees the Bible as a combination of history, metaphor and sacrament.[47] It sees the Christian life as relational and transformational. Borg

---

47. In this context, a "sacrament" can be viewed as the way God comes to us, and the way we come to God.

gives examples of metaphorical interpretation in the story of the wedding feast at Cana of Galilee and in the exalted titles given to Jesus after his death. Finally, we have considered excerpts in which Borg describes the Wisdom Woman, Sophia, to be the feminine form of God and, for your consideration, I have included this Sophia Theology within the Emerging Paradigm.

The Emerging Paradigm, says Borg, brings about a powerful and committed Christian life. What more could be asked of a new Reformation?

This completes our visit with Marcus Borg and the description of his vision of the Emerging Paradigm, the new Reformation of the Christian church.

Five

The Spirit of the Historical Jesus

The Christ of Faith

BACKGROUND

ORIGINALLY I HAD INTENDED to confine this book to the historical Jesus alone and that is, indeed, what the previous chapters of the book are all about. However, Christianity cannot be based solely upon the historical Jesus. If the Jesus tradition had ended with Jesus' death, the worldwide religion of Christianity never would have developed. Following the historical Jesus, no matter how faithfully, never would have produced a full religion.

It is the same today. We can study and follow what we can reconstruct of the historical Jesus but that alone cannot and will not re-vision Christianity. The elements that built Christianity in the first century, and the elements that can re-vision Christianity in the twenty-first century, are a *combination* of the memory of the historical Jesus and the traditions that developed after Jesus's death which interpreted his life. In scholarly language, these later traditions have been called the "Christ of faith." In the words of John Dominic Crossan:

> I never presume that we find the historical Jesus once and for all. I never separate the historical Jesus from the Christ of faith. Jesus Christ is the combination of a fact (Jesus) and an interpretation (Christ). They should neither be separated nor confused, and each must be found anew in

every generation, for their structural dialectic is the heart of Christianity.[1]

Thus, finding the historical Jesus is a continuous process. But it is equally true that finding the Christ of faith also is a continuous process. The term "Christ" literally means the "anointed" but it has come to mean much more than that. It has come to mean the interpretation of all that Jesus said and did in the imagination of his followers. But there must be limits to this imagination. Originally, the Christ of faith was an extrapolation based upon the oral traditions about the historical Jesus. But, in fact, the Christ of faith soon was separated from the historical Jesus and took on a life of its own. The Christ of faith, in Christian doctrine and art and literature, became a symbol of spirituality, which, as the decades and centuries rolled on, was divorced entirely from the historical Jesus. This was so much the case that in many contexts the Christ of faith bore no resemblance at all to the historical Jesus that had generated its beginnings. In our day and time, when scholars are becoming more adept at finding the historical Jesus, it is essential that we make parallel strides at finding the Christ of faith that is in harmony with and linked to the historical Jesus. The whole point of this chapter is that the Christ of faith must always be linked to the historical Jesus. Then, a re-visioning of the Christ of faith calls for a re-examination of the various interpretations of Jesus's life to determine which doctrines of Christianity actually reflect the values and life of the historical Jesus.

Thus, a re-visioned Christianity must have a re-visioned Christ of faith. But, because of the long abuse of its divorce from the historical Jesus, I propose that we abandon the "Christ of faith" language altogether and use, instead, a completely different term. I suggest that there was a certain Godly Spirit that enveloped and permeated the historical Jesus that attracted his followers. That Spirit lived on after his death. We can call it "the Spirit of the historical Jesus." I am proposing, therefore, that the two elements upon which we can base our faith are the historical Jesus and the Spirit of the historical Jesus. With this terminology, it can never be possible to separate the Spirit of the historical Jesus from the historical Jesus himself. Unfortunately, the replacement of theological terms requires their use over a period of time. Therefore, although I use the term "Spirit

1. *Fourth R Magazine*, September/October 1993

of the historical Jesus" as a primary term to express the concept, often in this chapter I will add for clarity the term "Christ of faith."

The earlier chapters of this book focused upon the historical Jesus. As we have seen, the quest for the historical Jesus achieved a decided breakthrough in the latter part of the twentieth century and now into the twenty-first century. Scholars have become adept at finding the raw material from which the portraits of the historical Jesus can be derived. Many scholars have made inferences in portraits of the historical Jesus using the raw data of what he is believed to have said and done, and each scholar inevitably paints a slightly different portrait of Jesus. The system is not perfect. But the scholars are dealing with probabilities not certainties.[2] And from these probabilities there have emerged the characteristics of the historical Jesus that we can use to take the next step, the step of combining the historical Jesus with the Spirit of the historical Jesus, the Christ of faith.

The earlier chapters of his book were based upon excerpts from other books. This last chapter is an expression of my own views because I found no similar expression in any other book.

THE SPIRIT OF THE HISTORICAL JESUS

The "Jesus" of John's Gospel is not the historical Jesus. It is likely that John's community was familiar with the oral tradition of the historical Jesus and possibly was familiar with one or more of the synoptic Gospels. From these sources, John's community must have recognized that there was a projection of godliness that emanated from the historical Jesus. That was possible because the historical Jesus showed us what God is like and what a human life full of God is like. That emanation and projection of Godliness from the historical Jesus, like a whiff of perfume which permeates the room, can be called the "Christ of faith" but which I prefer to call the "Spirit of the historical Jesus." It was a spiritual presence that saturated the historical Jesus during his lifetime and that continued to exist after the historical Jesus's death—existing in the memory and lives of his followers. But this Spirit of the historical Jesus still bore the imprint of the historical Jesus himself. It contained his values and his vision. Sometimes it helps me to have a visual image of this Spirit of the historical Jesus. I often think

---

2. Perhaps the most accurate portrait of the historical Jesus can be seen from a combination of the portraits described by several different scholars.

of the human Jesus in his earthly life as surrounded by, covered by, and permeated by, a luminous coat. It covers his head, his arms, his body and his legs. I visualize it as sparkling. This luminous coat not only covers him, it also indwells the historical Jesus and saturates his soul. But this Spirit was visible to some people and invisible to others. Some could see this sparkling coat and could see the human Jesus through it. After his death, the Spirit of the historical Jesus is the sparkling coat alone. It still bears Jesus's image and contains his essence, but his physical body is not there any more.

During Jesus's lifetime, was he God incarnate? That is, was he God in the flesh? The church councils of Nicaea and Chalcedon would have us believe so when they proclaimed that Jesus had two natures, one human and one divine, and that these two natures were not commingled in any way. But perhaps those statements of the councils should no longer be taken literally but instead should be interpreted to say that Jesus's human Spirit was so completely motivated by God and so completely responsive to God that he was a *metaphor* of God incarnate.[3] He was like God. Thus, under this reasoning, the Spirit of the historical Jesus which permeated him during his lifetime and which survived his death was metaphorically like the living God.

Are you at all familiar with the *Divine Comedy* by Dante Alighieri, the poet from Florence, Italy in the thirteenth century? In his masterful poem, Dante goes on a guided tour of the afterlife in three stages: Hell (*Inferno*), Purgatory (*Purgatorio*) and Heaven (*Paradiso*). Dante sees and converses with deceased people he has known in Florence and people from history that Dante knows about. *Purgatorio* XXV.88ff. describes how Dante can see bodies of the deceased people. They have an apparent body formed by air that Dante calls a "shade" similar to the refraction of light in a rainbow that is formed in a cloud. In Dante's poem and theology, this "airy body" will take exactly the form that is required of it at any given time, being palpable or not palpable as the need arises.

Dante's companion in Hell and most of Purgatory is the Roman poet Virgil, who is palpable to Dante in canto XXV of *Purgatorio*. But the persons with whom Dante converses in that canto have a non-palpable body. Previously, in the *Purgatorio* III.20–33, Dante discovered that his own body cast a shadow from the sun but Virgil's body did not. Virgil explains

---

3. I borrow freely from the thoughts of John Hick, *The Metaphor of God Incarnate.*

that his physical body is in a tomb in Italy and therefore he is shadowless in Purgatory. The point that I want to emphasize is that the airy bodies in the Divine Comedy always have the imprint of the person they represent. Dante could recognize these people if he knew them in Florence or could recognize historical people if he knew about them from their history. I have found that the imagination of the poet Dante gives me another way to visualize the Spirit of the historical Jesus after the death of the human being, the Spirit that still contains the imprint of the human Jesus.

MODERN SCHOLARSHIP AND THE GOSPEL OF JOHN

It is my thesis that we must combine the historical Jesus with the Spirit of the historical Jesus to find true Christianity. Does modern scholarship affirm this notion? I believe it does. Our window to understanding the Spirit of the historical Jesus is the Gospel of John and the subsequent Letters of John. Those are the scriptures upon which we must focus. The "Jesus" of the Gospel of John and the Letters is not the historical Jesus. Instead, in theological reflection, the writers of John's Gospel and the Letters considered in depth this Spirit of the historical Jesus, this godliness, this emanation and projection from the historical Jesus, and named it simply "Jesus." Thus, the "Jesus" of John's Gospel and the Letters is the Spirit of the historical Jesus, not the historical Jesus himself. The real question is whether or not the Spirit of the historical Jesus in these scriptures is free-standing and unattached or whether is it linked and grounded in the historical Jesus. It is my contention that those who wrote the Gospel of John and the Letters held this necessary link. It is my contention that in both the Gospel of John and in the Letters, the Spirit of the historical Jesus is grounded in the historical Jesus himself. We will begin with an examination of the Gospel of John and then we will have a brief look at the Letters.

Perhaps the best place to amplify an analysis of the Gospel of John is with J. Louis Martyn's monumental book, *History and Theology in the Fourth Gospel* (1st ed., 1968; 3rd ed., 2006), and with a subsequent book by the same author, *The Gospel of John in Christian History* (1978). An essay by D. Moody Smith is attached to the third edition of *History and Theology*.[4] In it, Smith examined the contribution of Martyn to the

---

4. Smith, "Postscript for Third Edition of Martyn, *History and Theology in the Fourth Gospel.*"

theological studies of the Gospel of John and states that Martyn "rightly gets credit for a sea change in Johannine studies for somewhat the same reason that the Wright brothers got credit for the airplane." Among the notable scholars that have approved of Martyn's work, directly or inferentially, and have supplemented it with their own insights are Raymond E. Brown, who wrote *The Community of the Beloved Disciple* (1979), and *An Introduction to the Gospel of John* (2003); and David K. Rensberger, who wrote *Johannine Faith and Liberating Community* (1988), and *1 John, 2 John, 3 John* (1997).

In summary, Martyn proposes that the Gospel of John can best be understood as a conflict between John's community and the nearby Jewish synagogue. He divides the history of John's community into three "periods."

In the Early Period, which probably began before the First Judean Revolt, there was a group of people within the synagogue who were Torah observant but who embraced the oral traditions about the historical Jesus, principally many of the miracle stories and elements of the passion-resurrection narrative. They came to believe that Jesus was the long awaited Mosaic prophet, the expected Messiah. This group invited others in the synagogue to "come and see" and their evangelistic preaching seems to have met with considerable success. The Messianic group differed from the unbelieving Jews in one aspect only: their confession of Jesus as the Christ.

Dialogue and debate within the synagogue continued until some point in the 80s when the leaders of the synagogue became so concerned with the growth and contentions of the Messianic group that they took the drastic step of excommunicating from the synagogue those who openly held Messianic beliefs. Excommunication from the synagogue was no small thing. The excommunicated person could expect to be ostracized by family and former friends. In addition, if the person had a job, perhaps it would be withdrawn and it might be that no new job was available. Excommunication was something to be feared and avoided if at all possible. According to Martyn, there was a group within the synagogue who did just that: they avoided excommunication by keeping secret their belief that Jesus was the Messiah. These secret believers Martyn calls the "Christian Jews." He calls those who were excommunicated the "Jewish Christians."

The Middle Period began with the traumatic expulsion from the synagogue of the Jewish Christians. Although now separated from the synagogue, the leaders of John's community continued to win a few new converts and even that limited success caused the synagogue leaders to take the next drastic action. A death sentence was issued against the Jewish Christian evangelists and in some cases execution was carried out. Those two major traumas, excommunication and execution, caused the separated community of Jewish Christians to turn inward upon themselves and to begin to form their own theology and identity.

As the Johannine community transitioned from the Middle Period to the Late Period, the time when most of the Gospel of John was written, their theology became centered more and more upon the Spirit of the historical Jesus even though they continued to view Jesus as the Messiah, indicating that their theology still was rooted in the teachings and traditions of the historical Jesus himself. The Johannine community began to take onto itself the characteristics of the Spirit of the historical Jesus, which was so spiritual that it is sometimes called the "stranger from above."

According to Martyn, in the Late Period, there were three groups centered around the synagogue in their city. First, there was the parent synagogue itself. Secondly, there was the Johannine community of Jewish Christians who had been excommunicated from the synagogue. Thirdly, there was the group within the synagogue who secretly believed that Jesus was the Messiah, the Christian Jews. Martyn finds within the Gospel of John an important insight about relationships during the Late Period. According to Martyn, although John 8:31–32, and the verses which immediately follow, purport to be a conversation between the historical Jesus and his opponents, the author of John's Gospel tells two stories at once. One story is about the historical Jesus during his lifetime. The second story reflects a conversation between two groups *at the time of the writing of John's Gospel,* some sixty years or so after the death of the historical Jesus. In the written Gospel, Jesus himself is saying the words in verses 31–32 but, in the second story, according to Martyn, it is the Jewish Christian leader and evangelist in John's community who is doing the talking and his audience is the group of secret Christian Jews who were still within the synagogue. Our focus should be on the second story.

Here are those verses from the Gospel of John with my explanations in brackets:

> Jesus [the Christian evangelist] then said to the Jews who had believed in him [the Christian Jews still in the synagogue], "If you continue in my word, you are truly my disciples; and you will know the truth, and the truth will make you free."

These secret Christian Jews within the synagogue were willing to accept the teaching and words of Moses, they were willing to accept the teachings in the oral traditions of the historical Jesus and believe in him as Messiah. But they were unwilling to accept and believe the teachings and word of the Spirit of the historical Jesus, the Christ of faith, who teaches *about* himself in so many of the parts of the Gospel of John. They were unwilling to accept the high christology that had been developed within John's community in the Late Period. According to the evangelist in John's community, these secret Christian Jews did not *continue* in Jesus's teaching over the period of time from the teaching of the historical Jesus to, and including, the *subsequent* teaching of the Spirit of the historical Jesus, the Christ of faith, in high christology. Therefore they were not truly Jesus's disciples. The truth that makes a disciple free is the acceptance of *both* the teachings of the historical Jesus *and* the teachings of the Spirit of the historical Jesus, and putting those in a primary position over the teachings and traditions of Moses. Acceptance of *all* these teachings would make the disciples Jewish Christians.

Viewed from another standpoint, the Christian Jews within the synagogue were willing to participate in a religion *about* the historical Jesus, which they could do while still participating in a religion *about* Moses. But they were unwilling to participate in the religion *of* Jesus because that would require that they place the life and teachings of the historical Jesus and the teachings of the Spirit of the historical Jesus above the teachings of Moses.

I think we can infer that the Johannine community itself did indeed adhere to the exact position that the Jewish Christian evangelist was urging upon the secret Christian Jews within the synagogue.

To put the issue in the language with which we began our search, there were two groups who were at odds with one another: the Christian Jews had only the historical Jesus but John's community had both the historical Jesus *and* the Spirit of the historical Jesus and the two were completely linked together.

THE LETTERS OF JOHN

It is instructive to examine two of the Letters of John in this context. By the time 1 John and 2 John were composed, the dispute between John's community and the local synagogue had died away. Instead there was an internal dispute within the Johannine community itself. Some people held not only to the high christology of the Spirit of the historical Jesus but also held to the acceptance of the historical Jesus himself, which they called "Jesus in the flesh." Others, it would seem, denied the flesh and blood historical Jesus and held only to the high christology of the Spirit. This latter group left John's community and much of the verbiage of 1 John, and 2 John is directed toward them in polemic language. For example,

> ... every spirit that confesses that Jesus Christ has come in the flesh is from God, and every spirit that does not confess Jesus is not from God. (1 John 4:2b)

> Many deceivers have gone out into the world, those who do not confess that Jesus Christ has come in the flesh ... (2 John 7a)

Thus, according to the community of John who wrote the Letters, truth is in the *combination* of *both* the historical Jesus and the Spirit of the historical Jesus. To put it in other words, the teachings of the Spirit of the historical Jesus must always be anchored and linked to the teachings of the historical Jesus himself.

THE GOD OF THE HISTORICAL JESUS

Before going further, we first must focus upon the God to whom the historical Jesus prayed, the God who he proclaimed and served. I will be using a term which probably is unfamiliar to most Christians, but which must be understood to comprehend the relationship I see between God, between the historical Jesus, and between the Spirit of the historical Jesus. The term which I wish to define is "the God *of* the historical Jesus."[5] This term follows ancient Hebrew tradition. In Exodus, God said to Moses:

> I am the God of your father, the God of Abraham, the God of Isaac, and the God of Jacob. (Exodus 3:6)

5. I have borrowed this phrase, slightly modified, from Stephen J. Patterson, *The God of Jesus.*

Thus, for Israelites, their God was (and is) the God of Abraham, Isaac, and Jacob. The Jewish religion is built on that *understanding* of God. The Muslim religion is built on a different *understanding* of God as articulated to Muhammad. Traditional Christianity is built upon a still different *understanding* of God. The three Abrahamic religious traditions may well worship the same God, but each religion has its own understanding of God, and in each case that becomes a limiting factor. For each of the Abrahamic religions, there is not a universal God, but instead there is a narrower scope in understanding God,[6] which, for each of these religions is unique.

I borrow and focus upon Marcus Borg's idea of the "Emerging Paradigm" found earlier in this book and I suggest that within this paradigm there is a Christian theology which has its own *understanding* of God, one that it is different from the understanding of God in traditional Christianity. This unique understanding of God uses the recent scholarship in the quest for the historical Jesus. I suggest that this new understanding of God can be called, "the God *of* the historical Jesus." It is the God to whom the historical Jesus prayed, the God who the historical Jesus taught and revealed. It is a different understanding of God. Certainly it is different from the Muslim understanding of God, different from the Jewish understanding and it is also different from the traditional Christian understanding of God.

FURTHER CONSEQUENCES OF COMBINING THE HISTORICAL JESUS WITH THE SPIRIT OF THE HISTORICAL JESUS (THE CHRIST OF FAITH)

To repeat somewhat and to amplify quickly, the Spirit of the historical Jesus was a palpable presence to some of his followers during his lifetime. But it was not apparent to everyone.

1.   To some, the Spirit of the historical Jesus was not apparent at all. All they saw was the flesh and blood man who said some revolutionary teachings about the Kingdom of God. These people tended simply to ignore him.

---

6. Islam and traditional Christianity, but not Judaism, may contend that they worship a universal God. However, upon close inspection, both Islam and traditional Christianity have their own understanding of God that is quite unique to their own religion. Hence, each of those religions has a narrower scope of God than something universal.

2. To others, such as the leaders in the Jerusalem Temple, the Spirit of the historical Jesus was visible but they believed his teachings about the Kingdom of God were subversive and constituted a threat to their way of life, a threat to their control of the domination system of their day. These people wanted to do away with him.

3. Others found that the Spirit of the historical Jesus was a manifestation of the living God and they would forsake everything to follow him.

After Jesus's death, this Spirit of the historical Jesus lived on and continued to elicit the same three responses among those who had known him or come into contact with him. For those in categories 1 and 2 above, all traces of Jesus had disappeared from the earth. But his close followers, those in category 3 above, could feel his presence with them still and began to relate to this Spirit of the historical Jesus more and more as full divinity. Many called it "resurrection." This is where the members of John's community found themselves. But the only language they knew to describe him and their relationship with him was not the "Spirit of the historical Jesus" but simply "Jesus."

Where did this godliness in the Spirit of the historical Jesus come from? I would argue that it had only one possible source, and that source was the God *of* the historical Jesus. Thus, the origin and sustenance of the Spirit of the historical Jesus was and is the God *of* the historical Jesus. Since the sustenance and origin of the Spirit of the historical Jesus is the God *of* the historical Jesus, it requires only a small step to see that the "Jesus" of John's Gospel not only is the Spirit of the historical Jesus but also is the God *of* the historical Jesus. Then the "I AM" statements of John's Gospel stand true on their own. "I AM," of course, is the name God gives to himself in the Book of Exodus.[7] Therefore, in the Gospel of John, within the Spirit of the historical Jesus, it is:

1. *God* (I AM) who is the Bread of Life (John 6:35)

2. *God* (I AM) who is the Light of the World (John 8:12 and 9:5)

3. *God* (I AM) who is the Door of the Sheepfold (John 10: 7 and 9)

---

7. Then Moses said to God, "Behold, I am going to the sons of Israel, and I shall say to them, 'The God of your fathers has sent me to you.' Now they may say to me, 'What is His name?' What shall I say to them?" And God said to Moses, "I AM WHO I AM"; and He said, Thus you shall say to the sons of Israel, 'I AM has sent me to you.'" Exodus 3:13–14.

4. *God* (I AM) who is the Good Shepherd (John 10: 11 and 14)
5. *God* (I AM) who is the Resurrection and the Life (John 11:25)
6. *God* (I AM) who is the Way, the Truth and the Life (John 14:6)
7. *God* (I AM) who is the True Vine (John 15:1 and 5).

The God they referred to, however, was not the tribal God of Abraham, Isaac, and Jacob, and it was certainly not the apocalyptic God seen in portions of the synoptic Gospels. But it was the God *of* the historical Jesus, the God of compassion and forgiveness, who was and is linked to the historical Jesus himself. Then the Prologue of John's Gospel (in John chapter 1) also can be taken at face value. Within the Spirit of the historical Jesus, it is *God*, (albeit the God *of* the historical Jesus) who was in the beginning and all things came into being through him.[8]

Please note that the proper viewing the Spirit of the historical Jesus starts with the historical Jesus himself. What could be more important to Christians than to learn all they can about the historical Jesus and then to learn of the Spirit of the historical Jesus intertwined with the God *of* the historical Jesus? What could be more important than to build again from the historical Jesus and see a new spirituality? How is that accomplished? The building and learning must be by responding to the actions of the God *of* the historical Jesus and from the words and actions of the historical Jesus himself. How God acts equates with who God is, in the mind of the historical Jesus. The Kingdom (Reign) of God was the historical Jesus' favorite term for God acting in this world. For Jesus, words and deeds are the same.

> And why do you call me, "Lord, Lord," and do not do what I say? (Luke 6:46)

The God *of* the historical Jesus and the interdependent Spirit of the historical Jesus should become the measuring rods. But the historical Jesus himself should also become a measuring rod. All doctrines of the Christian church should be tested by all three of these measuring rods.

---

8. Viewing the Jesus of John's Gospel as the Spirit of the historical Jesus which also is the God of the historical Jesus becomes an adequate explanation when John's Jesus is talking about himself or is talking about others. But what about the scriptures when John's Jesus is talking to the Father? The God of the historical Jesus is an immanent God. Hence the Spirit of the historical Jesus also is immanent. When John's Jesus (the Spirit of the historical Jesus) is talking to the Father, it can be viewed as the immanent Spirit of the historical Jesus talking to the transcendent God.

For example, suppose that a doctrine is based upon a church teaching about Jesus derived from the Spirit of the historical Jesus (the Christ of faith). If the historical Jesus never said or stood for any such thing, that doctrine must be called into question.

The Gospels are a combination of confession and history. Confession means the telling or making known—a proclamation. Confession of sin is one kind of confession. But here I am using the term in an altogether different sense. In the Gospels, what is important is the confession of Jesus. Within that framework, the question is "What is being confessed?" Or, better yet, *who* is being confessed? The traditional answer to that question is Christ *alone* is confessed without reference to the historical Jesus. In Christian churches around the world, Christians see only Christ.

It was not always so. When the Gospels were written, each author's confession was linked to the oral tradition of the historical Jesus. To understand Christ in our own day we must once again find a link to the historical Jesus. Otherwise Christ becomes a God-like man who came down from heaven, said a few wise things and returned to heaven. That is a hollow definition because it is not grounded in human history. True Islam, Judaism, and Christianity have always been religions that are grounded in the history of God's revelation: Islam through the words of Muhammad in the Qur'an, Judaism by the Exodus and Passover traditions, and Christianity through the life and teachings of Jesus. A departure from this grounding in history removes the stamp of authenticity. When Christ is confessed *alone*, Christianity is in grave danger of losing its link to human history. Christ becomes an empty symbol into which wild fantasies can be poured. Then, Christianity becomes a religion *about* Jesus instead of the religion *of* Jesus.

In defining Christ, however, if the one confessed is the God *of* the historical Jesus, that will determine what Christians believe about the Spirit of the historical Jesus and it will be grounded and anchored in history by its link to the historical Jesus himself. John Dominic Crossan said it succinctly:

Christian belief is always

(1) an act of faith
(2) in the historical Jesus
(3) as the manifestation of God.[9]

9. Crossan, *Jesus, a Revolutionary Biography*, 200.

Although not exactly in the terms I am using, Crossan found the necessary connection between the historical Jesus, the Spirit of the historical Jesus, and the God *of* the historical Jesus.

As we have seen, if the historical Jesus is the starting point, the devotional statements in the Gospel of John are an embellishment on that foundation. It is the God *of* the historical Jesus who is the light of the world, the bread of life, the way, the truth and the life. It is the God *of* the historical Jesus who is the Spirit of the historical Jesus. In this context the historical Jesus and the Spirit of the historical Jesus (the Christ of faith) are two sides of the same coin. They are that linked. They are inseparable.

Why has the church strayed so far from the link between the Spirit of the historical Jesus and the historical Jesus himself? Perhaps it was because until the advent of modern scholarship, it was not possible to get back to the historical Jesus. But now we can do so with reasonable probability. The churches must now take that next step.

I would remind you that each scholar has a slightly different portrait of the historical Jesus, as each Christian who studies these matters will also. Since the historical Jesus is the starting point, each scholar and each Christian will have a slightly different understanding of the Spirit of the historical Jesus as well as a slightly different theology. That diversity gives us grounds for continuing dialogue and growth.

If we are to follow the pattern of the Gospel of John in following the Spirit of the historical Jesus, the Christ of faith:

1. We will ground our belief system in the historical Jesus, his values, his vision of the Kingdom of God, and his vision of God—the one he worshiped and served.

2. Upon that foundation, we will participate in the religion of the historical Jesus by participating in high christology, the life of the Spirit of the historical Jesus. We will worship both the Spirit of the historical Jesus and the God *of* the historical Jesus. And, finally, we will see that same Spirit in others and let that Spirit lead us into fellowship and community.

THE EUCHARIST, LORD'S SUPPER, OR HOLY COMMUNION

As a postscript, I would add a few thoughts about how this understanding of the Spirit of the historical Jesus fits with the Eucharist in Christian churches. The Lord's Supper, the Holy Communion, or the Eucharist (as it is called in the various denominations) consists of the distribution of the bread and the wine in accordance with the mandates of the Gospels. I would suggest that in the context of the Spirit of the historical Jesus, these elements have the following meaning:

> Bread = symbolic of Jesus' self, his earthly body which contained the Spirit of the historical Jesus = symbolic of feeding on the Spirit of the historical Jesus

> Wine = symbolic of a new covenant—a new promise that God will be present through the life and the teachings of the historical Jesus and therefore through the Spirit of the historical Jesus. (Technically, wine is a symbol of blood, and blood in the Israelite tradition always was a symbol of the life of the animal or person) = symbolic of the ingesting the life of the historical Jesus = symbolic of ingesting the Spirit of the historical Jesus as well.

Viewed in this way, the elements of the Eucharist are directly tied to the Spirit of the historical Jesus and thus to the historical Jesus himself.

Epilogue

THIS COMPLETES OUR JOURNEY in this book. You might ask yourself
how many of the thought patterns in chapter 4 of this book are present in your own life or the life of your church. Is the Church in need of
Reformation? Can the quest for the historical Jesus play a role?

You have started on the long path of biblical literacy and I hope you
have enjoyed the ride. If this "taste" of scholarship has whetted your ap-
petite and you are ready for more, you might want to search your local
library or bookstore to find one or more of the books that I have quoted.
This book has intentionally not been comprehensive to include all important books on the topic of the historical Jesus, but in your further reading,
you may wish to delve into some of these.
Books that contain portraits of the historical Jesus:

- N. T. Wright, *Jesus and the Victory of God*. Christian Origins and
  the Question of God 2. Minneapolis: Fortress, 1996.

- Gerd Theissen and Annette Merz, *The Historical Jesus: A
  Comprehensive Guide*. Translated by John Bowden. Minneapolis:
  Fortress, 1998.

- E. P. Sanders, *The Historical Figure of Jesus*. London: Penguin,
  1993.

- Pieter F. Craffert, *The Life of a Galilean Shaman: Jesus of Nazareth
  in Anthropological-Historical Perspective*. Matrix. Eugene, OR:
  Cascade Books, 2008.

Books that also introduce readers to the subject of the historical Jesus or
contribute to the historical background of the quest:

- James M. Robinson, *The Kerygma and the Historical Jesus*. Eugene,
  OR: Cascade Books, 2008.

- W. Barnes Tatum, *In Quest of Jesus*. Rev. ed. Louisville: Westminster
  John Knox, 1999.

Books that explore the social and archaeological world of the historical Jesus:

- John Dominic Crossan and Jonathan L. Reed, *Excavating Jesus: Beneath the Stones, Behind the Texts*. San Francisco: HarperSanFrancisco, 2001.

- K. C. Hanson and Douglas E. Oakman. *Palestine in the Time of Jesus: Social Structures and Social Conflicts*. 2nd ed. Minneapolis: Fortress, 2008.

- Jonathan L. Reed, *Archaeology and the Galilean Jesus: A Re-examination of the Evidence*. Harrisburg, PA: Trinity, 2000.

- Richard A. Horsley, *Sociology and the Jesus Movement*. 2nd ed. New York: Continuum, 1994.

Thank you for your interest in this vitally important subject. You are no longer a beginner. Open your mind to the possibilities.

Bibliography

Allison, Dale C. "Jesus Was an Apocalyptic Prophet." In *The Apocalyptic Jesus: A Debate*, edited by Robert J. Miller, 17–29. Santa Rosa, CA: Polebridge, 2001.

Borg, Marcus J. *The Heart of Christianity: Rediscovering a Life of Faith.* San Francisco: HarperSanFrancisco, 2003.

———. *Jesus, a New Vision: Spirit, Culture, and the Life of Discipleship.* San Francisco, CA: HarperSanFrancisso, 1987.

———. "Jesus Was not an Apocalyptic Prophet." Pp. 31–48 In *The Apocalyptic Jesus: A Debate*, edited by Robert J. Miller, 31–48. Santa Rosa, CA: Polebridge, 2001.

———. *Meeting Jesus Again for the First Time: The Historical Jesus and the Heart of Contemporary Faith.* San Francisco: HarperSanFrancisco, 1986.

———. "Re-visioning Christianity." In *The Once and Future Jesus*, edited by The Jesus Seminar, 55–61. Santa Rosa, CA: Polebridge, 2000.

Brown, Raymond E. *The Community of the Beloved Disciple.* New York: Paulist, 1979.

———. *An Introduction to the Gospel of John.* Edited by Francis J. Moloney. Anchor Bible Reference Library. New York: Doubleday, 2003.

Cain, Marvin F. *Jesus the Man: An Introduction for People at Home in the Modern World.* Santa Rosa, CA: Polebridge, 1999.

Craffert, Pieter F. *The Life of a Galilean Shaman: Jesus of Nazareth in Anthropological-Historical Perspective.* Matrix. Eugene, OR: Cascade Books, 2008.

Crossan, John Dominic. "Almost the Whole Truth: An Odyssey." *Fourth R Magazine* 6/5 (1993).

———. "Jesus as a Mediterranean Peasant." In *Profiles of Jesus*, edited by Roy W. Hoover, 161–68. Santa Rosa, CA: Polebridge, 2002.

———, and Jonathan L. Reed. *Excavating Jesus: Beneath the Stones, Behind the Texts.* San Francisco: HarperSanFrancisco, 2001.

Funk, Robert W. *Honest to Jesus: Jesus for a New Millennium.* San Francisco: HarperSanFrancisco, 1996.

Funk, Robert W., Roy W. Hoover, and the Jesus Seminar. "Introduction." In *The Five Gospels: The Search for the Authentic Words of Jesus*, 1–38. New York: Macmillan, 1993.

Hanson, K. C., and Douglas E. Oakman. *Palestine in the Time of Jesus: Social Structures and Social Conflicts.* 2nd ed. Minneapolis: Fortress, 2008.

Hedrick, Charles W. "The 'Good News' about the Historical Jesus." In *The Historical Jesus Goes to Church*, 91–103. Santa Rosa, CA: Polebridge, 2004.

Hick, John. *The Metaphor of God Incarnate: Christology in a Pluralistic Age.* 2nd ed. Louisville: Westminster John Knox, 2006.

Hoover, Roy W. "Incredible Creed, Credible Faith." In *The Once and Future Faith*, edited by The Jesus Seminar, 81–100. Santa Rosa, CA: Polebridge, 2001.

————. "The Art of Gaining & Losing Everything." In *The Historical Jesus Goes to Church*, 11–29. Santa Rosa, CA: Polebridge, 2004.

Horsley, Richard A. *Sociology and the Jesus Movement*. 2nd ed. New York: Continuum, 1994.

Jesus Seminar, editor. *The Once and Future Faith*. Santa Rosa, CA: Polebridge, 2001.

————, editor. *The Historical Jesus Goes to Church*. Santa Rosa, CA: Polebridge, 2004.

Levine, Amy-Jill. "Introduction." In *The Historical Jesus in Context*, edited by Amy-Jill Levine, Dale C. Allison Jr., and John Dominic Crossan. Princeton: Princeton University Press, 2006.

Martyn, J. Louis. *The Gospel of John in Christian History: Essays for Interpreters*. New York: Paulist, 1978.

————. *History and Theology in the Fourth Gospel*. 3rd ed. New Testament Library. Louisville: Westminster John Knox, 2006.

Miller, Robert J. *The Jesus Seminar and Its Critics*. Santa Rosa, CA: Polebridge, 1999.

————, editor. *The Apocalyptic Jesus: A Debate*. Santa Rosa, CA: Polebridge, 2001.

Patterson, Stephen J. "Wisdom in Q and Thomas." In *In Search of Wisdom: Essays in Memory of John G. Gammie*, edited by Leo G. Perdue, Bernard Brandon Scott and William Johnston Wiseman, 187–221. Louisville: Westminster John Knox Press, 1993.

————. *The God of Jesus: The Historical Jesus and the Search for Meaning*. Harrisburg, PA: Trinity, 1998.

Reed, Jonathan L. *Archaeology and the Galilean Jesus: A Re-examination of the Evidence*. Harrisburg, PA: Trinity, 2000.

Rensberger, David K. *1 John, 2 John, 3 John*. Abingdon New Testament Commentaries. Nashville: Abingdon, 1997.

————. *Johannine Faith and Liberating Community*. Philadelphia: Westminster, 1988.

Robinson, James M. *The Gospel of Jesus*. San Francisco: HarperSanFrancisco, 2005.

————. *The Kerygma and the Historical Jesus*. Eugene, OR: Cascade Books, 2008.

Sanders, E. P. *The Historical Figure of Jesus*. London: Penguin, 1993.

Schweitzer, Albert. *The Quest of the Historical Jesus*. 1st complete edition. With a Foreword by Marcus J. Borg. Translated by W. Montgomery, Susan Cupitt, and John Bowden. Fortress Classics in Biblical Studies. Minneapolis: Fortress, 2000.

Smith, D. Moody. "Postscript for Third Edition of Martyn, *History and Theology in the Fourth Gospel*." In J. Louis Martyn, *History and Theology in the Fourth Gospel*, 19–26. 3rd ed. New Testament Library. Louisville: Westminster John Knox, 2006.

Spong, John Shelby. *Why Christianity Must Change or Die: A Bishop Speaks to Believers in Exile. A New Reformation of the Church's Faith and Practice*. San Francisco: HarperSanFrancisco, 1998.

Tatum, W. Barnes. *In Quest of Jesus*. Rev. ed. Louisville: Westminster John Knox, 1999.

Theissen Gerd, and Annette Merz. *The Historical Jesus: A Comprehensive Guide*. Translated by John Bowden. Minneapolis: Fortress, 1998.

Wright, N. T. *Jesus and the Victory of God*. Christian Origins and the Question of God 2. Minneapolis: Fortress, 1996.

The Donkey
A Novel

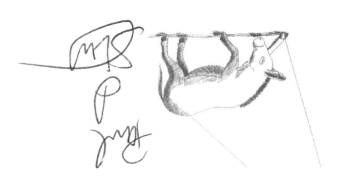

By
Paul Stuligross

The Donkey

First Edition Printed 2013
Copyright © 2013 by Paul Stuligross
All rights reserved.

ISBN-13: **978-0-9888930-7-8**

Technical Review Editor: Nelson O. Ottenhausen
Managing Editor: Dari Bradley
Sr. Editor: Doris Littlefield
Cover Art: Cartoon Studios
Donkey Sketch: Lindsay Bochenek

This is a work of fiction and is not intended to refer to current places, events, or living persons, however, some events, characters and locations are based on historic records. The opinions expressed in this manuscript are solely those of the author and do not represent the opinions or thoughts of the publisher.

Published by Patriot Media, Incorporated
Publishing America's Patriots

P.O. Box 5414
Niceville, FL 32578
United States of America
patriotmediainc.com

Acknowledgements

In thanksgiving for my family's help and the Salvation Army's goodness; for my wife's quiet patience and support which means so much to me; and for my two daughters—my shining stars that allow me a small glimpse into the heart of God.

Introduction

During September of 1918, and before the end of the Great War (World War I) in Europe, the United States sent a military unit of 5,500 men to Northern Russia, officially named the American North Russian Expeditionary Force (ANREF) to help thwart the Bolshevik revolution occurring in that country. Because of the frigid conditions where they fought, enduring temperatures of 40 to 50 degrees below zero, the soldiers called themselves *Polar Bears*.

Then President of the United States, Thomas Woodrow Wilson, dispatched the troops in response to requests from the governments of Great Britain and France to join an Allied Intervention Force in Russia to help prevent Bolsheviks, a Marxist political group, from taking control of the Russian government, a regime that would later become the Russian Communist Party.

After leaving Camp Custer, Michigan in July of 1918, soldiers of the 85th Infantry Division believed their assignment would be at the Western Front in France. Unknown to them, President Wilson had agreed to a limited contribution by the American troops in Russia, and these Custer Division troops would be the ones used, but only for guarding stockpiled war materials.

When U.S. Army General John J. Pershing received the directive from President Wilson, he changed the orders for the 339th Infantry Regiment, along with the 1st Battalion of the 310th Engineers and other ancillary 85th Division units. Instead of heading for France, these units trained and re-outfitted in England with Russian weapons then went to North Russia. Arriving in Arkhangelsk on September 4, 1918, they were attached under British military command.

For the next eight months, left only with memories of home and with little hope of defeating the advancing Bolsheviks, the *Polar Bears* and their families felt as if they had been forgotten. Following the Allied Armistice with Germany in November of 1918, family members began writing letters and petitions to newspapers, asking for the immediate return of the *Polar Bear* soldiers.

Aware of the change in their mission and the fact the port of Arkhangelsk had frozen over, thereby closing down all shipping, the morale of the American soldiers plunged. They would ask their officers why they had been sent to fight in Russia, but they didn't get specific answers other than they must fight to survive and to avoid being pushed into the Arctic Ocean by the Bolshevik army.

In February1919, President Wilson directed his War Department to begin planning the withdrawal of all American units from North Russia. U.S. Army Brigadier General Wilds P. Richardson arrived in Arkhangelsk aboard the icebreaker *Canada* with orders to organize a coordinated withdrawal of American troops, "at the earliest possible moment". On May 26, 1919, the first half of a British North Russian Relief Force arrived in Arkhangelsk to replace the Americans.

In early June, the bulk of the *Polar Bear* units had been rescued and brought home to America, two-thirds of them coming back to Michigan. During the withdrawal, the American ANREF veterans began to officially call themselves *Polar Bears* and were authorized to wear the *Polar Bear* insignia on their left sleeve.

On August 5, 1919, the military formally disbanded the ANREF, and then on May 30, 1930, Troy, Michigan erected a monument to honor the *Polar Bear* units at the White Chapel Memorial Cemetery where it still stands to this day.

Information Source
—Wikipedia

Dedication

This book is dedicated to John Stuligross; the real *Polar Bear* who brought us the story of the *Candy Bar*. Corporal John Stuligross, grandfather of the author Paul Stuligross, is standing in the middle of the back row.

*NCOs of Company G, 339ᵗʰ Infantry Regiment, 85ᵗʰ Division,
American North Russian Expeditionary Forces, 1918,
wearing Russian Valinkas (fur or felt knee-high boots).*

Rejoice greatly, Daughter Zion! Shout, Daughter Jerusalem! See, your king comes to you, righteous and victorious, lowly and riding on a donkey....

—Zechariah 9:9
The Holy Bible

Prologue

Private First Class John Sloan sat huddled in a frozen trench, the Bolshevik enemy less than a farm field's length away. The sun set a mere hour before, plummeting along with the mercury. However, it seemed like a warm spell compared to the last few nights—fifteen below zero, much better than the nights before.

John blew into torn, hardened gloves to keep his hands warm, his rifle firmly pinched inside the crook of his left elbow. He could barely recognize his friend, Billy Nichols, crouched beside him.

Glancing at John through the rising vapor of his own breath, Billy asked, "When you wanna get it?"

Smiling, John responded with, "Get what?"

"You know."

"It's a mile's walk."

"You're telling *me*? You're the one that wants one."

"I don't expect you to go with me."

Billy smiled back at him. "I'm your best friend. You'd go with me if I wanted one."

They looked at each other for an instant, frozen in time.

The shelling would begin soon. Like clockwork, artillery from behind the enemy lines pounded away at them twice a day, once in the morning, once at night. Sometimes, the assaults came too.

John peered down through the trench at a stockpile of food and supplies on the other side of a makeshift bridge. The mission for his unit, protect the food.

He often pondered the irony of it. *Why are we guarding oatmeal? It's frozen so damn hard that eating it is impossible. The rest of the world went home after the Armistice ... and Lord only knows why it's so damn important for us Polar Bears to stay.*

Settling into a comfortable squat, he recalled something from the past. He stared at his friend beside him, watching Billy hold onto his rifle much like a baseball bat. The men grew up together, played ball together, farmed together and rode horses together. They sat beside

each other wondering the same thing as the rest of the men in the unit, *When can we go home.*

Then the shelling began.

An artillery round struck the trench berm above them. The blast shook the earth and showered them with snow and frozen dirt.

As the sergeant made his rounds, he declared, "They're comin', boys. They're comin' sure as the dickens!"

Rising up enough to get a clear look through the barbed wire, John peered at the figures trudging toward him—Bolshevik troops, grasping frozen weapons, their heads donned in padded gear.

Then he looked over at Billy.

Billy rose up a little then stood all the way up as if something overtook him, something absent of common sense.

John yelled, "Don't get yourself killed, Billy."

Shrugging it off, Billy grinned at John then both men directed their attention to the advancing enemy, waiting for their orders.

More artillery shells landed nearby, one to their front, another to their rear.

Again, John yelled out, "They're bracketing us!"

The sergeant barked an order from the other side of the trench, "Fire on my command!"

Lifting his rifle, John leveled it toward the enemy then found his sight picture. He grasped the bolt and tried to pull it back—frozen solid. Jolting his weapon, he pulled on the bolt again, but it wouldn't budge. John glanced over at Billy who appeared to struggle with his weapon too.

They looked again at the approaching troops and knew they had to make a decision, and fast. They both glanced up and down their trench and saw heaps of frozen bodies within it. There was hardly anyone left at their end, barely a *Polar Bear* left to guard the food.

Panic overtook John as he tried again to rack the bolt. He saw Billy secure his bayonet to his rifle then climb from the trench.

John lunged toward his friend and yelled, "Billy!"

Without responding, Billy jumped the barbed wire, overcome with rage as if he wanted to end it right then and there. Reaching the first line of enemy troops, he struck one with the butt of his rifle and

ran his bayonet into another. Amidst a sea of Bolshevik troops, he forged through them one at a time.

Climbing up and over the side of the trench, John's eyes locked onto Billy's helmet. An enemy soldier emerged suddenly from the mud beside Billy. Turning his rifle toward the enemy, Billy shoved cold metal into his gut. Another one came his way and he landed the rifle butt against the Bolshevik's head.

John looked back into the trench and saw enemy soldiers making their way toward the food supplies. Then he glanced back toward his friend and became torn, but he remembered his mission, *Guard the food*, so he jumped into the trench and fought his way toward the supply tent.

A moment later, a Bolshevik knocked the rifle from his hands and the sheer strength of John's size was put to the test. He threw one enemy soldier aside and turned another's bayonet back into him, all while moving ever closer to the food supply.

He heard another loud explosion. Glancing back at the frozen field, he watched his friend's body fly apart. Bits of Billy scattered onto John. Then a sudden hard thud struck John's face, the butt of an enemy rifle hit him in the jaw, sending him to the frozen earth.

Fighting for consciousness, John opened his eyes long enough to see Bolshevik soldiers running away with oatmeal sacks. He stayed conscious long enough to assess what he'd seen; his friend killed rather than he, with nearly a hundred more dead men beneath him.

A thought flashed through John's mind, *All for sacks of oatmeal.*

The Armistice for the Great War had been signed almost half a year before, but he lay on the cold Russian ground and witnessed the unfathomable, wondering for an instant if he might die. He closed his eyes and thought of what could give him peace: the thought of God, the thought of home, the perception of something familiar.

John reopened his eyes and lay still, watching the enemy escape with the oatmeal, aware only that his friend had died and he lived.

The Donkey

Chapter 1
The Fire

Explosions rang out, sending curtains of fire high into the dark summer night, its aura contrasting against the Detroit skyline. Dan Mertz saw through his car window, the orange above the rooftops as he approached it while weaving his red Mustang through the streets. In his two decades of street reporting, he couldn't remember a month as bad as this one, perhaps not a year.

He thought, *A double-homicide, a local government scandal, and now this, a third firebombing in a week. The gang activity was supposed to have been down in July, but it's August and things still look as hopeless.*

As he drew nearer, he peered through a dusty windshield with his deep-set eyes, surrounded by wrinkles, knowing he would again find little more than the screams to which he'd become accustomed. Traversing through traffic, he felt like Penske driving through Belle Isle. As the city lights glared off the glass buildings, he wove his red ragtop sports car between them, pondering why he was in such a hurry to get to these things. *If I just slow down, perhaps they will all be gone by the time I get there.*

Feeling compelled to reach for the radio knob, he pushed it.

A female reporter's voice sounded serious over the radio as she announced, "This is the third reported firebombing in a week and the police are beginning to see a pattern."

He mumbled, "Enough with this crap," then flipped the knob to another station.

A new voice said, "Heroin use is on the rise in the city ... that according to the latest FBI report."

Sighing, he spun the dial again then slowed his car to a more manageable speed as he drew nearer the aura of the distant fire. He had grown used to the media noise in his car, perhaps desensitized.

Staring through his window, it surprised him to see the size of the fire—the largest one in a while.

Another reporter replaced the silence inside his car. "The mayor was sentenced to six months in jail and our murder rate has reached an all-time high. Many people are wondering ... how does Detroit find hope in the midst of it all?"

Breaking from his trance, Dan yelled at the radio as he pulled behind a set of fire trucks, "No kidding. Ya think?"

Sliding old credentials around his neck, he emerged from his car at a trot. Drawing nearer to the chaos, he eased into a mode he had grown comfortable with: one that allowed him to be stoic. The sounds of distant screams meshed with the popping red and yellow flames. Easing his way between two fire engines, he accessed a group of bystanders. He had learned that victims are often among the bystanders or with families of the victims. From them he could get the real stories and declare the real tragedies—ones that would sell more papers.

He edged up beside a group and found himself once again out of place, a white reporter standing in a sea of black faces, many with streams of tears glistening in the early morning light of the sun and the fire before them. He only had to wait and listen. Experience taught him to be patient and soon a group of firemen gathered before him. He presumed one of them to be a battalion chief.

The chief barked, "Listen ... two kids still unaccounted for!"

A fireman answered, "Chief, that roof's ready to go any minute."

Dan heard screams from beside him; someone said something about her baby still inside. A fireman assessed the risk to the other firemen and the picture became clear in Dan's mind. *There are still kids inside the building.*

"He's right," the chief said. Then looking around, he waved another man over and ordered, "Get your men out ... Now!"

One of the firemen looked up at the building, his face covered in soot. Dan's eyes felt drawn to the soot spattered name on the back of his jacket. He mouthed it—*Jenkinson*.

As Jenkinson pled his case, Dan watched then heard the man say, "Chief, I've got time. Trust me. I need to get those kids out!"

Emphatically, the chief disagreed. "Damn it, Mike, listen to me. We've got accelerants all over the place!"

Dan's senses heightened as he watched Jenkinson ignore the chief's orders and race toward the building. Cries of despair grew amid the bystanders and Dan felt himself drawn to an older black woman being held back by another. He understood her to be the mother. Instinct replaced compassion in an instant and he stepped toward her, iphone and microphone in hand.

His voice rose among the noise. "Ma'am, can I get your name? What is your child's name?" He would need to be louder as her attention remained directed to the building, her tears shimmering in the firelight. "Ma'am, your kids ... are they still inside ... inside the building?"

Another woman turned toward him, a tight grip on her friend who tried to break free as her friend's screams pierced the air. "Somebody done firebombed it! Both her kids are still inside. Please, Jesus ... Oh, please, Lord!"

Stepping back again to watch, Dan waited for a reaction, waited for something to write about.

The mother of the trapped children grew more adamant and her screams got louder. "Please, Jesus ... oh Lord, save my babies!"

Drawn again to the flame-engulfed building, Dan noticed the three-story apartment complex had wooden boards covering half the windows. The poverty of the families living in the other half became evident and all too familiar to him.

A sudden horrendous screech sounded. Dan's eyes rose to the building's roof as it crumbled, exploding into a twisted pile of wood and flames. Sparks flew off and floated into the early morning air.

Then out of the ashes came one of the firemen.

As the courageous firefighter emerged through the thick smoke, Dan could see he held a small boy about four years old. The child's mother broke free from her friend's grasp and ran toward him.

Embracing her son, she cried, "My baby. Where's my baby girl? My daughter's still inside!"

The fireman handed off the young boy then turned back toward the building—Jenkinson.

Another fireman stepped up and tried to get her behind the fire line. "Ma'am, take him to the ambulance and have him checked. You're gonna have to step back."

Pleading, the woman said, "But my daughter ... she's still—"

Dan tried to separate himself from the scene in front of him, but this time he felt different. He felt weak.

Then it happened.

Another explosion rang out, this one bigger than the other. Dan stepped back and watched the firemen scatter as if in slow motion. He saw a distraught mother collapse into a bystander's arms, her son saved and being treated, but her daughter would not be so lucky.

It all became surreal to him again.

The chief cried out, "Sweep the area! Pull everyone back!"

Another fireman approached the chief, his face covered in soot as he shouted, "We lost Jenkinson. Jenkinson and the girl are gone!"

Though Dan felt the urge to step toward the grieving mother, he held himself back. *Not again*, he thought. Instead he reconciled with an internal bedlam.

Things got to him this time—another murder, another fire, another calamity. He clinched his eyes shut and felt a mist of water upon his face. He would relive it again later and try to allow the emotions to flood through his fingertips onto the computer keys. He had to feel the emotions, the hopelessness and to allow his readers to do the same.

It would all have to wait until later. His bosses would have to understand this time.

He drove home with the radio off and the top up. Although warm enough to put it down, he felt most comfortable in the silence of his own presence. It wouldn't be enough. He pulled into the driveway of his suburban condominium and parked. Dark when he left, a bit lighter when he returned. This time he noticed the garage lights lining the winding street, soldiers at attention: clean, exact. He turned on the radio to see if it still worked and sorry he did.

"For the third straight year Detroit has reached a list it hoped to stay off of … the highest murder rate in the nation—"

Angered, he pushed the radio off button and found himself in isolation. He thought, *Tomorrow will be a new start, but then again ... maybe not.*

~ ~ ~

Starving … that's where I find myself, where I find this city. Starving for respite from the bedlam with which I am daily faced. I cannot escape it, even within the confines of my own car. It follows me through my silvery, metallic antenna. I need only turn the knobs of my radio to hear about the chaos, not even marginally different from the tragedies I report. If I could find even the slightest reclamation from the murders I covered this week, it would render my job more bearable. I find instead only tears, wailing and hopelessness. I find myself in a dream, imprisoned in a field of overgrown weeds, trapped between rows of depreciating homes. I look down at myself from the Heavens as I cry out, my face shrouded in the shadow of the clouds, "Won't somebody do something?" And yet I find my voice drowned by the sound of a roaring fire that has consumed a house, a home directly next to the field in which I stand. I wake to find that it is not a dream. I am immersed with the reality that I will cover yet another murder, another fire, another human tragedy in a city that will likely never escape these conditions, at least not in my lifetime. If hope is dead within these limits, I know not how to erect it. And so I will trudge along certain only in the knowledge these forms will strike again and again. I will find them absent of redemption.

The hallway light glints off the laptop keys as Dan clicks save three times. The glowing screen cast light on his features and dark wavy hair. Bent forward recording details of the latest firebombing, his unruly locks revealed a spattering of gray. Although he promised

himself he would hold out until fifty before reading glasses, he found his eyes covered with them at forty-eight.

Sitting in the dark, early in the morning, felt therapeutic, and it afforded him the opportunity to contemplate his job with the Detroit Free Press. More than once, he would gaze at the plaques on the den wall and be reminded of his long career—*Society of Professional Journalists; Journalist of the year, 1995; Detroit Local Hope Initiative, 1996; Investigative Reporting Award, 1998.* He would often convince himself that it was another person, someone that hadn't been there for two decades, someone less jaded by years of contemptuous reporting.

"The facts," he remembered his college professor proclaiming, "just report the facts. Anything else can be toxic."

He thought back to those idealistic years, times when he actually believed he could change things.

Looking at the clock in the dark, he hoped he hadn't awakened his wife then mumbled, "Toxic. How could it be anything else?"

From the hallway, his wife asked, "Talking to yourself again?"

Startled, he jumped, spilling a cold cup of coffee across his desk. "Damn. You scared the hell out of me."

Frantically, he scrambled for some napkins nearby and found them among his cluttered desktop. His glasses fell off as he worked through the mess.

His wife Cindy tried to hide a laugh. "I married you because you're so entertaining," she said.

Dan continued to assess the damage. "What? Yes. Well I'm glad I keep you so entertained."

"If you clean up that clutter, it won't be so bad."

He exclaimed in a voice that put her in mind of an amateur night at Chaplin's Comedy Club, "Well, thank you for that advice, wife … much good it does me now!"

She knew his comedic outbursts acted as a cover-up, something to hide the frustration into which his career had him pigeonholed. She often stated so to her friends. And often, Dan would overhear those conversations and shrug them off in his flighty way.

Shaking his head in self-disgust, he glared over at her as she continued to contain her giggles. Then he followed her gaze across the room to his trophy-covered, red wall.

Dropping the napkins into a bigger mess on the floor, he mumbled, "I'm no Mr. Clean."

He watched her smile melt into a stare then she flung her wavy blond hair and stood with her hands on slim hips. He watched her when she got like this, certain she didn't ponder about their age difference of her being three years his senior. During their fifteen year marriage, the nostalgic glare would turn into a proclamation, somewhat of a perspective upon which he felt compelled to reflect.

As their eyes looked upon his past, hung on the walls of his office, she whispered, "Remember that guy?"

With a slight smirk, he emphasized, "What guy? What ... you mean the guy that didn't know how to wipe his mouth?"

Cindy continued staring at the wall.

He added, "You mean the guy who thought he was gonna solve the city's problems? Right. That guy left town ... about twelve spilled coffees ago."

She glanced back at the stained papers across his desk and said with a smirk, "I don't know what's worse. Spilling the coffee... or letting your desk get that bad in the first place."

"Yeah, well ... when I figure it out I'll let you know."

Cindy laughed and he glared at her again.

She asked, "Don't you have to be at work?"

As she tried to peek at his computer screen, he held up three fingers. She looked at him and appeared curious.

He blurted, "Number three ... the third firebombing in a week!"

As Dan rose from his chair, she succeeded in hiding the laugh then asked, "What about Nelson?"

Dejected, Dan walked past his trophy wall, looking sad as he fumbled through his pockets and came out with a set of keys then glanced over at more falling papers. "Apparently he's too busy. So once again, Dan gets dumped on. I'll finish the story at work."

"I don't suppose you'll be home for dinner?"

Dan looked at her, certain they understood each other so he said, "The only thing I suppose is, I can't suppose anything."

She understood it in a way that only she could.

Before disappearing into the garage, he promised, "I'll call you later."

Chapter 2
A New Assignment

He considered six hours of sleep a luxury, but still found himself running late. A wrinkled shirt, undone tie and mussed up hair announced his entry into the newsroom. He felt the busy sounds of the morning a welcomed distraction at times and other times he found himself unable to go to the office.

Adopting a low profile, Starbuck in hand, Dan hoped to reach his desk without being noticed.

Someone shouted from across the room. "Nice job, Danny. Three house fires in a month!"

"A week," someone amended. "Three in a week."

Dan arrived at a cluttered desk, not unlike the one at home. Shuffling papers around, he overlooked the urgent notes stuck to his phone.

Trying to ignore the teasing, he mumbled something then let it spill over. "Real funny. Yeah, laugh it up. Very funny."

The jabs continued. "You goin' for a record, Danny?"

Filing through a pile of papers, he flipped one over spilling his coffee. "Damn it! Not again."

Picking up the flimsy cup he crushed it and threw it hard into the wastebasket. All of a sudden, it got quiet. He scanned the room and saw his cohorts' eyes staring at him.

"Sorry." He smiled. "Sorry … been a hell of a few weeks."

They nodded and went back to work. Dan's chief emerged from his office across the room. A plump man with black-rimmed glasses and the world's largest collection of suspenders, Doug shouted at him; his voice carried above the noise of the newsroom and all eyes stopped to watch.

Holding up a coffee-drenched piece of paper, Dan muttered, "Great … now what?"

Doug bellowed, "Dan, I need to see you a minute."

"Yep … yep. Be right there."

Dan wiped down his shirt and tried to tuck it in. A few more papers fell and he couldn't help but notice the chuckles emerging from around him. The walk to the chief's office seemed long and he soon found himself in Doug's absorbing presence.

"Sit down," Doug said.

Dan took only a corner of the seat.

"Been a rough couple weeks, hasn't it?"

"Couple months, more like it," Dan replied.

"Couple months … right?"

"Yes," Dan replied then said, "No … I don't know. Has it?"

With his chin resting upon two fingers, Doug inquired, "What happened?"

"Same as what always happens … someone died … a fireman and one of the kids."

After a brief silence, Doug said, "I shouldn't have sent you."

Dan turned toward the newsroom then responded with, "Don't worry about it. I was just blowin' off steam."

"No. I shouldn't have sent you." Waiting for a reaction that didn't come, Doug reached into a desk drawer and pulled out a note. Glancing over the top of his black rims, he reached across the desk and offered it to Dan. "Here."

Reluctant at first, Dan took the note and glanced at the writing on the front.

"I've got something else for you … ought to keep you busy for a while."

"What is it? What … you're not taking me off the assignment board are you?"

"Just for a while Dan—"

"Listen, if this is about my outburst—"

Doug held up a hand. "I'm asking you to call this lady."

Dan read the note aloud. "Claire Henning."

"She's turning one hundred years old this year." Then Doug explained, "Apparently she's got a story to tell … a miraculous chapter in her life … some chance encounter with God, I guess."

"Aw, come on Chief. I'm not up for this."

"You are up for this!"

Dan tried to object again but an intern walked in and interrupted him. "Chief, Mitch has some questions about Sunday's layout."

After he rose from his chair, Doug reached for a worn, brown sport coat and said, "Be right there."

Compelled to follow him, Dan stood and tried to plead his case.

Doug glared back at him. "Listen Dan, I don't want to hear it. Her number's on the note. She lives in Saint Johns."

"Saint Johns? That's half way across the state!"

"Well then … you better get going."

"How long is this gonna take?"

"I suppose as long as it takes her to tell her story."

Dan followed Doug's long strides between the desks. "This isn't going to be quick. That's why you assigned me, isn't it? To get me out of here."

"Just call the lady. Go out and interview her." Doug stopped, turned to look directly at him. "You used to be a hell of a reporter, Mertz. Get your shit together."

Dan watched Doug disappear behind another door. Standing alone, no one paid him attention this time. He felt certain it was on purpose. Glancing at the yellow note in his hand, he took another quick look at his desk. *Nothing there worth dealing with,* he thought so he read the note again.

"Claire Henning. One hundred."

I'll call her … today.

~ ~ ~

Winding through the streets of a town he had never been to, he found himself with one hand on his earpiece, the other hand tapping a malfunctioning GPS.

He answered Cindy's questions. "Late, I'll be home late."

She asked, "How long will this take?"

"Today," he answered. "I hope I wrap it up today. Believe me."

Pulling down a long, straight dirt road with his clean, red Mustang, he mumbled, "I just washed this thing."

Cindy had a girls' night out planned and promised to be home before he was.

"Fine … that's fine," he said. "What a waste of my time this is. Can we get another GPS this week? This is ridiculous … over an hour to get here."

She promised they could. Then he slammed on the brakes.

"Wait. Here it is. Here it is. I gotta go."

She told him she loved him and he found himself pulling slowly down a long, tarred driveway. Flower boxes adorned the white trimmed house and a well-kept yard with spurts of white picket fencing around the front. His brakes squeaked as he came to a stop and before long, he stood on a quaint porch, a set of rocking chairs and a mesh table nearby. When a few knocks and rings produced nothing, he stared down at his notes.

A middle-aged woman emerged from around a corner of the house. Her partially gray hair lay matted underneath a yellow scarf, her hands donned in soiled gardening gloves.

"You must be Dan," she said, pulling off a glove to offer a hand.

He nodded.

She introduced herself. "I'm Catherine, Claire's granddaughter."

Dan took hold of her hand then wiped his clean. "Dan Mertz. Detroit Free Press."

"Come on around."

She led him to the back of the house. He glanced at the grounds, impressed with the simple settings. Gnomes lined a well-groomed garden trimmed with annuals and hydrangea bushes.

Catherine explained, "I live right next door, my husband and I … our kids. I'm the only family she's got close by. She likes to garden when she feels up to it. I'm over here a lot."

Ascending the steps to a clean, painted porch, Catherine opened a squeaky screen door and welcomed him in. He insisted she go first and he followed her into the small brick home.

"She's been looking forward to this. It's been a long time since she's talked about the donkey."

"I'm sorry," he said then asked, "The donkey?"

Catherine nodded.

"I'm here about a donkey?"

He wound through a thin hall into a gaudy living room decorated with dark tin photographs and lace doilies about the furniture.

Catherine leaned over an elderly woman asleep in a rocking chair. "Nanna? Nanna?"

Dan wanted to sigh. He wondered if she would be awake long enough for him to interview her. The old woman arose from her slumber and raised her wrinkled face. White hair well groomed fell into curls and revealed gray baroque earrings. She wore a white and pink flowered sweater. Her knitting lay atop her lap along with two silver needles resting nearby.

"Nanna, this is Daniel Mertz," Catherine announced.

She seemed confused as she responded, "Dan? Dan Mertz?"

"Right, Nanna. Daniel Mertz, from the paper."

Claire's eyes widened. She held out her hand. "Oh, Mr. Mertz."

Startled by her discerning eyes, Dan hesitated a moment at their sincerity then grasped a cold, limp hand and said, "Dan Mertz. It's a pleasure to meet you."

Bracing herself against a table, she began to stand, her footing firmly against the blue shag carpet. Catherine stood beside her, guiding her to her feet.

"Mr. Mertz. Let me take a look at you," Claire said, appearing awkward while standing before him, her slight frame no match for his. She scanned him up and down for what seemed like minutes before saying, "You don't look like a reporter, Mr. Mertz. You're quite a cake-eater."

Dan looked at her. Perhaps his cohorts had gotten to her first.

He smirked, scratched his head and said, "I guess I don't know how to take that."

"A lady's man," Catherine interjected. "She means a lady's man. You'll learn quickly Nanna isn't afraid to speak her mind."

"Good," he assured. "That's a good thing. Well then, shall we get started?"

Before sitting he pulled a notebook from his satchel. Fumbling for a writing utensil, he revealed a pink fluffy-tipped pen he received at the pre-school he spoke at a few years before. Quickly apologizing, he took the time necessary to find a better one.

Catherine exchanged a final pleasantry before leaving them alone. "I'm sure I'll be seeing a lot of you."

"A lot? What do you mean? How long—"

Settling in a chair, he shot a nervous glance at the old woman seated once again in her rocker. She smiled back at him.

He whispered, "Cake-eater."

Claire maintained her curious gaze in his direction.

Clearing his throat he found himself ready to venture forward. "So ... where do we begin?"

Claire's eyes glazed over a bit, and Dan felt she wouldn't be able to get through much, but later he would learn it was her way.

"How long have you been on the job, Mr. Mertz?"

He reminded her. "Dan ... well ... a long time."

Glancing at his watch, he adjusted his body in his seat. "Could we ... I mean do you mind beginning?"

Smiling back at him, she seemed to accept his impatience and asked, "Where should we begin?"

Dan tried to crack a smile. "How about you tell me?"

"Nineteen twenty?"

"Nineteen twenty it is."

Claire settled in, her century old mind wandering to a time Dan knew little about. Eyeing something invisible to him, she found it then shut her eyes to revive it within. A strong-willed woman, well spoken, she narrated the past plain and direct.

"We grew up on a farm in the middle of Michigan ... my brother Will and I. It was a grand life. Plenty of land to play on ... lots of animals to keep us company."

Dan wrote with zeal and checked his recorder from time to time. She paused often, though the pauses were slight.

"My father inherited the farm. It had been in the family quite some time." Stopping again to recall something less pleasant, her eyes squinted shut. "Things got tough when Dad left for the war ... the Great War. A girl never likes to say goodbye to her father. They got even tougher when he returned. A few bad harvests can do that. Largely, though, it was because he wasn't the same man. Do you know what I mean, Mr. Mertz?"

"Please," he said, eyes looking to his notebook, "call me Dan."

Claire's eyes remained closed as she continued. "Even through the rough years, most of my memories were good ones, especially

when it came to school … Johnson school. It's where I met my closest friends, Liza and Lucie."

Dan's writing slowed. He stopped when she opened her eyes and stared at him in a way that invited him back with her.

"It's also where I met Becky Brewer, the class snob."

He accepted her invitation and soon felt himself in 1920.

Chapter 3
The Sloans

Spring, 1920

The sweltering heat radiated from the old wooden floor of the schoolhouse. Children sat motionless, their backs pasted to the wooden chairs, wool clothes uncomfortably clung to them. A young female teacher paced about the front of the one-room schoolhouse, pointer in hand, as the students studied a clock on the far wall.

A young Claire sat directly in front of her brother, two years her junior—she nine, he seven. Her curly brown hair rested atop thin shoulders. She often wondered how long she would have to endure being in the same class as him, firm in the belief he rarely missed a chance to terrorize her and her friends.

Occasionally, Claire glanced at Becky Brewer who sneered back at her, finding it within herself to fluff a newly purchased dress while Claire looked down at the loosely stitched holes in hers. As Claire recalled her mother's words, 'Waste not, want not,' she thought, *Why does it always have to do with clothing for a young girl's survival at school.*

Today was different than the rest—the last day of school. Eyes stared past the stoic woman in the front of the room, out to the breeze inclined trees and the sway they incurred.

Then the bell rang.

Jumping from their desks, children scampered toward the green-trimmed door and out onto the dusty playground: first Claire, then Liza, then Lucie. Will snuck up behind Liza and pinched her, leaving her with a familiar disgust that lasted most summers.

Mornings brought farming chores for Will and Claire and other duties for their friends. Swim breaks, though frequent, weren't frequent enough for the lot of them, but it seemed like Will usually had time for games.

After school recessed for the summer, not a day passed before Claire knew her brother was up to something. The wooded area

south of the Sloan farm had always been a perfect spot for his tricks. Their father had built a tree fort between two of the tallest oaks in the forest, the words *The Sloan Fort* printed in paint on its facing.

One day, Will hid in the thick woods, waiting for Claire and her friends to arrive. Claire walked with her best friends, Liza and Lucie, through the trees and as they strolled between the pines and into the brush, Will jumped out. Trying to hide a bucket behind his back, he failed at his ambush. Finding it too heavy, he swayed with its weight, spilling sour milk over the weeds below.

Frowning, Claire asked, "Will Sloan, what have you got there?"

"Nothin'."

Will stood still and didn't move. He had a thin frame, peaked brown hair crewcut, freckles and a few missing teeth.

Lucie stepped a bit closer and said, "Looks like milk."

Liza asked, "What do you mean to do with that?"

Smirking, Will said, "Come here and find out."

Their eyes widened.

Leaning into Claire, Liza whispered, "To the fort."

Will blurted out, "I heard that!"

Claire cried, "To the fort!"

Dragging her friends behind her, the three of them darted off between the trees.

Yelling, "I'm comin' to get ya!" Will followed, spilling milk from the bucket as he ran.

The Sloan children knew the forest well. Ascending the first hill and crossing a winding, thin creek, drying like clockwork every summer, they then headed to the sprawling oaks just beyond. Claire and her friends crossed the creek first, Will a bit behind. Finally, the girls reached the tree fort and the makeshift ladder that descended from it. With Will too close, Claire hid behind a tree and watched as her friends scrambled up the ladder.

When Will reached the base of the fort, he looked up at Liza and Lucie, unaware of his sister's location. "I'm comin' up to get ya!"

A sudden strange voice sounded from another direction, a voice the Sloans had grown used to. "What ya doin'?"

Will recognized it immediately as Curtis Atkins, the town bully. Will spun around and watched as Curtis emerged from the other side of a tree, sneering at him. Big for his age, Curtis appeared to the

other children as larger than life and often displayed the ugliest bruises. Will thought, *Proof of his toughness.*

Curtis's brother Elmer also stepped out, appearing much bigger than Curtis.

Elmer announced, "Didn't we tell you before? This is our fort!"

Claire peeked out from behind her tree as Will stepped back, set the bucket of milk down behind him and objected, "Is not your fort! My dad built it before he went off to fight."

Lunging toward him, Elmer shoved Will hard and spat out, "Well it's ours now."

Will shouted, "Is not!"

An argument began, echoing among the trees as Elmer and Curtis taunted Will. Claire found a clearing between her and the ladder. She reached for the bucket of milk and looked for the right moment to climb up.

Shoving Will again, Elmer taunted, "Listen, a punch in the kisser will make it mine!"

"Will not!"

"Will so!"

Silently, Claire found herself within arm's reach of the ladder. Grasping the bucket, she climbed up to her friends; then hiding the milky weapon, the three waited for a chance to dispense it.

As the shoving continued, the boys circled a few trees and then stopped directly beneath them.

Curtis yelled, "What do ya think, Elmer, shall we take the fort?"

Hollering back, Will replied, "Go chase yourself! It's our fort!"

Elmer stepped up, grabbed Will's collar, clenched his fist and said, "Well, we're takin' it. What're you gonna do about it?"

Will's expression changed as he dipped his head from the laughter of his deriders. Quietly, Will clenched his fist shut. Reeling back, he lunged forward, delivering a solid punch to Curtis's jaw, sending him to the dirt.

The fight was on.

From above, the girls cheered for Will, watching as he held his own. Will shoved Curtis down, then Elmer, then Curtis, but it all became more than Will could handle and he suffered defeat. Curtis

rose from the dust and grasped Will's arms from behind as Elmer prepared to punch him, all three bloodied.

Glaring at Will, Elmer snarled, "Now you're gonna get yours."

Ranging back a fist, Elmer prepared to deliver a punch when a sudden slimy white substance from above interrupted him. The sour milk projected a solid stream from the fort onto Elmer's head.

Will raised a boot and kicked Elmer, sending him to the dirt, drenched in milk.

Releasing his grip, Curtis stooped to tend to his brother. "Elmer, Pa is gonna see that."

Elmer rose from the ground, glared at the three laughing girls in the tree fort and howled, "I'll be seeing you … real soon!"

Curtis cried out, "Come on Elmer. Let's get outta here."

After Claire and her friends' laughter subsided, Elmer levied another threat to them before wiping himself off and disappearing with Curtis between the trees. As they ran off, Claire thought she heard one of them say the other would get *whipped* at home. For what, she didn't know.

Claire and her friends climbed down from the fort and once their feet touched solid earth, Lucie stepped toward Will, staring at a shiner about his left eye. "They got you good," she said.

Leaning in, Claire touched her brother's eyelid. "You're gonna get it, Will."

He winced. "I didn't start it."

"You know how father feels about fighting."

"*You* dumped the milk!"

"Well it wouldn't have happened if *you* hadn't chased us in here."

Will winced again as his sister explored his shiner. "Ouch … you're hurting me."

"That's what big sisters are for," she said.

Liza pulled a handkerchief from her sleeve and handed it to Claire. "I wish those boys would leave us be."

"They've been bullies as long as I can recall," Lucie said.

Claire looked up to the sky and could tell it was getting late. She grabbed her brother by the arm. Reluctantly, he followed her, holding Liza's white hankie on his eye.

"Come on," she said. "We're going to be late for supper."

Lucie and Liza reminded Claire she was forgetting something. As a tradition, the three friends gathered in a circle, locked pinkies and spoke simultaneously, "Daisy girls … all for one … one for all."

After exchanging hugs, they disappeared in different directions.

Claire smirked at her brother as she dragged him toward an open field. "Why I take care of you, I don't know. You'll get yourself killed someday, William."

Rolling grass swayed in the wind as the two ran toward the homestead. Settled between two forests, the farm's landscape suffered only now and again the troubles of simpler times. A red barn rose high into a blue sky and lay braced against two silos. The livestock looked placid, at least for the time.

Present

"My father was a real *baby grand*," the elder Claire told Dan. "A real—"

"Let me guess," he said then asked, "A real cake-eater?"

"A hard-boiled man," she replied. "Big and strong."

Dan returned to his recorder and notebook.

Again she took him back to a dinner table, many years before.

Spring, 1920

John Sloan sat patiently beside his children, eyes focused on the farm reports before him. A bracing solid man, he wore overalls, his sleeves rolled up to reveal battered, steel wrists, his frame nearly too big for the slight kitchen chair. Helen, his wife, hurried between the stove and the worn cedar table, delivering the mashed potatoes.

With his head hung low, trying to hide the shiner, Will said, "I hate potatoes."

His mother warned, "Eat them, young man."

John's eyes remained buried in the paper. "Farm reports just came out for the month."

Glancing at John, Helen asked, "So soon?"

"Looks like another dry summer."

Helen sat across the table from him as Claire and Will dug in, faces pasted to the steaming supper, forks in hand. Interrupted by their mother's cough, they glanced up at her briefly.

She asked them, "Aren't we forgetting something? Will, Claire?"

The children grasped hands with their mother and began to bow their heads for a solemn prayer when Claire glanced at her father, wondering, *Why doesn't he ever say prayers with us.* She assumed it was by design, but he never participated since coming back from *over there.*

Helen glanced at Will, "Why don't you lead us?"

All three began until Will took over. "Rub-a-dub-dub, thanks for the grub. Yay, God."

Releasing his mother's hand, he grabbed his fork and dug in, until he caught her gaze. Frowning, he set it down again, took her hand and waited for her to begin. Together they bowed their heads.

"In the name of the Father and the Son and the Holy Ghost. For what we are about to receive, may we be truly thankful. Amen."

Both children answered in unison, "Amen."

Will's face rose and caught his father staring at his shiner.

Through a stern glare, John asked, "Is there something you want to tell me, son?"

His voice faltering, Will replied, "I don't know."

Claire added, "He didn't start it, Father. It was the Atkins brothers … Curtis and Elmer."

"I don't care who started it."

Helen reminded him, "John, you know how those boys can be."

"That still don't make it right."

Will piled beans onto his plate. There weren't many.

"But, Dad, he pushed me down."

His tone firm, John answered, "Then walk away."

Claire looked from her father to her brother. "We wouldn't have been there if you hadn't chased us with that sour milk."

Will exclaimed, "It sure did come in handy when you dumped it on Elmer's head!"

Helen began to laugh. Covering her mouth, she tapped the table as their battle continued.

John spoke again. "That's enough! Both of you! Now, I told you both … stay away from those boys … you understand? I don't condone fighting … for nothin'." A tense silence ruled until John's voice softened a bit. "It never leads to nothin' … nothin' at all."

The argument rested, interrupted only by Helen's snickers at the thought of her son's antics. Dinners weren't as filling as they once were so Helen tried to laugh more. Aware of her mother's attempts, Claire watched her mother's face as she reached for her father's hand. He pulled it away, stretching as if uncomfortable.

"Sunlight's wasting," John said. "Gotta get that planter fixed. Son, you got chores to finish."

As John rose, Will acknowledged then finished his last gulp of milk. Stretching again, John walked out, leaving the family at the table in silence.

Claire shot her mother a glance. Helen's smile at Claire appeared to be false. She didn't remember such indifference from her father before he went away, and although she was years younger, she recalled a man much different, one who had certainly changed. For a nine-year-old, she found it difficult to ignore the pain she saw in her mother's eyes.

That night, as she and her mother worked at the sink, their hands buried in warm, soapy water, they peered out through sheer curtains covering the window, Claire scarcely tall enough to see what her mother could. The room filled with sounds of the spring breeze as the two of them looked off toward the barn and a light emitting from where John worked, a man neither one seemed to know as well since his return home from the war.

Claire asked, "Mother, do you and father still love each other?"

More comforting than convincing, Helen replied, "Of course we do. Why would you ask such a thing? Just because we don't hold hands … your father's just got a lot on his mind."

"Like losing the farm?"

"Why would you think we're going to lose the farm?"

"Well, Lucie's mother said they might have to sell. And Liza's father's out of work too."

Helen forced a smile while saying, "Claire, this farm has been in the family for three generations. We're not going anywhere."

Claire's eyes softened a bit, then her mother made a sudden change in subject, only in a way she could. "How was school?"

Carefully, Claire answered. "Becky thinks my clothes are ugly."

"Becky Brewer? Becky's all wet … and so is her mother for that matter."

Confident that her mother knew best, Claire smirked, "Bet she's going to the county fair … bet she'll have a new dress on too."

Helen paused then said, "Never you mind about Becky's new dress."

Together, they finished washing in silence, interrupted only by the swaying of the kitchen curtains and the sounds of livestock moving in for the night.

Leaning over to kiss Claire's brown, wavy hair, Helen said, "All your friends will be there … at the fair."

Claire nodded. She knew it to be true and looked forward to it every year.

~ ~ ~

John knelt, covered in dirt, intensely consumed in a partially rusted planter. The setting sun shone through a window and cast long shadows across the rafters and hay. Grasping a hammer, he tapped hard at a screw but it wouldn't budge.

Appearing from around a corner with a steaming cup of coffee in her hand, Helen asked, "Cup of Joe?"

He didn't break his trance. "Put it over there."

She set the cup down and began playing with her apron, searching for a lost connection. She walked over to a tool bench and picked up a wrench then went back to fiddling with her apron.

Her voice sounded forced as she said, "I was just talking with Claire."

John continued working.

"She's excited about the fair."

Again, no answer.

"It'll be good to get away from this place for a few days," she continued then glanced down at her worn nails, not as manicured as the day they married. "Velma said a colored man bought the old Conway farm. Wonder if he'll be there?"

John's voice came from beneath the planter. "Right next door ... don't know. Guess that depends on how brave he is."

It surprised Helen that she received an answer and she said, "It's not right for men to treat them any different."

"I know it ain't right," John added. "That's just the way it is. There's a lot of things that ain't right about this world, Helen. It's enough to test a man's faith."

Glancing at the hay beneath her feet, she searched for an answer. "John, the war's over."

Wiping a sweating brow with his sleeve, he rose and said, "I don't want to talk about the war. I've got enough on my mind tryin' to keep our heads above water on this farm."

She edged toward him. "What do you want me to say, John? I can't pray anymore than I do."

"Yeah, well ... there's a lot of men praying these days ... and God ain't listenin'."

Glancing over a shoulder she checked to make sure they were alone then found the courage to ask him. "John, how bad is it? Be honest with me."

For once he looked directly at her and said, "You see our silos lately? We got two-dozen head of cattle and about enough feed to last until mid-summer. After that, it's anybody's guess."

Wanting desperately for them to be the team they once were, she held her sigh and asked, "What else can we do?"

"I intend to auction some cattle ... and pigs at the fair. If it gets too bad, the kids could stay awhile at your sister's."

"John, we can't do that, I'll try to find work if I have to."

He shut his eyes, something she hadn't seen in quite some time. "A man should be able to provide for his family without his wife working."

Meanwhile, Claire made her way to the barn. Hidden on the other side of the door, she knelt by the foot of a post, a silent listener to that which she already knew. Her young head rested against the red painted wood, and she felt her stomach get sick as she heard her father speak again.

"Let's see how we do at the fair. We can talk about what to do with the kids later."

Claire rose. Burdening her mother further wasn't something she desired. Instead she pushed on her stomach, swallowing the nerves and tried to find the maturity about which her mother often spoke. Old enough to understand the war *over there* had ended; she knew the conflict at home remained. She ran off in silence, left only with the budding worries of the future.

Chapter 4

A Solemn Request

Crickets sang to the moonlight and the tranquility of a farm at rest. A peaceful breeze danced through open windows, paying respect to the fleeting security that the night brought to those inside. Helen breathed peacefully as she lay next to her restless man, something she'd grown used to. The night's deepness brought another *episode* as he tossed in his sleep.

Small beads of sweat formed on John's brow gleamed in the moonlight. Wrenching in his sleep, he experienced a time even less certain than the ones in which he lived. The sounds of artillery fire and explosions rang through his mind along with flashes of a friend's face from whom he became separated far too soon.

Her mother felt the effects of her father's nightmares more than Claire, yet she often awoke too. And as often. Claire thought about the pain of a man she knew little about, perhaps the greatest man she had ever known. Those nights allowed her to see through a window into her father's soul and perhaps an answer to his apathy, but only from a distance.

One night, she moved closer as she listened outside her parents' room, a night worse than it had been in awhile.

John flailed in his sleep, crying out, "Billy! Billy!"

He blurted a horrific scream and found himself in the arms of the woman who knew him long before the demons did. He lay in her grasp, sweat dripping from his brow.

Claire heard her father moan, "How long. How much longer?"

Jaded silence.

A tear that welled in Helen's eye began to run down her cheek. "Only as long as you let it, John. Only as long as you let it."

Overcome by her mother's anguish, Claire scampered down the long hallway toward the front door, trying to remain anonymous. She found herself standing on the front porch, her face reflecting the moon's light, cheeks wet with her own worries. Raising her eyes to the Heavens she sighed then prayed.

No answer came, only the quiet wind of the prairie, but the wind soon became her friend and she spoke with certitude that her voice would somehow not fall on deaf ears. "If you're there God ... please help us. We need your help ... now, more than ever. Please send us a miracle ... a miracle."

The neighbor's farm sat atop a distant hill and Claire stood against a post to watch it. Her still, small voice harmonized with the night and the post to which she braced herself stood tall, perhaps a reflection of the sentinel she had always believed her farm would be.

The world was changing, in more ways than one.

Present

Claire stopped for a moment, waiting for Dan to catch up. He did, so she moved him ahead to the County Fair.

"It was always a highlight for me," she said. "Something to look forward to. It was the only vacation we took as kids."

She stopped a moment, waiting for him to acknowledge. He broke from his trance, jumping out of his funk. "What? The county fair ... yes ... the only vacation you took."

Hesitating, she looked directly at him. "Mr. Mertz, may I ask you a question?" Dan's clumsiness became evident to her as he struggled to give her his attention. "Are you in a hurry, Mr. Mertz?"

He reminded her. "Please, it's Dan ... no, I mean ... I don't want to take all month or anything—"

"Because, your boss called me," she said.

"He did?"

She nodded slightly, her eyes appeared suspicious. "Yes, he did. You know what he told me?"

Dan hung his head and whispered, "I'm not sure I want to—"

"He told me you need to get your shit together."

"Great ... that's ... yeah ... he told me the same."

"I suspect, Mr. Mertz, his idea was to make this a retreat of sorts."

Dan appeared boyish, his wavy hair a bit mussed. He adjusted in his seat at her assessment.

"So can we get started again?"

He cleared his throat, a nervous cough or two. "Certainly."

Without missing a beat, she brought him again to the past. "Everybody who was anybody attended the fair. People came from all over ... Lansing, Mount Pleasant, West Branch. We always had a marvelous time."

Dan offered, "Sounds like you got along with most everybody."

"Most people," she said. "Especially my parents. But there were some men my father just didn't trust. Mayor Gavel was one of them."

Spring, 1920

During the long and winding caravan trip to the county fair, children ran between carriages and a few Ford trucks plastered with dust from moving on rough gravel roads. The Sloan children found themselves in Lucie's caravan for much of the time then back to Liza's. Will followed his sister for lack of anything better to do.

The holiday began like clockwork with a stop at Charlie Logan's store in town. Claire found herself amidst the creaky wooden floors and rows of penny candy, enduring her brother's presence as he bounced a rubber ball beside her.

John seemed more interested in the hardware on the boring side of the store, rifling through a bucket of old, metal washers, wearing large overalls and the same plaid shirt, rolled at the sleeves.

The store's owner, a friend of John for years, poked his head around a corner. A middle-aged man with receding hairline and an infectious smile, a friend willing to forgive John his debt, a burden John had lots of.

Wearing a worn, white shop apron about his thin frame, Charlie grasped a broom firmly in his hands and greeted them. "John, Claire, Will, how are you today? Headed to the fair, are ya?"

Helen called from across the aisle. "Charlie, how are you?"

Sweeping methodically, Charlie said, "Helen, you're looking fine today. Headed to the fair?"

John replied, "Same time every year."

Mayor Gavel emerged from behind another aisle. A plump man with a round nose whose greetings always rang artificial, he engaged John. "John Sloan, our local war hero. Fancy meeting you here."

John said in a tone that addressed the insincerity, "Mr. Mayor."

"Heading to the big event I see. Is your lovely wife with you?"

Peering from across the store, Helen waved politely.

"Good, good," said the Mayor. "Listen, this year's cakewalk is bound to be a real treat. Mabel's rhubarb pie is a real dandy this year … a real dandy."

John moved toward the register, hands filled with nuts and washers. "I'll be sure to remember that."

Claire walked up beside them, acknowledging the mayor.

Gavel followed them to the front of the store then asked, "Claire showing any horses this year?"

John shook his head. "No, none to show."

The mayor chuckled then said, "Well, she can still catch a pig, can't she? I see your boy's getting big too."

While tugging on her father's overalls, Claire asked, "Father, how about the hog calling contest?"

As he chuckled his belly bounced then Gavel asked, "Hog calling contest? Why honey, you wouldn't stand a chance."

Will came toward them and said, "Oh yes she would. She's got a big mouth."

Charlie rang up John's sale and John glanced at a two hundred twelve dollar balance owed to Charlie since last spring, scribbled neatly on a paper in the drawer. Slamming the register shut, Charlie smiled at him in a way that said he didn't care.

Pocketing a small bit of change, John nodded once to Charlie then to the mayor, whose smirk remained.

"You have a great day, Sloan," Gavel said.

John turned toward the door, fisting a pocket full of change. Reaching the edge of the counter, he stopped before a worn, blue poster nestled beside a change jar framed inside a peeled, red bucket. Outside the bucket lay a sign embossed with tan letters that read, *Salvation Army War Lassie: Keep her on the job.*

Reaching out to the Salvation Army jar, John dropped in the change then whispered, "For a candy bar," before heading toward the door.

Confused, Will said, "But Dad, we didn't buy a candy bar."

As the Sloans filed past the door onto the dusty wooden porch, John nearly bumped into a tall, thin black man on his way in.

The man's long and lean face had profound eyes, deep wrinkles and a smile that exposed ivory teeth. John tipped his hat and the stranger acknowledged.

Before she climbed aboard their wagon, Helen nudged John and said, "That's him."

John looked at her with a strange expression.

"The one that bought the Conway farm," she said.

Nodding, John grabbed the reins. The Clinton County Ribbon cutting ceremony would begin shortly.

Helen climbed into the wagon to follow her husband toward their week of respite with livestock in tow, certain of little more than the fact they would be home in a week.

~ ~ ~

After settling in at their camp, the town women collected in the field house kitchen and listened to the men boasting about last year's harvest, something they likely wouldn't be able to do this year. Children ran past long tables lined for supper as women maneuvered heaps of food toward seated guests.

Helen grasped a metal pot filled to the brim with baked beans. Slipping between low-backed wooden chairs, she felt herself bump up against someone. Turning, she saw a white Roman collar and a middle-aged man she had come to admire with undercut hair and engaging eyes. He smiled at her. He had been at her parish for a shorter time than the others and most had wished it were longer.

"Father Cunningham. How are you? I didn't think you were going to make it this year."

He caught the splendid aroma. "Are you kidding? The corn roast is the highlight."

Some locals spun in their chairs and called his name. He smiled at them then leaned in and complimented their cooking.

Helen asked him about Monsignor Cobalt.

His tone rhetorical, he said, "You know him. He never comes to these things. How's your husband?"

She set the pot down and waved off the heat. "John's fine, Father … as cantankerous as ever. You know how he get's come planting time."

"I can only imagine."

"Can't get him to go to church with me, Father. What's a woman to do?"

"Helen," he replied, "talk to John less about God … talk to God more about John."

She smiled, removed her apron and joined her husband at the far end of the table covered with a red and white checkered cloth. Helen leaned over to kiss his head, but he turned away, his eyes looked distant and cold.

Sitting across from them, Charlie Logan pounded the table to draw John out of his trance. "Johnny. Food's gettin' cold. Eat up friend, before I get impatient and eat your bit."

Helen said, "Gracious, Charlie, you don't have to worry about that. Eating has never been much trouble for the Sloan family … at least not John."

She tried to smile wider, but wondered silently if her words might someday ring less true.

~ ~ ~

After supper, Claire and her friends found themselves with a bit too much time. Claire lay beside Liza and Lucie in the livestock barn, peering down from a loft at the dry hay and the dust that settled into a stream of sunlight. Livestock moved below, settled into stalls for the night: pigs, horses, cows and a few donkeys.

Sighing at the presence of Will, Lucie wondered why he always tagged along until Claire reminded her friends of her sisterly duty.

Will supposed Liza liked him, so he tossed a spot of hay at her.

She yelled back at him, "Pest!"

He tossed more at her so Claire scolded him. "William, that's enough!"

"She started it."

"I did nothing of the sort—"

He shouted, "You're a sissy!"

Liza shouted something back then they all turned toward the sudden sound of an opening door at the far end of the barn. The livestock startled and Will shushed the girls. Settling into the

shadows of the loft, they watched as the two Atkins boys came into the barn, a long stick in Curtis's hand.

Will sighed while Claire peered through a crack, brushing aside a tuft of hay to get a better look. She felt it odd that Curtis focused his attention on a mangy donkey at the stall closest to them. He stepped toward the animal, bullying eyes fixed on the gray and white mane tangled with dirt and small twigs, its hoofs filthy. Elmer stepped next to his brother and began taunting the animal. Rearing back, Curtis struck the donkey with the stick and the donkey brayed in pain. Reaching back Curtis struck the animal again.

Indignant, Claire jumped up and Will shoved her back down.

He whispered, "Are you crazy?"

Again, Curtis struck the animal and then both boys taunted it.

Breaking loose from her brother, Claire stood up and announced their presence from above. "Stop it! Leave him be!"

As the Atkins brothers looked up at them, Will covered his face.

Claire shouted, "Leave him alone! Both of you!"

Elmer challenged, "You wanna come down and make us?"

Curtis pointed the stick at Will. "You're next on our list, Sloan!"

Will glanced through open fingers at the two boys he had grown to hate. Fear gripped him as he waited for what was sure to be another shiner.

Elmer went to the ladder leading to the loft. As he placed a foot upon it, another door swung open and in staggered a thin, unshaven man, grasping a bottle wrapped in a brown paper bag. Dirt buried deep under his fingernails, he took a swig, wiping his mouth with a sleeve, glaring at the two boys before him.

Claire recognized him—Coy Atkins, the boys' father. As he moved closer toward his sons, their eyes widened in fear.

Taking another swig, he addressed them, words slurred in moonshine, "I dun told you boys once if I dun told you a thousand times to stay near the tent."

Elmer stuttered, "S-sorry, Pa, w-we was just—"

The sudden sound of slapped skin filled the barn as Coy hit Elmer across his face, sending him hard to the ground.

Coy screamed, "I don't give a damn! Get your asses back to the tent ... now!"

Dropping the stick to the ground, Curtis pulled his brother up from the hay and dragged him out of the barn, leaving Coy alone, oblivious to the witnesses above and less aware of the witness standing on four legs in front of him.

In his drunken state, Coy swayed a bit then raised the bottle to parched lips and took another sip, peering sideways at the donkey gazing back at him. Slowly lowering the bottle, he locked eyes with the animal. The donkey looked back at him as if peering into his soul. Appearing ashamed to look more, Coy turned away, searching the ground for an answer.

He raised his eyes and sneered back at the animal, mumbling, "What're you lookin' at?"

Then he took another swig and staggered away. The door squeaked again as he disappeared and left the children alone.

Safely down from the loft, Claire felt drawn to the donkey. She went to him with a handful of hay. The animal remained still and kept his eyes on the other children.

He wore a tattered saddle, green and red in color, with an odd broach affixed to it, patterned in a way Claire had never seen. It looked foreign, perhaps Hebrew. She edged toward him and he moved toward her then his snout nudged her hand and she opened it.

As he nibbled on the hay, Claire spoke softly to him, "Here, sweetheart. Take this."

Liza moved closer, nudged Claire's arm and said, "I think he likes you."

Claire shushed her. "Let's make sure he's not scared." She stroked his dusty, gray and white mane. "See, all he needs is a little attention."

They heard a sudden creak from the door, resonating from across the barn. This time, a small, older man emerged out of the shadows, carrying a bucket, wearing a curmudgeon like expression. A small potbelly hung over a loosely fitted belt and small strands of gray hair spun off the top of his balding head.

He glared at Claire as he approached and motioned her away from the donkey. "Darned kids. Stop feedin' him. Stop it, I say!"

Pulling her hand away, Claire and the kids stepped back trying to conceal laughs.

"You feed him too much and all he does is crap all over the place! More trouble than he's worth, I tell ya."

Claire said, "Doesn't seem like he'd be much trouble."

The man reached over the crude wooden corral. "Yeah, well you don't know the half of it, little girl. Try owning him for awhile. Dang nabbit! Between the dreams and the commotion and the seizures and the antics—"

Unable to contain their laughter anymore, Liza and Lucie nudged each other.

"It's past his feedin' time anyway," continued the man.

Lucie spun to look at a clock across the barn then blurted out, "Claire, what time is the contest?"

Will looked annoyed as he asked, "What contest?"

Liza and Lucie answered in unison, "The hog calling contest!"

Claire answered, "Seven … we're late. Let's go!"

Chapter 5
The Contest

People packed the field house to the brim. Children scampered in from outside and adults sat beside the same long tables at which they had eaten, chairs turned toward the stage.

Large double-doors stood open, exposing the wind and a pen filled with prize animals being offered for sale throughout the night. A portly man stood on the wooden platform made into a stage and a few people scowled when they realized who it was—Mayor Gavel. However, he did have a few admirers in the crowd.

The mayor stepped toward the microphone and quieted the crowd. "Ladies and gentlemen, welcome to the tenth annual Clinton County Hog Calling contest."

Sparse applause sounded as Gavel's speech continued: the same speech he gave every year, and it had more to do with him than anything else.

Father Cunningham located John and Helen and eased his way between them then asked, "Are you two ready?"

John tried to be polite and asked the priest about his supper.

"Always a highlight," the priest replied. "Mrs. Sloan, your beans and cornbread were superb."

Helen smiled and then nodded toward the stage. "Father did you see Claire up there?"

The priest said, "Sweet little Claire … a hog-calling contest?"

Helen concealed a laugh in a way that told the good Father that he needed to learn more about the Sloan's daughter.

Gavel raised a large finger toward the sky and continued, "As a first prize, we have a selection of pet animals that have been offered as gifts." He pointed toward a pen past the open doors. "Many generous farmers we have this year … many generous people."

Claire stood on her toes, glancing over the heads of contestants in front of her. Beholding a host of farm animals, she noticed the one in particular that looked familiar.

Gavel continued, "The winner will be given first choice. Now, let's get started with Norma. Norma Conner."

The crowd settled onto cold, wooden chairs. John leaned against a freshly painted post and Helen stood next to him, glancing from time to time at Will seated motionless, looking bored.

Becky Brewer sat in the front row, showing off a new dress, waving at Claire with the hopes she'd notice it. Claire moved her hand to try and cover the small hole in hers.

Next to Claire, children took turns holding cupped hands over their mouths to shout out their own hog-calling adaptations—first Norma Conner, then Billy Nichols, then Brendan Knittle and Stanley Olson. Claire waited patiently beside her friends.

Lucie stepped toward the small podium, pulled her dark black hair back into a ponytail, then cupped her hands and screamed a call. Sparse laughter and applause rose from the crowd.

Next, Liza's turn. She took the stage and bellowed a call, louder than Lucie's. A few more clapped.

Then Claire stepped up. She took her place at the front, feet planted firmly beneath her. The crowd grew silent as she paused for more than an awkward moment. Head hung low in thought, she raised it again to peer at Becky Brewer in the front. She breathed in deep, hawked up a wad, leaned forward and spit on the ground. It landed close to Becky's feet, drawing a few gasps.

Rearing back, she reached down within and bellowed an ear-wrenching call. It resonated off the walls of the field house and echoed deeply into the rows of tables. At first, an odd silence fell over the scene then loud, spontaneous applause exploded from the crowd. A standing ovation meshed with bouts of laughter and praise as people clapped, hailing Claire's efforts. Father Cunningham joined in the applause, nudging Helen, glancing toward John who nodded with a small, forced grin.

Tired, plus his large girth, the mayor ascended the steps with effort, grabbed the microphone and shot a frown at Claire. Then he motioned for the contestants to stand around him.

Liza and Lucie scampered to the end of the line, congratulating Claire on her performance.

Gavel addressed the crowd. "What a great group of performers. This will be a difficult decision. You, as our audience, will be the deciding factor. First, let's give a big hand to all our performers."

The gathering erupted into applause.

"Who shall be this year's winner? Shall it be Norma Conner?"

Some cheering came from the back of the hall as Gavel moved down the line of contestants.

As Helen watched, Will rose to get her attention. She shushed him, half annoyed at the interruption.

Continuing down the line, Gavel held a hand over each of them. Applause sounded, more for some than others.

Then the mayor reached Claire.

Holding a hand above her head, he asked the gathering, "Shall the winner be ... Claire Sloan?"

In unison the crowd stood, erupting into ovation and cheers. Visually bewildered, Gavel scanned the line of contestants and nodded. Turning toward Claire he shook his head, unable to deny she won the contest.

Raising Claire's hand as the victor, he bellowed, "Very well, the winner shall be Claire Sloan. Claire, tell us, which of the farm animals before us will you choose?"

Claire scanned the pen beyond the guests then pointed a finger toward one of them and blurted, "Him ... I'll take that one!"

Looking toward the pen, Gavel said, "The sheep. She wants Mr. Calhoun's sheep."

"No," Claire responded, "the donkey! I want the donkey!"

Heads turned toward the donkey with a gray and white mane, standing in the midst of the other animals in a pen. Liza bumped Lucie and nodded toward him—the same donkey they met earlier that afternoon.

Gavel took a quick look at the donkey then turned to look sideways at Claire. "Claire, you want that dirty thing? You'd better ask your parents about—"

She blurted again, "I want the donkey!"

The mayor glanced at the Sloans, and Helen nodded then looked to her silent husband, perhaps an implicit approval. Gavel scanned the crowd to find the donkey's owner.

The same curmudgeon Claire had met earlier stood atop his chair. "I am the animal's owner."

Gavel held a hand up to his eyes to peer in the man's direction. "You are Mister—"

"Lenter. Saul Lenter," the man replied.

"You are willing to give this animal ... this ... donkey as a prize to Miss Sloan?"

"She's damn welcome to him."

Gavel approved to the sound of more applause. "So let it be. Let's all congratulate Claire Sloan as this year's winner of the Clinton County Hog Calling contest."

Will tugged on his mother's shirt again and she turned toward him, "What is it, Will?"

"I told you she had a big mouth."

Cunningham leaned between John and Helen. "She did it. John, Helen, congratulations."

John nodded and said, "All we need ... another mouth to feed."

Helen understood his concern. Had it been before the war, she would have placed a hand on his shoulder and rubbed one of his arms. Instead she kept idle. No livestock had been sold yet and she felt a deep apprehension they would return from the fair no better for it. Kissing a finger she planted that finger on his cheek, smiled at Father Cunningham and walked away. She had learned it was about all she could do.

Present

The elderly Claire settled into her chair beside a steaming cup of tea, something she'd learned would ease her to sleep each night. Dan glanced at his watch as the time flew by quicker than he had hoped.

He asked, "So, you won ... and that was it?"

After a long awkward pause, Dan wondered for a moment if she hadn't already fallen asleep. He waited through the silence until he had enough of it then thought of another question.

Claire's voice broke the silence first. "Nighttime at the fair was the greatest ... a time for the grown-ups to dance ... and the kids to

play. I couldn't wait to play with my new friend. Neither could Lucie or Liza. Will, on the other hand, could not have cared less."

Dan smirked, "Reminds me … of me."

Claire went on, "Yet, when we got to the donkey's pen, he was gone. At first I was worried then we heard him braying from another part of the barn. Something was wrong. I knew something was wrong. It was as if he was trying to tell us something."

Spring, 1920

Claire walked at a brisk pace beside her friends to the barn, square dance music blaring from the hall. Striding faster, she hoped they would lose her brother.

Will grumbled, "I don't want to see your stupid donkey!"

"Go chase yourself, William."

Claire's patience with him was tried most often in the summer months, times when they were forced to work and play together for long hours.

Entering the barn, they rounded the corner and peered into the donkey's stall, but saw no donkey there. Neither Claire nor her friends had an explanation. When Will sneered, the girls wondered if he was up to something.

Then they heard the donkey's frantic brays from across the barn. Peering down the long thin aisle, past piles of stacked hay, a light shone from beneath the door. The commotion coming from the other side sounded like a fight.

As the children edged toward the door, the sounds got louder and the braying continued. Their steps cautious, they all moved forward, ducking between posts. Then Claire caught a glimpse of the animal, bucking and neighing, perhaps a warning of some sort.

The children rose long enough to look through a window into the next room. Two large white men with dirty overalls harassed a lone man, a bit more moderate in stature. They had shirts unbuttoned and mud on worn boots. The smell of alcohol emitted from them, even to the next stall.

The thinner black man wore a plaid shirt and blue jeans. It didn't take Claire long to recognize him—Wilson Washington, the new owner of the Conway farm. The man they'd bumped into in town.

The children hunkered down and watched in horror.

One of the men punched Wilson in the stomach. "I told you once before, spades don't go round here. You don't listen too well."

The other man grabbed Wilson's shoulders, shoving him hard into a concrete wall then picking up a rope laying in the hay, he threw it to his partner who jeered Wilson with it. "The only good spade is a dead one."

The donkey bucked and brayed again until one of the assailants glanced in his direction.

Taking the rope to the animal, he held it up and bellowed, "Ya want some of this, ya stupid animal?"

Hunkering down further, Claire peered through a thin crack in the wood. One of the men grabbed Wilson by the throat and Lucie swallowed a scream, Liza's hand over her mouth.

Claire leaned against her brother and whispered, "I'm going to get Father."

He whispered back, "It won't matter."

"Yes it will!"

Will gripped her upper right arm. "He don't fight. Remember what he told us?"

She pried his fingers away. "Let go of me!"

The punches on Wilson continued as Claire rose to her feet. Scampering off, she slipped out of the barn into the starry night, the sounds of a disturbed animal left behind. She knew her parents would be at the dance hall. She would be sure to find help there.

~ ~ ~

A scrawny caller barked orders to the sounds of a bluegrass band as ladies and gentlemen locked arms to begin a square dance. Tables had been cleared from the floor and sounds of quick stepping boots and cheers replaced those from dinner.

John leaned against the same post with a lifeless expression on his face. Helen stood beside him.

Charlie Logan, who had closed his store early to join the fun and festivities, edged up next to John, nudged him and asked, "What's eatin' ya, John? You're not gonna dance?"

John shook his head a bit. "Never been much of a dancer."

Helen interjected, "He thinks he'll embarrass me."

"You used to be a hell of a swinger, Johnny," Charlie recalled.

John noticed an older lady wearing patriotic colors and a war bond hat, gliding from group to group holding a bucket that read, *Salvation Army*. Ignoring his friend, John stepped toward the lady. Plunging a hand into his pocket he came out with a fist full of change. He dropped it in the bucket and the lady nodded.

"For a candy bar," he said before returning to his post.

Charlie glanced at Helen and asked, "Candy bar?"

She shrugged. "Don't ask me. He won't say why."

"What is it with you and candy bars, Johnny? There something you been hiding from us?"

John became lost in the moment; his eyes appeared empty as he gazed about the room then asked his friend, "Hiding?"

Turning again toward the music on the stage, John disappeared into his mental recesses, quietly melting into silence.

Charlie stepped closer to Helen and whispered, "He ain't the same, Helen."

She concealed her nostalgia. "None of us are, Charlie."

Claire burst into their presence. She grasped her father's arm. "Father, come quick! Please!"

Looking down at her, John asked, "What is it?"

"It's Mr. Washington. They're beating him … bad!"

His trance appeared to break. He glanced at Helen in a way that nearly looked for her approval. His eyes locked with hers for an instant until he turned back to Claire.

"Show me where."

~ ~ ~

Liza, Lucie and Will remained crouched in the adjacent stall, paralyzed with fear. Wilson, his lip bloody and left eye swelling shut had weakened. One of the white men panted hard from his effort. Blood dripped from his hand and his partner's shirt had a long tear in it. He glanced down and kicked the straw with his boot, uncovering the rope that had fallen into it. Grabbing it again, he lifted it up and taunted Wilson.

Tossing it around a beam, he sneered. "You know what you got comin' to you after you dun ripped my partner's shirt."

Out of the shadows, a sudden set of large white hands appeared. One grasped a shoulder, the other the rope. Yanking the rope down from the rafters, the faceless man stepped out—John Sloan.

Rearing back, John punched the man, knocking him off his feet and into a wooden fence, splintering it into pieces. The other man came at him. Clenching the man's overalls, John sent him into a box of crates.

The first man rose, shook off a blur then wiped his bloodied nose and scowled at John.

Lunging toward John, the man yelled, "You son of a bitch!"

John sidestepped him, slugging him in the stomach and the face, spinning him backward and knocking him unconscious.

Staggering to his feet, Wilson's eyes hazed over from sweat and blood. Gradually, the second man stood again with a shovel in his hand. Moving behind John, he raised the shovel above John's head.

A large fence post struck the man in the back, knocking him to the ground. John swung around and saw Wilson standing over the man, holding a fence post.

Wilson coughed and winced from pain. Together he and John labored to breathe, their opponents lying unconscious in the hay.

Will emerged from the shadows, assessed the damage and stammered, "Holy shit!"

Aggravated, John stepped toward him and grasped his shoulders. "Get your things and get back to our camp."

Will saw the two crumpled men on the ground and gasped, "You cleaned their clock!"

"Get back to camp. Now!"

Claire and her friends came out of hiding and John ordered, "Claire, tell your friends you'll see them tomorrow."

The children filed past John and Wilson, the donkey quiet in the next stall. Claire stopped a moment to look at him. Their eyes met and it was as if she understood him, and he understood her. Then the donkey watched as she followed her friends out of the barn, leaving John and Wilson alone.

Breathing hard and bent over, Wilson began to nurse a wound to his face then said, "Wilson ... the name's Wilson Washington."

Offering his hand, John said, "I'm John Sloan. Welcome to the neighborhood."

Wilson laughed hard then winced again from the pain.

Nodding, John turned again to assess the two unconscious men. *They'll be all right. They'll live.*

He smirked at Wilson, acknowledging a sense of humor. "You got a planter I can borrow?"

Wilson laughed as best he could.

All John did was smile, but it was more than he had done in quite a while.

Present

Claire nodded. "Wilson and my father became friends that day. And if it were possible, we gained a newfound respect for my father ... perhaps because he was willing to do the very thing he so hated ... because it was the right thing to do."

Dan checked his recorder and jotted a few notes. He took a long, careful sip of the coffee sitting next to him. Shirt untucked, he caught Claire's glance at his uncombed hair. Disregarding what she thought, he set the cup down so as not to spill it.

"I've been having trouble with that lately," he said, nodding toward the coffee. "So ... the fair ... and now you own this donkey."

"Indeed," Claire smiled. "Do you have children, Mr. Mertz?"

He adjusted in his seat. "Dan. Call me Dan ... me? Probably never ... I mean ... too busy. My wife works two shifts. Too much crap in the world. I'm not sure I'd wanna bring them into it."

"Too much crap?"

"Well, you know." She didn't so he thought he'd bring her back on track. "Can we get back ... so, you spent one week at the fair?"

She smiled, almost as if she knew something about him then conceding to him, she continued, "One week. But for a little girl, a week was like a lifetime. And before we knew it, it was time to return to the life that awaited us."

Dan stopped a moment. "Wait. The livestock ... did you get rid of the livestock?"

"My father sold two horses and three swine. That was it. That, with the drought … none of it helped."

"The drought?"

"One of the worst dry spells ever."

He asked as if it were a statement. "So, you were no better off after the fair … and your father?"

"His nightmares continued … at first. Yet even in the midst of all, this damaged man always made sure we got to church."

He nodded. "I see."

Claire shook her head. "But he never went."

Spring, 1920

The dark-blue Sloan wagon, drawn by a team of horses, pulled up in front of St. Mary's parish, leaving clouds of dust in its path. Helen shuffled her kids out of the back, making certain to keep their Sunday clothes away from the animals in the wagon bed. Nothing sold that would have helped them, and they now had a new animal to care for, a donkey. Helen motioned Claire and Will to the front steps then watched as the children scuttled past a praying statue of Christ at the Garden of Gethsemane.

Going to her husband, she asked a rhetorical question, "Can we settle up with Charlie?"

He shook his head and without expression said, "Headed there now. Don't imagine he'll mention it."

Helen leaned to catch a glimpse of the donkey, tied to the inside rear of the trailer. "Don't forget about him."

Kissing her fingers, she placed them on his, meeting the usual indifference. Though he tried to acknowledge her, he only nodded once before driving off. He had to go less than two miles to Logan's store and about ten to the farm.

Going to town became an indulgence. When they got there, they stayed longer. Less hassle and less wear on the horses in the heat.

John parked the team in front of the well-worn porch at Logan's store and climbed off. Walking past the wagon's rear, he glanced at the newest member of the family, the donkey tied to the wagon's gate. As he pushed open the flimsy screen door, a bell announced

his entrance and he made his way to the hardware aisle. Rifling through more bolts and washers, he grabbed a handful and walked toward the front, stopping at the feed aisle.

He shook his head and whispered, "What the hell do they eat?"

Grabbing a bag of feed, he took the long walk to the front of the store and plopped it on the counter.

Charlie's wife greeted him. "For Claire's new friend?"

He replied, "I never owned one before."

She rang up the sale. "Claire must be happy."

He asked, "Charlie still at the fairgrounds?"

Velma nodded then looked at the feed. "Another bad harvest?"

John nodded once as the drawer opened, revealing the same past due note. *Sloan: $212 credit.* His eyes gravitated to it and Velma tried to draw them away, shutting the drawer again.

Tipping his hat, he promised, "I'll settle up when I can. You have my word."

She understood and smiled. He collected what little change he had in his pocket then made his way to the door. As he passed the Salvation Army bucket, he stretched a hand out and dropped it in.

Before pushing open the door, he whispered, "Candy bar."

Stepping onto the porch, he walked past the back of the wagon then slung the feed onto the front seat. Hesitating before climbing aboard, he went back around to take a closer look at something. He saw the rope still attached to the back of the wagon, but no donkey. He stooped to pick up the empty rope then swung around and looked in a few directions, but he saw nothing.

His mind raced as he walked to the side of Logan's. He peered around a corner then another, but no donkey in sight anywhere. Glancing in the dirt for a clue, he saw hoofprints so he followed them to a dirt path across the street and between a few posts.

Striding toward the middle of town, he shook his head and said, "Dumb animal."

Cupping his hands to call a name, he realized he didn't know it. He walked between shops, peering off toward Main Street. Two men sat on a bench outside a Buckley and Nunn store.

One of them called to him, "Mister, you lookin' for a donkey?"

John acknowledged the man who then pointed toward the north end of town. "He ran off that way ... up toward city hall."

The other man bellowed, "Up toward the church."

Tipping his hat, John said, "Much obliged," then glanced back to check on his wagon, still tied to a post in front of Logan's.

Moving on, he climbed a large hill that led to a field between city hall and St. Mary's church. He heard the service going on as he reached the peak, his family engaged inside. Edging closer, he peered to get a better look at something. He saw a gray animal feeding off the grass adjacent to the small grotto. Nestled in the middle of the field stood the statue which his family passed by weekly: Christ kneeling by a rock, praying at Gethsemane, his eyes looking to the Heavens in turmoil.

John moved closer and mumbled, "Stupid animal."

A young man, waiting outside the church doors with a cigarette in his mouth, hollered to John. "Mister, is this your donkey?"

John answered, "Thanks. He got away from me."

After approaching the animal, John grabbed the broken rope attached to the bridle then looked directly at him and asked, "What the hell's wrong with you?"

He tugged on the rope, but the donkey wouldn't move, so John pulled harder and said, "Come on."

Standing solid, the donkey began eating grass, refusing to move.

Pulling again, John muttered, "Come on, ya dumb animal."

Half embarrassed, he glanced up at the man on the steps who seemed interested in his comedic struggle. Wrapping the rope around his hands a few times, he bore down again and tugged. This time, he lost his grip and landed on his rear. He sat on the ground for a moment, glaring at the donkey.

"Oh, yeah? You think so?" Rising again, he jerked the rope and frowned as the donkey's nose remained in the grass. He sighed, sat in the field next to the animal and said, "Fine, I'll wait you out."

~ ~ ~

Inside the church, with the service underway, Helen sat beside Claire, who wore one of the two dresses she owned, the blue and less tattered one. Next to Claire sat Will, slouched in a way that spoke of the pain with which he dealt in such stillness. Wearing a

Sunday best pant suit, his brown hair only long enough to be combed, swirled to one side.

Monsignor Cobalt, the pastor of St. Mary's as long as Helen could recall, stood at the front of the altar whispering prayers. She felt more distant from him than with Father Cunningham, and she noticed, more than once, the two of them never stood together. That morning, Father Cunningham greeted them at the door alone. She reckoned because of Cobalt's ego. She hadn't said more than a few sentences to the monsignor over the years, and he hadn't said as much to her either.

Cobalt bent at the waist, kissing the white-covered altar, "*Te igitur, clementissime Pater, per Jesum Christum Filium tuum Dominum nostrum supplices rogamus ac petimus.*"

Will yawned loud enough for others to hear so Claire nudged him in a way that allowed her to scan the congregation. She saw Becky seated next to her mother and wondered why it seemed it was scarcely more than a place for them to be seen.

Claire prayed through the pomp and circumstance, aware her family was no better off for the time being. She carried those worries with her as she followed her mother to the Communion rail, and sang the dismissal hymn, *Crown Him with Many Crowns.*

Shuffling out of their pews, Will stared at a younger lady wearing a white and yellow frilly dress, her hair pulled into a tight bun and covered with a doily. Claire noticed her brother focused on the woman's crutches and her legs locked firmly in metal braces.

She anticipated his question, "Polio, dummy ... and it's not polite to stare."

Helen shushed them as they filed to the gathering area at the back of the sanctuary. Helen eased next to the crippled woman, who nearly fell despite the crowd, her name Eleanor Russell. She glanced behind Eleanor to see Mildred Brewer, Becky's mother, shoving people and trudging her way to the front of the line, a quicker route to Monsignor Cobalt and the one person who could feed her sanctimony.

Reaching out, Helen offered a hand to Eleanor. "I'm sorry. Please forgive my clumsiness."

"Thanks, Helen," Eleanor replied.

It surprised Claire that her mother knew the woman. She shot her mother a curious glance.

Helen whispered, "That's Miss Russell. She lives in town."

Will bellowed from behind, "Claire says she has polio."

Helen shushed him. "William. Let's discuss this later."

Upon reaching the gathering area, Helen slid past a large group of *Cobalt followers*. Mildred stood at the front, inviting Cobalt to dinner loud enough for all to hear. Helen smiled politely at Mildred as she pulled Claire and Will toward the large, wooden door.

They stepped outside and the spring sunlight hit them. Claire shielded her eyes from the brightness. Briefly, she caught a glimpse of someone leaning up against the grotto in front of the church, next to the statue. Then she noticed the donkey grazing in the grass. Squinting to get a better look, she recognized her father next to the animal she'd won. She skipped down the steps and around a short fence where John stood staring at the donkey.

Helen approached him and asked, "What are you doing here?"

John shook his head. "He got loose. Then he decided to wander all the way over here. I couldn't get him to move."

Edging closer, Claire stroked the donkey's mane. Easing a hand toward him, she seemed to get his attention without any difficulty. She pet his nose, grasped his rope and he followed her away from the grotto. John's glare followed them.

Concealing a laugh, Helen wondered, "So, where's the wagon? You expect us to walk home, Mr. Sloan?"

Shaking his head, he glanced once at the statue of Christ then back at the donkey. "I'm beginning to believe what the old man said about him. More trouble than he's worth."

Helen walked beside her husband as they followed Claire and the donkey back through town. She thought about slipping her arm inside his, *but hearing him talk is enough for now.*

Chapter 6
Elijah

Present

It was his second visit to her home. Dan wrote with a fever pitch, something he had learned to do, supplementing the recording. It helped him to anticipate better and absorb more of the material. Glancing at his watch, he tried to be obscure then felt drawn to peek at the sun outside Claire's daintily decorated picture window.

"That was the first of many episodes we had with him," she said.

He sat still, emitting a false smile, wondering, *How many more visits will this take.*

Claire stirred a fresh cup of coffee and he politely passed on the offer for more, hoping she would get the hint. He began to understand that she pulled few punches and felt glad he had no need to stand on ceremony with her.

She asked him, "So, tell me, do you like your job, Mr. Mertz?"

Feeling awkward by the question, he looked to the kitchen and saw the coffee pot simmering away. He thought, *It'll be a good diversion,* then said, "You know, maybe I will have a cup."

Standing, he saw her nod for him to help himself. He found a porcelain cup on the counter and poured half a cup. Setting it down, he reached for the sugar and knocked the coffee over. It streamed from the counter, down the cupboard and onto the white, tiled floor.

"Sorry for being so clumsy. I don't know what my problem is these days."

Pulling on a roll of paper towels hung beneath a cabinet, the roll came loose and crashed to the floor. Pieces of plastic shattered on the countertop. Politely smiling in Claire's direction, he felt her gaze on him, warm as it was and patient too. Bending to pick up the pieces, he cleaned the mess, straightened his shirt and took what was left of his coffee back to the living room.

Claire watched his every move then said, "Mr. Mertz, you're quite a mess today."

Dan's eyes widened, surprised at her candor. "Thank you, Mrs. Henning. Thank you for pointing that out. Not just today, though. It's been a mess for awhile. Just ask my wife."

"Your job?"

He answered abruptly. "That too."

"So, you don't like it anymore?"

"I used to."

He sat cupping his drink then set it on a table beside him.

She asked, "What changed?"

Dan looked directly at her, trying to stall for an answer then gave her the first thing that came to mind. "I don't know. I'm a reporter. I cover unpleasant things."

"And, do you ever find any hope … in all this unpleasantness?"

Dan cleared his throat. "Listen, can we … can we just get back to nineteen twenty?"

A slight smile formed on her expressive face. "Wait on hope, Mr. Mertz. Be patient and wait on it. It's always there."

Dan gave her a false smile and said, "Dan. Please, call me Dan."

"Waiting isn't easy, though, Mr. Mertz. We had to wait too, especially for my father. His nightmares were the same. At least they were at that time. I still remember his screams. It's something a little girl never forgets."

Dan's eyes grew thoughtful as he stared directly at her then he reached over and hit the record button again.

"We assumed it was because of what he'd seen over there," she said. "It changed him. Do you know what that's like, Mr. Mertz?"

Dan nodded, pulled a pen cap off with his mouth, opened his notebook and began writing again. "I think."

Claire's face melted into a smile as she recalled and referred to the best summer of her life. "The summer of nineteen twenty."

He asked, "Because of the donkey?"

"All because of him," she replied.

"And, what did you name him? I mean … did you name him?"

Claire looked at him. "Why, of course we did. I named him ... Elijah. The four of us were inseparable. It was the best summer of my life."

Summer, 1920

Claire finished her chores, but Will's took a bit longer. She felt he hadn't finished because of all his swim breaks in the cold but refreshing pond behind the silos. She noticed her brother watching her from across the field as she, Lucie and Liza took turns riding Elijah toward the woods, dressed in Helen's feather boa. Seated atop the leather saddle, they were careful not to kick off the strange patterned, odd-looking, red and green broach.

They prodded Elijah across a parched field, dry enough that cracks emerged the size of their hands.

Carrying some hay in from the field, Will approached them, studied the scarf around the donkey's neck, frowned at them and said, "Aw, for cryin' out loud, don't dress him like that!"

She snubbed him. "He's mine and I'll dress him how I like."

Will noticed they carried a set of their mother's best tea cups and said, "Mom sees that and she'll have your hide."

"Never you mind, Will. I don't suspect Father knows about your swim breaks, either."

The daisy girls, as they liked to be called, had a custom. At least weekly, they led the donkey to the woods and the tree fort, hoping not to run into the Atkins boys. They hadn't lately and Claire reasoned it was because Coy Atkins kept a tight grip on his sons, though with his moonshine habit, she knew it wasn't a pleasant one.

She felt it was only a matter of time until Will emerged to terrorize them so they always prepared themselves to fight back with pitchers of water, fruit salad, or tiny tea cups filled with goat's milk.

It had threatened to rain one day so Claire and her friends stayed near the farm as John drove horses in the small field on the north side of the barn. Plow blades entered the parched earth, kicking up pebbles and clouds of sand. Stopping to wipe a brow, John took a long sip from a leather canteen. Another patch of dust kicked up by Mayor Gavel's approaching car drew his attention.

The mayor had started making rounds from farm to farm, trying to muster support, and funds, for a commemorative clock tower to *honor* the war's fallen. He tried to spin it as a need, but John knew better. In the midst of so many drought laden farms, the only need they had any concern for was one that hadn't fallen from the sky.

John watched his wife exchange pleasantries with the mayor and thought about driving the horses forward. Perhaps it would send a message that the drought ate any Sloan donation that might go toward the tower. He saw Gavel turn and point in his direction.

Sliding a planter brace around his back, John grasped the reins and drove the large, black horses on. Nearing the end of a row, he found himself stuck as one of the blades hung up on a large rock. He heard his name called from behind him and pretended not to notice.

Gavel approached him, handkerchief in hand, waving the dust away from a brand new suit and coughing. "John Sloan, our local war hero."

John became more interested in the rock.

The mayor asked, "How are things for you, my good fellow?"

Dusting off a plow blade then wiping a brow, John's attention remained on the planter as he began kicking at it. "Take a look at my field, Mayor. That oughta tell you."

Gavel glanced around. "Yes. I see. It's that way all over these days. Listen, you're aware of what we're trying to do in town?"

Unable to move the rock, John asked, "We?"

"Why, yes. We think it would be a proper tribute to a town so affected by the war … see?"

John began walking toward his barn. He needed a shovel to move the obstructing rock.

Gavel followed him like a lost puppy. "We figure we can get it done for less than two-thousand. Would cost the tax-payers minimal … that is, if we can get some goodwill donations."

John opened the gate leading to the barn. "You said *we*, Mayor. Who're *we*?"

"The whole town, John." The mayor swelled with arrogance, delighted that John sensed the half-truth. "You of all people should know what this town has sacrificed for the war."

John stopped, looked at Gavel; the mayor felt compelled to take a step back.

The mayor said, "I mean, you were in the thick of it, weren't you, John?"

"Is there anything else I can do for you, Mayor?"

With a false smile, Gavel asked, "So, you were a *Polar Bear*? What exactly did the *Polar Bears* do?"

John turned toward the barn, allowing the gate to swing shut.

Gavel opened it, followed John and continued talking. "Oatmeal … you guarded a large supply of oatmeal, didn't you? I'd say there's nothing wrong with that, John … nothing to be ashamed of."

"I'm glad for your approval."

"John, should I tell the town that our war hero doesn't want to contribute?"

The two men walked to the far side of the barn, past half-open silos, the conversation one-sided then John stopped long enough for Gavel to stand next to him and catch his breath.

"People respect you, John," Gavel said. "What can I put you down for?"

"Nothing."

"You want to remain anonymous?"

John glared at him for a moment, picked up a fork full of straw and began walking. Gavel followed him as they rounded one of the silos and drew near the open barn door. They stepped across dry ground and broken sticks as their bodies cast shadows against the barn's weathered wood.

As they entered the barn, something flew at them from inside one of the stalls, multi-colored and wet. It landed on Gavel's blue suit jacket. A second batch launched and landed on his head. John stepped back and looked at the mayor's red face. Gavel pulled a handkerchief from his pocket and wiped the mess away.

Three heads rose from the adjacent stall and Claire, Lucie and Liza emerged, faces red with embarrassment.

Claire stumbled forward. "I'm sorry, Father … we thought—"

"We thought it was Will," Liza said.

Lucie said, "Yes, Mr. Sloan. We thought it was Will. He put chewing gum in my hair last week. And, well, it took my mother three hours and a gallon of vinegar—"

Their words met deaf ears. Instead, the two men stood silent, staring at a large clump of sticky, wet fruit splattered about the pinstriped suit.

Then Will rounded the corner. His eyes widened as he looked at the mayor. Pointing at Gavel, he laughed.

John picked up a shovel, threw it to the ground and erupted. "Damn it, Claire! What the hell's wrong with you?"

Claire gasped and jumped back, seeing a side of her father that she hadn't known before.

"Who do you think you are, wasting food like this?"

A sudden silence and Claire's eyes welled then she broke into tears, running off toward the house.

The other two girls froze and Liza said, "We're sorry, Mr. Sloan. It was our fault."

Getting a towel from a nearby stall, John handed it to Gavel.

Exasperated, the mayor snatched it and began wiping off his suit then looked at the remaining girls. "Miss Nichols ... Miss Cantor ... your parents would be disappointed in you ... very disappointed."

Peeking around the corner of the barn door, John watched his daughter run away. For some reason, his eyes felt less jaded this time. Searching for the sudden, odd regret, he couldn't find its source. Had he been able to laugh again, he likely would have when Gavel got soaked. Torn between the mayor and his daughter, he left the barn to get a better look at the house.

He watched as Helen embraced Claire then saw Helen look at him from across the yard.

Present

Claire's voice sounded solemn. "He had never said a cross word to me before. I was too young to understand why he did it ... yet, there were other changes happening before my eyes."

Dan wondered, *What does she mean.*

"You see, since Elijah's arrival, I saw something different when I took him into town ... when mother would allow me to take him. Will said it was my imagination, but it seemed as though people

were kinder ... gentler and they began to help each other. And strangers ... well, they just smiled more."

Dan looked at her and wondered again, *Is she finding things that aren't there.*

"I was happy to see such a change," she continued. "Our town needed it. But I was especially happy when it involved Elijah's new corral. Wilson Washington promised to help my father build it as his way to pay my father back."

Chapter 7
A Curious Fear

Summer, 1920

Helen allowed Claire to take Elijah into town more than once. It gave Claire a bit of joy as she stood beside him in front of the tannery building, waiting for her mother to finish at the seamstress. It was Helen's way of earning a bit of money, something she kept from John. Claire often noted how her mother secretly placed what she earned in the satchel stashed beneath the bedroom dresser. It allowed her father to keep his pride.

In the midst of the steamy afternoon, Claire watched, counting the people as they greeted each other across the street. She never took the time to notice before, but with Elijah by her side, her innocence allowed her to believe their kindness was because of him.

Wagon traffic picked up in town, kicking up large clouds of dust that migrated onto the windows of the nearby buildings. Elijah stood beside Claire as her small hands grasped his lead rope. She watched him as some of the horses passed and he appeared more nervous today. The sounds of buggy whips rang out from time to time and each time one cracked, Elijah jumped.

Then a stubborn team blocked the road, frustrating their owner. He leaned forward and cracked his whip into the dry air. And again. As Elijah's uneasiness grew, Claire tried to calm him. A sudden loud whip snap sounded, louder than the last, and Elijah broke free from her grasp.

Claire cried out, sprinting after him as he ran off, braying and trotting from one side of the street to the other.

"Elijah!"

Her voice did nothing, so she yelled again. "Elijah! ... Elijah!"

The donkey ran faster, almost as if deafened by fear. Eventually, she lost sight of him between some buildings. She glanced up to read a few signs. One of them read, *City Hall*. She looked to the left

and to the right until she heard a commotion coming from around the way.

Sprinting toward it and hoping to catch sight of him, she reached a corner and stopped in her tracks. There stood Mayor Gavel's partially constructed clock tower with metal framework built around its base and a large square of freshly poured concrete beside it. Hoof-prints dotted the wet cement, and one of the frames had toppled into it. On the other side stood Elijah, covered in cement.

A group of workers glared at him then at Claire.

She moaned over the damage. "Please tell me he didn't do this."

No one said a word. They only nodded and then she realized this wasn't something she could keep from her parents.

~ ~ ~

Helen promised to break the news to John, so Claire kept herself busy with chores in the barn until her friends arrived. Perhaps the most distressing, not knowing how her father would react. She knew he would want to make amends, with money they didn't have. That afternoon, she sat quiet, pensive and hugging her knees, watching as Lucie rode Elijah around an open barnyard.

Will marched in from a field, sneering at them from a distance. He found his father pondering the recent damage. Matching his father's large strides between the stalls, he watched as John slung feed into each of them with a scoop shovel.

After reporting his chores as finished, Will asked, "Why does she get to play with her friends?"

John tossed the shovel aside and walked toward the silos on the other side of the barn, saying, "Get your chores done quicker."

"It's not fair. I got more chores than she does."

John remained silent.

He stood and watched as his father approached the two silos. Side by side, they rose into a clear, blue sky, symbols of the prosperity that was once theirs. John climbed the ladder to one of them. Reaching one of the middle doors, he unlatched it.

"Horses all fed?"

Will whispered, "No."

John swung the door open to assess the level and Will watched patiently for a reaction. None came.

"It's bad … isn't it?"

John remained motionless, staring at the meager supply. "Get to the horses, son."

"Yes, sir."

Hanging his head, Will walked past the open field and paused long enough to glare at his sister and her friends.

~ ~ ~

That afternoon, Claire followed Will in from the field, dawdling behind him after the evening milking with two buckets filled to the brim. Stumbling forward, Will carried two large bags of feed. He always carried more than he should, his way of showing how strong he was. He got as far as the first stall and dropped one. Then he slammed the other into an empty cattle stall and watched his sister stagger in behind him.

With a sarcastic tone in his voice, he said, "You'd better hurry up with that, Claire. Your friends are waiting."

"Mind your own business, William."

Will wiped his brow then stopped as something attracted his attention on the far side of the barn. He saw a whip wrapped tightly, resting on a hook against a wall. He walked over and unraveled it.

"You'd better be careful," Claire said. "Father doesn't want us playing with that."

He stretched it out, mischievous eyes resting on an empty spot on the wall. "Hey, watch this."

Rearing back he snapped the whip into the air. Then reaching back again, he found a spot on the wall and cracked it. He cracked it again, and then again.

They heard a sudden commotion outside the barn. Claire ran to see what it was and saw Elijah tied up on the other side of the wall. He brayed, visibly shaken over something.

Will cracked the whip again, and the donkey got louder. Claire came back inside to watch Will then looked out at the donkey again. There seemed to be a connection. Racing back outside, Claire's eyes

locked with Elijah's and she understood. Hurrying back to the barn, she saw Will reach back and crack the whip again.

She screamed at him, "Will, stop it! Stop it. He doesn't like it!"

Ignoring her, Will continued and the donkey kept up his fierce braying, pulling against his tether. The force of his bucking rattled the barn wall, sending his saddle off the shelf and onto the ground, knocking off the broach.

"Will, stop it! He's scared of it. He doesn't like it!" Claire grasped her brother's shoulder and he pulled away. "It's bothering him, Will! Stop it!"

A sudden shadow appeared in the doorway across the barn and Will stopped in mid-stroke. Claire looked to the intense figure filling the entire space—her father. The silence was deafening.

Will dropped the whip and muttered, "Oh, no."

John stood solid, large hands on his hips. "Put that thing away before someone gets hurt."

Will answered, "Sorry, I was just—"

"He wouldn't listen to me," Claire interrupted. "He never listens to me! Elijah was getting upset, and—"

"I'm well aware he doesn't like it," John said.

Walking over to the whip, John calmly picked it up and hung it in its proper place.

Claire glared at her brother. "You ... you're such a pill!"

He exclaimed, "I can't help it if your donkey's off his nuts!"

"He's not off his nuts. He's just scared. Why must you—"

John blurted out, "That'll be enough! Will, get back to work."

Hanging his head, Will mumbled, "Why is it always my fault?"

Catching his father's glare, Will found his way out of the barn.

Picking up the broach from the ground, Claire then led Elijah back into the barn, petting him, calming him. She thought she saw a slight smile form on her father's face, but reasoned it was only her imagination. Tending to the donkey's peace, she stayed a bit longer and studied her father as he gazed off into nothingness. She thought, *His troubles must run deep today.*

After picking up her buckets, she smiled at the donkey then said, "It's okay, Elijah. It'll be just fine. I'll fix the broach and saddle tomorrow after morning chores."

~ ~ ~

Wilson and John stood beside each other near the completed corral and stable, reveling in their accomplishment on the hottest day of summer. Wilson dipped a cup into a bucket beside them and took a long sip, water drenching his shirt, gleaming off his dark skin in the midday heat.

John knew little of the Washington family, only that they were black and had few friends. Perhaps the two families had something in common.

"Thanks for the help," John said.

The Logans were generous too. A week before, Velma Logan pulled Helen aside and told her to take the wood for Claire's new friend. John would have none of that kind of charity. He promised it would be added to what they already owed. With Elijah's propensity to run off, he felt eager to get the corral done.

Wilson wiped his mouth with a sleeve. "Least I can do. Can't do much farmin' as dry as it's been."

There was a peace to the silence between them.

Wilson said, "Not every day white folk help a black man."

Recalling the trouble at the fair, John reasoned aloud, "Some men don't amount to much. Those thugs been on a toot as long as I can remember ... even before it was illegal."

"You learn how to fight in the war?"

John buried his face in a cup of water then said, "Don't much talk about it."

"I ain't much fond of confrontation either," Wilson said. "Most summers, I take my family over to Idlewild."

"Idlewild? Never heard of it."

Wilson laughed. "That's why we go there."

~ ~ ~

The drought remained and the heat unconscionable, but John appeared to sleep better. He scarcely awoke anymore and his screams came less frequent. Perhaps he'd learned to be quieter.

Claire knew her mother never spoke of her father's dreams, but she didn't know the dreams hadn't stopped, they just changed.

The night after finishing the corral, John lay immersed in sweat. Though less fierce, he dreamed of mysterious unfamiliar things. Helen refused to ask him, perhaps out of fear the old ones would return. She felt it better not to know.

She lay quietly beneath the covers as John climbed out of bed. Finding his way to the kitchen, he discovered a way to process his dreams. He stood, looking out the kitchen window at the horizon, pondering over the passing summer. He held a scratch pad in one hand, a pencil in the other. He began writing. Perhaps if he could make sense of his dreams they would vanish altogether. For now, he contemplated their change and the mystery of their meaning.

Shoving the pad and pencil back into the drawer, he glanced up again and caught sight of something in the distance, an aura of light emitting on the horizon. He looked at a clock across the room. The sun wasn't due up for hours. He took a closer look and realized the light didn't come from the east. Wiping tired eyes, he leaned into the glass window and identified its source. It came from the farm next door, the Washington farm.

A sudden hard and frantic knocking at the front door startled him. Hurrying to the door he pulled hard on it. A frantic black woman stood before him—Penny Washington, Wilson's wife.

As John opened the screen, Penny grasped his shirt and shrieked, "Our barn is burning and there is no one there to help!"

Chapter 8
Let it Rain

Summer, 1920

Helen hurried from upstairs. The ruckus woke Claire and Will as well. John shut the door and turned toward them.

She asked, "What is it?"

John answered, "Wilson's barn is burning!" Turning to a closet near the porch he pulled out boots and a jacket. "I'm goin' to help."

Disappearing into another room, Helen reappeared with a set of boots and jacket of her own. She sat hard on a chair and slid the boots on then followed her husband onto the porch.

He turned to her and asked, "What do you think you're doing?"

Answering bluntly, she said, "Coming to help."

"No way, Helen."

As he stood staunch and still, she ignored him. She then brushed by and hurried into the barn where she pulled shovels out of a stall.

Something told him he couldn't stop her as he said, "Helen, no."

Slipping on a set of gloves, she declared, "John, I'm not a china doll. I can take care of myself."

Aware he wouldn't win the argument, he shook his head then headed for the truck.

Will and Claire stood on the porch, watching as their parents piled shovels into the bed of the truck.

Helen called to them from a distance. "You kids stay put. Claire, watch after your brother."

Claire shouted back at her, "Can we come?"

John ordered, "Absolutely not!"

"But Father—"

"You two are to stay here. Is that clear?"

John slid into the driver's seat, turned the key and pushed the starter with his foot. The sound of the engine rang into the night. Soon the old prewar pickup chugged down the long driveway and disappeared toward the Wilson farm.

Standing quietly in each other's company, Will and Claire saw the aura of light atop the trees. In unison, they glanced at each other and for once, they had the same idea.

They blurted together, "Come on," and then quickly changed to their work clothes.

Trudging through the long, dry field, Claire marched ahead of her brother. The light grew more intense as they drew nearer. The Washington farm wouldn't be far: past the north field and a line of trees, over a dried up creek bed and through a slight forest and they would be there.

Climbing over a small trench that lined the old creek-bed, Will looked up at the sky. The small volunteer fire department vehicle heading down the county road toward the farm startled them.

With his face toward the flames, Will exclaimed, "Jeepers, that's one big fire!"

Claire yelled at him over her shoulder. "Hurry up! Let's get there before it's out!"

Will's smaller legs worked hard to keep up with her. "If we get caught, this is your idea."

"We'll only stay a minute," she promised.

Stopping at a fence, over which they had difficulty climbing, they heard footsteps behind them. The steps grew louder so they peered into the darkness to see who it was.

Will started to speak, but Claire shushed him. Coming out of the shadows, they saw an animal and as it drew nearer, the light of the flames reflected off of his smooth gray and white coat of fur.

Claire's eyes widened as she exclaimed, "Elijah!"

Will exclaimed, "Great! What's he doing here?"

Running toward the donkey, Claire declared, "Elijah! No!"

"How did he get out? I told you his corral wouldn't hold him."

Claire pointed toward his pen and ordered, "Go home, Elijah! Get back home!"

The donkey remained still so Claire turned her back on him and walked toward the fence again. Elijah took a few steps toward her and she then realized he wasn't going anywhere.

She repeated, "Get back home!" Again she turned toward the fire and Elijah followed her. "Go home, Elijah … back to your pen!"

Straddling the fence, Will shook his head. "He's not listening, Claire. I told you he was off his nuts."

Claire commanded, "Get! This is no place for you to go!"

The fire crackled in the distance and the sounds of yelling men pierced the night. Claire knew her attempts at getting Elijah to return to the farm were in vain. Sighing loudly, she looked again at the fence then noticed an open gate about twenty yards away.

Smirking at her brother, she pointed to it and said, "You should have used the gate, dummy." Then she turned again toward Elijah. "Fine, come on."

As she walked toward the gate, the donkey followed her.

Will shouted, "What! Are you kidding? Dad is really gonna kill us if we take him over there."

"He'll never know if you keep your big mouth shut."

They reached the outskirts of the Washington property, lined with trees. Crouching in the bushes, they knelt beside each other, Elijah standing nearby. They watched the horror before them as flames engulfed the large, brown barn as sparks lifted through the night sky, wind-blown toward the house.

Will pointed toward a well about half a field's distance from the garage. They could see their parents there as Helen pumped water and handed buckets to a line of people stretching to the barn.

The two Washington children, a boy and a girl, frantically led horses away from the fire engulfed structure, grasping bridles as the animals bucked violently to escape the heat. A few other people stood by, but not many. A small fire wagon remained parked, a few men pumping frantically as small spurts of water dusted the roof.

John appeared and grasped Helen's arm. "If we don't get some water on this thing, there isn't gonna be a house left either!"

Helen nodded then signaled the others to look at the house. Sparks began landing on the roof, and the water became scarce.

John grabbed hold of a bucket and ran toward the flames. He dumped the water onto it sending little more than some smoke into the night. Loud cracks filled the air and the sounds of dry twigs and burning timbers ruled the darkness as another horse escaped from the flames.

Claire and Will looked on as John approached Wilson, two shovels in hand. Together, they dug a ditch between the house and the barn. Soon, the flames were too hot.

The battle close to being lost.

Wilson's son Frederick, a teenager, approached the men and pointed to the house.

Claire heard his voice break through the chaos. "Daddy, look. The house is burnin'… the house dun caught fire!"

Wilson saw a small patch of flames toward the corner of the roof. Trying to get the firemen's attention, he pointed to the spot.

His wife cried out behind him, "Sweet Lord, help us!"

As the heat intensified, Will and Claire crouched further down. Claire's eyes remained glued to the chaos before them.

Whispering loud enough for her brother to hear, Claire said, "I don't believe this."

"How do you think it started?"

She answered with a calm, almost entranced tone, "I don't know. But this is awful … just awful."

Elijah remained calm beside them as Claire stretched over to pet him. The far-reaching flames reflected well into her eyes and—

Present

Claire didn't complete her sentence and Dan felt compelled to look up at her. He sensed there was more, but the old woman squeezed her eyes shut. He tilted his head to get a better look at her. It looked as if she tried to relive the moment.

Waiting longer than he normally would, Dan cleared his throat then said, "So?"

She remained silent and he wondered if she was okay, but then she opened her eyes and looked at him.

"You're not gonna leave me hanging there, are you? What happened? Did they lose it? Did they lose the house?"

A small grin appeared on her old face, reveling in the past. The smile melted into a confused stare.

"You would have thought so," she said. "So did I, Mr. Mertz. But you see, just about the time we arrived with him … about the time we arrived with Elijah … the strangest thing happened."

Summer, 1920

For once, Will became interested in his sister. He glanced over at her, somehow secretly understanding her concern. Then something fell from the sky, hitting her arm. She broke her trance to stare down at a wet drop as it spilled onto the ground. Another one hit then another. Before long, they became aware of the rain increasing. Together they stared at the raindrops about her arm. Then the sky opened up and torrents of water fell to the earth.

Claire lifted her face to the heavens and allowed the rain to pound away at it. Holding her hands out from her sides, she raised her palms upward as if to catch it and perhaps to keep it.

Will smiled for the first time in awhile.

Then the cries of relief came, first from Penny then Wilson. The rain poured onto the barn roof, sizzling in the flames.

Wilson shouted, "It's raining! It's raining!"

In a matter of minutes the fire waned and the tide had turned. John stood still, hand grasping his shovel as Wilson embraced him hard. He patted Wilson's back and watched as the flames that had consumed the barn began to lose their grip.

From across the yard, Helen brushed the rain away from her brow and smiled at her husband. He gazed back at her in a way that established a connection for the first time in a long while.

Overcome with joy, Claire jumped. "It's raining! It's raining!"

Bursting with emotion, she felt a compulsion to embrace Will. Reaching over, she hugged him hard.

Captured by the moment, he reciprocated then shoved her away as she kissed him. "Yuck."

With the elements no longer on its side, the fire lost its battle and smoke rose from the barn. Claire's clothes dripped as she stroked Elijah's soaked mane. She and Will would have time to get him back home and change before their parents knew. Keeping their presence at the fire a secret from their father would be easy, but perhaps not so with their mother.

Present

Claire Henning remained thoughtful, her voice solemn. "It wouldn't have been so odd … except the rains were felt nowhere else that night."

Dan asked, "Nowhere?"

"Nowhere … not at our farm … not in town … not anywhere, nowhere else except on Mr. Washington's farm."

He inquired further. "So, let me get this straight. You want me to believe this donkey was miraculous?"

"No, Mr. Mertz. I want you to cover my story."

Visibly taken aback, he stopped recording, stuffed his pen into the pocket of his briefcase.

Scratching his head, tucking in an unkempt shirt, he mumbled, "It's just … a little stretch to call that a miracle, that's all."

Claire looked at him. "What we learn from experience depends on the philosophy we bring to it, Mr. Mertz."

Buttoning up his briefcase, he said, "Sounds like something from C.S. Lewis."

"Indeed," she answered. "Mr. Mertz, may I ask you a question?"

He shrugged, uncertain he wanted to hear it.

She asked, "When did you lose it?"

The question made him feel uncomfortable. "What makes you think I lost something?"

Glancing at a copy of the Free Press atop the coffee table in the room, she answered, "I can read."

Surprised by her candor, he stood and put on his windbreaker then said, "You're a spunky one." She reinforced his assessment with a steady look. "So, you've read my stories? You know what it is I cover … the city I cover?"

"I know what you write about," she said.

"Detroit's a rough city. I write about truth, Mrs. Henning … brutal and unsightly."

He felt sure she wanted more. Instead, he hurried himself along. It had been two days of interview and still not close to being done. Nor was he certain he liked it when she asked about his personal life. For her, there must be a connection between her story and his, regardless of his desire to ignore it.

Claire smiled, shut her eyes and continued. "Truth ... it really isn't truth ... unless it's laced with compassion, is it?"

He nearly made it out the door when her words reached him. He felt a sudden compulsion to stop so he turned around to face her. The assuring silence made him feel it okay to divulge something.

Dan forced the false smile away then asked her, "You want to know what I lost?"

Her expression said she did.

"Hope," he said.

Something told him she already knew that.

That something reassured her he would be back to finish and she said, "See you next week, Mr. Mertz."

"Next week," he said then stepped out onto the porch.

Chapter 9
One Hundred and Counting

Present

Dan felt happy when he realized his name hadn't been taken off the assignment board at work, at least not totally. He had spent enough time with Claire that he hardly recognized his desk, cluttered with piles of messages and interdepartmental memos. He would have time for a quick lunch with Cindy before work.

Their favorite diner rested on the city's west side, about halfway between his office and the hospital where she worked. The food at Providence Hospital had become boring to her so she suggested their favorite diner. Plus, it gave Dan another excuse to get away.

Cindy sat across from him wearing light green scrubs, her blond hair pulled into a tight bun. She asked him about this assignment to which he became so attached.

He said, "It has nothing to do with any attachment. I just can't wait to get back to regular work. Doug will have my rear end if this takes too long."

She asked, "Isn't Doug the one who sent you?"

Nodding, he set his coffee near the edge of the table. "Yes, but I've got to show my face in the office now and again."

Glancing at his cup, she mentioned, "You know what's gonna happen to that … don't you?"

He dismissed her concern and expressed his frustration over the lack of cohesiveness in Claire's story. He told her a bit about it.

"A candy bar … and a donkey?"

"Somethin' like that," he said. "That's all I can get from it so far. Anyway, it's taking forever."

"Well maybe you needed this."

Dan scrunched his eyes and appeared indignant, his way of disagreeing, then stood and leaned over to kiss her. "I've got to go."

"Do we actually get to eat dinner together tonight? You're not going back there?"

"No. Her birthday's not until next week."

Cindy shrugged. "One hundred doesn't come every day."

He picked up the tab before slinging the briefcase around his shoulder; an open flap on the case caught the porcelain cup, sending the coffee to the floor. She laughed and covered her mouth as Dan stood still, gaping at the mess as if he expected nothing less.

"I told you," she said.

He knew she had.

~ ~ ~

Walking into the newsroom later, Dan saw some cryptic looks coming from his cohorts. Someone told him, "Doug is looking for you," so he ducked his head and tried to hide at his desk.

Checking so many messages could be difficult. Scrambling to tidy things up a bit, he piled papers into more manageable stacks and some of them fell to the floor. He rose from his seat to escape before being noticed.

A sudden loud voice erupted from across the room. "Mertz!"

Dan froze, hoping Doug would go away.

"Mertz! My office!"

All eyes followed him as he traversed between the desks toward his editor's office. After he entered, the door closed behind him. Dan saw Doug's caustic stare and a single piece of paper pointed directly at him.

Doug asked, "Mind telling me how I'm supposed to print this?"

He held the article Dan had written a few weeks before, the one that revealed a little too much.

Looking at the paper, Doug read from it. "If I could find the slightest reclamation from the murders I covered this week, it would render my job more bearable. I find instead, only tears, wailing and hopelessness. I find myself in a dream … imprisoned in a field of overgrown weeds, trapped between rows of condemned homes."

Dan looked up at Doug and shrugged.

"You really think Detroit needs to hear this?"

Pointing at the sheet, Dan asked, "Did you … did you read the rest of it?"

"I don't need to read the rest, Dan. This is crap. I can't print this! You're painting the city as something without—"

"Hope?"

His assessment caught Doug by surprise, who thought about it a moment. "Listen, how much longer is this assignment gonna take?"

"You're asking me? You sent me."

Doug sat in his chair, adjusted his suspenders then his black-rimmed glasses. He shook his head, absent of further advice.

"It's her birthday next week. One hundred years old," Dan reminded him. "I imagine a couple more weeks ... maybe a month or two at the most."

Holding the article high in the air, Doug peered at him and said, "All right. Take some more time. In the meantime, I'm gonna ditch this. I need you in the office at least twice a week from now on. I'm overloaded. I need to send a few your way. I'll try to make 'em more ... manageable."

Dan thanked him with a nod then pointed toward his desk and muttered, "I'll get that desk cleaned up too. I promise."

Doug concealed a smile then shook his head and commanded, "Get outta here, Mertz. Go cover that lady's story. One hundred doesn't come every day."

~ ~ ~

Dan sat squeezed in between two great-great-grandchildren of Claire's, wearing a party hat they'd forced him to put on. He held a blower firmly in his teeth as a candle-covered cake made its way through the gathering and onto the dining room table.

Her granddaughter invited him weeks before, and he hadn't found a decent excuse to miss it. He sat among the chaos, tooting his horn and found it more fun than he would likely admit. He backed away and tried to take off his hat, but the youngest ones made him keep it on. Finally, the cake appeared and brightened the purple flowered tablecloth. Catherine promised she could fit one hundred candles on it, and it seemed like she had.

Claire sat near the flames, her face warmed by the fire and Dan watched as wetness formed on the other faces nearby. Those kinds of tears weren't something he was used to these days and he found

himself joining in on a resounding rendition of *Happy Birthday*. Then the kids tried to count to one hundred, but were cut short.

Catherine asked if Claire needed help to blow out the candles.

Dan chuckled, "I know some Detroit firemen if you need 'em."

Her young relatives blew on the flames until they extinguished and Dan jumped in on the applause.

One child blurted, "What'd you wish for, Nanna?"

Claire glanced across the room, a half hidden smile.

Another one asked, "Yeah. What'd you wish for?"

She answered, "If I tell, it won't come true."

They didn't press her further and the party continued. Dan made rounds, grasping hands, embracing people he had never met in a way that reflected otherwise. Surprised at being treated like such royalty, he meandered about and tried hard to remember all their names. Children hung from his arms and climbed about his back and the afternoon melted into evening.

Her family is odd, he thought. They shook his hand before they left as if he belonged to their club: one that knew about the donkey, one that needed no apologies, no explanations. They all knew, but he hadn't quite been initiated.

After the commotion, he figured Claire would be too tired to talk. Instead she waited, hands folded on her lap, as he dug into his third piece of cake. The two of them sat together in the silence, his party hat still on his head.

"Damn, this is good cake," he said. He felt a bit embarrassed at her patience. "I'm sorry ... I'm sorry, this is my third piece."

Setting the cake down, he wiped his mouth with a sleeve, then brushed off his hands, sending crumbs to her floor. He bent down to pick them up while Claire sat still, a smile across her face.

He noticed it and pulled out his recorder and notebook and said, "I thought you might be too tired."

She shook her head. "I'm fine."

Opening his notepad and securing his recorder, he stopped for a moment then asked, "So ... what'd you wish for?"

She looked at him as though she didn't understand.

He nodded at the half-eaten cake. "You know ... what'd you wish for?"

"You want to know?"

"Sure."

"The third miracle."

"I'm sorry?"

"The third miracle," she said. "The third healing."

He didn't understand. *Perhaps she's tired.* He studied her a moment longer then realized she wanted to press on despite the day. It was her birthday, after all, so he allowed her to jump back in.

Chapter 10
Silos Anew

Late Summer, 1920

Claire's thoughts turned to the weeks since the fire, and the small crowds that had gathered at the Washington farm since then. Her father started the trend, and soon others followed. Sometimes Claire wandered to the Washington farm with her friends and Elijah, often struck by the joy she saw in those working to rebuild the burned-out barn. It brought people together, she reasoned, in ways she hadn't seen since the war ended.

They also had conversations and casual talk in town about the drought, the fire and the rain. More than once, Claire heard the speculation. For days after the fire, she watched her father kneeling on his own land, lifting a handful of dry earth and letting it fall through his fingers.

Her mother didn't know she had taken Elijah to the fire that night, but something told her that her father did. When she told her friends, the word of the rains at the Washington farm spread faster than her parents would have liked. In her young mind, she reasoned everyone would believe it a miracle too, but it wasn't that simple.

One day at the mill, she watched as her father ground and sifted the last bit of corn while men stood in the background, Gavel at the helm, laughing at him for allowing his daughter to forward such claims. As for the cause of the fire, no one came forward with opinions, although her father had his own.

The next day at church, Claire sat between her mother and Will, her back leaning against a wooden pew, vainly comprehending Latin prayers from the altar. Though service was often difficult to follow, today one of the readings from the book of Zechariah struck her. As they returned home, she recalled the passage. *Rejoice heartily, Oh daughter Zion, shout for joy, Oh daughter Jerusalem. See, your king shall come to you; a just savior is he, meek and riding on an ass....*

John drove the truck up the long, slender driveway, hauling a load of bagged flour. Will sighed at his mother's request to help his father unload it. He met his father near the silos as John stepped from the truck.

John directed, "Stack 'em next to the elevator son."

Will grabbed an armful, wishing he had the strength to carry more. John followed him to the elevator where they stacked the bags next to the base. John recalled Elijah hadn't been fed yet. Grasping a forkful of hay, he carried it through the barn and tossed it into the donkey's pen. He glanced around a bit, but couldn't see Elijah so he eased closer to get a better look at the stable.

No Elijah.

Confused, John searched the grounds then circled back to take a second look at the corral. The donkey had disappeared.

Hurrying around to the far side of the barn, he shouted, "Elijah! Elijah … come!"

Frustration welled up then he turned to look at the gate—open.

Mumbling, he said, "Not again."

Then he heard Will calling for him from the other side of the barn, near the silos. "Father, come see this!"

He didn't answer, but instead, he scratched his head, wondering, *How can this animal be so elusive.*

Will shouted again, "Father!"

Dismissing Will's voice, John shook his head, scanning the horizon. He returned to the gate's latch and pounded on it, but saw nothing wrong with it.

"Father … oh, Father … I think you want to see this!"

Studying his workmanship, John said, "Just a minute, Will."

"Father, I think you want to see this!"

Closing the gate, John followed his son's voice past the stables, toward the far end of the barn. Rounding the corner, he caught sight of Elijah wandering in the field adjacent to the silos, his nose buried in the grass.

John barked at him. "Get back to your pen, ya dumb animal!"

Will called him again. "Father, I think something's happened. You might want to see this!"

John grasped the donkey's mane and tried leading him back to the pen, but Elijah wouldn't budge. Clapping his hands, John shooed him away from the silos.

"Dad!"

"What is it, Will?"

Then retreating a bit, John turned, looked at Will and noticed an unusual expression on his son's face. He saw Will staring at the closest silo and a pile of silage spilling forth from an open door. John edged toward him, stopped and stared at the same pile on the ground. Though it didn't register at first, John saw more silage than he had seen in the entire last month. He felt compelled to check the silo so he climbed up to the top, unlatched the door and saw more silage. He hurried back down the ladder and once on the ground, he stumbled backward, almost falling.

The silos were full.

John then looked over at the oats bins inside the barn and saw them full too.

A wary silence embraced John and Will as they stood looking at the heap of oats. They turned in unison to look at one another for a moment. John turned and looked back at the donkey, grazing in the field. He studied the animal for a moment then turned to stare at the silage then to the oats bin again, and then back at the donkey.

This has to be a mistake.

~ ~ ~

As Claire stirred a butter churn plunger, Helen said, "You've got to churn it thoroughly," then guided Claire's hand. "That's it … just like that." She backed away, tended to dishes in the sink then smiled at Claire. "You're turning into quite a young lady. You'll make a fine wife someday."

After a brief silence, Claire asked, "Momma, do you think Elijah is special?"

"Your donkey? Of course he is, Claire. He means a lot to you."

Mother doesn't get it, Claire thought. *But special is enough for right now.*

The side door opened and John entered the kitchen. He walked to the sink, wiped his brow with a sleeve and pumped a glass of water. He took a long sip then stared out the kitchen window.

Then in a casual tone, he broke the silence. "Helen?"

"Yes?"

"When did you get home from church?"

Shrugging, she said, "About half past twelve."

"And, did anyone stop by today?"

Helen turned and looked directly at him. "Not that I'm aware of … why? Is something wrong?"

Again the side door slammed and Will dashed into the kitchen sounding winded. Helen looked at him and her expression changed.

Catching his breath, Will proclaimed, "Mom, Claire … someone filled the silos! Someone filled the silos! The oats bins are full too! Come and look!"

Helen dropped the wooden spoon then followed Will and Claire out the door, by the chicken coop and toward the barn. In the past, he would have beaten her. Today, she passed him as they sprinted over clumps of weeds and piles of busted fence. Through the barn, past a row of stalls, she emerged on the other side and stopped dead in her tracks, her eyes fixed on the pile of silage before her. Will caught up then Helen and finally John.

Claire's eyes widened then she spun around to face her mother.

Lunging toward Helen, she grasped her mother's apron and exclaimed, "Elijah filled the silos, Momma! He did it."

Will protested, "That's ridiculous … stop being stupid."

"God gave him to us, Momma … God gave him to us."

Again, Will objected, "You're so dumb. You should stop telling people that."

"Momma, he did it. I just know he did!"

Their arguing voices rose.

"You're so stupid, Claire! Why would you think—"

"He did it, Momma. You gotta believe me."

From behind, John stepped in between the two and demanded, "Claire, get him back to his pen. Son, you got some grain bags to unload. Get goin' on it."

Will and Claire scowled then disappeared in different directions, leaving John and Helen alone to consider the sudden windfall. A moment later, Claire wandered back into their presence.

Drawing close to her mother, she whispered, "I told you he was different, Momma. I told you."

John stood motionless until Claire walked away.

Helen said, "John, someone had to do this."

"Do you know how long it would take to fill these silos? They're filled to the brim, Helen."

Breaking his trance, he strode to the barn and grabbed a shovel.

Helen followed him and asked, "What're you going to do?"

Thrusting the shovel into an oats bin, John took hold of a nearby wheelbarrow and said, "I'm gonna do what we should've done a long time ago ... pay Charlie Logan a visit ... then I intend to figure out how that animal keeps getting out of his pen."

That night, Helen slept as John dreamed without the screams and without an understanding. He awoke and quietly rose so as not to wake her and wrote with a dull pencil from a kitchen drawer.

Present

Dan arrived at her house for the third time in a week. It got easier, more engaging, or maybe because of Doug's assurance his job would be waiting for him. Today she reflected longer on her father and mother, but he wanted to know what her father's writings meant. Instead she spoke about how quickly the summer passed.

"It flew by ... quicker than I ever remembered."

He understood and sipped his coffee before placing it atop a coaster beside him. "And your father ... he paid the Logans back?"

She nodded. "Seemed like Father made a trip there every week after our sudden windfall. He felt obliged after owing for so long. He was a man of deep pride."

Dan agreed.

"Yet even after our newfound abundance, things didn't change as quickly as I'd hoped for my father ... at least I didn't think so."

Late Summer, 1920

John rested against the counter at Logan's store. Charlie stood on the other side, a copy of the State Journal spread open wide across the register. On the counter beside them lay a piece of paper denoting John's paid debt, lines scratched through the old amount.

Charlie scanned the article. "They're still talking about that influenza thing. It's a real dandy ... a real pandemic."

John agreed then turned to watch his children running through the aisles. Will chased Claire past him.

"Not in the store, son, take it outside."

They tore through the screen door and onto the porch. Claire scampered across it as Will chased her past their wagon, toward the corner of the store. She found a thin alley between Logan's and the barbershop and slipped into it, a space barely wide enough for her shoulders. Then she saw Will on the other side, following and it surprised her. As brave as he acted, she knew he didn't like dark spaces—too many spiders.

She turned to look back at him, sticking out her tongue then ran toward a grain house across another road. Catching up, Will lunged for her shirt and she tripped, stumbling to the ground. Shaking off the frustration, she waited for Will to tag her. As she glanced up from the dust, she noticed a set of larger boots standing directly in front of her.

They weren't Will's.

Slowly, she raised her eyes up the boots to a set of torn, dirty pants then saw a boy standing above her and next to him, another boy. Blocking the sun from her eyes, she peered up at them and recognized the Atkins brothers. As she got to her feet, they stood in front of her, hands on their hips.

Will stood behind her and sighed, "Oh, no."

Curtis pointed at him. "Sloan, I still got a beef with you."

Claire jumped in front of him and commanded, "Leave us be!"

Elmer shoved his brother aside, puffing out his chest. "Keep quiet you chunk o' lead."

Over Claire's shoulder, Will snarled, "Don't you talk to my sister that way!"

Approaching Will, Curtis plunged a forefinger onto his chest and sneered, "Or what? You wanna fight me?"

Recalling his father's warnings, Will stood silent.

Pulling Will away, Claire said, "They're not worth it, Will. Come on. Father's waiting."

Dragging him around the far side of the barbershop, they picked up speed when the Atkins followed.

Curtis yelled, "What are you, yella?"

Elmer hollered, "Look, he's goin' to get his daddy."

Claire shouted back at them. "Leave us be!"

Curtis replied, "Or what? You gonna sic your donkey on us? Maybe he can do a miracle."

Laughing, Elmer said, "Yeah, maybe he can make us disappear."

Reaching the front of the store, Claire and Will caught sight of their father seated in the wagon.

Again, Curtis taunted, "Yeah, sic your donkey on us, Claire!"

Will said to Claire, "I told you not to spread such nonsense. You had to keep flappin' your gums about your stupid donkey, didn't you? You never listen to me!"

As they reached the front of the wagon, John turned to look at the Atkins brothers. Elmer followed them bravely to the front, but Curtis waited behind.

Defiant, Elmer boasted, "Your pa can't do nothin' to us!"

"Yeah," Curtis yelled from the back. "You ain't a real war hero either … Polar Bear! My pa could take you! You ain't nothin'."

Will and Claire climbed up behind John then watched their father get off the wagon. The Atkins took a step back as John looked them over. Edging backward, they watched as John turned away from them and disappeared into the store again. Will and Claire glanced at each other then at the Atkins who also seemed interested in what John was doing.

As hard as they tried, they could see little through the screen, only that their father carried something to the counter. They watched as he offered a coin to Charlie and another to the Salvation Army bucket then the door swung open again and he emerged, carrying two ice cream cones.

A large grin appeared on Will's face. "Look. Dad got us some ice creams."

He held out a hand to accept his, but his father turned toward the Atkins instead.

Curtis and Elmer retreated, cautious and uncertain. John took a step toward them. They glanced down at John's two fists, pondering the treats. Suspicious, they looked at each other then back at the ice cream. After a moment, they edged toward him and reached out. John handed them the cones and they accepted.

John responded with a nod then tipped his hat and climbed back aboard the wagon. Claire watched the brothers as they stared at their ice cream, aware of something she hadn't seen before. Then John picked up the reins and drove the horses toward home.

As they pulled onto the dusty road, leaving the Atkins boys behind, she looked over at her father and asked, "Father, why did you do that? Why did you give them ice cream?"

He answered without regret, "Because, Claire, it doesn't look like those boys have been given anything ... for quite some time."

Present

Dan looked directly at Claire, a bit misty.

The old woman continued, "That was the moment for which I had somehow waited. As turning points go, that was one of the grandest. I never looked at my father the same after that. Perhaps I hoped he was journeying back to the man I knew before the war. And after that day, the Atkins boys ... well, they never bothered us again."

Chapter 11
She's Only Sleeping

Fall, 1920

The smells of old leather, the swaying of trees blowing in the fall breeze and burning leaves in the cool air silenced the winds of summer. Claire and Lucie rode Elijah as much as they could the last few weeks of summer break.

But Liza hadn't been around. They assumed she'd been visiting her grandparents in Flint so the two of them took liberty with the donkey, dressing him and his saddle in feather boas before climbing aboard. By summer's end, he'd grown used to the attention and Claire had grown used to calming him by rubbing his faded red and green saddle broach before mounting him.

After Labor Day, school began and Claire and Lucie once again sat in the stiff wooden desks at Johnson school with Will seated in the back of the room for at least one more year. This year began differently, though, because a seat remained empty—Liza's seat.

Claire glanced over at it from time to time, wondering, *Why isn't she here. She couldn't be in Flint for this long. Perhaps the work of the fall harvest is keeping her away. After all, her parents are getting on in age.*

When school dragged on and Liza had missed nearly a week, both Claire and Lucie wandered over to her farm to see how she was doing and to drop off her homework. No one home, nothing looked out of place. Claire thought, *She's scarcely missed a day since we've been friends, but now it's been weeks since I've seen her.*

The second week came and still an empty seat so Claire cut through the woods on the way home, past Liza's farm. This time, Liza's mother Mary, answered the door. Claire handed Liza's schoolwork to her and considered the casualness with which she spoke about her daughter's plight.

Present

"Her mother told us she'd been sick," Claire said to Dan. "She promised Liza would be back at school soon … once she got better. And I promised to bring Liza's homework to her."

Dan asked, "So, when did she get back?"

Claire sighed, paused a moment then continued, her voice quivering, "She didn't at first. Finally, one day we stopped by and could see something was different."

Dan sat up in his chair and leaned forward a bit.

"People were gathered on her porch … some were crying."

Dan looked at Claire and she hesitated then closed her eyes. Familiar with her ways, he waited through the silence until she opened them again and continued.

"No one could have prepared us for the news we would hear. Seemed she had contracted the Spanish Flu. None of us wanted to believe it."

Fall, 1920

Claire and Lucie sprinted across harvested fields, tears streaming down their cheeks. What they saw would always be burned into their memories. It flashed through Claire's mind as she walked from the small row of oaks into the Sloan cornfield.

Having stopped by to see her that day, they had noticed all the people gathered, most of whom they had never met. Creeping onto the large, green steps in front of her porch, they peered through the screen door at a white-haired man with a full, bushy mustache, a man she knew only as Doctor Kipling. They watched as the doctor embraced Mary, Liza's mother.

Mary screamed, "Oh, God … help us! Please, God … not my baby! Not my baby!"

As Claire stepped onto her porch, the visions seemed indelible. She felt certain Lucie had the same battles as she ran toward home to report the news.

In her bedroom, Claire clung to a bedpost, her mother stood beside her, brushing her shoulder with an open palm. Helen always

knew when she hurt. While her silent presence often comforted her, today it was different.

Helen offered, "Claire, honey, I wish I could tell you something to make you feel better."

Claire sensed her mother knew about Liza for a while. It wasn't the type thing that kept silent in a town like theirs.

She asked, "She's going to die … isn't she?"

Her mother hesitated long enough for Claire to question her answer. "Liza's a strong girl."

"Isn't she?"

Turning toward her mother, Claire saw her father standing in the doorway. "Father, is she going to die?"

John evaded the question. Instead he looked at Helen and said, "I'm going over there … see if they need anything."

As John disappeared down the hall, Helen answered, "There's food in the pantry, John."

Jumping up, Claire ran into the hallway. "I want to come."

His tone firm, John said, "No, Claire. You're staying home."

She shuffled behind him as he continued outside. "But Father, she's my friend."

"I said no."

"But Father, I want to!"

He stopped suddenly, pounded his hand against the side of the house. "Damn it Claire, listen to me!"

She stepped back and her eyes welled up. Shaking her head she peered through the wetness then ran off toward the barn. John moved forward as if he wanted to stop her, but something didn't allow him. Instead he only whispered her name as he watched her disappear toward Elijah's pen.

Standing beside a partially loaded wagon, John assessed what goods he could part with. Then Claire appeared behind the wagon, holding a rope attached to Elijah. He looked at her and she came toward him.

"Father, I'm coming and I'm bringing him with me."

He glanced at the donkey, his tone less vehement. "Claire, you can't bring him. And you shouldn't go either."

With a firm tone, Claire said, "Father, you know he's different. Please … can I take him?"

He tried to dissuade her, but she pressed him further. "He came from Heaven, Father. God gave him to us. He came from Heaven."

"Claire, your hopes are gonna be shot," he answered. "I know you want to believe, but—"

"Please," she begged again.

For a moment, she saw her father look beyond her, beyond his own jaded perception. The silence felt awkward yet peaceful then he sighed in defeat and motioned to the back of the wagon.

"All right ... tie him to the back and climb in."

The trip to Liza's farm seemed longer than Claire remembered it. As they drew near, it surprised her to see the large crowd gathered in the front yard. People milled about the porch, elders and young people alike. Claire recognized some, others she didn't.

As her father pulled the wagon up the sandy driveway and parked, she jumped down and untied Elijah. She caught sight of Lucie standing next to her parents. She also saw Wilson there, and next to him stood Charlie Logan and his wife, Velma.

Claire went to Lucie and they embraced then Lucie stroked Elijah's mane, following it with her hand, down to the brown, worn saddle and the broach attached to it. No one said anything for a moment, waiting in silence. Then they began to mummer.

Someone said, "Doctor Kipling is in Liza's room, checking her."

The murmuring stopped. The white haired doctor appeared in the doorway and pushed on the screen then stepped out onto the porch. Claire reached over and rested her hand on Elijah's saddle. Taking off his glasses, the doctor pulled his stethoscope off his shoulders and rubbed his eyes.

He spoke loud enough for everyone to hear. "She's gone."

Screams filled the air as Mary collapsed into her husband's arms. "No, dear God … no! Not my baby! Not my baby girl!"

Tears streamed down Claire's face as Lucie embraced her again. The crowd migrated toward the porch, offering embraces. Pulling away from her friend's grasp, Claire looked at the family long enough to see Liza's mother, still limp in someone's arms.

Something in Claire's eyes intensified and she moved toward the porch, pulling the donkey behind her.

"No, wait," she said. "This can't be. You haven't let me bring him in yet."

John took hold of her and guided her back toward the lawn. "Claire, come on."

She pulled Elijah closer to her and with an emphatic tone, she proclaimed, "But he can heal her."

Wilson came toward her, but she shrugged away from him, turning toward the people on the porch and spoke louder, "But he can heal her. No, wait, you didn't let me try yet!"

John gently placed his large hands about her shoulders, trying to shield her from the pain.

Breaking away from her father's grip, she moved closer to the crowd and shouted, "Elijah can save her! You don't understand! Let me bring him in!"

Charlie came out from the crowd and along with John, they grasped her shoulders.

Spinning her around, John stared into her eyes. "Claire, stop it. There's nothing—"

Breaking loose, she ran to Elijah then lunged toward his saddle, grabbing the broach and tearing it away. Sprinting toward the porch, John intercepted her long enough to grab her arm. She swung loose from his grasp, ran toward the house and up the steps.

She cried, "He can save her! Elijah can save her!"

As she reached the front door, Kipling grabbed hold of her shirt. "Sweetheart, there's nothing you can do now—"

Peeling his fingers away, she reached for the screen. "She's not dead! She's only sleeping!"

After pulling the door open, Claire ran down the long hallway to Liza's room, her father chasing her. As she rounded the corner she could see a thin, slight body covered in a sheet. Peeling back the covers, she saw her friend, a bluish tint to her bony face, arms resting about her side. She plunged the broach into Liza's cold hand and watched as the hand fell onto the bed and opened, the broach resting within it.

Claire screamed, "He can save her! He can heal her!"

John grabbed her from behind and slung her over his shoulder.

"No, I have to stay! He's going to heal her!"

John carried his daughter through the sea of adults gathered in the hallway. They parted to let him by, alarmed at his daughter's behavior. When John reached the front lawn he placed Claire down in the grass beside Wilson and Charlie.

Positioning himself squarely in front of her, John said, "Claire. Claire. Listen to me! Listen to me!"

She panted heavily and sighed to catch her breath.

"There's nothing *we* can do. There's nothing *he* can do."

Wilson patted her curly brown hair. "Come now, child. You'll be fine. You'll be fine."

John embraced Claire's head as tears streamed down his arm.

Charlie whispered in John's ear, "John, if they need anything send them over."

John agreed and cradled his young daughter's head and heard sounds of weeping about them. Eventually, people wandered away, shouting to each other, promising to be there for any unmet needs. The surreal lull became extensive as Liza's family meandered onto the porch again, talking, mumbling and embracing people.

Claire raised her head and felt arms from behind her. She turned and saw Lucie. The two of them embraced.

Lucie lamented, "She can't be gone. She just can't be."

John put his arms around the girls and held them to him.

A sudden loud scream came from the porch, piercing the silence. Then more screams emerged. Heads rose and bodies turned to the commotion. Something about these cries seemed different. They weren't like the ones before.

Someone shouted, "Oh, my God! My God!"

Another cried, "Jesus, Mary and Joseph!"

With her head buried in her father's embrace, Claire could only hear muffled voices, but as the volume rose she felt compelled to pull away and glance in their direction.

Steadfast, John's attention remained on Claire until he saw the remaining guests, staring at the porch. Charlie, Wilson, and Lucie looked in that direction too. John felt a strange compulsion to look also. His eyes squinted, despite the falling sun, and intensified when he saw the slight, frail figure of Liza amidst her family.

Liza stood with Elijah's broach grasped in her hand, appearing before them, clearly her color had returned.

Dumbstruck, people faltered with a guarded excitement. Claire shrugged away from her father and moved closer to her friend, peering out at them.

John wiped his eyes and stumbled toward the porch to get a better look then whispered, "You gotta be kidding me."

The bridled discretion melted and the gathering ran toward the porch. Claire watched as Mary screamed, embracing Liza, dried tears upon her face. Claire moved closer, lost in the sea of gatherers as John looked above their heads as people spilled onto the steps.

Someone shouted, "It's a miracle … a miracle!"

Another cried, "She's been raised from the dead!"

John lost sight of his daughter, shoved away by the crowd. Looking around behind him, he could see the donkey standing alone in the field. Someone ran up to it, embraced it then raised her hands toward the heavens. Looking around, John called for Claire and she turned toward him, her sorrow gone. She called back to her father, but Doctor Kipling's shouts from the porch drowned her out.

A man in the crowd shouted, "I thought you said she was gone!"

Kipling replied, "I checked her. I tell you, I checked her." Then he motioned for people to give Liza more space. "Back up, people! Back up, I say. Give her some room. Let me look at her."

Resigned that he would get no closer, John stepped back and Charlie moved beside him. They looked at each other, placid and speechless. Voices rose from people neither had met.

"The donkey did it," someone screamed. "Jesus' donkey … he did it! Jesus' donkey did it."

One of the children shared in the euphoria. "It's Claire's donkey. He performed a miracle."

Finding herself trapped on the steps, Claire climbed the wooden post that rose to the porch's roof and watched as the adults guided a confused Liza back to the open screen door. Kipling positioned his hand on her shoulder, checked her forehead and waved people away.

He told the family, "I checked her, I swear. I'll stand on that."

Claire looked on until her friend disappeared into the house then she scampered to her father, who stood in the grass. She embraced him hard then pulled back and looked into his stern eyes. A solemn stillness overcame them when John looked directly at her.

She spoke to him as confidently as she ever had. "He came from Heaven, Father. I told you. He came from Heaven."

His silence seemed different this time. She studied his eyes and could tell they said something more profound. He stared back into hers then turned to look at the donkey grazing in the field, unaware of his own hailed status.

The people gathered inside Liza's home, riding on the hope that she would live.

Present

Dan tried to appear disinterested. His college professors had warned him to stay neutral because to act otherwise may send the wrong message.

He adjusted his body in his seat, checked his recorder and said, "So this miracle ... any of this documented?"

A solemn nod as she answered, "Most of it."

He paused to gather his thoughts. "Well, what ... what I mean, who wrote about it? Who documented it?"

She smiled. "I'll get to that, Mr. Mertz."

He quietly reminded her, "Dan. Call me Dan."

Slowly, Claire sat up to open a drawer on an adjacent table. He leaned forward to help her, but she shunned his assistance then filed through a pile of doilies, pens and cards. He noted the expression on her face as she found something. Pulling it out and resting it upon her lap, she unfolded the cloth napkin in which it was wrapped. Leaning toward him she opened her hand and offered an oval-shaped broach to him.

Reluctantly he took the faded Hebrew-patterned stone, painted with earth-tones blue, green and red.

He looked at her and asked, "What is it?"

"You wanted documentation."

"The broach? From his saddle?"

"Keep it," she said. "Use it for your story."

He objected and tried giving it back to her. "This belongs to your family. I can't take this."

She insisted, "By all means, please do. My family doesn't need it ... to believe."

He pulled it back and looked at it then wrapped it again in the white, cloth napkin. He silently slid it into his briefcase and waited for her to speak again.

She asked him, "Do you believe in miracles, Mr. Mertz?"

Tapping on his recorder, he hoped to deflect the question. Instead he surrendered to the compulsion to raise his eyes and look directly at her. "No. I don't."

"I'm sorry," she said. "I'm sorry if my story is difficult for you to listen to."

"It's intriguing," he said. "So far."

"But too farfetched. I understand."

"Do you?"

He stared at her, wondering, *How could she.* "When you've been a journalist as long as I have, you set the bar low … start expecting the worst."

"And I'm certain it leads to questions?"

"About life."

"About God?"

He answered with a somewhat harsh tone, "About whether there is one. Listen, can we get back to—"

She interrupted him, adjusting as if to listen to his answer. "And what have you concluded thus far?"

He allowed the smirk to disappear from his face. "I haven't."

Fall, 1920

The school year wore on. It had been less than two weeks since the *incident*, as the adults coined it, and word had spread, as much from Claire's inability to bridle her excitement as from Liza's own family. Helen had warned Claire not to say too much. But in Claire's young mind, she couldn't figure why and thought, *Why keep quiet. A miracle is a miracle.*

Things began to calm down a bit on the farm, and although John could scarcely afford any time away, he glanced at a hand-scratched address written on the ripped out corner of the newspaper. He stood standing on the front step of a man he had never formally met, a

man the town knew little about. After knocking on a solid wooden door, a Mr. Lenter greeted John.

Accessing the man's information had required the unfortunate contact with the mayor's office. Gavel made sure to walk John past the clock tower under construction, the one to which he refused to contribute, as Gavel reminded him.

Walking with the donkey's former owner, John recalled how he had offered the animal at the fair as a prize won by his daughter. He also noted how Lenter could not have acted less interested.

"How'd you say you found me again?"

"Mayor's office," John said.

"Well, let's make it quick. I got a lot to do."

Lenter headed to a Ford truck parked in the driveway. After grabbing a wrench from a table, he stepped onto a small stool and despite his slight frame, he buried his head beneath the open hood.

John asked, "Where'd you get him?"

"I bought him off an old miner last year. Thought he might keep me company. All he did was cause me grief."

"You remember the guy's name? The guy you got him from?"

From under the hood, Lenter said, "How the hell do I know? He gave him to me for a song though. Then he started talking all kinda crazy stuff … said he inherited him awhile ago … said he might be trouble, but he'd be worth it … the donkey, that is." He went back to work for a moment then stopped, set the wrench down and leaned out toward John to make a point. "Say … why you wanna know so much about him? I'm not takin' him back from you, see?"

John nodded and watched Lenter bury his head again under the truck's hood then clearing his throat, John continued, "So, what kinds of things … I mean … why was he so much trouble?"

Lenter exclaimed, "For one, he's stupid! He wouldn't stay in his corral if his damn life depended on it." John waited through a long pause as Lenter dropped a tool into the engine block and swore under his breath. "Moreover, I don't remember getting a full night's sleep the whole damn time he was with me. Kept havin' dreams."

John's interest piqued. "Dreams? About what?"

"I don't know. The animal's cursed, I tell ya."

Wondering about more, John asked, "Not too many good fates?"

"I wouldn't say that. Had some good fates, I guess. None of it had to do with him, though."

Waiting for answers, John realized they wouldn't come so he shook his head, glanced around the property and waited until Lenter offered more.

"The straw that broke the camel's back was when he dumped the can of varnish on my head. I'm workin' outside a shed ... the stupid animal gets the shakes about something, bumps the ladder and knocks the whole damn gallon on me ... waste of good varnish too."

A small smirk emerged on John's face. "Don't imagine you were hammering nails when that happened, were you? Or using a whip?"

Poking his head out from under the hood again, Lenter said with a stern tone in his voice, "Listen, I answered all your questions. I'm not takin' him back from you, see?"

Nodding, John thanked him and turned to leave, but Lenter called for him again. "Hey, take the satchel with you."

Curious, John only looked at him.

"The rest of his property ... some papers. They might tell you more about him. They're in the shed."

Lenter motioned toward a decaying, wooden structure adjacent to the barn and John took the long walk toward it. Grasping a handle affixed with only one screw, he pulled on the door and the handle broke off. Stepping past the creaky door, he moved into the darkness past piles of rusted tractor parts and planter hinges. He scanned the contents then he saw a brown, leather satchel setting under a folded white tarp.

Crouching to get a better look, John flipped open the cover and pulled out yellowed papers. Holding them up to a small sliver of light, he could make no sense of the writing, so he slid the papers back into their place.

Before he closed the cover, he looked closer at something carved into the leather. Leaning again into the light, he stared at what appeared to be a name—Rufus, Shahhat. Shaking his head, John put the cover back in place and sealed it shut. His questions had merited little today, but he thought about someone who might change that.

~ ~ ~

John stood in front of the rectory, looking up at the ornate, stained glass inset within the red brick and the deeply varnished door before him. He rang the bell, hoping no one would answer because Saint Mary's hadn't seen much of him lately. He tucked in his shirt then heard the sound of an unfastening latch on the other side. He stepped back as the heavy door opened, and then he saw the smile of the young priest he knew as Father Cunningham.

The priest slid his Roman collar back into its place and wiped his mouth from a late lunch. "John, to what do I owe this surprise?"

John tolerated the pleasantries, something he usually ignored, as the two walked through the long hallway to a high-ceiling office and looked at a stack of books that required shifting to find a place to sit.

Father Cunningham apologized to him. "Sorry, John, we don't get too many visitors." He noticed John seemed interested in a few of the paintings on the far side of the room. "You oughta recognize the first one," he said. "I don't know much about the second."

He walked up behind John who began looking at a picture of Christ and the one next to it, a less familiar painting.

Pointing to the first one, Father Cunningham said, "That's the Sacred Heart ... Jose something or other. The other one I found at a garage sale."

John appeared to study the paintings, as much to find the right moment to speak as anything else.

Cunningham pointed to the second one, a picture of a man and two boys standing on a cobblestone street, witnessing a crucifixion with a host of other people and animals meshed behind them. John focused on a donkey in the painting, his mane not unlike Elijah's.

"I guess that's Simon," Cunningham said of the man. "Standing next to his sons ... at least that's what I'm told."

Nodding, John then cleared his throat.

The priest offered John a seat then asked, "So, what can I do for you, John?"

As John sat, some books fell off the back of the chair. He bent to pick them up until Cunningham motioned for him to leave them.

John asked, "Did you ever hear of, or know of a man named Rufus in these parts?"

After thinking about it for a moment, Cunningham replied, "No ... can't say I have ... at least not in this parish." Then he noticed

John's expression appeared to be one of disappointment so he asked, "Everything all right, John?"

John shrugged, thought about how he could begin then said, "Things have been different lately ... around the farm. I've been having dreams."

Aware of John's struggles by speaking often with Helen about them, Cunningham said, "I see, well, war isn't an easy thing—"

"No," John interrupted. "These are different. They're not about the war ... not anymore."

Reaching into the pocket of his overalls, John pulled out a crinkled sheet of paper and handed it to the priest, the same paper he'd been writing on each night. "What do you make of this?"

Taking hold of it, Cunningham held it up and read it in silence then shaking his head, he mumbled, "I don't know ... looks like another language. I can't quite tell. If I didn't know any better, looks something like ... Aramaic." He smiled as he glanced back at John and said, "You didn't tell me you know Aramaic."

"I don't," John answered. "I have no idea what that says. I just wrote it down as I heard it ... as I saw it."

"I beg your pardon?"

John hesitated a moment then he handed the priest the leather satchel. Cunningham flipped it open and filed through yellowed parchment paper.

He noticed a name etched into its inside pocket, shook his head and read, "Rufus, Shahhat. Nope, don't know a Rufus. There's a city named Shahhat in Libya ... that's about all I can tell you."

Sighing, John said, "Some strange things have been happenin' since Claire brought him home ... the donkey."

"I see," Cunningham answered.

Feeling certain Cunningham tried not to treat him as though he were crazy he continued, "My daughter believes ... well ... she's been telling everyone—"

"About the rains at the Washington farm ... and your family's silos," Cunningham said with a smile. "I've heard some of it. People are generous, John, but I don't think there's any harm in her believing in miracles. Don't trample on her fantasies."

"There's something else," John added.

The priest sat back in his chair as John adjusted his body in his then he asked, "You know the Nichols family?"

Cunningham answered, "Yes, Claire's friend Liza. She's been sick ... hasn't she?"

"Not anymore."

Chapter 12
Weary Pilgrims

Present

Claire settled with a warm cup of tea, something she attributed to her old age. Cupping it with both hands, they trembled as she set it atop a doily beside her. Dan studied her, waiting for her to ask him if he wanted some and waiting to decline again.

She looked at him and continued, "Word of Liza's healing spread fast. Mother always said the telephone was the devil's gossip tool. Soon, people started showing up in town ... strangers ... thrill seekers, mother called them. Elijah would still get out of his pen from time to time. Other times, I took him into town with us."

Then her face grew more solemn as she said, "But mother didn't think that was such a good idea anymore. I figured it was because he'd been so much trouble. Mother must have known there were other things brewing."

Fall, 1920

Helen took Will and Claire to town more than once during the week. One day, she needed their help carrying a load of dry goods back to the farm. The routine hadn't changed much, though this time they came without Elijah because he had been causing a bit of a stir among the town folks lately.

Claire studied her mother's face as they carried the last load from Logan's front door to the wagon tied off in front. She noticed her mother looking at a group of strangers standing in a pack at the Tannery across the street.

"There are more of them around," Claire said. "Strangers."

Helen only nodded, mentioning she noticed that too, then watching as the strangers made their way to Charlie's counter asking about *the farm*, and Charlie sent them away. Unfortunately, more

than once in the past, Gavel intercepted them, and didn't take to the stirring as amicably. Instead, he seemed to blame the Sloans for the disruption, glaring in their direction as he sent the thrill seekers packing.

The ride home was peaceful and as they came up the driveway, John walked about, at a distance, carrying two bags of feed into the barn. Helen parked the wagon and directed her son to tend to the horses then told Claire she needed to speak with their father.

Helen found John forking some straw into a stall and stopped short of a waist-high pile. She asked him how it went at the church and at Lenter's, aware of the answers for which he'd been searching.

John explained things to her, but she felt none the wiser for it. Then she asked about the priest and he explained what he told him, aware only that Cunningham had listened, with little to say.

Helen's voice peaked as she asked, "You told him everything?"

"Everything … about the silos … the rain. He already knew about most of it."

Turning to see if Claire was around Helen said, "I know. She's been talking."

"I told him about Liza Nichols too," he said.

"How did he react?"

"How do you think he reacted? He looked at me like I had a third eye. How dumb of me. People are startin' to look at us different now."

Concurring, Helen said, "I spoke to Velma yesterday. She heard about it from her Aunt in Wixom … Wixom! That's near Detroit. I don't want this to spin out of control, John."

Setting down the pitchfork he bent to draw a cold cup of water from a bright metal bucket. "It's Claire I'm worried about. I don't want to see her get hurt."

Helen cupped her lips, eyes to the ground and agreed by her silence. She watched as her husband actually stood before her, his presence unabated.

John shook his head. "You know, for a minute it looked like he actually believed me. How's he supposed to believe it if I don't."

She edged closer, offering a hand to his stiff arm. "You don't believe in much, do you?"

He backed away and stared at her. "No, I don't."

Helen retreated and John returned to work. Then she rested her empty hands on the only hips they'd felt in a while—hers. Turning toward the house, her bottled passion unmet, she took a few steps then stopped to face him again.

"You know, John, you're so worried about Claire all the time." She paused to look at the donkey's pen at the far side of the barn. "Did you ever think he might have come for you?"

John halted long enough to watch his wife walk away and noticed the setting sun reflecting off her light brown hair.

~ ~ ~

John sat in the stiff-backed wooden chair, an elbow rested on the kitchen table as Helen slivered potatoes into a large pot. He scanned a fresh copy of the State Journal newspaper spread across his lap, something he rarely found time to do.

The screen door slammed shut in the hall and Claire followed Will to the ice box, setting two buckets of freshly squeezed milk beside each other. Will moved to a window and looked outside, interested in something at the front of the house. Helen glanced out too and saw the county road with a line of cars along it.

Will asked, "Mom, what's going on in town today?"

"Nothing I know of. Why?"

Claire came up behind Will and looked out at the winding road then said, "It looks like a bunch of cars are headed that way."

John peered at the paper's headlines, oblivious to the other conversations. His eyes widened as he folded the paper to stare out the screen door then back at the paper, and again out the door. Holding the paper close to his face, he let the words seep into his consciousness. Glancing out again at the long, bending row of cars, he rose from his seat and walked toward the door, paper firmly in his hand and looked at the endless line.

"I don't think they're headed into town," he said.

Helen wiped her hands, removed her apron and came up behind him then asked, "What is it, John?"

"Remember when you said you didn't want things to spin out of control?"

"Yes."

"I think they just did."

Helen snatched the paper from him and opened it. Her eyes stopped on the words printed across the front page, near the top— *Miracle Donkey Heals Girl.* She realized then that her husband was right. The cars weren't headed into town. Instead, they slowed as they reached the front of the Sloan driveway.

John pushed open the screen and Helen followed him out. Stumbling off the porch he hastened to intercept the strangers as they spilled out from their cars onto the lawn. He held up his hands as they meandered toward the barn.

"No! Go back! There's too many of you!"

People emerged from creaky wooden wagons and Model Ts. Confused eyes squinted through the sunlight as they came closer, hoping for direction. Some of them were crippled, strapped in metal braces, others wheelchair bound, yet others too weak to walk were carried by family members. They all ignored John's dismissals.

One man asked, "Where is he? We want to see him."

John shook his head as the questions intensified. He hurried toward a group moving in on Elijah's pen.

They shouted and pointed in Elijah's direction. "The donkey! Look, it's Jesus' donkey!"

Helen stood a few feet off the porch, resigned to the masses, and watched as John disappeared among them. She turned toward the house and saw Claire and Will gazing open-mouthed at the numbers. The tide overcame them, hundreds, perhaps thousands of people. Helen knew her family needed help so she went to town for that help, and hopefully, in time, all the people would be gone.

Claire counted more than a thousand. Within an hour, the line stretching from Elijah's pen became more orderly and less chaotic. Sick people, some dying, came from as far away as Detroit, wrapped around his pen to the far side of the barn and back. A mass of pilgrims sat about the front lawn, waiting and hoping. At the corral, Will sat atop the rail fence holding onto Elijah's lead rope while Claire stood beside him stroking his nose to keep him calm.

People waited patiently to get close enough to touch him. They stretched, reaching to make contact. Some stroked his mane, others his saddle, others the saddle-broach, thanking the God they believed facilitated the meeting.

One cried out, "Please, heal me ... Lord!"

"Keep my loved one's safe," another prayed.

Helen returned with reinforcements, the Logans and Wilson with family, and meandered through the crowd. John spotted Charlie from across the way and waded between patches of standing and sitting pilgrims.

As he approached Charlie, he said, "This has gotten outta hand. Help me keep them away from the rest of the livestock."

Helen milled between groups, offering water from a metal bucket slung across her arm. Occasionally, she glanced at her husband and at her children seated in the donkey's corral. Alarmed at the gratefulness of the strangers, she looked at them with pity.

Offering more drinks, she heard Eleanor Russell thank her from a wheelchair. She couldn't help noticing how Eleanor had worsened since the last time she'd seen her. She glanced at Eleanor's legs, still in braces, but scarcely able to support the weight of her own body. Helen moved the wheelchair out of the crowd and embraced Eleanor then turned and saw John coming toward her.

He said, "Helen, these people are sick!"

She lowered her tone. "I'm aware of that, John."

"We can't do anything for them. They need a doctor."

"You can see they're not going anywhere."

Standing silent for a moment, he scanned the masses then said, "And what happens, Helen ... when nothing happens?"

She didn't know how to answer. Instead, she backed away and offered someone more water. Then she turned to look at a few cars approaching up the county road.

John saw them too.

The cars kicked up large clouds of dust as they slowed at the end of their driveway and pulled in. John immediately recognized them, the sheriff and Mayor Gavel.

John whispered, "Thank God."

Trudging a path through the people, he headed to meet them.

The two cars came to a halt and their doors flung open. Out of one stepped the Clinton County Sheriff, the other, Gavel, Monsignor Cobalt, and Father Cunningham. Cobalt scanned the crowd as Cunningham stood behind him.

John intercepted them as they came toward the lawn. "Mayor, Sheriff. Thank God you're here."

Gavel glanced around, scoffed at the chaos. "John Sloan ... 1 see you've created quite a ruckus."

John said, "I assure you, Mayor ... I had nothing to do with it."

Gavel folded his thumbs inside his waistcoat. "How am I supposed to get done with my tower with all my workers here? You know ... this is causing quite a stir in town. You make deceptive claims and this is what happens."

"Listen," John said. "I just want these people off my property."

Gavel came toward him. "This can't happen, John. It isn't good for the town."

"Maybe you should thank the State Journal," John answered.

As Gavel shook his head and walked away, the sheriff began dispersing people.

Then Gavel stopped, long enough to sneer, "The healing of a girl? Really, John ... you should know better."

John stood silent.

Then Gavel cupped his hands and shouted to the crowd, "Clear out, people! Clear out and head on home!"

Monsignor Cobalt made his way to the donkey's pen and found a wooden crate to stand atop then bellowed, "Children. My children. Listen, all of you! There have been no miracles surrounding this animal! Do you understand? No miracles. This is a trick of the devil! Do not allow yourselves to become beholden to these lies!"

The sheriff yelled, "This is private property. You must leave at once. At once, I say!"

Helen stood still, her arm throbbing from the weight of the water bucket. She watched as wheelchairs and people moved off the grass, toward wagons and cars. She caught a sudden glimpse of Mildred Brewer. Mildred smiled back at her, appearing a bit friendlier than usual. Beside Mildred stood two young children, one, Helen recognized as Becky, Claire's rogue schoolmate. The other, she hadn't seen before, an older girl, perhaps fifteen, walking with braces and crutches.

Dismissing Mildred, she turned toward the departing guests, forcing a smile as she watched them leave the same way in which

they arrived. Then she watched Eleanor Russell wheel herself closer to Elijah's pen, perhaps for another goodbye.

John sighed with relief as the last guests strolled off the patchy grass, returning to their wagons. Someone called to him. He turned to see Monsignor Cobalt standing nearby and smiled at the prospect the monsignor knew his name.

"Mr. Sloan?"

"Monsignor."

Cobalt sneered at him. "I would like to meet with you at the rectory ... sometime soon."

"Certainly ... this week?"

"Soon," Cobalt said.

John stood still. He saw the mayor's glare before Gavel stepped back into his Model T. Then Father Cunningham walked by. An odd reluctance, he tried to smile at John and the two of them stood staring at each other for a moment as if they knew something the others didn't. Cunningham nodded once, and John returned the gesture then the priest climbed in the back seat.

While John stood and watched as the final two cars backed out of the driveway, his family looked on as if they had his back. Something told Claire that he had theirs and would protect them.

Later that evening, the sun set behind a patch of clouds low on the horizon. The west side of the barn next to the donkey's pen always caught the twilight, holding it amidst the red, faded barn paint. It had been hours since people left, yet one person remained, a solitary figure seated in a wheelchair among the shadows adjacent to Elijah's stable. Claire noticed the woman as she came inside from feeding the horses and asked her mother if it would be okay. Helen assured her it was ... for a time.

Then John asked about the woman. "Who is that?"

"Eleanor Russell ... from church," Helen said. "She wanted to stay a bit. I told Claire it would be all right."

"All right? Helen, we just got through clearing everybody out."

"Just for a bit."

John withheld further objections so Helen sent Claire out with cold water for Eleanor, and told her she could stay as long as she

liked. Eleanor had arranged for her husband to pick her up, and if it gave Eleanor something to hope for, Helen knew it couldn't hurt.

An hour after the sun set, Claire sat beside her mother as she sewed patches onto worn overalls and torn dresses. She glanced over at Claire from time to time, peering over the top of her bifocals in the dim light. Claire felt her warmth. No one had heard anything from Eleanor and the clock said nearly nine o'clock. Helen thought, *Perhaps her husband picked her up.*

They heard a sudden knock at the door and the two glanced at each other. Then another knock sounded, louder than the last. Helen set down her knitting and answered it.

At first, Helen didn't recognize the woman who stood there. She squinted, peering into the darkness through the screen.

Eleanor Russell stood in the light of the moon. Helen took a step back to get a better look as Claire moved beside her. They both looked at the woman's face and could see tears streaming down it.

They looked at her legs, less the braces and whole. Helen's eyes intensified and rose slowly to Eleanor's hands, absent a crutch, filled only with the braces she had previously worn. Eleanor stood firmly on the porch, complete, and with feet planted firmly beneath her.

Helen's legs faltered and she reached for the door post to keep from falling. They hadn't witnessed what had happened, but the extraordinary result of something happening stood before them, something miraculous. Although they tried to accept its certainty, they felt it was enough for now.

~ ~ ~

In less than a week, John and Claire went to the rectory and met with only Monsignor Cobalt because Father Cunningham had gone to Lansing to visit the sick. Claire had begged to go with John, and since she came to town with him, he had no choice but to allow her to come along. They sat in silence, hearing only mumbling sounds coming from behind the door and a loud, ticking grandfather clock standing in the corner of the room.

John sat in a chair outside Cobalt's office, watching the clock. Then he noticed his daughter looking at a painting across the room, a painting of Christ riding a donkey.

The door opened and Cobalt stood before them, tall and lean; his thin, drawn face rose to a high forehead with brownish hair pasted back. He motioned to John who then rose slowly and looked at Claire before disappearing into the office.

He said, "Wait here."

Transferring his cap from head to hands, John held it in front of him as he stepped into what felt like a gauntlet. Scanning the office, he saw Gavel seated in a chair across the room and the tone of the meeting appeared to change.

John glanced at the mayor and asked, "What's *he* doing here?"

Gavel answered, "This is just as much a town matter now—"

"Since when is it a town matter?"

"Since people have been sniffing around town because of your stories," Gavel said.

Cobalt held up a hand. "Gentlemen … gentlemen."

John stood fast, glaring at the mayor he had learned to dislike, and the other man he scarcely knew. Cobalt offered him a seat and he accepted. Then the monsignor took a seat behind a solid oak desk littered with books.

The monsignor leaned back and stared at John then cleared his throat and said, "Mr. Sloan, it has come to my attention that some … some curious and unusual things have been happening recently. There have been rumors."

John stirred a bit and sat up.

Nodding toward Gavel, Cobalt continued, "These rumors have made their way to the city, and now to the paper. They have fueled what I fear is an unquenchable fire. And have filled many with a false sense of hope."

Gavel interjected, holding up a stack of papers. "Do you know what these are?"

John shook his head.

"Formal complaints … fifteen formal complaints filed on my desk … all because of outsiders bumming around, asking questions about your farm … the donkey's farm. It's disrupting town business. Frankly, we don't have the resources—"

John asked, "What business is that, Mayor … your precious clock tower?"

"I find it interesting," Cobalt said. "I find it interesting that an un-churched man such as you can uphold claims like these." He picked up a copy of the State Journal and slid on his spectacles. "Seems your daughter believes your silos were miraculously filled. Miraculous rains at the Washington farm. Then there's this claim of a healed girl." He stopped to look at John over the top of his glasses then stated, "Preposterous."

John said nothing and only stared at Cobalt.

Cobalt asked, "Do you think this is the way God works? I am the spiritual authority for this district. To think that the Lord would impart such blessings on the likes of you is absurd. You are filling people's minds with heretical fantasies. It must stop."

With a lighter tone Gavel said, "John, every time Claire brings that donkey into town, he attracts attention. You're gonna have to keep him locked up."

John defended himself. "What am I supposed to do? I built him a corral and sometimes he gets out. I'll tell her she can't take him—"

Interrupting John, Gavel said, "Keep him away from town ... away from city hall *and* away from town."

The monsignor added, "That order stands for my parish. Word of this has already reached Bishop Gallagher. He expects me to handle this and I intend to."

After a short silence, John asked, "Have you spoken to anybody else about these incidents? They can tell you what they saw."

"Miracles elicit investigation," Cobalt said. "Delirium does not. He remains on your farm ... and I will hear of no further claims."

Silence again overtook them and John felt it was misinterpreted. As the three men stood, John looked at them then reached for Cobalt's limp hand and shook it.

Gavel offered his hand. "Come on, Sloan. No hard feelings?"

Staring at it, John nodded once, turned and walked away, leaving the two men standing in the doorway. Claire followed her father out the rectory door.

Neither said anything on the way home. John thought it best because it was his way.

Chapter 13
A New Perspective

Present

Dan shook his head as he wrote then looked up at Claire and with a disgruntled expression on his face he said, "Jerks."

His sincerity surprised her.

Half-embarrassed, he added, "Well, you know ... not very nice."

Claire agreed and casually moved him forward into the fall and November. To her, the seasons ran together that year. He understood why, but hoped for more detail. Instead she sipped more tea. He had grown used to surrendering to her, and once he did, time moved faster. It was his fifth visit with her.

She glanced out a picture window over Dan's shoulder. The trees had started to turn and the seasons of the present shadowed the ones of which she spoke. Claire's granddaughter entered the room and poured him more tea despite his objections.

Her voice soft, Claire began again. "Thanksgiving was grand that year. Mother saw to it everyone was invited ... the Logans, the Washingtons ... even Father Cunningham. Conversation was light that year, except when it came to the election. It was mother's first."

Dan looked at her, confused.

"Women's suffrage ... the election of nineteen twenty. And you can bet the women had lots to say."

Dan agreed.

"But as the night wandered on, I saw something happen with my father. It was as if he allowed himself to relax. He was less vigilant ... less pensive, but now, the intensity seemed to rest with Father Cunningham."

"Cunningham?"

She nodded. "He was the last to leave that year ... by design, I felt. Perhaps he was hoping we'd have something else to tell him."

"Something else?"

"About him … about the donkey," she said. "He seemed more distant than I ever remembered him being. Mother felt the same. After all, we'd thrown enough at him to make most priests run the other way. It had been weeks since Eleanor's healing … longer since Liza's. And though he assured my father he was interested, we could see the uncertainty in his eyes."

Dan waited through another silence.

"The quietude these events rendered was a double-edged sword. Bad in some ways … good in others. But it was the first night my mother would see my father smile. The first night … since he'd come home from the war."

Thanksgiving, 1920

The weather outside forced John to split more wood that soon disappeared into flames pouring heat out from the stone fireplace. Cunningham had brought some vinyl records over that night and left them behind. As Helen laid siege to the kitchen's mess, she played them, one by one. After the kids went to bed, John sat on the davenport, looking at the fire.

Helen snuck into the living room and watched him, entranced by the flames. She opened the Victrola oak doors then slid beside him as another record started, something from the American Quartet, *Moonlight Bay*. The soft sounds of their voices melded with those of the crackling fire. She moved closer to him, hoping he'd have something to say.

He did.

"Some meal you cooked today."

"Thanks," she said, waiting for more.

She had become accustomed to his silence, and lately, from people in town. As she studied the dancing flames, the couch began to bounce beside her. She looked at John, laughing. His smile looked unforced. Taken aback, she wondered, *Why*.

John noticed her confusion. "Was just thinkin' … thinkin' about the look on Gavel's face when Claire threw the fruit salad at him."

"Fruit salad … I remember."

"I got mad at her … probably shouldn't have. It was a long day."

Helen smiled, but the smile melted along with his.

John whispered, "Long nights … I'm used to long nights."

She agreed and her breathing got heavier, more exact. Edging closer she forced her eyes to gaze directly at his.

Continuing, he said, "There were some long nights in Russia, I'll tell ya … nights I dreamt I could be home … sitting right here."

Immersing herself in him, she waited for more.

"Some days we didn't have but a few hours sunlight … that was it. *Polar Bears* they called us. I guess we were supposed to take it."

Holding her breath, she tried not to interrupt his somber tone.

"When we shipped out from Battle Creek, I thought sure we'd be going to France. It surprised us all when we ended up fighting the Bolsheviks. Then, about the time the rest of the world went home, things got worse for us. Limeys led us into battle against Trotsky. After seeing three days of what men can do to each other—"

He fell silent again for a moment and she wondered if her breathing caused it. She wanted to ask for more, but knew she was getting more than expected.

Turning to her, he said, "Then Billy died. You remember Billy?"

She did.

"Do you know what we were doing over there? Guarding a shipment of oatmeal. We talked the night before he died. We missed home, but you know what we missed most that night?"

She shook her head.

"A candy bar," he said. "He wanted one … I wanted one in the worst way. So after the shelling stopped, we promised each other we'd walk together to get one."

Helen didn't want to ask him to expound.

Instead, he asked, "Did you ever want something that reminded you of home? Something so bad you'd walk the earth for it?"

She nodded.

"When the Bolsheviks advanced on us, he jumped up out of the trench. I think he was half crazy. Then I had a choice to make … help my friend, or do what I was charged to do … protect the supply. I chose the latter … and he died … instead of me."

A tear formed in her eye.

"So, the next day I went for that candy bar. I walked a mile back to a post. Damn cold, too. I came up on a tent, and I couldn't believe

it. There was a candy bar … right there. I pulled out a dollar and slapped it down. Do you know what … they wouldn't sell it to me."

Helen shook her head.

"They wouldn't take my American money. 'Russian rubles only', the man said. So … I kept walking. I walked another mile, maybe more. Finally, I came across a Salvation Army tent. There was another candy bar … right there. I pulled out my American dollar and slapped it down. Do you know what the man said to me?"

Again, she had no idea and shook her head.

"He looked me directly in the eye, and said, 'Keep your money, soldier. This one's on us.' That was a damn good candy bar … maybe the best one ever. I tried to pay him for it, but he wouldn't let me. It was then I told myself … I'll pay him back till the day I die."

Gradually, John recognized the music's words. "You remember this song?"

She whispered, "Like yesterday."

He reached for her hand and she looked down at his. A rough hand covered her fingers and he grasped them. Guiding her upward, they rose together and John pulled her close. He felt awkward and frustrated in the moment. As she moved her feet gracefully across the hard wooden floor, emotion welled within her. They danced in silence, and for the first time in years she found her face close to his. Her breathing became heavy and somehow she knew she had never fallen out of love with him.

"I've missed you so, John."

His words spilled out as eloquently as they ever had. "I've loved you ever since the first time I laid eyes on you, Helen Sloan. I've never stopped."

They danced alone in the warmth of the fire while outside the picture window, the donkey stood in his pen under a starlit sky.

Present

Claire's eyes glistened as she recalled the night. "I never told my parents, but I watched them dance. I snuck out of bed and hid in the shadows. I remember it like it was yesterday. My mother had waited for so long—"

Dan jolted from his trance and noticed the time. He shut his recorder off and fumbled with his notepad.

Claire asked, "Leaving so soon? I thought you would stay longer this week."

He couldn't stay, but didn't know how to tell her. Doug began pressuring him. *Too much coming in. I need to catch up for a few weeks before I come back.*

"I've got other assignments too, you know ... if I want to keep my job."

She peered at him, more profound than she had in awhile. "Your mind is wandering today."

He tried to shake off the feeling, but she leaned forward and pressed him further. A false smile spread across his face. Too uncomfortable to stare back, he took longer packing up his things.

Then he spoke. "So, I'm at this apartment fire not long ago. Two kids in the house. This woman is praying ... crying out to God, I suppose. Anyway, a fireman loses his life. So does one of her kids."

"So, your story was about a hero?"

"No," he said, a bit annoyed. "My story was about one dead kid and a dead fireman."

"You see, Mr. Mertz, maybe that's your problem. You choose to focus on the bad and ignore the hope that comes from it."

Dan looked at her as if he wanted her to believe he was insulted.

"Hope? Some kid dies and you want me to spin it as redemptive?"

"Well, you're the reporter, Mr. Mertz. Aren't you the one who decides what the story's about?"

For the first time, he became cross at her. "Why does God let man suffer, Claire? If He really exists ... why—"

"Why does *man* let man suffer? You have the power to choose what you see, Mr. Mertz. You can either cover a tragic fire, or a hero who dies to save a child. You used to be a talented reporter."

He agreed.

"Talent is nurtured in solitude," she said, "but character is forged in the stormy billows of the world. Look for the good, Mr. Mertz. Look for hope. It is then that you'll find God."

For the first time in awhile he didn't have a joke. Instead, he stood, nodding at her. Perhaps he would heed her words, though he could promise nothing.

Stopping short of the door, he turned toward her and said, "See you in a few weeks."

~ ~ ~

Dan sat across the table from an empty seat, waiting for Cindy to arrive, the phone to his ear. A light snow spattered the sidewalk as the wintry air reached the city earlier than predicted. He listened as Doug barked a few more orders to him then glanced up at the sound of a bell. Cindy walked in, a jacket covering her hospital scrubs and planted herself across from him.

He spoke into his earpiece. "Yes, Doug. I don't know how much longer … Doug she's a hundred years old, she moves slow. Yes. I can cover that. Yes. Thanks, Doug. Thanks, Doug."

Hanging up, he grinned at Cindy.

"Doug?"

He nodded.

"Is he trying to work you to death?"

"He's the one who told me to interview her … remember?"

"So … it's his fault I haven't seen you?"

"Not exactly," he said. "She's just … slow."

"I see," Cindy answered. "It's almost Christmas. Do you think you'll be done before Christmas?"

"I don't know, but I hope so. Doug needs me to do a piece on some lady who got screwed by a contractor. I told him I would do it before I go back to Claire's."

A waitress came to their table, notepad in hand. As she took their order, Dan saw a homeless man huddled in a doorway across the street. Cindy wondered what interested him so and he quickly reeled in his attention. Reaching into his briefcase, he pulled out something folded in a white napkin and placed it on the table.

Cindy looked at it as he shoved it close to her and asked, "What do you make of this?"

She unfolded the napkin and saw the saddle broach Claire had given him, dark green with faded red Hebrew patterns.

"It's the broach from his saddle … allegedly."

"Allegedly?"

"Well, she believes it. She thinks he healed some people. I think she's waiting to tell me about a third miracle. There have only been two healings … allegedly."

"And what do you believe?"

"What is this … twenty questions?"

Cindy pushed for an answer as he put the broach in his briefcase.

"I don't know … I guess I believe people can fool themselves into believing whatever they want."

During the meal, Dan remained quiet. His odd compulsion to complete Claire's story puzzled her, and she noticed his mind wandered more than in the past. She felt uncertain whether or not she liked his new disposition and she watched him carefully, until they were through.

As they approached the register together, Dan promised to walk her to her car. He zipped his dark-green jacket before pushing on the glass door then Cindy looped her arm with his. As the door flung open and a blast of cold air hit them, Dan looked again toward the homeless man seated against the brick doorway. He would have turned away from such poverty in the past, but something compelled him to pay attention this time.

He quickened his pace as he escorted Cindy toward the parking garage a block over. A sudden force spoke to him after he heard a sound he'd grown used to ignoring, the ringing of a bell. He stopped and turned then looked across the street and saw a Salvation Army bucket. He had passed it by so many other seasons, perhaps because he was too familiar with its beckoning. It had become lost in his world, enveloped in a sea of hands outstretched at this time of year.

Today he watched, long enough to plunge a fist into his pocket and come out with something. He left Cindy on the sidewalk, trotted across the street and approached the bucket then cracked a smile. He leaned toward the man and said something before dropping the money in. He ran back to Cindy, waiting patiently on the other side.

She asked, "What'd you say?"

He looked at her, but didn't answer.

"What'd you say to the man?"

"Nothing," he answered.

She kissed him on the cheek before they parted ways for the day.

Dan returned to his car, and then drove to the office with the radio off.

~ ~ ~

The next few weeks he found himself back in the bedlam from which he'd been spared for the last few months. He responded almost as if he never left: a fatal car crash, a house fire, a despondent senior. This time, though, he waited a bit longer. He watched more and spoke less, the rewards clearer.

He studied the tragic fire and watched as a bystander draped a blanket across the shoulders of an exhausted fireman. He peered out at the torn wreckage of a family's car then noticed a cold, drenched police officer carrying a small child away in his arms. He looked upon a few people from whom he had, in the past, drawn little hope, and waited longer to see a stranger buy a meal for a homeless man. He saw a teenage girl run down the street to track down the elderly owner of a wallet that had fallen out of his pocket.

Dan thought, *These people, the same ones who lived within the city limits before, have they changed that much or did I.*

Chapter 14

A Gift from a Friend

Heading across slick streets to an address on Detroit's west side, Dan double-checked his GPS and whispered the address, "Two-six-five-three-five Brammell."

Pulling into the driveway, he winced when his brakes squeaked. He looked at the roof, partially torn up and covered in plastic.

On the porch, he met a middle-aged woman who introduced herself. "I'm Laura ... Laura Jenkinson."

She invited him to come inside. He made a brief statement about the reason for his visit. "It's an investigative report. I'm covering an assignment for a colleague."

After she invited Dan to sit beside her at the kitchen table, he agreed. He noticed contractor bills strewn about, and as much as he tried to ignore them, he saw medical bills too, some of them rather large. He studied her deep-set eyes and brown hair with gray streaks and wondered for a moment, *What could have driven her to such an early gray. Perhaps there's a reason for it.*

He glanced over his notes to see if he understood the basics then said, "Let me get this straight, you gave this man a three-thousand dollar deposit and he disappeared?"

She nodded, as if embarrassed to have done such a foolish thing then said, "Well, not at first."

As Dan wrote, he said, "I see."

"He worked for about two weeks stripping and replacing tiles. Then he said he needed more money."

"So you gave him more?"

"Another thousand," she said. "He's quite a scam artist. I wish I would've checked some references. How did you come to ... I mean ... who called the Free Press about this?"

Dan said, "I don't know. I was given the assignment yesterday. Do you mind if I take a look at the damage?"

"Not at all."

She rose with him and together they walked down a long thin hallway, rooms on either side with pictures of firemen and family members strewn about the walls.

"I've got two kids," she said, "Cal and Sara. I wouldn't mind it so much … except all the water damage is in Sara's room."

Reaching the end of a hallway, she stopped and pushed open the door of a bedroom. Dan stepped in and saw a young girl that looked about twelve years old, lying in bed, an IV and breathing tube attached to her body. Her hair appeared thin and wiry from disease.

The girl turned her head toward him and mustered a faint smile. Above her, a damaged ceiling with wet plaster, meshed in tarred ceiling tile and covered in plastic. A moldy damp smell infused the air and Dan briefly assessed it, but his attention came back to the girl again.

Laura introduced them. "This is my daughter Sara. Sara, this is Mr. Mertz. He's here to help us with our problem."

As much as he tried to pull his eyes away, they remained focused on the girl until Laura motioned him out of the room and into the hall. He followed after glancing one last time at the ceiling.

Shutting the door, Laura waved him away and whispered, "She has JPA (Juvenile Pilomyxoid Astrocytoma). It's a rare form of brain cancer. I just want her to be comfortable. We don't know how long—"

"And her father?"

"He passed away months ago. It's been hard on her. She was the apple of his eye."

His tone sincere, Dan said, "I'm sorry."

"You may have heard about it," she said. "He was a fireman. Dan Jenkinson?"

Dan's face hardened. His mind shifted to a night not long ago: dark, hopeless. Recalling a fireman lost trying to save a child, he swallowed hard as if reliving the tragedy, reviving the emotions. He had covered the story and wished he hadn't.

She continued, "Anyway, if we could just get the roof fixed."

As she rambled on, he felt a sudden urge to ask her a question so he held up a hand to interrupt her then said, "Would you mind … I mean … could I give your daughter something?"

Dan reached into his briefcase and pulled out the napkin he had become so familiar with. He unwrapped the broach and took it out. Laura studied it for a moment with a puzzled expression on her face then took him back to Sara's room. Following her in, he went to Sara's bedside and placed the broach in the young girl's hand.

Folding her fingers around it, he gripped them tight and said, "Here, you can use this more than me."

The young girl asked, "What is it?"

"A gift ... from a friend."

Laura smiled at her daughter. "What do you say?"

Sara gave Dan a forced smile and said, "Thank you."

Nodding once, he assured Sara it was all right then followed Laura back to the kitchen. She delivered the rest of the facts to him and he promised he would pass it on to the right people.

Before he left, he noticed a small memorial of her husband atop a credenza across the room, a picture framed in redwood with an adjacent lit candle. As much as he tried, he could find little reclamation.

Instead, he spoke words that he knew would be of little relief. "I'll get this to our people. They'll be in touch."

Laura Jenkinson thanked him as best she could.

On the drive home, Dan began to feel the unfathomable nature of her struggles.

~ ~ ~

He was glad to be back at Claire's and this time they sat on the front porch with Dan shivering and Claire bundled from neck to feet. She wanted some fresh air, she told him. He didn't have the heart to tell her his recorder didn't work as well in the cold. She rocked methodically, her thin frame centered in the wooden, green rocker, and again she took him back.

"Winter seemed shorter for us that year. Eventually, it melted into spring."

Dan nodded. "So, let me catch up here. You got two miracles ... allegedly, and your dad smiles and dances with your mother. So what happens all winter with this donkey?"

"Not much," she recalled. "In fact, not much was said either. People looked at Eleanor as casually as they had before she'd been healed. And it wasn't any different with Liza."

"How can that be? Didn't anybody wonder?"

"Farmers don't see much of each other all winter, Mr. Mertz. We don't get out much. When we did, it was then we could see a difference. We started to learn who our friends were … and those who weren't. Eventually, even the papers would turn against us. I could see the pain in my father's face as he read the disparaging remarks about his family. I thought maybe another miracle would make people like us again, but God's timing is not ours."

Spring, 1921

Helen hurried her children through the streets toward Logan's Hardware with Will lagging behind again. The cold winter air had departed, replaced by the approaching spring's warm air. As much as Helen was pleasant to those in town, the gestures weren't always returned. Spring planting had begun, so Helen stopped in for a few dry goods, shielding her children from the dirty looks of a few.

As they pushed on and said goodbye to Charlie, someone walked in and asked, "Where is the farm?"

The bedlam hadn't yet ceased and a few stragglers appeared occasionally. Charlie sent them packing, promising they would find nothing there of interest. Helen thanked him in her own way before loading the wagon and heading toward home.

On the farm, John focused on his work. When Helen arrived, she tried to hide the newspaper from him, but the first thing he did after coming in from the fields, he picked it up. His eyes changed when they read the headlines, placed just below the story about the new clock tower.

`Donkey Farce Fuels False Hope.`

Things had changed, though Claire couldn't understand why. She had kept Elijah out of town and he had stayed in his pen. She remembered what her father was told, what the mayor warned.

She knew her father's dreams had changed, though she hadn't a clue how, aware that he'd been writing them down in silence.

That night, John stirred again, and not unlike others, he awoke to a sea of confusion. Though he no longer felt terror, he tried, nonetheless, not to wake Helen. He processed the dreams alone, in the kitchen, present only with his heavy breathing.

He found light from the moon coming through a window. Rummaging through a drawer, he pulled out a dull-tipped pencil and wrote again. Most nights it was easy to remain placid, but tonight, his attention was scattered and the words he wrote less legible, less exact. Perhaps something different was happening.

As he wrote, something attracted his attention toward the barn and a small light emitting from Elijah's stable. He went to another window to get a better look and leaned toward the glass. A peculiar brightness came from the structure, unlike anything he had ever seen before. He wanted to get a better look so he slipped on a coat and headed outside.

Pushing on the fragile screen door, he caught it before the wind blew it shut. He hurried off the porch into a small sliver of moonlight, staring through the shadows at the donkey's corral as he trotted toward it. Drawing nearer, his eyes focused on the open gate. He looked again at the light from the stable and saw a shadow of a man kneeling beside Elijah.

John thought about the shovel hanging in the barn. *It would make a good weapon*, he reasoned, *something to fend him off with*. As he started that way, he felt compelled to stop first to find out who this person is and what he wants. Edging closer, he focused on the figure, still on his knees. Then he held a hand up to shield his eyes from the intensity of the light surrounding the man.

As John entered the open gate, he rubbed his eyes then stared deeper through the light. A stranger, wearing a robe like John had never seen before and a hat he couldn't recognize, silhouetted by the light that enveloped, yet penetrated him. Drawing nearer, John saw more. The man didn't wear a hat, but a crown of branches about his head. John called to the stranger. No answer, no movement. So he called out again.

A sudden explosion of light burst from the stable, sending John to his knees. The light then disappeared in an instant, leaving John kneeling in the darkness. He looked up at the stable, both man and

donkey were gone. Rising from his knees, he scanned the corral and looked inside the stable. He spun around to glance at the gate and noticed it still open. He ran toward it to get a better look in the field.

There was no man and no Elijah.

As the evening wind howled, John turned to see Claire coming out of the house, a concerned expression on her face. Behind her followed Will and Helen. Something woke them. John tried to keep Elijah's absence from them, but they pressed him. Waving them back to the house, he brushed by them as they walked to the barn.

Claire asked, "Where is he?"

John kept silent and she followed him.

Will looked around the grounds and said, "I told you it wouldn't be long. I told you he'd get out again."

Grasping her father's arm, Claire asked, "Where is he, Father?"

Flustered, John went from stall to stall, trying to shake off the confusion. "I don't know. He was here … but now he's gone."

"We're supposed to keep him locked up!"

Helen tried to intercept John.

He moved past her and picked up a shovel then shouted into the wind. "What did you do with him?"

Following him, Helen grasped a shirt sleeve. "John, what is it?"

"There was a man here," John said as he stumbled between the barn and the silos, scanning the countryside. "There was a man here. He must have taken him!"

They watched as John hurried about the grounds, scanning the horizon. Perhaps he hadn't woken up yet from a dream.

Dropping the shovel, John answered his own question. "Town ... he's wandered into town."

Sliding between her parents, Claire asked, "What night is it?" Helen didn't answer so Claire pressed her further. "Mother, what night is it?"

Helen knew what Claire meant—Easter weekend and the night of shadows.

Claire cried, "I know where he is. Father, I know where we'll find him!"

John went to the barn and grabbed a harness then bridled the horses and readied the wagon.

As midnight approached, John said, "Hopefully we'll find him in town before he draws more attention."

Returning to the barn, John picked up a shovel and tossed it into the back of the wagon, his silence invited the others to come along. Together they all grabbed their coats and climbed up inside the wagon behind him.

Heading for town, John drove the horses fast.

Chapter 15
Keeping Watch

The moon hid within a swatch of blue clouds while the wagon kicked up invisible dust in the spring night blackness. As they entered the outskirts of town, Claire tugged on her father's shirt and yelled to him from behind. He followed her directions and yanked the reins toward the long path leading toward St. Mary's. Drawing nearer the church, they could see a few figures outside by the grotto, shadows painted amidst the skyline in the brief shafts of light coming from the nearby buildings. John stopped the horses short of a gravel path then reached back for the shovel.

As Helen glanced at him, John nodded toward one of the figures and said, "That's him … the man I saw. He's got him."

She stood to get a better look and saw a statue kneeling at a rock, the same one they passed every week. Helen guided her hand over John's as Claire and Will jumped down from the wagon. John stood, shovel in hand.

"It's a statue, John," Helen said.

"It's the same guy I saw—"

"John," she said. "It's a statue."

Dropping the shovel, John let it rattle against the hard wood of the wagon floor. Jumping down, he followed his children toward the grotto of Christ praying at Gethsemane and a familiar donkey standing by the statue's side.

Another man stood nearby and as they approached him, they recognized the Roman collar and Father Cunningham.

John's breathing became heavy and his voice emphatic. "Sorry, Father. He got away from us. I'll get him home."

Cunningham smiled. "No. Let him be. He wants to be here … with Him."

John stopped short, moved beside Claire and Will, watching the donkey amidst the silence. A few lights brightened in the distance, and some people peered at them from across the way.

Father Cunningham didn't mind and broke the silence. "I saw him wander up ... from up there."

They all looked up to his bedroom window encased in red brick, located at the top floor of the rectory.

"It's like he wanted to be here. Funny thing is ... do you know what night it is?"

Claire nodded and a few more lights turned on around them. Doors opened across the street and people meandered onto their porches to see what was up.

Cunningham recited words reminding them of their significance. "And going a little farther, he threw himself on the ground and prayed, Father, if it be possible, let this cup pass from me."

The rustling around them grew louder. They saw torches and lanterns accompanied by more people. Their voices pierced the night's silence and John watched them approach as he tugged on the donkey's bridle. When the mob crested the hill near the church, Claire looked up and saw Monsignor Cobalt beside them. Behind him came Mayor Gavel, his green and silver housecoat glistening in the lantern light.

Cunningham turned back to the grotto. "See, the hour is at hand, and the Son of Man is betrayed."

John tried to pull Elijah away, but a sheriff's deputy replaced him then Gavel and Cobalt came out from the crowd.

Cobalt waved people away. "Go back home, people. It's late. This is no concern of yours."

Someone shouted from the back. "We want to see him!"

The monsignor turned toward the Sloans and said, "I see you have not heeded my warning."

Responding to Cobalt, Cunningham interjected. "They were just leaving, Monsignor."

Wiping his brow with a white handkerchief, Gavel scolded, "It's not like you haven't been warned, Sloan."

"He got out. It's that simple," John said.

Gavel added, "And you led him here."

Nodding toward his window, Cunningham replied, "He came here on his own. I watched him."

Moving closer to John, Cobalt grumbled, "Isn't it interesting that the Sloans would know exactly where to find him."

"He's attracted to the statue," John said.

"A warning is a warning. I must consider—"

Cunningham interrupted, "Monsignor, he's causing no harm."

Cobalt sneered at him. "I'll hear nothing from you, Father."

The priest's face went placid, as if he expected nothing less.

As the number of bystanders grew, they began to jostle around as people positioned themselves to get closer, even at that late hour. The chaos grew, and then the rain picked up. A few people slipped in the mud around the grotto, and one of them, Charlie Logan, slid in with the group, his hair disheveled. He wiped his brow and glanced at John then at Claire, a gesture implying support.

Turning to the Sloans, Cobalt asked, "Now do you see what his presence promotes?"

Claire shoved past her mother and embraced Elijah. "He's done nothing to hurt anyone. You people are causing the stir!"

Gavel motioned to the sheriff's deputy to remove the animal. "Sloan, you leave us no other choice."

The deputy made a move toward the donkey again, but John intercepted him and took hold of the bridle and said, "We're leaving with him now, Mayor."

He tugged on it, but Elijah wouldn't move and started braying and bucking. "I'm afraid that won't be possible right now, Sheriff."

The sheriff shoved John's hand away and pulled on the bridle as Claire held onto her pet, tears forming in her eyes.

"We're taking him with us," Cobalt announced.

John exclaimed, "The hell you are!"

Bunching a fist, John reared back and slugged the deputy in the jaw, sending him to the mud.

Charlie emerged, holding him back. "Mayor, you have no right to do that."

"Logan, I suggest you stay out of this. It's only until—"

"Only until we can prove it," Cunningham blurted. He turned toward John, and lowered his voice, his tone urgent, "It's only for a time … until we can verify. I'll work this out, John. Let me work this out."

Claire clung to the donkey's shoulders, her tears mixing with the spring rain. The deputy rose, wiped off his clothes and nodded at John, as if to say that John owed him one. Then he peeled Claire's hands away from the bridle, to the sounds of steady, livid brays.

Despite the rain, the crowd remained as Cobalt tried to calm them. "Everything is fine, my friends. Go home. This is no place to gather on this holy night."

Gavel looked down at Claire and said, "Claire, this is only until we have time to investigate."

Cutting in, Cobalt said, "Until I can have time to review this fully ... and make no mistake, Mr. Sloan. I will review it fully."

Cunningham tried to appeal to Cobalt, "Monsignor. I think if we look at this—"

Cobalt cut in again and ordered, "Deputy, take the animal!"

As the deputy dragged away the unwilling animal, Will reached down and grabbed a handful of mud. He reared back and tossed it at the mayor, striking him about his face and neck. Helen pulled her son back as Gavel took out another handkerchief and wiped the mud off his face.

The mayor glared at Helen and sneered, "I see the apple doesn't fall far from the tree."

Shoving past her brother, Claire fell into her mother's arms and sobbed, "God gave him to us, Mother. They can't take him! God gave him to us!"

Helen calmed her daughter as best she could, watching the donkey as he disappeared into the darkness. "It's only for a time, Claire. It'll be all right."

While the crowd began to dissipate, Charlie Logan slapped John about the shoulders, trying to calm him.

Father Cunningham looked squarely at John and nodded once, and John then knew the young priest would do what he could. "An investigation," the priest told him, "one that would come to the answers for which all had been searching."

Standing in the rain adjacent to the grotto, John watched as his family walked toward the wagon, leaving him alone with the statue. He glanced at it, and the 'Man of Sorrows' appeared to gaze back at him. It was as if John wanted to say something, but knew there

would be no answer. Instead, he watched the rain coat the marble. A single raindrop fell upon the statue's head and streamed down across the crown of thorns then into His eye and across His face, a defeated tear caressing a white, stone cheek.

John stayed long enough to watch Christ weep then nodded once and tipped his hat in a way that told Christ he understood. Turning toward his family at the end of the path, he felt the urge to embrace his own weeping daughter. Instead, he shot her a glance that told her it would be all right. He climbed aboard and drove the horses home.

Present

Claire sat forward, her voice strong. "We knew the investigation would be lengthy. And we knew the odds were stacked against us."

Dan didn't understand. "How can someone … I mean, how can they just take property like that?"

"People can fool themselves, Mr. Mertz, when authorities feel threatened."

He shook his head.

She recalled, "Easter came and went for us … without Elijah. Father Cunningham assured us he was fine, though he never divulged his location. Something told us that even he was kept out of the loop."

Dan's eyes intensified. He looked past her.

"I prayed for Elijah every day," she said. "Somehow I trusted I would see him again … especially after I learned the hearings would be starting soon."

"Court hearings?"

"You could say that. More like town hall meetings … with a bit more force. You see, we learned of another possible healing. It came to light about the time they took him. Mother was suspicious when she heard who it was. Constance Brewer, Mildred's niece. She'd been on the farm that day."

Dan recalled it.

"Father Cunningham tried to assure us this was anything but a witch-hunt. Somehow, it didn't seem that way. Judge Scanlan was chosen to preside over the hearings. He was a local judge. Everyone knew him and trusted him. He agreed to rule on the civil complaints

filed with the mayor's office. However, when it came to miraculous events surrounding the donkey … well, that was a different story."

Spring, 1921

Helen shuffled Will and Claire past the seated Brewer family outside the town hall and ignoring Mildred, Helen pretended to be more occupied with Claire's hair than she was. Outside the large, oak doors leading to the meeting room, Claire smiled and embraced her dearest friends, first Lucie then Liza. She asked Liza if she was ready to testify and the young girl assured her she was.

Judge Scanlan sat firmly behind a long, semi-circular table, a hard wooden gavel at his side. In the front row sat both priests. Beside Cobalt sat the mayor, fussing and talking loudly.

The benches squeaked as they sat. Helen shushed the children as the judge cleared his throat, preparing to begin. She looked around once more to find John, but knew he wouldn't be there because of plowing season.

With a solemn voice, Judge Scanlan began, "Gentlemen. Ladies. If you are wondering about my opinion in regards to this matter, it is only my intent to maintain the civility with which these hearings should be conducted."

Monsignor Cobalt looked on as Father Cunningham nodded, a defense prepared in the files atop the bench beside him.

"In fact," continued Scanlan, "I will not rule on the validity of the miracles. That, Monsignor, will be your job. As I see it, my position is solely to facilitate these hearings. All else are matters of faith. It shall be up to you to bring these before your bishop should you see fit."

Cobalt interjected, "I am responsible for quashing any false claims that might cause scandal within—"

Cunningham blurted, "I'm sorry, but isn't your job to come to the truth?"

Scanlan held up a hand. "Gentlemen … Fathers. I am no man of God, nor will I stand in God's way. Conduct your investigations. Hold your testimonies before me, but know this … my authority rests solely with the civil aspects of the complaints … nothing more.

Now, perhaps you should come to an agreement as to how I am to rule on this. Upon what criteria shall my decision be rendered?"

After a long silence, Cobalt leaned to Gavel and whispered as Claire watched. Then the accusers came out of their huddle.

Cobalt stood and said, "Three miracles ... three healings ... proven and certain. It's one of the ways we validate sainthood. I propose we use the same criteria here to merit their legitimacy."

Scanlan sat back and answered, "Agreed. Fine then, gentlemen, three healings it shall be." The judge looked directly at Helen and said, "Mrs. Sloan, I see you are with us today. Do you understand the need for this hearing?"

Helen shuddered as she braced herself against the bench in front of her, her voice loud and clear. "I do not."

The judge asked, "Mrs. Sloan, do you feel that these hearings are out of line?"

She nodded.

"And your husband ... Mr. Sloan?"

"He's in the fields ... he has work to do."

His voice projecting off the hard, wooden walls, Gavel said, "Judge, I find it interesting that Sloan wouldn't be here. After all, he's the one who made these claims."

Cunningham interrupted. "You're out of line, Mayor. You've taken property from a man—"

Cobalt sprung from his seat. "He is spreading claims that are dangerous to the people in this district!"

Taking off his glasses, Scanlan rubbed the bridge of his nose and said, "Gentlemen. Gentlemen. Shall I lose order this soon? Three miracles ... that is what you're calling for. Three."

"Documented," Cobalt said. "Unequivocal healings."

Both priests agreed, as did Gavel.

Scanlan confirmed, "Fine, then gentlemen, three healings it shall be. Take your time. Review your records. We will begin testimony next week."

Present

"And so it began," Claire recalled. "It seemed like forever for me ... largely because we were kept in the dark. Still, I carried a

strange peace about it. And I knew it wouldn't be long until I saw him again."

Dan asked, "How long?"

"Weeks, months, I didn't know." She shifted in her seat, silent in thought. "They called over thirty witnesses. The ones they were most difficult on were the ones who supported our beliefs ... my beliefs. Among the first was Mr. Washington."

"Wilson?"

She nodded. "His word was somehow diminished in the eyes of some ... the rains about his farm on that night. No one wished to ponder them ... it would have meant they had to ponder who started the fire in the first place."

Dan shook his head and rubbed his eyes.

"Soon, it was my friend Liza's turn to testify, but she scarcely remembered a thing."

Chapter 16
A Familiar Trial

Spring, 1921

Liza's frail, young frame, surrounded by the arms of a brown, leather chair, sat beside a long, curved table. Leaning forward, she spoke loud enough so her small voice reverberated off the hollow walls. Father Cunningham stood before her, his voice comforting to the ten-year-old child. He winked at Liza once or twice and she broke a slight smile, but only for him.

She said, "I don't remember much after I got sick."

Cunningham asked, "What *is* the last thing you do remember?"

While thinking about her answer, she looked at Monsignor Cobalt, but when she caught his glare, she looked away.

"Doctor Kipling," she replied. "I think I recall him being in my room … tending to me. I remember the coldness of his stethoscope. After that, I fell asleep."

"Thank you, Liza. I'm finished for now."

Hoping for more, Cunningham sighed then nodded at her, glared at his opposition and sat down.

Monsignor Cobalt stood, and with a false smile and caustic tone, he asked, "So, you don't remember being sick?"

Lowering her head down, Liza shrugged her shoulders.

The judge reminded her. "You must answer, Liza."

"I don't know … maybe."

Cobalt nodded then began pacing the floor. "Who told you that you were ill?"

She glanced at her parents. "They did."

"I see. Are they doctors?"

Rising, Cunningham appealed, "Judge, is this really necessary?"

The judge asked, "Monsignor, where are you going with this?"

"I'm trying to establish a pattern of imagination and unfounded information." The monsignor paused then rephrased the question. "Let me ask this. You don't recall being sick enough to die, and

your parents were the ones who told you that you were ill. How is it you came to the conclusion that you were raised from the dead?"

Liza nodded toward Claire. "She told me. They told me."

He looked to the Sloans, "I have nothing further."

Cobalt took his seat beside Gavel and the judge excused Liza. She scampered down to find her family.

The monsignor called on Doctor David Lewis from the Detroit Diocese. They fired nominal and superfluous questions at him then allowed Doctor Lewis a shot at Doctor Kipling, the one who had pronounced Liza's death. Kipling sat in the witness chair beside Judge Scanlan with his legs crossed and dressed in a dark blue suit. As Doctor Lewis paced with a medical book in his hand in front of Kipling, he asked about the diagnosis.

"I had misdiagnosed her weeks before," Kipling answered.

Lewis asked, "How did you diagnose her?"

"I was certain it was a form of cholera. I treated her accordingly. Eventually, she suffered from pulmonary hemorrhages and then she was gone."

"You're certain of this?"

"Yes, I'm certain of it."

"Well, you misdiagnosed once. Who's to say—"

Kipling exclaimed, "I know how to tell if someone's dead!"

"Nothing further," said Lewis then he whispered something to Cobalt, nodded at the judge and took a seat.

The afternoon melted into dinnertime. Cobalt called a dozen other people to the stand, all of whom were at the farm that day and none of whom experienced a thing other than an empty stomach and excessive thirst.

Then Cobalt called Eleanor Russell. The town knew her as the crippled one—the one who wore braces on her polio-stricken legs for years—but she had none on as she strolled up the center aisle. All heads turned to watch, scanning her body. Yet they maintained a silence that did little to help the Sloans's cause.

She sat as Doctor Lewis conducted the first line of questioning. Promptly, he asked her about her diagnosis. Her answers were less than medical—generic and common—she knew only what she had been told. She had been diagnosed with poliomyelitis years before.

The prognosis hadn't changed, but for worsening. Her answers sounded little more than hearsay until Lewis brought her attention to the day on the farm.

"I don't know what healed me. I just know it happened after I left him … directly after I left him."

Lewis paced the floor in front of her. "Isn't it true, Mrs. Russell … isn't it true that you were already getting better?"

Alarmed by his directness, she responded, "I had been getting treated with a convalescent serum. It was helping, but I don't know how much it helped."

"So it was the medicine that healed you?"

"No. I don't know. I just know—"

Lewis interrupted, "The medicine was helping you."

Cunningham rose and stated, "Let her finish, Doctor."

Lewis swung around to look at the young priest. Retreating a bit, he smirked and turned again toward Eleanor.

She cleared her throat and answered, "I just know … I know that I couldn't walk when I got to the farm. And I could when I left."

As mumbles erupted from the onlookers, Cobalt whispered loud enough for all to hear. "Preposterous."

Doctor Lewis spun around again and faced the judge. "Your Honor, her claims are simply unbelievable. We have no way of knowing what her original diagnosis was … and the use of therapeutic serums have been known to—"

Interrupting, Cunningham said, "I've got her records here."

The judge called Cunningham forward and looked at the bundle of paperwork then nodded and mumbled, "There's more within these than I can possibly read in the time remaining here today. Therefore, I'm calling a recess to these proceedings until I've had sufficient time to study these records."

~ ~ ~

The next day, Claire sat between her mother and Will while Becky Brewer conveniently planted herself across from them. As the court prepared for the hearing to reconvene, Claire looked at Becky then Mildred. As much as Claire wanted to trust them, her expression spoke otherwise.

Constance, Becky's cousin, sat nearby and appeared nervous as she sat on her hands, rocking in a way far too young for her fifteen years of maturity. Her healing claims seemed wary, and Claire scarcely remembered her being at the farm that day. Because of their past uncertain relations, Claire had far too many questions.

Judge Scanlan called Constance to the stand and swore her in. Both Cunningham and Monsignor Cobalt questioned her then Doctor Lewis spoke to her and asked her about her past.

"I was crippled," she said, "stricken with polio at a young age."

Lewis circled her, his black, dress shoes moving across the floor like a shark. "And your claim is that you were healed?"

She nodded.

"How long after you left the farm?"

"Immediately."

The crowd stirred and Helen's expression changed when he failed to ask anything further, appearing to already know something.

Judge Scanlan called a short recess then spoke to both priests. A moment later, the double doors in back opened up and in walked an older man, balding with gray hair, his face wore a persistent frown as he drew near the front. Visibly irritated at the prospect of being there, he fumbled with his cap as he stepped toward the judge and refused to place his hand over the Bible to be sworn in.

Claire recognized him immediately—Saul Lenter, the donkey's former owner.

Lenter sat in the witness chair, fussing. Then Cobalt stood, approached him and began pacing the floor.

Cobalt asked, "How long had you owned the animal?"

"Almost a year. Wish I'd gotten rid of him sooner."

"And why is that, Mr. Lenter?"

Agitated, he answered, "I done told you this story three times."

Monsignor Cobalt commanded, "You *will* answer the question, Mr. Lenter. This hearing has already wasted enough of my time." When Lenter frowned, the monsignor rephrased the question. "Why were you so eager to get rid of him?"

His answer guarded, Lenter proclaimed, "He was cursed. He was nothin' but trouble."

"Cursed ... I see." Cobalt turned toward the Sloan family and continued with a sarcastic tone. "So, this donkey ... this agent of God was cursed. Tell me, Mr. Lenter, of what religious persuasion are you?"

"My father was Jewish ... my mother Protestant. I have none."

Cunningham stood and Scanlan, acknowledging his objection, asked, "Where are you going with this, Monsignor?"

Dismissing the inquiry, Cobalt continued. "So this donkey ... this miraculous animal falls into the hands of an agnostic son of a Jew and a Protestant. I think I've heard enough."

Cobalt's silence meshed with the crowd's stirring as he took his seat again.

Before beginning to question Lenter, Cunningham paused, his chin resting upon fingers as he pondered his line of questioning then asked, "Do you recall the name of the man who gave him to you?"

"How the hell am I supposed to remember that?"

"Just answer the question, sir."

"No. John Sloan took the belongings with him. Why don't you ask him?"

"Anything else you can tell me about him?"

"Yeah," Lenter said. "I should've trusted my gut when the guy started tellin' me about him. He couldn't dump him fast enough."

"What kind of stuff did he tell you?"

"That he was trouble ... that he'd seen some trouble ... some violence that stayed with him."

"Violence? What kind of violence?"

Lenter's patience began wearing thin. "I don't know. Listen, the animal's cursed, I tell ya. Now, I'm not takin' him back. I done my civic duty. Am I finished?"

Father Cunningham nodded. Lenter rose, addressing no one, he returned the cap to his head and marched down the aisle then out the double doors.

Midday passed through the hearings' recess before everyone sat in silence again, waiting for Scanlan to take the bench. Eventually, he called the next witness, a polished, distinguished looking man dressed in a gray suit. With a briefcase in his hand, he stepped to the front of the room.

Claire read the title etched on the side of his case: *Doctor Dewey James, Michigan State College, Department of Archeology.*

Doctor James took his place beside the judge in the witness chair and the questioning began. Eventually, the priest produced a leather pouch and a few pieces of parchment paper for Dewey to mull over.

After examining them for a moment, Doctor James, said, "They were given to me by Father Cunningham some time ago. I was told he got them from a Mr. Sloan."

Judge Scanlan asked, "Am I to believe these belonged to the former owner?"

"I have no direct knowledge of that," Doctor James answered. "The satchel has a name etched into it. The few parchments appear to be records of something. They're difficult to read. Part of it is written in Greek and some in Aramaic."

"What do they say?"

"They talk about healings, as far as I can tell. And they claim to date back a while."

The judge asked, "Date back to when, Doctor James?"

"The first century."

As Cobalt leaned toward Gavel and whispered something, the crowd stirred.

Continuing, Doctor James said, "One of the entries claims to have been made by a first century historian ... somebody named Flavius Josephus."

Scanlan asked, "Flavius Josephus?"

Pulling out the leather satchel and unfolding it, Doctor James, said, "The satchel has a name etched on it ... *Rufus* of Shahhat. Shahhat is a city located in Libya. That's about all I can tell you."

Father Cunningham spoke from his seat. "Is it? Is it really ... all you can tell us?"

Doctor James shrugged.

Cunningham asked, "What was the name of that city in the first century, Doctor?"

"Cyrene."

"And how might that city be related to this case?"

"If you're referring to the name Rufus etched on the satchel, I think it's a stretch."

Standing up, Cunningham asked, "What notable figure lived in that city during the first century, Doctor?"

Doctor James paused then said, "There is a Rufus of Cyrene mentioned in the Bible. It's in Mark's gospel."

"And?"

Clearing his throat, Doctor James continued, "He was the son of Simon, the Cyrenean pressed into service during the Crucifixion."

The monsignor erupted, "I object to this nonsense."

Father Cunningham said, "It would have been impossible for—"

Cutting the priest off, Cobalt roared, "You *cannot* expect me to believe that this animal is anything other than a mining donkey!"

Scanlan pounded the gavel. "Gentlemen. Gentlemen. Please."

The two men quieted and returned to their seats. Scanlan then offered Cobalt a chance to cross-examine. After a long attentive pause, he embraced the opportunity. Stepping up to Doctor James, Cobalt took the parchments and read them in silence.

Finished, he turned and asked, "These names that appear on this paper ... were these early century Christians?"

Doctor James answered, "I don't know. I can't tell."

Cobalt answered sarcastically, "Oh, I see. Well, let me read them for you ... One Fifty-Four, Anno Domini, Emmaus, owned by Miriam from the family of Manaheh, a Jew ... Three Twenty-Six AD, Corinth, owned by Philip of the family of Annias, a polytheist. Here's the best one ... Seven-Thirteen AD Persia, owned by Waleed, the family of Hashim, a Muslim."

Waiting in silence, Doctor James stared at Scanlan who asked, "Doctor, can you, with certainty, tell us that these documents can be dated back to first century Judea? Can you, without doubt, tell us whether you believe this satchel and papers are legitimate?"

After scanning the room, Doctor James looked at the papers in Cobalt's hands. "From what I can tell, these parchments date back one hundred years ... one fifty at the most ... that's it. There is no way this paper could have stood the test of time. The paper has a consistency with something found in Egypt, but I have no evidence that tells me they are legitimate. In fact, I think they're fabricated."

"And the satchel?"

"Could have been branded by anyone."

The gathering grumbled and a few people stood to leave.

"I have nothing further," Cobalt said then returned to his seat beside the mayor.

Present

Claire said, "When it was my time to testify, the monsignor spoke to me and I felt like a scolded child."

Dan's frown indicated his disapproval of Cobalt.

"He tried to blame my father for filling my head with fantasies. He said our claims were a trick of the devil."

Spring, 1921

Monsignor Cobalt stood in front of Claire, her pink and white sundress draped across her lap. Though Cobalt began with timid questions, his tone became more fierce with each question and on occasion, Claire would glance at her mother for an answer, but mostly, she drew the answers from within.

"So, Claire Sloan, you claim to have been present during many strange events surrounding this animal … is that right?"

"Yes."

"May I remind you, young lady, you are under oath, and a lie would constitute a mortal sin."

Cunningham stirred in his seat and Helen breathed deeply from the back of the room.

Continuing, Cobalt said, "So, first the silos were filled then the rains came to the Washington farm, then—"

"No," Claire interrupted. "First, he made it rain … then he filled the silos."

"I see. So *he* made it rain, then *he* filled the silos. Did *he* turn water into wine, too?"

A few snickers spilled from the seats and Cunningham sprung from his chair. "Judge, I object to this treatment."

The monsignor rebutted, "Your Honor, it is my intent to—"

"His demeanor is condescending, and—"

"I will not have my character challenged by the likes of you!"

Cunningham sneered at Cobalt as the room quieted, "Perhaps your problem is your unwillingness to challenge it yourself."

Scanlan pounded the gavel. "Gentlemen, please. If you expect me to keep order in these proceedings you must do the same."

All fell silent until the double door sounded from the back. A few heads turned to see who came in. John Sloan stood in the doorway long enough to find his family then went to sit beside them.

Cobalt looked at him then returned his attention to the judge. "Again ... the claims ... these fantasies about miraculous rains and silos being filled. They are conveniently suspicious and should not be considered as legitimate."

Father Cunningham asked, "Are these your closing arguments, Monsignor?"

"These have been my arguments all along, Father. There has been nothing here that has been of a miraculous nature. And I don't understand why they have not been dismissed thus far."

"Are you finished yet?"

"We have heard three, weak accounts of possible healings—"

"I know the first two to be legitimate. I know nothing of Mildred Brewer's claim."

Scanlan appeared fatigued. "Three healings, gentlemen. Three documented healings. That was my understanding."

Both priests nodded and Cobalt fell silent. Scanlan removed his glasses, rubbed his eyes then replaced them. He smiled at Claire and winked at her. "Monsignor, do you have any further questions for this young lady?"

Cobalt paused a moment, nodded once at the judge then stepped uncomfortably close to Claire and said, "Just one more. Answer me this, young lady ... do you believe you have witnessed legitimate healings associated with this animal?" He pointed an accusing finger at her. "Do you, Claire Sloan, actually expect us to believe that this animal ... this donkey ... is the same donkey that was ridden by Jesus Christ?"

A deafening silence filled the room until she spoke.

"Yes."

The gathering stirred as a few more rose from their seats.

Someone said, "These hearings are a farce," then walked out.

Helen studied the room with her husband beside her. She felt enveloped in the sea of doubt.

A few people rose at the back with paper claims in hand and one man said, "He caused us five hundred dollars worth of damage."

Another cried, "A thousand to me."

After quieting the crowd, Judge Scanlan promised, "I will hear all your complaints after these proceedings."

The judge called Mayor Gavel to the stand next where he went into a diatribe about his tower. "It was built to honor the fallen of the Great War and it cost three hundred dollars more because of the donkey's mishap." The gathering stirred as Gavel paused then he raised his voice and continued. "That day, I was told he got away from Claire Sloan. Somethin' must've spooked him. The next thing I know, he ran across the wet cement and toppled over one of the walls. Cost at least three hundred to fix, maybe five."

He paused to peer over the top of people's heads at the Sloans seated in back. "I got nothing against the Sloans, although I never understood why John wouldn't contribute to this tower, being the war hero he is. I know he was a Polar Bear ... and, well, they didn't do much. But it ain't his fault. It's just ... you throw in all these claims of miracles, and this is what happens." He held up a binder with civil complaints. "And it ain't like they haven't been warned. I just think, Judge, it's prudent to keep these claims in mind."

Scanlan thought about Gavel's words for a moment then asked the mayor to take his seat with the rest. As the judge spoke, a door swung open behind him and a short, stocky court reporter entered, making his way to the judge.

The reporter whispered something in the judge's ear, rousing the spectators until the judge quieted them and announced, "This court is in recess for now. Monsignor, Father ... I would like to see you in my chambers."

Rising from their seats, the two men glanced at each other then disappeared with the judge into a meeting room behind the wall.

After following Judge Scanlan into an office, he invited the priests to sit. Taking his own seat behind a solid, wooden desk, he leaned back in his leather chair and removed his glasses.

"Why I let you talk me into doing this, I will never know."

Both priests remained silent. Scanlan quietly read a note handed to him by the court reporter then he glanced up at them, as if waiting for a punch line. "It seems we have a problem. I've just learned that one of the healings … is a fake."

Both priests sat up.

"It appears as though Mildred Brewer's niece Constance was never ill and it seems as though her illness was fabricated for more reasons than I care to speculate."

Father Cunningham said, "What reasons do you need? She's slandered herself."

"There is no force behind these testimonies, Father. This is not an official court of law. I couldn't find her liable if I wanted to, but this doesn't mean I disbelieve the first two claims. There is simply too much evidence to ignore. Now then … we agreed … you agreed … that three genuine healings are my criteria. If you have more to say before I render my judgment—"

Cunningham interrupted, "What about closing arguments?"

Cobalt disagreed. "If we haven't met the criteria, why should we continue to—"

Interrupting the monsignor, Cunningham asked, "Don't we have a chance to close this out properly?"

Scanlan thought about it while rubbing his chin. "Fine," he said. "Closing arguments will be heard, but understand this … they will be brief, and respectful. Do you understand, Monsignor?"

His answer seemed forced as Cobalt sneered, "Yes."

Both priests rose then left the judge alone to his thoughts.

Chapter 17
A Final Plea

Present

Claire spoke softly, "Monsignor's closing arguments were short and to the point. The third miracle had been fabricated … the third healing was a lie. And though the first two seemed legitimate, their details were yet in question."

Dan shook his head. "People wouldn't know a miracle if it bit them in the ass."

Claire smiled, "Perhaps, but the questions ran deeper than the alleged healings. Now, the questions about who owned Elijah would surface. To us, it didn't matter much, but to Monsignor Cobalt—"

1921

The announcement of the fabricated miracle sent shocks to those who had watched and waited for the truth. Only a few remained, hoping and waiting for more.

Helen promised, "Claire, it isn't over yet. There is still hope."

When Claire looked at her father seated beside them, she didn't see such optimism.

The monsignor paced the floor and began his closing arguments as his voice thundered while the Sloans and their supporters looked on. "You have heard the testimony before you. Prior to these hearings, we established the criteria by which these matters would be judged … upon which these claims would be passed on to Bishop Gallagher. Three miracles … three healings. It appears as though our criteria have not been met."

Claire clung to her mother's arm, uncertain of the outcome.

"We are also aware of the civil complaints this animal has elicited, at great trouble to the city."

The mayor nodded and beamed a smile.

Cobalt pointed to the records beside Cunningham. "According to these alleged documents, the animal was owned by the agnostic son of a Jew … worse yet, polytheists and Muslims."

Cunningham shook his head, his chin buried in a hand.

"Finally, and much to my consternation, there are claims by some that this animal … this donkey … is the same donkey that was ridden by Jesus Christ during his triumphant entry into Jerusalem. I ask you … shall I, as the spiritual authority of this district, allow you to become enthralled in the stories of a misguided family?" He stretched out his hand and pointed toward a door at the far side of the room. "Let us *not* revel in this fantasy a moment longer."

The door swung open. Through it walked a man holding a rope stretching to a dirty bridle and an unkempt, mud laden Elijah. He appeared weak, his mane dirty and his hooves covered with dirt.

Claire sprung from her seat. "Elijah!"

Pointing toward the animal, Cobalt stretched out his palm and said, "Ladies and gentlemen, I give you … Jesus' donkey!"

Laughter erupted from the room as they saw the stained donkey, saddle and broach caked with dirt, a slight scar on one of his legs.

"Now, I ask you," he continued, "would this mangy animal have been the ass that carried the Anointed One? Would God allow the same donkey that carried the Redeemer to fall into the hands of polytheists or Muslims … or Jews? No, I believe not, Your Honor. My recommendation is the removal of this animal from the county and the return of life to normal in this town. I will await your thoughtful response."

Some in the crowd began murmuring, a reflection from others as monsignor returned to his seat while the deputy led Elijah out.

Cunningham fussed with some papers at his table then rose and paced the floor. He shut his eyes for a moment, as if to pray, forging through the tension. Clearing his throat, he scanned the room and focused solely, if but for an instant, on the young girl seated in the back of the room.

He saw Claire smile back at him so he turned to face the judge and said in a loud and clear voice, "Judge Scanlan. Ladies and Gentlemen, I too am a man of God. I have difficulty understanding why someone would feel the need to lie about a healing … unless, of course, they were put up to it by someone else." His eyes locked

with Mildred's and she dropped hers to the floor. "I can likely say little to sway you that somehow this donkey … this inadequate animal, and the Sloans have been touched by God. Perhaps I can do best to remind you of Christ's earthly plight … a man of sorrows, acquainted with grief … should we expect the plight of his steward to be any different? Meager and unassuming were His ways. No less so with this animal."

Scanlan leaned forward, intent on listening.

Cunningham continued, "Have we become so wise that we can surmise all God's forms? We set out on these hearings to establish criteria … three unequivocal healings ... that is true. While it appears that we have not met our end, perhaps we should consider how we define miracles. We are told in the Gospels that God will not send signs to faithless generations. Nor are His ways ours. Monsignor sees no third healing. That may be so. Yet I see a family who has found hope."

Helen pulled Claire to her and there she found the solace of her mother's shoulder.

The priest went on. "Monsignor sees division. I ask you … is it any different than the division wrought by Christ? In fact this animal has only been divisive to those who have something to lose. I propose his presence has been a blessing to all else."

Wilson nodded and placed a hand on Charlie Logan's shoulder as Lucie and Liza looked on.

"As for the alleged former owners, Monsignor is distressed over the fact they were purportedly polytheists, Muslims, Jews … I ask … who do we think we are? Is God not allowed to bless those whom He wishes? Is He not the God of all? Or have we become so fettered with the ideologies of the Pharisees that we refuse to see?

"I don't know why we have not met our last miracle," he continued. "Perhaps God's timing is not ours. I can say only this … for the Sloans, hope has returned. A man can last forty days without food, three days without water, about eight minutes without air … but only one second without hope. Fear is but the parent of cruelty, and all hope surmounts despair. Ask this town if they've learned what that means, Your Honor. Ask John Sloan if he's learned, because of this donkey. Then you can tell me if he came from God."

Cunningham went behind his desk again and Scanlan promised he would deliberate in good faith then ordered a recess.

His answer wouldn't come quickly, but Claire hoped it would be just. Filing out of the hall, she locked arms with Lucie and Liza as they walked step by step together toward a row of wagons parked around the street. Time would pass slowly for her until she knew more, but living on a farm, she was used to that.

Present

Claire said, "As eloquent a message as Father Cunningham's was, it did little to sway the judge's opinion. And once again, we were faced with a decision that was out of our hands."

Dan looked dismayed.

"We didn't bother reconvening when Judge Scanlan called us to do so," she said. "Instead, we simply waited for the letter to come to us. It was delivered by none other than Father Cunningham. My mother insisted that Monsignor Cobalt should have been the one to deliver it, but he was too yellow."

Dan asked, "So … what did it say?"

1921

The sun set, painting the rolling landscape a bright orange, and the outline of the hills danced in the distance. John rested his elbows against the wood of a split rail fence. Cunningham shook his hand before handing him the letter.

Tilting the paper toward the reflecting sun, John read the words aloud. "After much testimony and deliberation, and pursuant to verbal contract established by all parties, I am faced with a decision that must weigh the needs of the many, most substantially the needs of our town. After careful scrutiny about each reported healing and the disclosure of one such report as false, it is apparent to me that the criteria set forth by all parties have not been met."

John glanced up from the paper and saw Father Cunningham turn toward the sun then John continued reading. "While I am inclined to embrace the validity of the first two healings, I am dissuaded from rendering a favorable judgment that might elevate

these events to further investigation by His Excellency, Bishop Gallagher. Of course, in such matters, it shall be up to the spiritual authority of the parish to forward such inquiries, and to my knowledge, no such intentions have been expressed.

"My deliberations have been tiring. They are leavened with concern for the Sloan family as contributing members of our community. Notwithstanding, due to concern over civil complaints levied by citizens and disorder the animal's presence has elicited, I am ordering the removal of the donkey from this district, indeed this county, within a time period of two weeks. The animal may return to the Sloan farm until such time arrangements can be made for his transfer out of Clinton County. After such time, should the Sloans fail to find a home, a civil petition will be filed to have the donkey removed immediately to an undisclosed location."

John looked up and saw Claire, Lucie and Liza in the distance leading the donkey toward the barn. Will ran after them.

The spring breeze folded the papers and forced John to look away for an instant. He felt the urge to read on but didn't have the heart so he folded the letter neatly and placed it in a pocket. The wind picked up, blowing his thin, brown hair aside from his face as he peered out again at the horizon.

Cunningham tried to find the right words. "I'm sorry, John."

"Don't be," he answered. "You did what you could."

"How's Claire?"

Turning toward the corral, John saw her sitting with her friends and said, "Better than I thought. Helen's sister agreed to take him. She can visit him anytime she likes. They live the next county over."

"That's good," answered Cunningham. "You know, John, you mustn't let this discourage you. The church has to look at these things with a discerning eye."

In his own way, John understood.

"They're doing the same thing with a young girl in Portugal."

"Are they?" Then after a pause, John added, "There's gonna be another war."

"You think so?"

"Men don't change much. I wish I could say they did."

"*You* did."

"I didn't have a choice. He made me."

John's eyes moved to Elijah's pen again then to the earth below, as if he wanted to say something else. Cunningham waited through the silence.

Looking at Cunningham, John confessed, "I used to dream of the war ... of all its carnage. Then the dreams changed after he came. Faceless men speaking to each other in a language I didn't understand. You remember those dreams I told you about? The ones I could make no sense of."

Cunningham nodded.

"The last one was different. The characters remained faceless. But this time, I understood everything ... every word they said." He shook his head and went on. "There's a man kneeling in the dust ... another man standing above him, holding a whip. The man with the whip asks a question. 'Will you die for them?' And the other man raises his head, covered in thorns, and answers the question, 'I will.'

"I had the sense that Elijah was there ... that I saw what he saw ... that I understood what he understood ... a reluctant witness to the scourging. It was as if I saw it all through his eyes. Stupid animal. I don't know what the hell to make of it."

The priest answered, "Maybe there's nothing to make of it ... except to realize we share in His suffering ... or maybe ... He shares in ours. One thing's for sure, though ... you're right about human nature. It hasn't changed in two thousand years." Shaking his head, Cunningham pulled out a pocket watch and said, "Well, I have to get to my breviary before supper."

John held out a hand. "Much obliged for your help, Father."

Taking John's hand, Cunningham smiled.

As John watched the priest go toward his black Ford parked in the driveway, a question stirred within him and the compulsion to ask it became too great. "Father?"

Father Cunningham stopped and turned around.

Swallowing hard, John then found the courage to ask, "Do you think He's real?"

Cunningham asked, "Who?"

John's eyes rose to the heavens. "Him."

Following John's gaze, Cunningham smiled and replied, "I think you know the answer to that question, John."

John thought, *Perhaps I do.*

As Cunningham disappeared toward the driveway, John's eyes never left him. With darkness coming on and storms brewing in the distance, John needed to batten down the shutters for the night.

Present

Claire looked tired. Dan surmised her story was near completion, so he interrupted less, listened more.

She continued at a whisper, "My father promised I could visit Elijah as often as I liked. Uncle Ken and Aunt Sue were scheduled to take him within the week, but first we had the storms to contend with. A line of twisters had taken root in northern Indiana. And they were headed toward town."

Dan watched her as if to grasp every word.

"When the night was over, a dozen buildings were reduced to rubble. One of those buildings was Mayor Gavel's beloved clock tower. Nothing was left of it … nothing. It had been leveled. And do you know what he was storing inside that tower?"

Dan hadn't a clue.

She smiled. "Two thousand pounds of oatmeal. He built a tower to store oatmeal. The irony was great. The very thing my father labored to protect during the war was left defenseless by the winds."

Pausing, Dan cleared his throat. "And your farm? Elijah?"

"Both were fine. The tornados passed just north of us. I would have a few days to spend with Elijah before my uncle arrived to take him and it made me feel better to know he'd be in the next county. But then, a funny thing happened … a family broke down."

"A family?"

"They had been displaced by the storms. The man said they were from Lansing. He hadn't been able to find any work so, they were headed to Ohio. He said he was a good tool man. When I saw his children, they looked hungry."

Chapter 18
Goodbye Elijah

1921

Claire carried two buckets of milk in from the barn. Glancing toward the county road, she saw the young family stranded beside their car and a wagon filled with meager belongings. She didn't mind interrupting Wilson and her father working to replace a gear on the tractor.

It wasn't long before the two men stood beside the car, assessing the damage and helping the strangers. Wilson had learned the trade on his own and John knew machinery. They towed the car back to the farm with one of the work horses and John assembled a new joint to fix the problem—a broken axle.

Watching as her father and Wilson finished, Claire tried not to stare too long at the three indigent children, their ages, nine, seven and three. They wore shoes with soles apart at the seams and well-sewn trousers braced by slight suspenders.

John closed the hood. "Should be all set now. Everything else looks good … just a couple flat tires. I can probably get to them tomorrow. You're welcome to bed down for the night in the barn … plenty of room for the kids in the house."

The man introduced himself as Harry and said, "Much obliged."

Later that afternoon, Claire cleared her bed, changed the sheets, tidied up her room a bit. Less eager to give up his room, Claire compelled Will to do so in her sisterly way. They wandered down to the kitchen and stayed close enough to overhear Helen and Harry's wife Rose, talking.

Helen said, "I'm sorry to hear of your struggles."

"We've been praying," Rose said. "Things are bound to change for us. Things are bound to get better."

Helen offered a hand. "You must believe they will. You're welcome to anything that's ours."

That afternoon, Helen baked some bread and Claire brought it out to the barn for them before they settled in for the night.

As the sun set and tall trees swayed in the wind, John stood on the front porch looking at the light emitting from the barn.

Helen approached him and handed him a steaming cup of coffee. "It's nice to see Claire so helpful."

He agreed. "She gave up her room easy enough, but Will—"

They both smiled, and it melded into laughter. Taking a good, long sip, his breath became visible as he gazed toward Elijah's pen and saw Claire with her friends sitting atop the fence.

Then looking toward the barn where Harry and Rose had bedded down for the night, he said, "I wish we could do more."

Helen agreed.

Bathed in the dim light of the barn and the moon, Claire sat between her friends and stared at Elijah's gray and white mane.

Lucie shoved her. "Come on, daisy girl. It's not like you're never gonna see him again."

"It won't be the same," Liza said. "Leave her be."

"Your uncle is coming in a few days," Lucie reminded her. "Why don't we visit him next week?"

Claire's voice sounded distant, somber. "Sure. Sounds great."

A deep voice spoke behind them. "Next week would be fine."

They all turned and saw John. Liza and Lucie jumped off the fence and stood erect. It was the first time they saw him with anything less than a scowl.

Lucie asked him, "It's getting late, isn't it, sir?"

He smiled. "A bit."

"Thanks for letting us stay," Liza said.

"You're welcome."

Liza turned toward Claire. "Brighten up, Claire. I'll go with you to see him next week."

She nodded.

"Me too," Lucie promised. "Next week."

The two friends ran off toward their farms and John watched as they disappeared toward the woods.

John moved closer to Claire and rested his elbows on the fence then broke the silence between them. "Nice friends."

Claire agreed and together they looked at a lantern burning in the barn where Harry and Rose were.

John said, "It was nice of you to give up your room for the kids. There's still hope for your brother, too."

Her eyes remained on the barn and the lantern. "We weren't much different ... you think they'll be okay?"

"I don't know. I think they'll do the best they can."

They watched the donkey for a moment. Elijah walked toward them and John stretched out a hand to stroke his mane.

"I suppose I'll miss him too. Dumb animal. Ken and Sue will be here in a few days. I'll take you to see him whenever you like."

She shrugged. "Sorry he was so much trouble."

He thought about it for a moment and compared the difficulties of the year with those of the war, but those comparisons had shifted, perhaps transcended. He looked at Elijah and pondered the change.

"Not all trouble is bad, Claire ... especially when it carries hope on its back."

He moved closer to his daughter and she placed her small head on his shoulder for the first time in years. Something formed in his eyes ... something he hadn't allowed since he'd returned from over there. Perhaps the emotions were too much.

"He brought me back, Claire. He saved me ... in more ways than one. So, I guess it doesn't much matter what anybody else thinks. You were right. He is from above and God as my witness ... you'll get your third miracle. I'll rest on that. Before your life is through ... you'll get your third healing."

Claire's eyes welled with tears and she called him by the name she'd longed to since his return. "I believe you, Daddy. I love you."

Reaching around her shoulder, he hugged her and nestled his head next to hers. "You hung the moon, Claire. I've always believed that about you. You hung the moon."

She squeezed her eyes shut and a tear rolled down her cheek. Then together they watched the horizon and the stars that glistened off its peak.

"I ever tell you the story about the candy bar?"

He had not, so she listened as his voice meshed with the wind.

Present

"That night went fast," Claire said. "The family remained the entire next day … longer than we expected. My father had fixed their tires by midday, but mother insisted they stay a while longer."

Dan wrote as fast as he could.

"Mother made supper for them before they left. She gave them some dry goods for the road, but there was more we could do."

1921

The family gathered in the Sloan driveway, the pickup filled to the brim with meager belongings. Yet it appeared they had room for more. Ohio was a long way off and the skies began darkening again. Harry explained how the storms had prompted them to move and how it was just a matter of time before they left home anyway.

John understood and promised him he'd find work in Cleveland.

Checking the freshly patched rubber, John kicked the tires as Harry glanced up at the gray, rolling clouds.

"Looks like rain, don't it?"

John agreed. "Yep. You'd better get movin'."

Harry offered a hand to John. "Thanks for all you've done."

Helen embraced Rose and Rose thanked her. As the kids filed closer, Helen offered each of them hugs. Then she realized Claire wasn't around. Spinning to look for her, she glanced at Will, who stood silent with his hands tucked into his overalls.

She asked, "Will, have you seen your sister?"

He shrugged as if he knew something. Rather than press him further, she helped Rose's kids into the back of the pickup. Harry climbed behind the wheel and the sky opened up. Large raindrops hit the landscape, spattering wetness across the wooden bed.

Resting a hand against the frame, John said, "You're welcome to stay another night. We got plenty of room."

"Can't," Harry said. "Cleveland's a good day away."

John offered a hand and Harry grasped it again. "Godspeed."

As the rain fell harder, Harry glanced beyond John's shoulder and they all turned to see what he was looking at. Claire stood with

Elijah by her side. She held his lead rope and it seemed as if she had been crying.

Helen asked, "Claire, what are you doing with him?"

Claire looked at Harry and asked, "Mister ... would you like a donkey?"

Harry looked at her then at Will, wiping tears from his own eyes.

"I think he might be good for your kids," she said. "He's quite a playmate, you know."

"I couldn't," Harry replied. "I don't—"

He stopped short then glanced at his wife who nodded once as if to say it was okay. He turned toward Claire and gave a single nod.

"I guess. For the kids."

John stiffened, his eyes widened. "Claire, what're you doing? You'll never see him if you—"

Against her father's objections, Claire led Elijah to the back of the bed and the kids pulled down a thin wooden ramp. As she guided him onto it, he walked to a small empty space beside the children. They hugged him and he looked back at Claire as she jumped back down to be with her family.

Harry started the engine, and Claire was overcome. She sprung forward, climbing into the wagon again. Lunging toward Elijah she embraced him hard and her tears streamed about his mane. Kissing him before backing away, she looked at his saddle then took off the broach and kissed him once more before climbing back down.

Tipping his hat to them, Harry put the truck in gear. As he pulled forward, Claire glanced at the broach and tucked it into a pocket. Will moved closer to her and placed a hand about her shoulder. Together they watched as the truck pulled away.

Standing next to her, John asked, "Claire, your uncle will be here in a week. Why did you do that? Why did you give him away?"

It didn't take her long to answer. "Because, Daddy, it doesn't look like that family's been given anything ... for quite some time."

As the truck with Elijah pulled away down the long and winding county road, the night shadows took his place and he disappeared over the horizon.

Present

Claire's voice sounded tranquil, "And just like that, he was gone. I would never see him again after that. I missed him so. Yet I knew somehow ... someway ... he might bear the same hope to another family the way he did ours. Not a day went by without me thinking of him, wondering where he was. But as I grew older, and the winds of change transformed me, I thought of him less.

"There have been times that I've felt like a daughter born of two fathers ... the one that left for the war ... and the one that came home. I lost my father to the First World War. I would lose my brother and my husband to the second. I can be most thankful that I got my father back ... that he was reborn in a way.

"Life is about loss, Mr. Mertz. Who would know this better than one who reports it daily? Yet, God always offers us a candy bar. He offered one to my father in the chilling fields of Russia ... and He offered one to us in the form of a donkey. As much as I wanted to believe my father's promise, the third healing never happened. I never did know of one. Now, as my life draws near its end, I suspect I never will."

Dan looked at her as if he didn't want her to believe that.

She continued, "God's timing is not ours nor will we always understand His ways. Even so, I have always remembered the donkey with fondness. And I hope you will too."

He answered, "I'll try my best to write about him. I promise."

Saying goodbye to her was more difficult that day. He felt as if it may be the last time. When he packed up his things and shoved them away, he experienced a tinge of sadness.

Claire's granddaughter, Catherine, followed him out to his car. She saw him off with a warm embrace then he climbed into his Mustang. "I'll miss her," he said.

Catherine smiled at him. "She has that effect on people."

"I'll be back soon to check on her," he promised. "It's not due to hit the press for a month."

She patted his shoulder and he backed down the narrow driveway then he drove the long trip home with the radio off.

Chapter 19
The Third Miracle

Dan had finished interviewing Claire almost two weeks before and still had written nothing. He never had a problem with writer's block in the past, but he did experience problems with organization. He went to the office every day and ignored the red light atop his phone, signaling voice mails he needed to address.

As he drove around the city with Cindy beside him, his mind raced between what needed to be written and what needed to be done. With Christmas less than a month away, in his world stress began mounting again. He pulled the car into Hiller's Market in Berkley, complaining about the deadlines.

"First part is due to hit the press next week," he said. "And I haven't written a damn thing."

"What have you been doing, Dan?"

"I don't know. Writer's block I guess."

He picked up his Tim Horton cup and took a sip. Together they walked past the produce aisle. He had agreed to shop with her for an upcoming dinner party so she sent him to find tomatoes.

"Big ones. Fat ones," she ordered.

Standing alone beside a sea of vegetables strewn about a table, he filed through them until a woman approached nearby and made him uncomfortable when she stood so close.

Then she looked directly at him and asked, "Dan? Dan Mertz?"

Glancing at her, he backed away, grasping his coffee cup. He didn't recognize her at first, though she looked familiar.

She offered a hand. "Laura. Laura Jenkinson."

It hit him. "Yes ... yes, of course. Laura ... the house ... the contractor problem."

She nodded.

"So how are things ... the work ... the roof?"

"Couldn't be better. Thanks so much for your help. I left a message for you the other day."

Dan looked over and saw Cindy heading toward him so he got busy with the tomatoes. "Message? Sorry. I haven't listened to anything in awhile. I've been busy."

Laura said, "I understand. Listen, I wanted to thank you for—"

"No problem," he said. "I passed it on to a good friend of mine … Jason Becket. He's a great investigator."

"Jason's been great. Not only did he recover our deposit, he found us a great contractor. They just started."

Cindy approached and Dan introduced them. "Cindy, Laura. Laura, Cindy … my wife."

"Pleasure to meet you," Cindy said.

Two children, Cal and Sara, rounded a corner and stood by their mother's side. Dan grinned at them then casually returned to his search in the tomatoes. Sara smiled back, the young girl's face full of color. She had an odd broach pinned to her red, down jacket.

Laura asked, "Cal, Sara, do you remember Mr. Mertz?"

They did and Dan nodded at them then Laura cleared her throat, thanked him again and said, "I'll let you get back to shopping."

Coming out of his trance, Dan responded with, "I'm sorry. I just … my wife gave me marching orders, and—"

"He moves slowly," Cindy joked. "Very slowly."

She understood. "It was great to see you, Dan. Thanks again for all your help."

As they walked away, Dan glanced up at them and sensed something different, though he didn't know what. He watched them disappear around a corner then he grabbed some tomatoes and followed Cindy to the checkout line. The long line gave him time to inspect the periodicals on the racks nearby.

He took a long sip of coffee then set it down on the counter. Flipping through a People magazine, he scoffed at the stories and put it back. Then he saw a National Enquirer whose cover had prophetic vows scattered across it. He stared transfixed at one of the pictures, a painting of Jesus riding a donkey.

Picking it up to get a better look, he bumped his coffee and it tipped. This time, though, he caught it, and his expression changed. An odd compulsion overtook him, one that prompted him to hand his coffee to Cindy and run back into the store.

"Wait here," he told Cindy.

He sprinted into the aisles again, searching for Laura and her children, running from aisle to aisle, until he saw the backs of their heads. He nearly knocked someone over as he ran toward them, calling her name.

"Mrs. Jenkinson! Wait!" He reached out to tap her shoulder then doubled over and tried to catch his breath. "Damn ... I'm outta shape. I gotta start working out again."

She looked at him, but didn't say anything.

Dan looked at Sara and asked, "Wasn't your daughter ... I mean, weren't you sick?"

Sara nodded.

Laura answered, "I'm sorry. I assumed you heard."

"Heard? Heard what?"

"Her tumor is gone. It was the strangest thing. She started feeling better about a day after you left. I took her in for a checkup, and the doctors couldn't find it ... anywhere."

Dan looked at Sara's red jacket and noticed the broach on it.

"She believes it was the charm you gave her," Laura said. "I told her, 'you keep wearing it then, child'. She's been fine ever since."

Sara asked, "What do you think, Mister Mertz ... do you think it was the broach?"

Something stirred within him and he fell to his knees. Stretching out his arms, he hugged Sara then leaned over and kissed the broach.

Rising again, he replied, "You don't know the half of it. I'll be in touch. I gotta go," then reached for Laura's hand and shook it. "I'll be in touch ... soon."

Shuffling through the aisles again, he sprinted back to his wife, waiting near the exit. He said nothing. Instead, he pulled her to the car, nearly spilling the groceries. Interested in the coffee in his hand, he recognized something. *I didn't spill it ... this time. I finally caught it ... this time.*

As he sped out of the lot, Cindy asked, "Dan, what's gotten into you? Why the hurry?"

"We gotta drop this stuff off and go."

"Go where?"

"To Claire's," he said.

"What?"

"I'm taking you to meet her."

"Dan, can't you just call her?"

He looked over at her. "Not for this."

A light snow had fallen, dusting the streets with uncertainty. The long drive to St. Johns gave Dan time to explain things to Cindy, though she didn't fully understand. Soon they arrived at Claire's driveway.

His tires made the first imprint in the snow. Sprinting up to the door, he knocked, but no answer. He glanced next door and it didn't look as if Catherine was home either.

A neighbor called to him from across the way, a man Dan had met only once during his visits. "She's not home."

Dan couldn't quite hear him, so he moved closer.

"They're at the hospital."

"Hospital?"

"She's at Crittenton Hospital ... she took a fall and her daughter found her yesterday."

Dan gasped, fumbled with his keys and raced toward his car as the man continued. "They're waiting for the rest of the family to fly in ... Crittenton Hospital."

He thanked the man and slammed the car into reverse. Then he turned to Cindy and warned her to buckle up. The drive to Crittenton would take a while and give him time to think.

Chapter 20

Another Candy Bar

A lone middle-aged woman sat at the information desk as Dan and Cindy ran through a double set of sliding doors to an empty lobby at nearly eleven o'clock. Dan approached the receptionist and waited impatiently for her attention.

When she looked up, Dan announced, "Claire Henning."

She checked her computer screen. "Fifth floor, Geriatric ICU."

Dan pulled Cindy and hurried toward the elevators then heard the woman say, "Family only at this hour, sir."

Ignoring her, he pushed the buttons in the elevator and the doors closed, leaving them in silence. While the numbers climbed in the display window, it became clear to Dan that Cindy hadn't inquired about anything more. He thought, *Perhaps she noticed a change these past few months and understands my need to complete this chapter in my own mind's eye before I can move on.*

The elevator doors opened to a large waiting area, rows of chairs to either side filled with many of Claire's family.

Catherine asked, "Dan, how did you find out?"

He replied, "We went to her house. What happened?"

"She fell yesterday … she's gone downhill since then."

"Can I see her?"

Smiling at him, Catherine said, "She's not going to know you're there. She had a stroke. She's held on for longer than we expected. We're hoping she'll be with us until my sisters arrive."

His voice cracked a bit. "There's something I need to tell her."

Looking around at the rest of her family, their smiles back at him told him that he was now part of it. Catherine nodded at him once then he turned to look at Cindy and promised to be right back.

Walking past a row of nurses seated behind a desk, he found his way to Claire's room. Stepping inside, he saw a sea of machinery and tubes spun about and attached to her frail body. The methodic tone of a heart monitor broke the silence.

Dan moved to her bedside wanting to joke with her, but instead, he leaned over and kissed her forehead then whispered, "Claire, it's Dan ... Dan Mertz. I've got something to tell you."

She didn't respond, yet something told him she would hear him and she would understand.

"It happened, Claire ... the third miracle ... the third healing. Her name is Sara ... Sara Jenkinson. Her father was—" He stopped because of an urging from within, a prompting to do the very thing he hadn't allowed himself to do in years. His voice quivered and his eyes glazed, tears welling within them. "Your father was right, Claire. You were right. He came from God. I want you to know that. Please know he came from God."

He stayed in her room longer than he planned then thanked her in his own way before leaving to be with her family, with Cindy. There was little left to say. Perhaps it had all been said. Instead, a flurry of emotions churned within him, and that peculiar writer's block suddenly disappeared.

The following days he pondered the irony of an old woman's story, one that could reluctantly lead him to overcome the depth of an impenetrable world view. He thought of the droves of people that would read what he learned: the police officers who would sit at the precinct desks, the Free Press spread open wide; the single mothers who would peruse their computer screens, hoping to uncover those opportunities that would change the direction of their children's lives; the auto workers leaning against presses, wondering who the Lions would beat next; the nurses whose frenzied schedules offered them scarcely enough solace to catch up on the day's events.

He hoped they would happen across his column so they could look beyond the surface for something a bit more. He wrote about what she had lived and what he had learned.

Then he saw it embodied in the press for which he worked. He noticed it through a frosted window of a paper stand that he and Cindy walked by. One night they strolled beside Laura Jenkinson, Cal and Sara. They watched as Sara deposited some coins into a Salvation Army Bucket, her face shining with a healthy glow.

"For a candy bar," she said.

And he smiled, knowing the rest would be read.

Candy bars are funny things. They come in all shapes and sizes. Some are chocolate, others are laden with nuts, many are offered in the aisles of our favorite stores, yet others are peddled by children hoping to corner the markets of their local grocery stores. Perhaps the most important candy bars of all are the ones given to us by God: morsels of hope in a world ripe with despair.

One such act was rendered on the wintry fields in Russia during the Great War. A century later, and a world away, the daughter of that man had a story to tell. It would be a true story from her perspective, and a story of faith from mine. Yet it is a story I intend to tell to a city that has bore so much loss and wallowed far too long in a diffident future.

It may take you some time to get to know Claire Henning. It did me. Faced with a father whose demons followed him home from the war and a farm flailing toward disaster, she found solace in a donkey she swore wrought the hope that saved them both—a donkey who healed some and divided others, yet one that will remain in the annals of her family's hearts forever, and perhaps in our own.

For a year Elijah would live with her. But his legacy would last a lifetime. Two miracles and some ninety years later, she would introduce him to me. Against my own designs, I took the assignment. She died three days ago at the age of one hundred. Now, over the next few weeks, I will tell you her story, perhaps a sorry attempt at assuaging the hopelessness I've heralded over so many years of reporting.

So, here, take a candy bar, Detroit. And look into the eyes of God. Perhaps together we can see Him looking back. Then maybe we can laugh in the face of fear and admit: not all trouble is bad, especially when it carries hope on its back.

About The Author

Paul Stuligross spent twenty-four years as a police officer with several as a detective. During his career, he received the *Officer of the Year* award for developing and implementing a comprehensive chaplain's program for his police department. He is the author of a novel ***The Birth of an Angel*** under the pseudonym Paul J. Stuart.

Education includes behavioral and psychological profiling as well as creative and screenplay writing. He has a Master of Arts in Theological/Pastoral Studies (2012) from Sacred Heart Major Seminary in Detroit, Michigan.

Paul writes for the *Michigan Catholic Newspaper* and is a member of the *Police Officer Writers Association, American Christian Writers Association, American Society of Authors & Writers and the Catholic Writers Guild.*

He teaches Theology at a high school in Michigan where he resides with his wife and two daughters.

Additional Books by Patriot Media, Inc.

Book reviews and descriptions can be seen at Patriot Media, Inc. website: patriotmediainc.com. Check the site often for discounts and special sale items.

D.M. Ulmer, Author:

Submarine Novels
Silent Battleground
Shadows of Heroes
The Cold War Beneath
Ensure Plausible
Deniability
Skagerrak

Mysteries &Novellas
Missing Person
The Roche Harbor Caper
The Long Beach Caper
Count the Ways
Where or When

Brett Kneisley, Author:
DVD-Tour of USS Clamagore,
Featuring Captain Don Ulmer

B.K. Bryans, Author:
Those '67 Blues
Flight to Redemption
The Dog Robbers
Arizona Grit
Brannigan Rides Again

Joseph C. Engel, Author:
Flight of the Silver Eagle

Nelson O. Ottenhausen, Author:
The Killing Zone: Evil's Playground
Jugs & Bottles
The Sin Slayer
The Blue Heron
The Naked Warrior

Paul Sherbo, Author:
Unsinkable Sailors: The fall and rise of the last crew of the Frank E. Evans

LTC Peter Clark, Author:
Staff Monkeys: A Stockbroker's Journey through the Global War on Terror

Dari Bradley, Author:
Hickory Nuts in the Driveway

Art Giberson, Author:
The Mighty O

Hannah Ackerman, Author:
I Kept My Chin Up

Hal Olsen, Author:
Up an' Atom

Jack Verneski, Author:
Scarecrow Season

Roger Chaney, Author:
Carquinez Straits